By Samantha James

A PERFECT HERO
A PERFECT GROOM
A PERFECT BRIDE
THE TRUEST HEART
HIS WICKED PROMISE
HIS WICKED WAYS
ONE MOONLIT NIGHT
A PROMISE GIVEN
EVERY WISH FULFILLED
JUST ONE KISS
MY LORD CONQUEROR
GABRIEL'S BRIDE

SAMANTHA JAMES

His Wicked Ways

AVON BOOKS

An Imprint of HarperCollinsPublishers

AVON BOOKS
An Imprint of HarperCollins*Publishers*
10 East 53rd Street
New York, New York 10022-5299

Copyright © 1999 by Sandra Kleinschmit
Excerpt from *Someday My Prince* copyright © 1999 by Christina Dodd
Excerpt from *Married in Haste* copyright © 1999 by Catherine Maxwell
Excerpt from *His Wicked Ways* copyright © 1999 by Sandra Kleinschmit
Excerpt from *The Perfect Gift* copyright © 1999 by Roberta Helmer
Excerpt from *Once and Forever* copyright © 1999 by Constance O'Day-Flannery
Excerpt from *The Proposition* copyright © 1999 by Judith Ivory
ISBN: 0-380-80586-3
www.avonromance.com

First Avon Books paperback printing: September 1999

Avon Trademark Reg. U.S. Pat. Off. and in Other Countries, Marca Registrada, Hecho en U.S.A.
HarperCollins ® is a registered trademark of HarperCollins Publishers Inc.

Printed in the U.S.A.

10   9

One

Scotland
Early 1200s

"Be not afraid."

The words slid past her ear, cold as a loch in the midst of a wintry freeze. Hearing it, Meredith Munro felt a chill that reached the very depths of her soul . . . a chill she'd known but once before.

Her prayer beads slipped to the floor. *Be not afraid,* the voice had intoned. Alas, but she *was* afraid! Indeed, she was terrified, for within her tiny cell stood three men—two hulking figures she'd caught a glimpse of from the corner of her eye . . .

And the one whose hand clamped tight about her mouth.

Men did not belong here at Connyridge Priory. Father Marcus was the only man who came here, and that was in order to say Mass and hear the transgressions of the nuns and novices who resided within these ancient stone walls.

Her mind reeled. Dear Lord, she was on her feet—snatched from her knees as she prayed at her bedside! The one who held her . . . his hand was immense. It covered her nose and mouth so that she could scarcely

1

breathe; all she could hear was the pounding of her own blood in her ears.

Fear pumped through her with every beat of her heart, a fear nourished by the dire certainty that these men meant her harm. A dozen questions tumbled through her mind. Where was Mother Gwynn? Sister Amelia? How was it possible they had invaded these hallowed walls? There were three of them . . . three! Had no one heard a sound? An awful thought reared high in her mind. Perhaps the others had heard nothing, for they were already dead!

Nay. Nay! She could not think thusly, for she could not bear it!

As if to remind her, the arm about her waist tightened ever so slightly.

Warm breath rushed past her ear. "A word of warning," came the grating male whisper anew. "Do not scream, for 'twill do no good, I promise you. Do you understand?"

His tone was almost pleasant, yet Meredith sensed that such was not his intent. Scream, she thought faintly. Shock and terror held her motionless. Why, the very notion was laughable! The muscles of her throat were so constricted, nary a sound could have passed had she tried!

"Nod if you understand."

Somehow she managed to raise and lower her chin. "Excellent," he murmured. "Now, Meredith Munro, let's have a look at you."

The world whirled all about her. He knew her. He knew her by name! How could that be?

Slowly, the man who held her lifted his hand. Meredith felt herself turned bodily so that she faced him.

As if to oblige him, the light of a full moon trickled through the narrow window set high in the outer wall.

Meredith felt the full force of his gaze dwell long and hard upon her. Though she still wore her coarse gray robe, she flushed, for she had neither wimple nor veil to cover the length of her hair. No man had seen her thus since the day she'd said good-bye to her father those many months ago.

No longer did he touch her, though they stood nearly toe to toe. She knew instinctively that this man was their leader. Gathering her courage, Meredith inched her gaze a long way upward to his face. In the frenzied brew of her mind, he embodied all manner of evil. His features were indistinct and blurred in the darkness, yet never had she seen such intense, glittering eyes, like chips of stone. Her insides turned to ice. Was this the face of death?

Her gaze dropped to the sword at his side. On the other side hung a dirk which looked just as deadly. A shudder coursed through her, for she was suddenly quite certain . . .

If there would be blood spilled this night, it would be hers.

One of the other men lit the stub of candle at the wooden table. "She is the one?" he asked.

Those eyes never left her. Indeed, they seemed to pierce through her very skin. "She is," was all the leader said.

"Aye," the man replied. "She's the look of a Munro."

Her mouth had gone dry, yet she forced herself to speak. "What do you here? I do not know you, yet you know me."

He neither agreed nor disagreed.

"You mean to kill me, don't you?"

He did not deny it. Instead he asked, "Are you deserving of death?"

Nay, she longed to cry. Instead her fingertips crept to the small silver crucifix which hung about her throat—it had been a gift from her father the day he'd brought her here. She fingered the finely etched surface, as if to draw both comfort and strength from it. Once again she heard his parting words to her: *Remember, daughter, God will always be with you . . . as will I.*

She gave a tiny shake of her head. "That is not for me to judge."

His smile did not reach his eyes. "Mayhap 'tis for me to judge."

Meredith gasped. Did the man have no respect for the Lord? Oh, silly question, that! a voice within her chided. His very presence here dictated the answer.

" 'Tis for no man to judge, only God himself." She sought hard to keep the quaver from her voice.

"Yet such is hardly the case, is it not? How many of God's creatures die from sickness?" He did not ponder, nor seek an answer from her. "Children and the aged, mayhap. But men . . . ah, well, men kill other men . . . and sometimes women, too."

A chill went down her spine, for this time there was no mistaking the threat implicit in his tone. Meredith could not help it—she felt herself go pale.

"The others." Her voice quavered. "Mother Gwynn. Sister Amelia. Are they—"

"They are alive and well, and snug in their beds."

Her breath came in and held. Slowly she let it out, trying desperately not to panic. Why had he come for her? Surely not to fetch her for her father! Oh, but she must escape this lunatic, for only a lunatic would dare to intrude into this holy place as he had done! Escape was foremost in her mind. In her heart . . .

She bolted.

Oh, but she should have known! Quick as she was, he was quicker. She managed not three steps and he was upon her. Strong arms encircled her, stopping her cold. She felt herself dragged backward, her entire length brought upright against his body—it was if she'd hit a wall of stone.

Her reaction was more instinct than conscious thought. She twisted and writhed, trying wildly to escape the shackle of his arms.

"Be still!" he hissed.

Nay. She could not. She *would* not. She renewed her struggle with vigor, only to hear a vivid curse resound in her ear.

"By God, cease!"

The forearm about her waist tightened, threatening to crush her ribs and cut off her breath. She could feel the strength in him, feel it in every muscle of his body. As she gasped for air, only then did the realization come to her that he might break her as easily as he snapped a twig from a tree.

Her body lost all resistance. Her head dropped. A choked sound emerged from her throat, a keening sound of despair. She hated the way she trembled . . . and hated the awareness that surely he must feel it, too. If she was to die—saints forgive her for being such a coward!—she prayed that death would come swiftly, a dagger sheathed in the heart just so.

It was not to be.

Without further ado, she felt her feet leave the cold stone floor. She was stunned to find herself deposited on the bench before the table.

"Now, then, you will do as I say."

But one thought ran through her mind, like the rush of the wind through the trees. Once before she'd been dragged from her bed in the midst of the night. Would the outcome be the same? Pray God, no. For if it was, she could not bear it . . . not again.

Little by little she raised her head. "If you mean to . . . to . . ." Faith, but she could not find it within her to even say the words!

Not that there was any need. "To defile you?"

She felt her skin heat with the flood of embarrassment. "Aye," she whispered.

His laugh was mirthless . . . and merciless. "I think not, Meredith Munro. Were I in need of a woman, of a certainty 'twould not be you. Indeed, I must force myself to suffer your presence."

Such assurance hardly brought her ease. She heard the snap of his fingertips. One of the others moved, producing parchment, quill, and ink. This was set down before her.

"You will write a note to Mother Gwynn, stating that, alas! you cannot give your life over to God, nor can you remain on this earthly world, for you are deeply ashamed that you are so weak in devotion and spirit."

Meredith gaped. God above, he would have her forfeit her own life!

"Nay, I cannot do it! Why, to take my own life would be mortal sin."

The dark stranger had only to place his hand on his dirk.

She shook her head. "I cannot write," she began desperately.

"You lie. You keep accounts for the prioress."

How did he know that? Who was he, that he knew all about her? Her attempt at a glare was pitiful—as *she* was pitiful!

Never had Meredith despised herself as she did this very moment! She lowered her gaze, that he would not glimpse her despair, then reached for the quill. Her eyes misting with tears, she watched as the words took shape.

Mother Gwynn, and my dearest sisters in Christ,

Though it pains me deeply, I have no choice in this matter. I fear I can no longer remain in the service of the Lord. I am deeply ashamed that I am so weak in devotion and in spirit, and so I must end it all. Forgive me, sisters, for what I must do, and pray for me, that my soul does not dwell in eternal damnation.

Trying desperately to still the trembling within her, she signed her name. With a crushing feeling deep in her breast, she looked up.

He was watching her, his gaze like the point of a lance. He picked up the letter and quickly scanned it. " 'Pray for me,' " he quoted. "Let us hope that someone does." He lowered the letter, leaving it on the table in the center of the chamber.

"Up," he ordered.

It crossed Meredith's mind to defy him . . . but only for an instant. In truth she was so relieved to still be alive that for one mind-spinning instant she feared her legs would not hold her.

"Your hands, pray."

Mutely she obliged. At a nod from him, one of his men dutifully stepped forward. Her hands were bound together before her with a length of rope. When the task was done, the man stepped back and opened the door.

Those burning eyes snared hers. "You will come," was all he said.

Meredith instinctively recoiled, but it was no use. His fingers curled around her elbow. She endured his touch as best she could. She had no choice but to follow, battling both a helpless frustration and a numbing fear. Who was this man? What did he want with her? Why hadn't he slain her? Indeed, why should he want her dead? Why should he want her *alive*? Or did he truly mean for her to slay herself?

They had passed Mother Gwynn's quarters. Meredith's gaze skipped forward, then quickly bounced away. She bit her lip, her pulse quickening. They were nearing the door to the dormitory where the nuns slept. If she were to call out and raise the alarm, one of the sisters might awaken. Indeed, perhaps someone was already awake, for surely it was nearing time to gather for Prime in the chapel. Then the intruders would be discovered—

He jerked her against him. The notion disappeared in mid-thought. The breath was jarred from her lungs. Her heart surely stopped, for suddenly they were wedded together, breast to breast, thigh to thigh. Meredith froze, even as it vaulted through her mind that his chest was like an immense wall of iron.

Panic raced through her, for he bent his head so that his lips brushed hers. Had he not held her in his grasp, she would surely have leaped from her very skin. Sweet Christ, surely he did not mean to . . .

"Do not," he warned in a voice meant for her ears alone, "for they would only be hurt should they seek to aid you. 'Tis a fight they cannot win . . . nor can you. I am set on this course, lady, and no one will stop me . . . *no one*." The arm around her back tightened ever so slightly before he stepped back—oh, yes, a warning indeed! she decided bitterly.

Despairing her weakness—despising it—Meredith clenched her bound hands into fists. To deepen her humiliation even further, those hard lips pulled into a tight smile, causing her own to press together.

Her eyes found his through the shadows. "There are ways to fight other than with swords." Where her words—or the courage!—came from, she would ever wonder.

There was a short, harsh laugh. "Aye, but there are indeed."

With that cryptic remark, he reclaimed her arm and led her into the passageway, down the narrow stairs. His men trailed behind them.

He seemed to know precisely where he was going, leading her through the nave of the chapel. They skirted the chancel and hurried through the cloister, turned left near the refectory. All too soon they emerged into the moon-drenched freedom of the night. His bold stride never faltered. Onward they continued, past the wooden outbuildings, weaving through the gardens and into the orchard. Before long they were outside the high stone wall that enclosed the priory, and only then did they halt.

They stood before the ringed granite cross of St. Michael, a cross which had been here for centuries. The smell of the sea was pungent and sharp, but Meredith scarcely noticed, for the ache of remembrance battered her. She fought a sudden, scalding rush of tears. Her lungs burned with a pain so intense it nearly brought her to her knees. It was here, on this very spot outside Connyridge Priory, that she had said her good-byes to her father. She had beseeched him not to return, not until she asked—*unless* she asked; for

Meredith feared that if he did, she might be tempted to leave with him, to return to Castle Munro and the home of her youth. Her heart wrenched, for she could almost see him again, the blue eyes so like her own shimmering with tears he made no effort to hide. He had wept openly . . .

So had she.

It seemed so very, very long ago . . . it seemed like yesterday. She vividly remembered how she had hated herself—hated that she had disappointed him. As his only daughter, his only child, she knew it was his heartfelt wish that she would someday marry and give him grandchildren.

Meredith knew that she would never marry . . . *never*.

She had not told Papa of that horrible night. She never would. In truth, she'd never told a soul on this earth! Though it tore her apart to leave Castle Munro, she could not stay. She could not live her life afraid of every man she saw, wondering if it was he who had touched her, who had shamed her so. Nor could she tell Papa the truth of what had happened that horrible night . . . Indeed, even *she* did not know the truth of it.

It was why she had left the father she loved so dearly . . . why she would never return to her home.

When Meredith had asked that he bring her to Connyridge to join the sisters he had been puzzled. He had questioned her, but in the end he hadn't refused. She was achingly aware that he fully expected her to remain cloistered here forever.

She had come to Connyridge solely to seek refuge. And it was here that the terror that night had wrought had finally begun to ease. She had found sanctuary within these walls; she had begun to regain a measure of the peace she had feared was forever lost to her. Though it had taken time, she was comfortable at the priory, no matter that the cold seeped through her sandals and into her very bones. Not so long ago, she had made the decision to give her life over to God. As a nun in the service of the Lord, she would be shielded from the lustful appetites of men . . .

Yet her struggle had continued, oh, in other ways! For she had been so very confused—in truth, she still was. Though the choice was hers, she was no longer certain . . . Would she be doing the right thing in taking her vows? Was this her chosen vocation? She should have known it in her heart, yet she did not! These past weeks she had prayed daily for guidance in that one particular endeavor—that she had made the right choice.

She was to take her vows within the month . . . but would she even be *alive* then?

To some, such a life might have been a prison, for life at the nunnery was comprised solely of prayer, work, study, sleep, and meals. Idleness was believed to be an enemy of the soul. With her mind thus occupied, she need not think of . . . other things.

But the sanctuary she sought was no more. All because of him . . .

Yet another man whose name she knew not.

Meredith could not help it. She stared at him warily. In the gloom of the night he appeared dark and featureless. She shivered, wondering what he might look like in the full light of day. She sensed he was young, not so aged as her father and Uncle Robert. Oh, but surely such a wicked man would be ugly as the devil's own sin! No doubt his teeth were gaping and yellowed and rotting, his skin mottled and pockmarked and dark as a heathen's. She shuddered, thinking that mayhap 'twas better this way. In daylight he might have frightened her to her grave!

She stood awkwardly as he spoke in hushed tones to his men; she could not hear what was said. The men nodded and strode away. Her mouth dry, she watched as he walked to a small cart that she hadn't noticed until now.

Her apprehension spiraled as he turned back to her, then beckoned to her. With a heavy tightness in the pit of her belly, Meredith moved forward. Unable to help herself, she peered inside the cart. A woman lay within, long red hair dirty and snarled, strewn across the wooden boards. Her head was turned at an odd angle; dull, unblinking eyes stared back at her.

The woman was dead.

A scream curdled in her throat. She felt herself sway, but mercifully remained on her feet of her own power.

Lean fingers curled around her arm. "Remove your robe," came his voice—a voice she had already begun to dread.

Meredith looked on as he removed the rope around her wrists, wondering if she'd lost her wits. Was this but a dream, a horrible trick of her mind? Her eyes squeezed shut, and she told herself she was back in her cell, huddled in her bed. Swallowing, she allowed her lids to drift upward.

Booted male feet came into view. Alas, *he* was there, a presence as unwelcome as ever . . .

And just as forbidding.

His jaw thrust out. "I'll not tell you again."

A foggy haze seemed to dance all around her. Nay, she thought, she couldn't have heard him right. Her mouth opened. She felt her jaw move, yet no sound came out.

"Fine, then. It matters little to me." Peremptory hands dropped upon her shoulders, seeking the neck of her robe. A jolt went through her as warm fingertips brushed her bare skin.

Meredith wrenched away as if she'd been scorched. "Nay!" she gasped.

"Do it . . . else I shall."

She could well believe he meant precisely what he said. She need not see his features to know that he meant it. She could hear it in his tone, see it in the set of his shoulders. Aye, there was an unswaying purpose about him that could neither be denied nor ignored.

His threat resounded all through her. Her fingers were clumsy with fright . . . and with wrenching shame, knowing that she would be naked before him. Awkwardly she did as he demanded, berating herself all the while. Ah, but she was a fool to comply so readily! Why couldn't she be stronger? she raged inwardly. Would she ever be meek and spineless? She was a weakling, in mind and heart and body, for she was powerless to fight him. Nay, she could not overcome his strength, nor his will, she thought, brutally chastising herself.

Her eyes downcast, she stepped from the coarse dark fabric now puddled on the ground at her feet. Burning with shame, she tried to shield her body with her hands—not just from the cool night air, but from the prying of those steel-edged eyes.

Yet he spared her not a glance as he bent and scooped her robe from the damp ground. Instead he strode to the cart, where he proceeded to strip the gown from the dead woman. To her surprise, he tossed it at her.

"Put this on!"

This time Meredith did not delay. With shaking hands she donned the dirty, ill-fitting gown, glad of the chance to cover herself once more.

By the time she finished, his men had reappeared, leading three horses. Meredith's heart leaped. Did they plan to take her with them? Her mind had scarcely formed the thought when the two men stepped toward the nude woman who still lay on the ground. Stunned, she watched as they dressed the woman in the robe she'd discarded—*her* robe! When it was done, they glanced inquiringly at their leader.

"Do it," came the low-voiced command.

One man grabbed the woman by her left arm, the other by her right. Together they dragged her some twenty yards to the east. What happened then shocked Meredith to the marrow of her bones.

The woman was cast down the cliffs to the jutting rocks below. Of course there was no scream—yet Meredith could hear it in the soundless chambers of her mind. There was only a dull thud . . .

Meredith cringed. The rocks below would tear into the woman's flesh like the gnashing teeth of a sea monster, leaving her body bloodied and broken . . . that poor creature! Perhaps it was a blessing that she was already dead . . . yet why would they kill her? Why kill her, only to throw her over the cliffs . . . ?

A paralyzing dread seized hold of her. Would she be next? No one could survive a fall from the cliffs. They were deadly; their height alone was enough to kill. Indeed, though Meredith had no fear of heights, she had always avoided the cliffs.

Her heart twisted as she thought of the woman. She'd been pretty. That much had been clear. Young and pretty and far too young to die . . .

Even as she sent a quick prayer heavenward for the

woman's soul, Meredith blanched. Only then did she begin to realize the significance of what she had just witnessed. The flaming red hair . . . dressing the dead woman in her robes . . .

Her eyes slid to him. He stood motionless, his gaze upon her, as if awaiting her reaction.

"Saints above," she said faintly. "I . . . they will think that . . ." She could not go on. Swallowing, she tried again. "You mean for the sisters to think that . . ."

"That the woman is you." His smile was rimmed with satisfaction, a satisfaction she could not even pretend to understand. "Her body will be mutilated on the rocks," he stated matter-of-factly. "Bloodied and broken."

God's mercy, he was right. Shortly after she'd come to Connyridge, the body of one of the villagers had washed up on the rocks—he'd been a fisherman. His flesh was torn to shreds, his face bloated and white so that he was unrecognizable. It had sickened her so that she'd nearly lost the contents of her stomach. Oh, aye, her note was damning indeed. The nuns would see the reddish blond hair of the woman and think that she had thrown herself from the cliff.

Meredith's heart wrenched. At least the poor woman had already been dead . . . Suddenly her breath caught. "You killed her, didn't you? You killed her!"

The tension spun out endlessly. He said nothing . . . a stifling silence that said far more than mere words.

Meredith shook her head. For one awful moment she feared she would be sick there and then. "Why?" Her throat ached so that it hurt to speak. "Why would you do such a thing?"

Again that debilitating silence.

"And I am next, am I not?" Drawing upon a daring she hadn't known she possessed, she straightened her shoulders and struck her breast with one knotted fist. "Kill me, then, if you will! Kill me now!"

"Kill you?" His laugh was harsh and brittle as he gestured to the cliff. "Come, now. Do you truly think I'd have gone to such trouble if I meant to kill you? Now, then. Will you come, or must I bind your hands again?"

Meredith lowered her head, battling within herself as never before. A woman lay dead because of her, and all she could think was how she might save her own soul! She was not only weak but selfish as well, and she could only hope that God would forgive her! Yet something within her protested—something refused to let this vile man win so easily.

Meredith knew she'd been dismissed as he glanced away. He made a sign to his men, who led the horses forward. He did not even deign to glance at her as he motioned her forward.

"Come," was all he said.

Meredith took a deep, fortifying breath. "Nay," she said clearly.

Now she'd done it, it seemed. She felt the touch of those ice-fire eyes return even before she forced herself to meet his regard.

"Y-you are a madman, and I'll go nowhere with you."

Beside her there was a curse. There was a stunning blow to the middle of her back that sent her toppling forward. It was *he* who caught her and saved her from falling headlong before his feet.

"Nay, Finn, leave her be!"

Meredith was half-afraid to breathe. She could feel his hands around her wrists like clamps of iron, imprisoning her as surely as a trap. Oh, aye, she could feel the strength in him and knew that were it his will, her life would be forfeit.

Slowly she raised her head from the awesome breadth of his chest.

"I'll go nowhere with you."

"Ah, but you will, Meredith Munro. You will."

"I will not," she stated again. She raised her chin, all at once not so sure of herself. In her heart she was appalled at her audacity. Mayhap *she* was the one who was mad!

"Who are you? Why are you doing this? What do you want with me?"

He released her. Meredith resisted the impulse to turn and flee. Instead she held her ground, her bare toes digging into the dew-draped earth.

"Who are you?" she said again. "You pretend to know me, yet I vow I've not laid eyes on you before this night!"

"Nay, lass, you have not."

"Then who are you?" Determination swept away her fear and uncertainty. If she was to die, she would at least know why—and she would at least know the identity of the man who would slay her! "*Who are you?*"

His eyes scraped over her, like a sword of molten steel.

"I am Cameron"—he stated but this one thing . . . and alas, it was all that was needed—"of the Clan MacKay."

Two

It was revenge that brought him to Connyridge—revenge and the blood feud that had been going on for a century and more.

It had not been a difficult task to find her. She was the only daughter—indeed, the only child—of the Red Angus, chieftain of the Clan Munro. Yes, a kiss given here, a coin there, and the information Cameron had sought became his for the asking.

Of course, there had been a few that balked at his plan. Murray had shaken his shaggy, unkempt head. "Ye canna do that! A woman of God, yet!" he'd cried. "What price will ye pay, man?"

"She has not yet taken her vows." Cameron was already prepared. "And whatever price I pay, I shall gladly yield."

Cameron was a God-fearing man, as much as any, yet it wouldn't have mattered if Meredith, daughter of the Red Angus, were the prioress herself. Nay, there would be no dissuading him . . .

He would have his revenge, no matter the cost. It was this which had driven him to heal . . . it was this which drove him to *live*.

As if to remind him, the jagged scar on his lower back began to ache. Raw pain ripped through him,

but it was a pain of the heart and not of the body.
Inside he cried out his anguish. Why had he been
spared, when no one else had been? Why had he
lived, when everyone else had died? His father and
his six brothers were gone. All had perished . . . *all* of
his brothers. Niall, the eldest. Burke, so handsome and
hearty. Bryan and Oswald. So vibrant. So alive. Kenneth, always ready with a laugh and a smile. Thomas,
but a tender lad of ten who could not yet wield a
sword . . .

Cameron was the only one left.

The weeks had not eased the fury within him; indeed, they had only sharpened it.

Remembrance went through him. Rage seared his
soul. His body tensed, like a red-hot sword plunged
into his gut. That was how his brothers had died.
Bloody and butchered . . .

Beneath the blades of Red Angus and his clansmen.

He sucked in a harsh breath. He had grown weary
of the years of hatred between the MacKays and the
Munros, the years of skirmishes and fighting, though
there had been a period of relative peace these past
few years. But all that had been shattered on a serene,
tranquil hillside not two months ago. In truth, he did
not want war or this blood feud continued, yet everything within him clamored for revenge.

He would not rest until he had it, for only then
would the deaths of his father and brothers be
avenged.

Now, having revealed his name, the memory assailed him anew. Cameron could not help it. A seething fury pounded in his veins. His hand crept to the
handle of his sword. His fingers clenched and un-
clenched. Now, as he watched her eyes grow huge,
the silence of awareness fell over her.

Recognition flared across her features. Her lips parted, but no sound emerged.

"I am the son of Ronald, brother of Niall and Burke . . ." One by one he named his brothers. "Perhaps you and the good sisters prayed for their safe arrival in heaven?"

He heard the breath she drew. She gave a slight shake of her head. "Heaven," she repeated, then swallowed. "Do you mean to say they are—"

"Aye," he stated flatly. "They are dead. Killed at the hands of your father and his men."

He did not imagine the blood draining from her features.

A primitive satisfaction washed over him, for he knew she awaited his next move . . . Would she cry? Beg for mercy? He relished the thought of either.

She did neither. Instead she stepped forward and bowed her head. Her lashes swept down, shielding her expression. She turned her head ever so slightly, baring her neck. Cameron knew that, despite his assurance otherwise, she fully expected him to strike her down that very instant.

That had never been his plan.

Indeed, he was darkly amused that twice now she had invited him to kill her. Clearly she thought him a barbarian, to strike her down—and a woman, yet! Never would he take a woman's life, for he had only the deepest scorn for a man who would prey on those weaker than himself.

He was not about to tell her the truth about the woman she was so convinced he'd murdered. Nay, they had discovered her on the roadside only hours before; 'twas this which gave him the idea to let the Red Angus believe that his only daughter had taken her own life.

How much better than to simply abduct the wench!

Aye, he thought with satisfaction. He would rob the Red Angus, chieftain of the Clan Munro, as he had been robbed . . . He would make the old man suffer . . . as he now suffered.

Dawn broke over the clouds on the horizon; her back was to the North Sea. Behind her, the sky was streaked with pale shades of yellow and gold. For an instant, it was almost as if a halo had crowned the peak of her head. She looked like an angel, but for the fire of her hair . . . She was no angel. She was a Munro. Ruthlessly he pushed aside a niggling guilt. She spoke of God. But God was on his side, not hers, he decided with a ruthless dismissal. Aye, Cameron was convinced that the Almighty was on his side. Why else would he have sent the red-haired woman by the roadside?

No, Meredith was no angel. She was a Munro, daughter of Red Angus.

His scrutiny sharpened. Her skin was deathly pale. He could see the ragged rise and fall of her chest. She was quaking where she stood, trying desperately to hide it . . . and not succeeding in the least.

She was afraid. Well, that was good. It was the nature of the Highlanders to cast an uneasy eye upon those stronger than themselves, and he was pleased she recognized it.

She was a strange one, according to those who had known her—small and meek and timid as a child, even more so now that she'd grown to womanhood. For nearly two years she'd been sequestered at Con-nyridge, yet it was only now that she'd decided to take the veil.

That would never happen. If he had his way, she

would never return to Connyridge . . . or Castle Munro.

Silently he watched her. Gleaming moonlight touched the slender, vulnerable arch of her throat exposed to him. An odd sensation gripped his belly. Lord, but she was a wee one! Cameron took a deep breath, filling his lungs with air. His gaze rested interminably long on the tangled skeins of reddish gold hair tumbling about her shoulders. A beauty, that's what she was, he thought suddenly. Faith, but he'd not expected that of a woman about to take her vows—nor from a woman of the Clan Munro.

A vile blackness swept over him. He was suddenly furious, with her for being so damned comely . . . and with himself for recognizing it.

Resolve clamped down upon him. He straightened his spine. He could afford no weakness. She was a Munro, he reminded himself. Enemies they were . . .

And enemies they would stay.

They had been traveling for hours. The noonday sun shone high and bright, as if in approval! In all truth, Meredith was amazed she was still alive. For one paralyzing moment, she'd thought he would kill her, for surely in that instant all the fires of the devil seemed to burn within him, as if from the inside out. Instead he'd set her jarringly upon his horse before him.

Not a single word was cast her way.

For Meredith, the morn had been the worst kind of torment. Her muscles ached, but not just from the unfamiliar hours in the saddle. His arms encircled her, brushing against her sides, an unwelcome reminder of his strength. His legs imprisoned her own, like bars of iron—the intimacy of it was almost more than she

could bear. She sought to hold herself stiffly erect, for
she stringently determined to avoid any contact with
his body. Aye, it was a physical pain, riding with
him . . .

And an agony of the heart as well.

By now surely the nuns believed her dead. When
she did not appear for Prime at dawn, someone would
have gone to her cell and found the note. No doubt
they had long since gathered in the chapter house,
shocked and stunned. Sister Amelia, who cared for
the vestments and altar cloths, would be weeping—
Mother Gwynn forever lost patience with the
woman's sentimentality. Perchance someone had already found the body at the cliffs, the body believed
to be hers.

Then there was Papa.

Cameron MacKay had come to Connyridge—but
had he come from Castle Monro? She shuddered,
thinking of the poor woman who lay at the foot of
the cliffs. Had Papa met the same brutal end? And
Uncle Robert? What of them?

It wasn't long before they halted. Cameron's men—
Egan and Finn, she'd learned they were called—led
their mounts to the stream, where they drank thirstily.
Egan was an evil-looking fellow—a giant, taller even
than Cameron MacKay, with a jagged scar that ran
down his cheek. His eyes were pale blue ice. Finn
was shorter and heavier and bearded. Behind her,
Cameron MacKay vaulted from the saddle in one lithe
move. Meredith hesitated, uncertain what was expected of her. When he made no move to help her,
she slipped from the saddle, falling hard to her knees,
for the ground was a long way down! She gasped as
a sharp stone dug into one knee.

The hairs on her neck prickled. She raised her eyes

to find him watching her, his regard infinitely cold. Brushing the dirt from her hands, she got to her feet.

She could stand it no longer. She had to know. She wet her lips. "My father," she said, her voice very low. "Is he—" She stopped, for she could not bear to say it aloud, could scarcely stand to even think it.

There was a taut silence. Standing with his feet braced wide apart, he made no answer.

She tried again. "Please tell me. What have you done with my father?"

She held her breath. It seemed to take forever before he answered curtly, "I've harmed none of your kinsmen."

Meredith lowered her head, that he might not see the tears that stung her eyes. She was endlessly thankful Papa was safe. But now she knew for certain . . .

It was her that he was after.

Throughout the day, every tale of MacKay savagery she'd ever heard had returned to haunt her, tales of Munro clansmen captured and tortured, of men beaten and murdered, of women raped and abused. A shudder coursed through her. The MacKays were a cruel, wild lot. As a child, whene'er she had ventured out, she'd been warned not to stray far from home, lest one of the MacKays had wandered onto Munro lands, up to no good.

Nervously she wet her lips. "What will you do with me?"

"That is none of your concern!"

The bite in his tone made her flinch. She longed to argue that it *was* her concern—indeed, it was her very life! Quaking inside, she sought to reason with him. "I am a woman. I've done naught to harm you."

His eyes seemed to light with the blaze of a lightning bolt. "You are a Munro! Your existence clouds the very air around me."

He spun around and she knew she'd been dismissed. "Wait!" she cried before she thought better of it.

He whirled.

"I present no threat to you. I will spend the rest of my days at Connyridge, I promise you, for I was to take my vows within the month. Indeed, I still may if you will only release me."

"Nay, Meredith, I think not!" Four steps had brought him before her. He smiled . . . oh, it was frugal, dangerous, that smile!

"I pray you, let me go." She prayed he wouldn't detect the tremor in her voice, in her very limbs. "Cease this madness."

His smile vanished. His hands shot out and she was snatched against him.

His lips stretched back over his teeth. "Madness!" he hissed. "Had you seen the way my brothers died, you would not dare to speak of madness!"

Meredith froze, taken aback by his outburst.

"Does that surprise you? That I am still alive? That I was the only one who survived? The only one your clan did not kill?"

"Nay!" she gasped. "I know naught of killing!" Her heart throbbed with fear. Never in all her days had she encountered such rage. The very air about him seemed to thunder and seethe. Her legs would have buckled had his hands not held her upright.

"You know naught of killing," he sneered. "And I promise you, I know naught of mercy, for your father showed none! Did my father receive mercy when his throat was slit from behind? When my brother Bryan was stabbed in the back and I was left to die?

Well, let me tell you of killing. My father—and all of my brothers—died beneath the swords of your kinsmen. Beneath the blade of your father, at the orders of your father!''

''That cannot be,'' she said, shocked to the core by such butchery as he'd detailed. ''My father would not do such things! He would not allow it!''

''Your father did!''

She shrank back from his fierceness. There was no denying the rage fired in his breast. It vibrated through him, so intense she could feel it in every part of his body. Sensing the demon within him, terror winged through her anew, but she was not so foolish as to challenge him now. Nay, now was not the time to argue.

His lip curled. ''Aye, you *will* go with me. You *will* remain with me. You may beg. You may plead. But know this, Meredith Munro. Do not try to run, for I will find you. I will hunt you to the ends of this land. Do not try to hide, for I will bind you to my side with a chain that will forever be unbroken.''

There was naught of mercy in his tone—in his very being. Meredith was shaking so that she could scarcely stand.

But at last she fully understood. It was not the feud alone which had brought him to Connyridge . . . to her. His brothers and his father had been killed. This was why he had taken her.

She was to be the instrument of his revenge. He would avenge the death of his kinsmen through her . . . *through her*.

Her lungs burned. Had Mother Gwynn even now sent word to her father that she was dead?

''Ah, I see you understand. Your father must live with the certainty that you, his only child, are dead.''

The thought tore her heart to shreds. He was right—the sisters would send word of her death, and Papa's grief would know no bounds. He would be devastated, thinking that she was gone. She well remembered her father's desolation when her mother had fallen ill and died one long-ago winter, though she had been but a child of ten. Aye, she thought bleakly. Cameron MacKay had chosen well, for such news might very well kill her father . . .

All too soon they were on their way again. Miserable beyond anything she'd ever known, Meredith scarcely noticed the purple haze of darkness creeping across the hill until they stopped again in a small clearing. As she leaped to the ground, her cramped muscles objected to such effort after the long hours in the saddle. One of Cameron's men, the bearded one called Finn, heaved a grating laugh as she staggered.

She righted herself with what dignity she could muster. She ignored him, for now that she was on her feet, she was aware of a most urgent need to attend to. Glancing around, she spied a copse of trees to the edge of the clearing. It was there she directed her steps.

"Where the devil do you think you're going?"

She stopped short. Cameron again, his glare as black as a moonless night. Dismayed and embarrassed, Meredith felt a hot stain of color rush into her cheeks. How was she to explain?

She drew a deep breath. "I . . . I fear I must . . ."

"What? You've a need to piddle?"

Faith, but the man was crude! Her nod was jerky.

He stared at her, long and hard. Her gaze cut away, but not before she'd glimpsed the stubborn set of his jaw. A flurry of panic touched her. If he refused, what was she to do?

"Go, then, but do not tarry."

His rudeness was not warranted. By the saints, she would not convey gratitude for such a delicate matter, not when he was so curt. Without a word, she turned her back and moved away.

"Meredith!"

Her name was like a clap of thunder.

Meredith glanced back over her shoulder.

"Do not run, Meredith! For if you do . . ." He drew a finger across his throat.

Meredith felt herself pale. Aware of his gaze stabbing into her back, she picked her way carefully toward the copse. Her feet were bare and the ground was heavy with needles that pricked her soles.

His warning stirred her mind anew. What would happen to her? she wondered. It was selfish, yet she couldn't help it. Throughout the afternoon, she'd tried so very hard not to envisage the fate that awaited her! Yet she couldn't erase the choking fear that he meant her dire harm. After all, he was a MacKay. Ah, but that was laughable, for what could be more dire than death? Bitterly she chastised herself. She should have screamed while she had the chance, no matter the cost to herself. Did it truly matter if she were dead?

But it did. Sweet Mother Mary, it did. Once she had thought she would rather be dead . . . *once*. But no more. Ah, but if the truth be known, she was afraid to die . . . afraid of everything! Why couldn't she be strong . . . strong like . . . like him?

Her shoulders slumped. She was but a woman—a pitiful one, at that.

Her bodily needs attended to, she gazed longingly at the gurgling waters of the shallow stream just beyond the trees. Quickly she moved to the edge of the water and knelt to rinse the dust from her hands and face. It was then a movement caught the corner of her eye—it was Cameron. With her hands curled on her thighs, she leaned back on her knees.

Quiet as the night, he strode to the stream, paying her no heed. It struck her that she'd never encountered a man so tall—why, she scarcely reached his shoulder! Yet for all his height, his body was leanly sculpted.

He claimed her gaze and there was naught she could do to stop herself. His hair was dark, the color of a raven's breast. An odd feeling touched the base of her spine. Last night, she'd been convinced he was grotesque, given the ugliness of his actions—why, to steal a novice from a nunnery was surely a sin! Was he a God-fearing man? 'Twould seem not. Aye, she'd expected him to be abhorrent.

Yet his was a face of supreme masculine beauty. His brows were strongly arched, as dark as his hair, his eyes thickly lashed. She'd already noticed the way his nostrils flared slightly outward, in perfect symmetry to the rest of his features. His mouth was thin, yet the slant of it was harsh . . . so very harsh. All at once she recalled with vivid intensity the way he'd bent his head last evening when he'd warned her not to scream. His lips had brushed hers . . .

The muscles of her belly clenched. Now he'd unwound his plaid from his torso and removed his shirt. Her gaze traveled over the sleek hardness of his arms, the wide breadth of shoulders and chest. For all that he was handsome, she could imagine no gentleness in him. She'd been a fool to fight him, a fool to try to run. He was hard through and through. Even his lips had been hard . . .

It was then she spied the wound in the lower part of his back, a long and jagged gash. The skin was puckered and still pink—the injury was recent. Meredith's mind raced. Had he suffered this wound in the attack on his family? She shuddered. It was only too easy to imagine a sword rending through his body, through sinew and muscle, grating against bone.

He turned then.

Wide blue eyes met those of darkest gray. She was the first to falter. She felt the searing score of his gaze—it slipped all through her, piercing like the keenest of blades. His eyes glittered, sharp as the edge of his sword.

"Come," was all he said.

Unfolding her legs beneath her, Meredith arose. Her muscles stretched, then stiffened. She ached all over, especially her legs and backside. His lips tightened, for apparently she did not move quickly enough to suit him. Taking her arm, he pulled her to her feet.

The moment she was standing, he released her, as if—as if she were some wretched creature he was loath to touch! For some reason she could not fathom, Meredith was hurt beyond measure.

In silence they returned to the clearing. Egan was crouched near a small fire that had just begun to burn; Finn was busy skinning two hares he'd caught earlier in the day. Meredith stopped near one of the massive oak trees that ringed the clearing. Easing to the ground, she leaned back against the rough bark.

Across from her, Cameron was on his haunches near the fire. With his knife he was busy fashioning a small spit from branches. Again and again her gaze came back to him, almost against her will. She stared at him as he worked, unwillingly fascinated. His hands were like the rest of him, long and lean and powerful. A knot gathered deep in the pit of her belly, for they were strong, those hands . . . hands that could

easily bend her to his will and force her to yield . . .
A man's body—aye, especially his hands!—held
naught but dread for Meredith. Indeed, her father was
the only man who held no fear for her.

She jerked as he jabbed the pointed end of a branch
into the skinned hare. Her mind bolted forward; there
was no help for it, for she was hardly ignorant of the
ways between men and women. Was that what he
would do to her? Plunge his hardness into her, tearing
her flesh even as he tore the pale skin of the hare's?
Images flashed before her, images she'd fought hard
to keep at bay these many months . . . the jutting hardness of a man's member. Her breath quickened. Cameron MacKay was not a small man. No doubt his
manhood was like a spear . . .

Fool! a voice reminded her. You heard what he
said. *Were I in need of a woman, of a certainty
'twould not be you. Indeed, I must force myself to
suffer your presence.*

She could only hope he did not lie.

The mantle of darkness began to thicken; night
crept across the world. Before long the delicious
aroma of roast hare filled the clearing. Juices dripping
onto the fire made it spark and sizzle. Shivering a little
from the cold air and damp earth beneath her, Meredith drew her bare feet beneath her ragged gown to
warm them. Though she longed to avail herself of the
fire's warmth, she decided a little cold was far pref-
erable to being near the three men.

The men tore into the hare, devouring it with gusto.
Watching them, Meredith's mouth began to water.
Until then, she hadn't realized how truly ravenous she
was. A glimmer of resentment sparked within her as
Cameron put his fingers to his lips, sucking the juices
from them. With an uncharacteristic crossness, she

wondered if he planned to starve her to her death.

With his knife, he hacked off one of the hare's legs. Leaning forward, he reached out and retrieved it. As he pulled it back, he chanced to glance at her. Their eyes caught and held. Meredith was the first to look away.

"Are you hungry?"

His voice reached her ears. Meredith was sorely tempted to ignore him, to pretend she hadn't heard, yet something warned her it would not be wise. Nor could she lie, for at that precise second, her stomach gurgled, loudly protesting its fast.

Her eyes barely grazed his. "Aye," she said, her voice very low.

He held out the leg in one hand. She hesitated but an instant, then moved toward him. She bent forward to take the morsel, only to realize her mistake—the gown she wore was mud-stained and ill-fitting, for the other woman had apparently been of larger stature than she. The neckline slipped, baring the naked curve of her right shoulder. Those eyes dipped low, an inspection that was all too thorough and missed nothing. Hastily she jerked the gown over her bare skin, searingly conscious that she wore nothing beneath. With a nod she took the tidbit, a wordless profession of thanks.

Quickly she resumed her place against the oak. While she ate, she considered all she'd learned this day. Aye, there had been blood spilled, on both sides, MacKay and Munro. Yet she could not believe that her father would sanction such butchery as Cameron MacKay had described. Was it possible he was mistaken?

Surely *he* didn't think so.

A horn of ale was passed among the men. Cameron

offered it to her, but she declined. Seconds passed into minutes. A weak light wavered from the fire. Cameron paid her no further heed, but Egan and Finn regarded her with ill-concealed hatred.

Egan stroked the scar on his cheek. A sneering smile curled across his lips. "Can ye imagine? The Red Angus has but one child!"

Finn nudged Egan. "He is nae a man! What do ye think ails him, that his seed did nae flourish!"

Meredith longed to snap that his seed *did* flourish! Was she not proof of the same?

"He has nae children, save *this* one!" 'Twas a sneer, a biting condemnation. "Aye, but one child, and a daughter yet!"

" 'Tis obvious why." Egan stared at her as he spoke. " 'Tis because he is a Munro!"

Finn poked him. "That may well be, for we all know the Munros are but spineless cowards. But methinks 'tis because his balls are like shriveled turnips!"

Ribald laughter filled the air. Their crudity embarrassed Meredith no end. Her hair sheltered her burning cheeks as she pressed her lips together and turned her face away, pretending to ignore them.

A flicker of movement caught her eye. It was him—Cameron. Deliberately he made his way toward her. Meredith felt herself pale. What did he intend now?

He sat beside her, stretching out his legs. He wore no kilt. The trews which covered his legs only emphasized their lean, taut length. His shoulders were wide and strongly muscled; his left was covered by his plaid. Her awareness of his nearness was overwhelming—and rattled her every sense. He smiled, as if he knew her every thought, her every fear. His air was that of a predatory animal.

Meredith longed to scurry away, like a rat in the night. Ah, she thought bitterly, if only she possessed the daring!

Her appetite had vanished. She tossed aside the rabbit leg. She did not look at him as she spoke.

"Why did you abduct me?"

His tone was falsely hearty. "Come, now. Your kinsman from long ago abducted the beauty who wed one of my forebears—and on the night they were wed! 'Tis only fitting that a Munro should at last be abducted by a MacKay, is it not?"

He referred to the feud. "It was a Munro bride who was abducted by *your* kinsman," she informed him heatedly, "not a MacKay bride!" She knew it was so, for she'd oft heard the tale when she was young. The poor woman had been utterly shamed. She'd taken her own life rather than return to her newly wed husband soiled by another man. Since then, the feud had boiled over with the slightest provocation. There had been disputes over boundaries, over land and water and thieving. There had been periods of outright war, and the occasional truce and time of peace as well. Would the death of his brothers—and her abduction—stir the furies anew?

"I know the truth. 'Twas a MacKay bride who was taken. But I wonder . . . will you kill yourself as she did?"

Meredith straightened her spine. "Is that what you're hoping?" she snapped.

An arrogant brow cocked high. He laughed, and made no answer.

A simmering heat sputtered within her, then grew with every second. Somewhere deep inside, she realized she was angry. The feeling was unfamiliar, for it had been a long, long time since she'd felt this way—at Connyridge, such emotion was frowned upon.

"I will not give you the satisfaction!" she said stiffly.

"Is that why? You spoke of mortal sin—'tis a state your clan knows much of. But indeed, it takes great courage to take one's life. Do you have it, I wonder?"

Courage. In truth, she had none, or she might have told Papa about that horrible, unforgettable night . . . But it would remain forever hers, a secret locked tight within her soul.

Yet something within her would not let him triumph so easily. Her chin tipped high. "And what of *your* clan?" She tipped her head toward Egan and Finn, who now lay sprawled on each side of the fire, snoring loudly. "Your clansmen spoke of the frailties of those who carry Munro blood. But 'twould seem I must be a fearsome woman indeed, that it took three MacKay clansmen to subdue one Munro woman." She made a sound of utter disgust. "And you speak to me of courage! You are naught but a coward!"

She should have known she would regret her rashly spoken taunt . . . and indeed, in an instant, she did.

He moved with the swiftness of one who was accustomed to relying upon agility to save both life and limb—and succeeded. There was no time to protest, to even draw breath, before she was caught squarely in the vise of his arms, tumbled to the ground at her back. She dared not fight—she dared not move . . . as if she even could! All she could feel was the heavy breadth of his chest, the immense width of his shoulders above her, dwarfing her own.

Eyes the color of storm clouds moved slowly over her features. "Tell me, Meredith. Do you look warily upon me now?"

Aye, she nearly blurted. Her gaze shifted, lest her expression betray her. Despite the weight of his body above her own, the rebellion within her would not be vanquished.

"Why should I?" Daringly she spoke, though inside she was a mass of quivering pudding. Beneath her scorn was an endless, dragging fear.

His slow smile sent a tremor all through her. "Because I am stronger than you, lass."

Lass. She shuddered, for upon this man's lips, it sounded like a curse from the devil himself. Oh, aye, she knew what he thought of her.

He hated her, with every fiber of his being.

There was an air of expectancy about him, as if he awaited her challenge. None was forthcoming, for in truth Meredith was aghast at all she had dared already speak.

At length he released her. Meredith let out an uneven breath, relieved when he arose and started toward the horses. Though she strained to see, 'twas impossible; the night was dark and moonless, and it was as if the shadows had swallowed him whole.

He was back within seconds, and it appeared he was not through with her. She stared—indeed, warily!—as he dropped to one knee before her.

Dangling within one large brown hand was a small length of chain.

Boldly he reached for one slender wrist. Meredith jerked at his touch, for he was so very warm! He paid no heed but placed the shackle deliberately around her right wrist. In shock she watched as he then proceeded to place the other end about his left.

She wet her lips. "Is there a key?" she heard herself ask.

He raised his head, his smile almost goading.

"Aye, but you'd best watch your tongue and mind your manners, lest I lose it."

A sizzle of anger shot through her. "Ah," she said sweetly, "but I wonder . . . which of us is the prisoner?"

His smile vanished. He bestowed upon her a look so quelling, her bravado was gone in an instant.

Without a word, he turned to his side and lay down upon the cold hard ground. Meredith felt herself jerked down beside him, for the length of the chain was such that she could not sit while he lay. His back to her, he drew the corner of his plaid over his head and slept.

Meredith was left huddling in the chill night air.

Three

Sleep departed little by little. Meredith was still caught in the murky web of the night's slumber. Somewhere in the back of her mind was the awareness that morning was nigh, the light of day trickling brightly upon the world. She lay on her side, but her backside was still wretchedly cold, and the chill damp seemed to penetrate to her very bones.

But there was warmth emanating from somewhere. She could feel it, and instinctively snuggled toward it, this wall of ovenlike heat . . . ah, warmth! Faith, but it was bliss. Like a cat nuzzling its mother, she stretched into it and against it.

A vile curse ripped through the air just above her. Meredith's eyes snapped open; the warmth she sought was no more, the swiftness of movement but a blur. She blinked as the shackle around her wrist dropped to the ground.

Cameron MacKay stood high above her, his feet braced wide apart. For the space of a heartbeat their eyes tangled interminably, his virulently accusing, hers still puzzled and confused.

All at once the air was filled with a thundering tension. He did not speak—and indeed, what need was

38

there? She glimpsed within those harshly drawn features a blistering condemnation.

Just when she thought she could stand it no longer, he spun around and was gone.

Slowly Meredith pushed herself upright. The venom she sensed in him pierced her to the quick. She could not fathom the burning in his soul. He regarded her as if she were some vile ugliness that stained the world, and all because she was a Munro.

Egan and Finn were just beginning to stir as she crept by them. After tending to her needs, she made her way to the stream. She splashed her face with water, then picked her way to a gnarled oak tree that stood guard near the pathway leading back to the clearing. It was here she knelt down upon the soft, mossy ground. The voices of the men flitted to her ears, but she ignored them. It was tranquil and peaceful here beneath the shade of the massive oak. Though her life was now in turmoil, she would begin this day as she had every day for the last year and more. Dutifully Meredith folded her hands, closed her eyes, and bowed her head low.

Her lips moved silently. She prayed for strength and vigilance, for the safety and wellness of her father and Uncle Robert, the sisters at Connyridge. She prayed most diligently . . . prayed for deliverance from Cameron MacKay.

A twig snapped behind her.

"It's time," intoned a voice that was already far too wretchedly familiar.

Meredith determinedly ignored him, continuing her prayers. Her skin prickled, for she could feel his regard as surely as if he touched her. Then, all at once, he *was* touching her. An arm slid hard about her waist, lifting her up and around and fully off her feet.

Her prayer—and her breath—were effectively cut off as she was turned to face him. His gaze slid over her, then fastened upon the silver crucifix which hung about her neck.

"Why do you wear that?" he demanded. "You said you'd not yet taken your vows."

Meredith winced inwardly. "I have not," she admitted.

"You should have taken them long ago. You've been at Connyridge long enough. Could it be you are not worthy?"

He sought to wound her. Meredith knew it and tried not to allow it, yet she couldn't help it.

What was it he'd made her write in her letter to the sisters? *I am deeply ashamed that I am so weak in devotion and in spirit.*

Was it true? Was that why she had tarried so long in taking her vows? Pain wrenched through her. Confusion roiled within her, confusion that the days past had not erased. Throughout she had prayed for guidance to make the right choice, for direction from above. A voice within cried out. Why had the God she so entrusted forsaken her? Was she being punished for her doubts? She had disappointed Papa, and now the Lord as well.

She inclined her head. Yet the fervor of her words belied the meekness of her pose. "God alone judges our worthiness—and our worth."

For an instant he looked ready to explode. Something raced across his features, an anger she could not begin to comprehend. He stepped close and raised his hand. Fighting back her fear, striving to ignore the power of the fist that hovered so near, Meredith braced herself for a stunning blow . . .

It never came. She gasped as warm fingers brushed

her skin. In shock she felt her crucifix ripped from about her throat.

"Do not prescribe to me, woman. 'Twould not take much to convince me that your blood would indeed be blood well shed." His lips barely moved as he spoke.

Meredith was shattered but determined not to show it. Mustering all her dignity, she lifted her chin. "I do not preach to you—I simply state my beliefs, for as you have said, I am not worthy. And for now I will entrust my crucifix to your safekeeping"—her gaze skipped to the chain dangling from his fingertips—"but I vow it will soon be back in my possession."

His lips compressed. Her heart leaped as he swung the chain and caught the whole of the necklace in his palm. His fingers tightened so that his knuckles showed white. For one awful moment Meredith feared he would fling it high and away and it might truly be forever lost to her.

His hand disappeared inside his shirt . . . and the necklace as well. All he said was, "Come. We dally no longer."

Meredith's fingers touched the place where the crucifix dwelled no more. She felt naked without it. But she would have it back, she vowed.

His low whistle cut through the air. Egan and Finn hurried forward, leading their mounts.

Panic raced through her. Beside her, she could feel his body—hard as a pillar of stone. The thought of riding with him again made her stomach curdle in dread. She could not do it. She would not!

She linked her hands before her to still their trembling. "I will come with you, but I will not ride before you on your horse." She swallowed. "Nor will I ride behind you, or with any of your men."

She knew she did not imagine the stiffening of his spine. "You will not ride with me," he repeated, "either before me or behind me? And you will not ride with Egan or Finn?"

Meredith shook her head. His tone was almost deadly quiet, yet the hint of a storm brewed in the depths of his eyes.

Behind him, Finn let out a growl. "By the Rood, woman, you will not dare such insolence—"

"Be silent, Finn!" Cameron sent his man a glare that was no less blistering.

"Yet you say you will come with me."

Still that disturbingly quiet tone. Though she was filled with trepidation, she held her ground. "Aye," she heard herself say.

"Mayhap you should explain."

Her heart had begun to race. Vaguely she wondered what madness possessed her, that she should challenge him so. "I will not ride," she said again. "I will walk."

His gaze dipped to her toes, bare and pink beneath the ragged hem of her gown. Some of the sizzle had departed his features. A brow arched high. Indeed, he appeared almost amused . . . Meredith was not sure which she preferred.

"You wear neither slippers nor sandals nor boots."

His unnecessary observation made her feel quite the fool. She angled her chin. "That is true."

"I warn you now, we will soon be leaving the Borders. We will not be traversing through soft, grassy meadows."

If her chin tipped any higher, her neck would surely snap! " 'Tis kind of you to inform me."

His eyes narrowed. "You're very defiant this morn, aren't you?"

"Nay, sir, 'tis not defiance."

But in so saying, so it was . . . and they both knew it. Meredith held her breath, wondering wildly what he would do. Given the circumstances, she was surprised he had not brushed aside her protest and proceeded to bodily place her upon his horse. Indeed, his reaction was remarkably restrained given the fact that he had snatched her from her bed.

'Twas only later she realized she should have been wary.

"Your feet will be bruised and cut."

"Your concern overwhelms me. But do not worry. What pain I may suffer shall be offered as penance for your sins."

The sweetness of her tone goaded him—as she had meant. Nor was there any doubt she referred to his abduction of her . . . Thus began the battle between them. Meredith could not deny that were this a test of strength, he would undoubtedly emerge the victor. Yet there was a part of her that would not bend to his will as readily as she had already done.

Something flitted across his face, something that might have been anger. But he spoke neither in fierce admonishment nor in anger—indeed, he did not speak to her at all! Instead he crossed to Egan. Laying a hand on his shoulder, he bent his head to the scarred man's ear. His instructions, whate'er they were, were quick and brief. In what seemed like mere seconds, Egan and Finn had gathered up their belongings and ridden away.

Meredith stared at the spiral of dust kicked up in their wake, then back to Cameron.

"Where are they going?" Her tone was sharper than she intended.

"Back to our home."

Her mouth was dry as parchment. "And what of you?"

"Do not worry"—his mouth twisted into a leer—"we shall soon follow."

Meredith spoke her thoughts aloud. "You sent them away, didn't you?"

"That I did, lass. That I did." He was suddenly far too relaxed, his manner far too easy.

"But now we are alone!" She colored when she realized how foolish that sounded.

She could not cast aside the sudden fear that clutched at her. Her thoughts were a wild jumble within her head. Her fears leaped apace with her heart. He had sent Egan and Finn away . . . yet why should he? Could it be he had another purpose in mind? Her breath came jaggedly. Would he rape her? Use her to slake his own base desire? Take her now that the others were gone?

She reminded herself he did not want her—he'd expressed his distaste quite plainly. Yet Meredith was not so innocent. She knew of the dark desires of men; she knew of the lust that drove them to think of naught but the lance between their legs. Nay, she was no innocent. A man need not feel desire or love to take a woman, to force a woman to his will . . . *against* her will. To some it was but a punishment. Was this what he intended? Did he seek to defeat her in the one sure way that man would ever defeat woman?

No. Surely he would not dare such a thing against a woman who had sought to be a nun . . .

But she was not a nun, nor would she ever be. Not now.

And he was a man who would dare anything. Had he not already? Why, he'd dared to invade the sanctity of the priory!

Or if not that . . . would he kill her? Yet if all he sought was her death, surely he'd have done so long before now . . . and before his men.

Her chin climbed high. "Know this, Cameron MacKay! I will never give myself to you!"

His lip curled. "Know this, Meredith Munro—chaste, virtuous lady, I have not asked you to!"

It spun through Meredith's mind that she was neither chaste nor virtuous. She hated the shameful remembrance that gripped her mind—and she almost hated him for bringing it about.

"You accused me of being a coward," he went on. His tone now rang with false heartiness. "You leave me no choice but to show you that I am not, that I do not need others to keep you in check."

He strode to where his horse, Fortune, was idly grazing the lush grass near the bank of the stream. The animal was quickly saddled and ready. Meredith remained where she was, unmoving. Never in her life had she felt so foolish! If only there was some way she could escape! But on foot, he would be upon her in an instant . . .

He returned far more quickly than she wished. High atop his mount, he appeared big and brawny and thoroughly indomitable, much to her everlasting vexation.

He did not stop where she stood. Instead he walked the horse right by her, on toward the next copse of trees without a pause.

The usually soft line of her lips pressed together in a straight, mutinous line. Meredith stared at the long line of his back, the square set of his shoulders. Did he expect her to run after him, like a child who was afraid of being left behind? By heaven, she would not!

Halfway there, he glanced over his shoulder. When he saw she'd not moved a muscle, he turned in his saddle and gazed back at her. His brows shot up before he retraced his steps.

"Do not tell me," he said smoothly, "you've changed your mind?" He shook his head. "Too late, I fear. You wished to walk, therefore we shall proceed at a more leisurely pace. But I do believe I should make myself clear, lass. I will not pity you when you plead to ride with me. I will not carry you because of your stubbornness, I will not pick you up when you falter or stumble. You will do what I say, when I say. If I tell you to call me lord—"

"I have no Lord save one." Meredith directed her eyes heavenward. "I will bow to no Lord save one."

His smile held no mirth. "Believe me, lass, had you not come from the priory, we would debate that very point. But let us make no mistake. I allow you to walk, not because it pleases you, but because it pleases *me*."

It pleased him! Meredith's jaw opened, then closed. Merciful heaven, what had she done? She wasn't certain if she was angrier at him or at herself for her own folly! Plead with him to ride, would she? Never!

Without a word he nudged his mount forward.

Meredith waited a full ten seconds before taking a step.

This time he didn't bother to glance behind.

Nor had he lied. They were soon deep in the rolling hills of the forest. Dried needles that had fallen from the fir trees pricked at the soles of her feet like the sharpest of thorns. Tiny rocks dug into her skin until every step made her wince. She had to force herself to walk, emptying her mind of all else, concentrating only on putting one foot ahead of the next. She plodded along, falling ever farther behind.

Near noon, he stopped his mount, waiting patiently for her to catch up.

He inclined his head as she approached. "How are your feet?" he asked pleasantly.

Meredith gritted her teeth. She was sorely tempted to retort that had he not snatched her from her bed in the middle of the night, she would not be in this predicament. Yet the choice to walk had been hers . . .

And he was right. She was too stubborn to change her mind.

"Do you truly care?"

"Only that you do not further delay our journey."

Meredith glared. The beast! Somehow she managed to keep her tone civil, disguising her anxiety.

"You've yet to tell me where this journey takes us."

It seemed he never would, for he made no reply.

She tried again. "We travel north and west"—she held her breath—"toward Munro lands."

His gaze narrowed. Meredith had the uneasy suspicion he'd not expected her to notice. Then all at once the corner of his mouth lifted in a baiting smile.

"North and west," he agreed mildly, "toward *MacKay* lands."

Munro lands. MacKay lands. In truth, what did it matter? Either way, she was his prisoner. These many months at Connyridge she had taken comfort from the repetitive order of the day, yet now the world was splintering all around her. She knew not what the day would bring. Indeed, she knew not what the hour would bring, if the truth be told, for her life was in the hands of this rude Highlander, Cameron MacKay! She had no say over it, over him, she thought with a rising hysteria.

Stop it! hissed a voice from within. She could not control the outside world, but she must take command of herself, she decided. Meredith forced a deep, calming breath, determined to seek respite from the turmoil in her soul. She knew but one sure way to accomplish this.

Sinking to her knees, she closed her eyes and made the sign of the cross, then clasped her hands against her breast.

Behind her, there was a long expulsion of breath and a brusque exclamation.

"God's teeth, woman! What the devil do you think you're doing?"

Her lips stopped moving. Her eyes did not open as she said simply, "I am praying."

"Again?"

Was the man blind? Meredith found little need to reply.

There was a foul curse, the jangle of a harness, and the noisy stomp of footsteps. In the next instant two strong hands shot out, cupping her elbows from behind. In a heartbeat she was lifted to her feet and turned bodily to face him.

"I have not harmed you, have I? Abused you or beaten you?"

He was angry again. She could feel it in the muted restraint of those hands which still curled warm about her shoulders. He was so tall! Far taller than her father, or even her Uncle Robert, who was by far the largest man at Castle Munro.

Her prayer had irritated him, irritated him vastly, she realized. She could well believe that here was a man who believed in no God, yet the notion that any man could be so foolish was almost beyond comprehension.

Ah, if only he would let her go. She hesitated, uncertain how to answer. Then, compelled by a force she was powerless to control, her gaze trickled slowly up the strongly muscled column of his neck, past the clenched line of his jaw, to the glitter of his eyes.

His expression was everything she expected, a reflection of his manner, hard and impatient. With his features so drawn and fierce, his mouth so very thin, he frightened her half out of her wits!

Her gaze veered away.

He gave her a tiny shake. "Answer me," he demanded. "Have I hurt you, harmed you in any way?"

Her eyes returned to settle on the broad expanse of his chest. "Nay," she said finally. Through some miracle she managed to sound somewhat normal. Her composure returned, little by little.

His hands fell away from her shoulders. "Then cease your prayers!" he growled.

That brought her head up anew. Now that he no longer touched her, she no longer felt so muddled. It seemed suddenly important that he not know of her fears—or, at least, the depth of them.

"You do not understand," she stated coolly. "I do not pray for myself. I pray for you."

"For me!" He appeared taken aback.

Meredith stared him straight in the eye. "Aye," she said quietly, "that God will forgive you your recent sins."

"Sins! To what sins do you refer? I've no doubt you're anxious to regale me with your account of my misdeeds." His smile was both false and brittle.

Meredith stiffened. "Very well, then. You took me

from Connyridge, and for what purpose, I ask? To make my father believe that his only child is no more.'' Her denouncement was stinging. '' 'Tis revenge you want, revenge for the death of your brothers and your father. But I tell you, you are wrong! The Red Angus is no murderer. He did not kill your father or brothers, for he would never be so cruel!''

His smile was wiped clean. ''And I tell you he was, for I was there!'' His gaze scraped over her like a sword of molten steel. ''You speak of God's forgiveness. But is not God a vengeful God? Aye, 'tis revenge I seek, revenge for the slaying of my family. I think I need not remind you that Scripture tells us, 'An eye for an eye, and a tooth for a tooth'!''

Her reply was swift and vehement. '' 'Judge not, that ye be not judged,' '' she quoted in turn.

He did not flinch in the slightest. ''I am prepared to face whatever consequences come my way in the days to come. But your father is responsible for the deaths of my brothers and my father. And I promise you, 'tis a debt I will see repaid measure for measure.''

Meredith shook her head. It was not defiance but genuine puzzlement that prompted her question. ''How? You chose to let my father live . . . and I have no brothers!''

He stepped near, so very near that her breasts brushed the folds of his plaid; so close she could see the dark steel that ringed his eyes.

''True,'' he said, his tone suddenly soft, ''but now I have you.''

Four

But now I have you.

That dark-featured face shadowed with a day's growth of beard . . . that ever-so-slow smile . . . that voice as soft as swan's down—any one of them might have sent a shiver throughout the length of her.

The three of them combined . . . it was enough to send a river of ice rushing through her veins.

His claim was true. He had neither harmed nor abused her . . .

But she had the awful feeling he was not yet through with her.

Bravely she held her ground, boldly drawing herself up before him. Somehow she managed to keep her regard entangled with his.

"I would ask you this. Did you see him?"

"Did I see who?"

"My father! You claim he was among your attackers, but I must know—did you see him? Face-to-face, I ask? For I swear to you, my kinsmen would not strike men down and leave them for dead. Never would my father sanction such butchery!"

It seemed an eternity yawned before he finally spoke. When he did, his lips were ominously thin. "I did not see him face-to-face. But I know well the bat-

51

tle cry of the Munros and the colors of their plaid—
and there was no mistaking the color of his hair.''

"You will not even consider that you could be
wrong? That there was treachery involved and someone sought to lay the blame on my father?''

"I will not, for I know who is to blame!'' Cameron's lips barely moved. "And were I you, I would
let this matter rest here and now.''

Meredith's nails dug into her palms. Suddenly
everything inside her chest was boiling and determined to be free. "You think you have defeated me
because I am a woman,'' she cried, "because I am
weaker and you are stronger. Were I a man,'' she
accused, "you'd not have dared to lay a hand upon
me. You are a wretch,'' she went on, for the spark
had been kindled and would not be doused. "Aye,
you are the slimiest vermin of the earth. I find your
actions despicable, as you are despicable!''

She stood with bare, dirty feet planted apart, the tilt
of her chin undeniably defiant. Cameron was
amazed—and angry beyond words. Despicable, she
called him. How dare she pass judgment upon him,
this—this pious little nun who was not a nun! And
how dare she imply that he was wrong, that it was
not her kinsmen who had killed his! What treachery
there was belonged solely to her father!

But he did not reveal the depths of his ire—he did
not dare, for he knew he would regret it later, as
would she for provoking it!

He forced an even calm he was far from feeling.
"Are you quite finished?''

The seconds passed, one into another, while each
tested the resolve found in the other's eyes. Cameron
was certain another outburst was imminent. Her lips
parted, then compressed tightly. Fury flared in those

dark-lashed eyes. Yet in the end she said nothing.

"I will take that as an aye." He whistled for his mount. "Let us depart, then. But just so you know, lass"—as he swung onto his mount, the smile he offered was tightly—"were you a man, you would be long since cold in your grave."

A heel on Fortune's side, and the animal sprinted forward. This time Cameron was in no mood to be mindful of his pace. It was not intentional—he was simply too angry with the wench!

Before long, the forest thinned. High above, fluffy masses of clouds cast huge shadows across the landscape below. Starlings swirled and veered and swooped with the currents of the wind. Before them, the hills rose in meadowed benches of bright yellow and verdant green.

Just then some small sound reached his ears—a tiny, choked-off sound of distress. It lasted but an instant . . .

Cameron's head whipped around.

Meredith was just behind him and to the right. He reined Fortune to a halt, then called to her.

"Do you need assistance?"

She shot him a fulminating look but said nothing. With her countenance set in smooth, implacable lines, she marched on. Whatever it was, she'd completely recovered, as if naught had happened.

"As you wish, then," he said coolly.

His gaze lingered on her a moment longer. A beauty, he'd thought last night, but such did not even begin to describe her. Impossible as it seemed, she was even more breathtaking in daylight! It mattered naught that her skin was smudged with dust, that her hair hung tangled about slim, narrow hips. The wretched gown she wore was ragged and torn—yet drooped in places that hinted of rounded pink tantalizing flesh that he had never thought to imagine—not in a Munro! A part of him could not reconcile such beauty, not when such vile blood flowed in her veins; yet at last Cameron admitted that which he had sidestepped throughout the day. Nothing could disguise the beauty beneath.

Cameron had slowed his pace. His gaze sharpened when he saw that she had begun to limp. A dozen times he nearly snatched her before him in the saddle, yet a dozen times he stopped himself. Why didn't she ask him to stop? She moved on with stoic persistence, the bonny wee fool!

They had just come upon the river that wound through the glen when she went down on one knee. A grimace twisted her features as she stretched out a hand to catch her fall, yet she was upright again in the next breath; had his regard resided elsewhere but an instant, he would never have noticed.

This time Cameron did not hesitate. He wheeled Fortune to a halt directly before her and swung to the ground.

Aware of the fierceness of his expression and the swiftness of his approach, she threw up a hand as if to ward him off.

"Stop!" she cried.

"Sit!" he countered.

She did not, but began to back away.

He snared her elbow and pulled her to him. With a growl, he laid his palms upon her shoulders, expecting her to fight him. She yielded, dropping to the ground as if she were melting, her legs folding beneath her.

Her eyes were huge. "Why do you look at me so?"

Only then did Cameron realize the fierceness of his

expression. Could it be this was a means to yield her compliance . . . a mere glower?

"Show me your feet," he said sternly.

"There is no need!"

Hurriedly she tried to draw her feet beneath her, but Cameron was too quick. He planted his hand squarely atop her thigh, just above her knee. Her reaction was immediate. She tried to recoil. With his fingers Cameron squeezed, just enough to convey the message that she was not free.

She froze. He had the feeling he'd shocked her to the saintly core. All at once her face burned crimson.

A potent satisfaction filled his chest. A look. A touch. This was proving most enlightening—it would seem either would quell her resistance.

Cupping his free hand around one shapely calf, he drew her foot forward, dimly aware of the softness of her flesh. She flinched, but did not withdraw.

His frown returned in short order.

His prediction proved correct, yet he experienced no gratification. The soles of her feet were raw and bruised. In places the flesh was torn and bloodied. In truth he didn't know how she could stand, let alone walk. He cursed her—and himself, for allowing her to continue to walk these many hours.

They sat upon a small embankment that sloped to the edge of the river. Rising, Cameron retrieved a strip of linen cloth from the pouch on Fortune's flank and walked through deep green ferns to the water's edge. She looked like a frightened doe ready to bolt, yet she hadn't moved by the time he returned. Her features, however, were decidedly nervous as he returned to kneel before her.

His mouth grim, he wiped the mingled grime and blood from her feet as gently as he could. When he was done, he slipped his dagger from the sheath at his waist. Her eyes flew wide, but surprisingly, she made no move to scramble back. Instead she clasped her fingertips before her. Dimly he noted her hands were dainty-looking and small, like the rest of her.

There were several thorns embedded deep in the heel of one foot. With the point of the dagger he set about removing the first. She inhaled sharply, yet no protest was forthcoming.

"Why didn't you tell me?" His tone was brusque. "You could have ridden."

He raised his eyes suddenly. He had the feeling he'd startled her, but she didn't glance away, as he suspected she would.

"To walk was my choice."

In all his days, he'd never known a soul so stubborn! He snorted. "And a foolish choice it was, too!"

Her chin thrust out. "I am not a simpleton!"

His lips thinned. "What, then? Or will you tell me now how our Savior went to the cross with bloodied feet—how you chose to follow in His steps with your antics?"

She gasped. "What? Do you dare to mock Him, too?"

"Lady, I believe in the Lord as much as you. But in my estimation, those who seek to martyr themselves are naught but fools."

A glare burned hot and bright in her eyes. "And I begin to see why you did not heed His call, though I see why He would turn aside a MacKay—in particular one such as you!"

Cameron's jaw snapped shut. Why, the insolent bratling! She not only insulted his clan, but the man he was! At times he wondered if he'd stolen the wrong woman, for this was not the meek and timid maid he'd heard tales of! One moment she was humble and trembling, timid and shy, the next she dared what no sane man would dare, unless he harbored an utter disregard for his life!

His mood was suddenly black as the pits of hell. With a whistle he got to his feet, then plucked her from the ground like a duck from its nest. Fortune appeared, his ears pricked forward. Cameron swung her atop the black steed's saddle and followed her up.

"You will ride," was all he said. Mayhap she recognized that he was possessed of little tolerance just now, for she did not argue . . .

At least not yet.

They continued several miles upstream. At length he halted near the water's edge for a quick assessment. The river was wide, cut here with upthrusting boulders. Normally it was fairly shallow, but there had been rains in the previous sennight; though the waters had not overflown its banks, the river was swollen higher than was usual during the early summer months. Still, he and his men had crossed safely on their way to Connyridge, and he judged they would do so again.

He leaped lightly to the ground, then pointed to a clearing across the river. "We will stop there for the night," he said curtly.

Her gaze followed the direction of his finger. He knew naught of the sinking flutter of her heart—that the sight of the calm, peaceful glade lent her no ease.

"There? Across the river?"

"Aye."

"But . . . we must cross."

"Aye!"

She persisted. "There is no bridge? No other way across?"

He mistook her dismay for stubbornness. "There is not. The river traverses east to west and we travel north."

"Can we not wait until morn?"

"We will not wait. We cross now."

She faltered. "But . . . it looks so deep—"

" 'Tis not."

She made one last rally. "How will we cross? Must we"—there was a slight quaver in her voice—"swim?"

"You may ride Fortune. I will lead him across."

He waded into the water, his hand on Fortune's bridle.

They were a third of the way across when the bottom dropped out from beneath Cameron's feet. The water was higher than he'd anticipated—there must have been more rain. He swore and kicked strongly. Fortune tossed his head, his eyes bulging. A word and stroke from his master, and the massive animal quieted. The water deepened, and soon Fortune could no longer stand, either. The beast began to swim. A quick glance behind revealed that Meredith had gone pale. Her fingers were twisted in the horse's mane. The water crept higher, clear to her hips.

Then suddenly it happened. The shifting currents of the stream pushed the animal to the side. The beast neighed and began to swim more strongly.

But for Meredith it was already too late. From the corner of his eye Cameron saw a flurry of movement. There was a cry and a spray of water high in the air.

Just before she went under, she screamed. She resurfaced but a second later, and for one agonizing heartbeat, their eyes collided—hers were stricken and filled with panic. His heart leaped. Too late Cameron realized what lay behind her reticence.

He started to swim after her, but a rush of water had carried her beyond reach—he knew he would never catch her this way. Abruptly he changed direction, swimming to the shore.

Lunging from the river, he ran along the bank, keeping her in sight. A more accomplished swimmer would have floated with the current, staying atop the water until it was safer. But she was fighting it. With flailing arms she clawed desperately at the air, bobbing up and down, pitching back and forth like a twig.

There was a bend just ahead. Cameron leaped across a fallen mossy log and nearly lost his footing. Somehow his feet found purchase in the mud and he managed to remain upright. He was just ahead of her now; in but an instant she would be delivered into a smooth, glassy pool. Inhaling deeply, he launched himself forward.

He surfaced next to her. Just before she would have gone under again, he caught her and hauled her up against his side.

She flung her arms about his neck. Stricken, glazed eyes lifted to meet his. "Do not let me drown!" she cried. "Do not let me drown!"

His arm tightened around her. "I have you now, lass." He placed his mouth near her ear. "Now listen to me. Keep your head above the water and do not struggle against me."

It took but ten strokes to reach the bank. When he was able to stand, he slid an arm beneath her legs and carried her from the river to the top of a grassy embankment. Unmindful of the two humans' ordeal, Fortune glanced up from where he munched the leaves of a bush.

Cameron stopped, a curious uncertainty within him. His lovely captive had yet to release him. The twine of soft, supple arms about his neck had not loosened;

her body still arched against his as if he were all that she sought in the world.

And he could still feel her terror with every uneven breath she took . . . just as he could feel it leave her little by little.

It was then that the oddest thing happened. The ghost of a smile danced on his lips.

"Lady," he murmured, "if you will but look about you, you will see you are in no further danger of drowning."

The top of her head brushed his chin as she raised her head.

"Oh," she said weakly.

Still she did not move. A dark brow climbed high. He cleared his throat, shifting her against his chest.

Only then did her perch in his embrace seem to penetrate her consciousness. Her daze left her in a flash. With a gasp she pushed herself away. Horror flitted across her face. As he lowered her to the ground, he couldn't help but be mildly offended.

She withdrew the instant she was free. He watched as she picked her way unsteadily toward the shelter of a stand of venerable oak trees, then sat beneath the outstretched branches. Cameron suspected the spot was not of any particular significance, but that her legs simply refused to carry her farther.

He was but a step behind her.

"Why didn't you tell me you cannot swim?"

She said nothing.

"Answer me, lass." His tone brooked no argument.

She turned her head aside. "You already think me weak." Her voice was scarcely audible. "If I had told you, you would but think me weaker still."

Cameron considered this. So. It was pride that dictated the absence of confession. Pride he could understand. Blind foolishness he could not.

The shadow of evening had begun to wash across the land, and with it a faint breeze.

Cameron did not miss the way she shivered. They were both drenched to the skin; her hair was a sodden waterfall down her back and her gown was plastered to her skin. Such discomfort did not bother Cameron, for he'd often slept in the cold, wet rain. For a moment he weighed a silent battle back and forth in his mind, sorely tempted to strip her dripping clothes from her back—it would be warmer that way. But she was already convinced he was the blackest soul on this earth, and were he to do so, no doubt he would surely plummet ever deeper into the depths to which she'd already consigned him.

Quickly he saw to building a fire. His stomach growled noisily as he dropped another branch on the leaping flames, reminding him that they had yet to partake of any food.

"We must eat," he said curtly. "If I leave, will you promise me you will not flee?"

Again no answer. She stared at him in that way he was beginning to dislike most heartily.

Cameron's mouth tightened. Her rebellion rankled— would that the river had drowned it!

"To return to Connyridge you would have to cross the river," he reminded her.

A shudder shook her slender form. "I will stay," she said at last.

Cameron smiled thinly. His statement was perhaps a peculiar means of ensuring her compliance, but 'twould seem a convincing one—and, he hoped, effective.

The possibility of her disappearance high in his mind, he did not tarry. Berries and wild turnips would have to do for this night.

At first he didn't see her. With a curse he quickened his pace.

It died unuttered in his throat. She had simply moved toward the warmth of the fire. Stretched out beside it, she was fast asleep, one arm extended toward the fire.

He was at her side in an instant, tucking her arm back toward her belly, lest she inadvertently thrust it in the flames.

Completely relaxed in slumber, she didn't even stir.

She was exhausted, he thought with a faint smile. Of course, he was aware she'd probably worked many a long hour at the nunnery; still, no doubt the hours traveled—the miles she'd walked—had surely been taxing. Then there was her ordeal at the river . . .

He was scarcely aware of moving. Putting out a hand, he started to brush away the damp strands of hair that streamed across her cheek. An odd emotion surged in him . . . tenderness? What was this? he wondered, amazed and aghast and annoyed all at once.

He snatched his hand away with a scowl. Why this sudden softness toward her, this strange protectiveness that surged in him? Was it protectiveness? He scoffed. Nay, not that . . . never that, for she was a Munro. It was only because she was a woman, and just as she'd said . . . weaker than he.

She moved then, easing to her back, her face upturned to the moonlight . . . to him.

A dark, avid gaze roamed her features—long silky lashes that shuttered eyes as pure as a bonny blue sky, the milky white curve of her cheek, the sensuous fullness of her lower lip. It struck him then, like a clenched fist low to the belly—a blatant desire that was stark and vivid and wholly undeniable. He remembered far too well the pouting press of breasts against his chest, the way his hand had fit the nip of her waist just so.

His staff stirred to almost painful life. Exhaling slowly, he pushed his thoughts away from the potent swelling between his thighs. A voice within reminded him of the chain in his pouch. He stared hard at the frailty of the wrist that even now lay between the tempting valley of her breasts. Yet in the end he discarded the need to see her fettered. She was already asleep, and there was no need to wake her.

His expression taut, he stretched out, near her but not touching her.

She rolled, burrowing into his side. Cameron went rigid, as if he'd been paralyzed. His lungs seemed to shut down. His body turned to stone, his insides to porridge. The entire length of her lay pliantly yielding against him. Her head was pillowed on his shoulder. He could feel the moist wisp of her breath trickling over the skin of his collarbone.

A shiver shook her anew.

His mood suddenly dark as the night, he lurched to a sitting position. In one swift move he'd dragged his plaid from his shoulders and dropped it over her form.

His mouth curled in scathing self-derision. Fiercely he berated himself, scorning both himself and this innocent temptress. Desire. Tenderness. What foolishness had seized hold of him?

This time, when he lay back down, he doubled the distance between them.

Sleep did not come easily for Cameron MacKay that night.

Meredith awoke with his plaid draped about her body.

Directly above, the sky was a perfect, brilliant blue.

Birds trilled a melodious tune, flitting through the treetops and rustling the branches. Yet the beauty of the day was lost upon her. One thought burned through her mind, as if it had been branded there.

He'd covered her with his plaid.

She lay very quiet, her fingers curling into the soft, warm wool. The scent of him still clung to the fabric—not unpleasant, just woodsy and musky and undeniably male.

Why? she wondered wildly. She didn't understand his concern—nor had she expected it. His face had been so hard as he'd examined her feet last eve. Why, the very sight of him reaching for her had made her recoil and long to make the sign of the cross. Yet the touch of his hands had been a direct contrast. Why did he even care? He was right. She could not blame him. She'd brought such injury upon herself solely because of her own obstinacy.

And he could have let her drown. Merciful heaven, he could have let her *die*!

Yet he had not. *He had not.*

She owed him her thanks . . . she owed him her very life.

What was it she'd said to him? *You are a wretch. The slimiest vermin of the earth.* In her heart Meredith was appalled at her behavior. Such slander against another was hardly benevolent! Of a certainty it was not behavior indicative of a servant of the Lord! She cringed inside. To think that she had dared to speak such things to another! Oh, but she was sinful and wicked and she must seek forgiveness here and now.

Clasping her hands together, she ducked her head to pray.

Her prayers never made it to fruition . . . oh, yet another sin! She stared at her hands. It dawned on her

slowly . . . she was unfettered. There was no chain
that bound them together. She was stunned that he
trusted her not to attempt escape, particularly after the
way he'd queried her last evening; but then she recalled his warning and a sizzle of resentment went
through her. More likely he simply believed she
would not do it. Mayhap because he was convinced
she was too much a coward!

She moved her head ever so slightly. He lay on his
back, one lean hand resting in the middle of his chest.
Swallowing, she allowed her gaze to slide upward.

Her stomach clenched oddly. He was older than
she, but still young . . . and aye, there was no help for
it, quite handsome despite the fact that he was a thieving MacKay. His face and neck were dark with several days' growth of beard, but there was a slight cleft
in his chin she'd not noticed before. Had he been
clean-shaven, it might have lent him a boyish air . . .
Faith, but there was nothing boyish about this man!
Nay, he was all brazen masculinity, all steely hardness
sheathed in muscle.

Oh, yes, his might was formidable, his control over
her unquestionable. But now he was asleep.

And Fortune was near, just beyond the next tree.

Deceit was not in her nature, nor was it her desire,
yet she prayed it would come easily. Nay, cunning
was the way of men . . . *his* way. She told herself it
was not so much deceit as desperation.

Excitement clamored within her breast. She must
flee while she had the chance, for she might never
have another. She must put her fear of the water aside,
and simply find a different place to cross the river and
return to Connyridge, one that was safe and shallow.
She could do it—she could!

But she had vowed she would have her crucifix

back . . . and by the Rood, so she would. It was her dearest treasure—indeed, her *only* treasure—and she would not leave it in another's possession, most particularly Cameron MacKay's!

Nervously she wet her lips. He'd tucked the necklace inside his tunic—there must be a pocket hidden within.

They did not touch, but she lay very close to him. Pushing aside his plaid, she eased to her side, taking care not to make any noise. Her hand stole out. As stealthily as she could, she slipped her fingers within the vee of his tunic.

He was so warm! She very nearly snatched her hand back. It was only the strictest effort of will that kept her steady on her course. Her fingers crept down, skimming across the taut plane of his belly. The prickly-rough sensation of hair brushing her palm made her mouth go dry. Were all men as hairy as this one?

He moved not a muscle. His breathing continued deep and even. Had she not been afraid to make a sound, she'd have released a long-pent-up sigh of relief.

Alas, she counted her blessings too soon, for the seconds marched slowly by. She damped down a feeling of panic. Where was her crucifix? There was no sign of it. Hurry! she commanded herself. If he should wake and discover her . . . why, his ire would surely know no bounds.

The thought had barely caught hold than she chanced to glance back at his face. A strangled cry caught in her throat, for her worst fear was upon her.

He was awake . . . and it appeared she'd managed to attain his undivided regard.

Five

Icy shock tore through her. She nearly cried out. What had she done, that her prayers remained unanswered?

"I presume 'tis not a maidenly curiosity that bids you trespass upon my person with such intimacy."

His tone yielded a lazy indulgence. Meredith was furious that he would mock her so. Why, the arrogant lout!

Her fingertips tingled with the urge to slap the smirk from his face. Indeed, she flexed them, sorely longing to do precisely that.

But the search for her crucifix had yielded a prize she'd not anticipated.

Her fingertips rested upon smooth metal—the handle of his dagger. Freedom. The readiest way to achieve it was within her power—indeed, within her very grasp. The awareness came dimly . . . action did not. Her fingers skimmed the handle. With a lightning reflex she snatched it from its berth in his belt and held it poised at the center of his chest.

In her heart she was aghast at the extent of her audacity; but for once the advantage belonged to her and she would be a fool not to use it.

"Do not move, else—else I will give you a wound

to match the other!'' She was all at once reminded of the puckered scar on his back.

He bestowed on her a smile like no other.

"You would turn my own weapon against me?"

"Aye!" she declared recklessly.

"You have not the courage."

"You are wrong!" she told him stoutly.

"What, then? Will you slit my throat? I warn you, lass, 'tis rather messy. You must move quickly, lest your hands and gown be sprayed with blood."

Meredith blanched.

"Of course, such things do not bother some, though blood can be a wet, sticky mess. Yet at least the end comes quick, or so 'tis said—"

He was doing this to try to rile her. She struggled to keep hold of her resolve. A blight on his soul! she thought furiously. This was the only way, she told herself. Somehow she had to convince him that he had to free her.

His calm was infuriating. "Be silent!" she told him.

He paid no heed. "Of course, there is always the heart. Your aim must be straight and true, though, for if you miss, there is the chance I will live. And of course you must then have a care, lest the blade encounter a bone. Aye, your grip must be firm and tight. If, however, you wish to cause me a slow and prolonged death, then mayhap you should try for a belly wound. Aye, that's the most painful of all. And if you turn the dagger just so—but quickly, mind you—you will feel the tearing of the flesh . . .''

His grisly details turned her stomach. All at once she was shaking. Could she do this? she wondered frantically. Rob a man of his life? But a turn of the wrist, a downward slice, and his life would be forfeit.

She could see the pulse throbbing strongly in his throat, the beat of his lifeblood . . . Could she watch as it ebbed to its last?

The prospect left her sickened. She could not. She despised herself for even thinking she could. Guilt such as she had never known forged a searing hole inside her.

She made as if to rise—the next moment, the dagger was struck from her hand and she was sprawled on her back. For one paralyzing instant, she couldn't move—could not even breathe, for the air had been driven from her lungs by the weight of the man atop her. Her panic was renewed. She sought in vain to free herself, but alas! he had only to wrap steely-hard arms about her own and trap her legs within the iron-taut vise of his.

At last she was still, exhausted by her efforts. Her breath coming in ragged spurts, she slowly raised her head.

It spun through her mind that she'd been right. She'd ignited a blaze and she was now caught fast in its fiery midst. His fury was unconcealed. It vibrated through him, so intense she could feel it in the tautness of every muscle as he lay atop her body.

"By God, I should kill you now!" His tone was scalding. He loomed above her, as hard and unyielding as the mountains.

A cry of bitter frustration broke from her lips. Blindly she confronted him. "Then do it," she cried. "Do it and have done with it, else *you* be the coward!"

Too late she realized the brash challenge issued forth. Scorching fire leaped in his eyes. Something splintered across his features, and for one awful moment, the taste of fear was like dust in her mouth. She was convinced he would indeed heed her cry.

"Lass," he said from between his teeth, "I marvel that I have not, so do not tempt me further! For rest assured, were I not such a benevolent soul, we would see who is the coward."

Something inside her twisted. Her daring was but a fool's defiance; it was just as he'd said.

She was a coward.

His expression dark as the evening shadows, he released her. "You leave me no choice. I will not soon forget how you repaid my trust. Were I you, I would bear that in mind."

Tears scalded the back of her throat, but they were tears she vowed she would never surrender in his presence. She had thrown down the gauntlet . . . and lost.

Now she must pay the price.

He whistled for Fortune, who obediently trotted forward. Meredith did not move as he made quick work of saddling the stallion. When he was done, he beckoned her forward with a nod of his head.

Meredith moved forward, stopping before him. Mutely she held out her hands.

Several seconds passed before Cameron understood . . . She expected him to bind her wrists! He did not— ah, though he'd have liked to!—but no doubt she would brand him a coward anew! Nay, he'd not give her cause to taunt him yet again that his manhood was not sufficient to keep her in check.

He scowled. Settling his hands on the narrowness of her waist, he lifted her to Fortune's back, then followed her upward.

He felt the way her spine went rigid, the way she strained to avoid his touch. His mouth tightened. His

arms came hard about her body; deliberately he pulled
her back against him.

Even as she tried his patience and his temper as no
other, he couldn't quite banish a twinge of reluctant
admiration.

Thrice now she had invited him to kill her. The
night of her abduction, she had neither cried nor
screamed nor wept. Nor had she begged for mercy.
Instead she'd stepped forward, and silently awaited
what she had believed might be her own demise.

She did not shrink from him, as she could have . . .
as she should have! Instead, her bravery rivaled that
of any man—and exceeded that of many.

What was it she'd said? *Do not move, else I will
give you a wound to match the other.* Why, if the idea
were not so preposterous, he'd have laughed! Had the
wench only realized she'd held his dagger as long as
she had because he allowed it! Only now did he find
her heartfelt declaration so amusing. At the time, the
bend of his mood had not been so inclined.

The hours passed. It was well into the afternoon
when her spine finally slackened. Cameron knew she
was unused to the hours in the saddle; he suspected
she ached to the very bone. He was given to wonder:
Would he have stopped if she had asked? Cameron
didn't know. He knew only that she did not ask, and
after her trick of this morning, he was not disposed
to offer.

The day was gloriously warm and sunny. It was
then he spied a crofter and several young lads in the
distance gathering stones from a field, a stocky cottage in the distance. As they neared, Cameron looked
on with a faint smile as the pile at the edge of the
field grew. From there the crofter and the lads carried
them over to join another stone fence that climbed

high into the hills. The sight hurtled him back many a year to his boyhood, for his father had often sent him and his brothers to complete just such a task.

They continued on, but a nagging restlessness brewed within him. He was anxious to be home, and yet the thought tore at his very heart. For his father and all his brothers were no more . . .

And the responsibility for the safety and well-being of his clansmen now resided with him.

It was a sobering thought.

A wave of greeting roused him from his reverie. It was the crofter.

Cameron raised a hand and gave a shout in return. Meredith's gaze had strayed as well—he felt the way her lungs filled with air, her flare of sudden awareness.

His smile withered. Briefly he entertained the thought of clamping her breast with the palm of his hand. Ah, now that would surely divert any intent she might have.

He leaned forward. His breath stirred the fine reddish blond hairs at her temple; his lips brushed skin that was incredibly soft. Even as the awareness rushed through his mind, he was furious that he should even notice.

"Do not," was all he growled.

Her lips compressed. Again her posture grew rigidly erect. The silence that had reigned supreme throughout the day continued.

Above the deep green of the treetops, sunset flamed across the horizon, lighting the twilit sky a misty pink and gold. Ever atuned to his prisoner, he felt her body relax. Was she asleep? Even as it crossed his mind, her body began to droop, only to jerk upright.

Cameron took pity on her. When they came to the

cool rushing waters of a stream and long, fragrant grass where Fortune could graze, he called a halt.

"We will stay here for the night."

He dismounted, then turned to offer her a hand. She had already slipped to the ground. His expression turned grim as she winced, but he said nothing. His gaze ever vigilant, he watched as she hobbled toward the shade beneath a tree. But she did not rest, as he thought she would.

She dropped to her knees on the mossy ground, clasped her hands, and bowed her head deeply.

A sigh erupted from him, of exasperation or temper, he knew not. Out of deference for a power mightier than he, Cameron forced himself to ignore her.

A quarter hour later, she had yet to rise, but her lips were still moving.

Something snapped inside him. For the second time on this journey, he pulled her roughly to her feet.

"For what do you pray so ardently?"

She focused on a point somewhere beyond his shoulder. "You are not my confessor," she said quietly. "I cannot tell you."

"Captor, confessor, to you they are one and the same."

Still she would not look at him. Cameron lost patience. "Tell me! For what do you pray? Nay, let me guess," he mocked. "You pray for my demise."

To his shock she ducked her head. "I do not pray for your demise."

Her denial came in a low, choked tone. He was puzzled now—but even more determined.

"For what, then?"

She gave a tiny shake of her head. "You would not understand."

"Then tell me."

Lean fingers beneath her chin demanded she look at him. Cameron expected the now-familiar rebellion. He expected a look that consigned him to the devil. What he encountered was something else entirely.

Never in his life had he seen such guilt—a soul in such torment. Her eyes were dark with pain, ringed with shadows.

The sight gave him a fleeting pause.

"Tell me," he said again. This time the gritty edge had left his manner.

"I held a knife to your breast," she confided, her voice scarcely audible. "I had within my hands the means to take your life . . ." She swallowed, as if unable to go on.

"And the thought was there," he finished quietly.

Her mouth trembled. "I could never have killed you," she whispered, and then it was a cry: "I could never have killed you, but aye, for an instant, the thought was there!"

Oddly, Cameron understood. He'd felt the same way the first time he'd killed a man. It was not he who had made the first move, but he had made the last. If he had not, he would not be alive on this day, and that was something he could never regret. It was on the tip of his tongue to say that if he were being held by another and a dagger was placed in his grasp, he'd have felt the same. Indeed, he'd have done the deed!

"You cannot know the shame I feel." Her voice caught painfully. "I do not know that I can ever forgive myself!"

Cameron had no answer. He believed in God. He went to Mass from time to time. On occasion he had prayed . . . not with her devoutness, but still, he had asked for the Lord's blessing and guidance. In truth, he could not fully comprehend her dilemma. Mayhap 'twas because she was a woman—mayhap because she had been a novice—and he was a man. For in his mind, there was God's law . . . and the law of the land.

There were times, he reflected, that instinct compelled the need to kill, the need to defend oneself and those one loved. There was killing . . . and then there was murder.

A bitter darkness seeped through him. Cameron could no more withhold the thought than he could stop the rising of the sun. He was reminded of his family. Of his father and his brothers, who had done naught to precipitate murder. Of young Thomas, who had raised neither sword nor hand toward the Clan Munro.

Her hands came together in the folds of her gown. "Please," she murmured. "Do you think I might have a moment to myself?"

His jaw tensed as he stared at her. "For what purpose?"

Her face had turned the color of the sunset. "You know for what purpose."

He did, but he was not compelled to be lenient just now. "Nay," he said harshly. "You go nowhere without me."

Her eyes caught his, then slid away. She plucked at her gown. "Please," she said again. "I realize that you are wary, but I vow I will cause you no further trouble."

Another refusal was but a heartbeat away. Yet in the instant before she glanced away, Cameron glimpsed a naked dismay. Damn, he thought viciously, feeling himself weaken. Damn her for swaying him!

"I will turn my back, but go no farther than there."
He pointed at a tall hedgerow across the clearing.

She did not argue, but fled wordlessly.

Cameron busied himself lighting a fire. Sitting back
on his haunches, he waited . . . and waited.

With a curse, he leaped to his feet. Ah, but it was just
as he'd always thought. She was no angel, she was a
treacherous witch! *I vow I will cause you no further
trouble.* It had been but a ploy to escape—her appearance of guilt had been but trickery! Twice now he'd
been taken in by the sweetness of her soft, feminine
form, her facade of innocence. He cursed both her and
himself—ah, more fool was he to have trusted her!
Well, he'd not be deceived so again, and she would
know it. He whirled, only to be brought up short.

Meredith stood before him . . . but she was not
alone.

A tall, bearded man dressed in a filthy ragged kilt
stood beside her, a ruthless look about him. Lank,
greasy hair hung down to his shoulders. Even as a
prickle of warning sped through Cameron, another
man stepped forward, this one stout and heavy-
jowled. Each carried a dagger strapped to his waist.
Cameron's gaze leaped to her face—her eyes were
huge, dark with fright.

Cameron's gaze narrowed on the stubby fingers
curled possessively around her elbow.

"So, lassie. Would this be your 'usband, then?"

"Nay," she said quickly. "He is my brother."

Her brother! What was this? Cameron groaned silently. It was obvious she was not acquainted with the
telling of untruths.

"You lie," the bearded one observed baldly. His
fingers bit cruelly into her flesh. Cameron heard her
sharp inhalation, but she made no outcry.

The man's fate was sealed in that instant. He would be the first to die, Cameron decided.

Cameron flexed his fingers. The pair did not know to heed the dangerous glint in his eye. "I am neither her husband nor her brother," he said coldly. "Indeed, what I am to her is none of your concern."

"Ah, but it is. Ye left the wee lass alone, and fair game to any and all."

"Aye, and a bonny wee lass she is!" The burly one chimed in with a leering grin. Beady eyes raked Meredith from head to toe. With a grating laugh, he reached out to pinch the side of one breast. "My taste runs to plumper tits, but no matter. Say, Davis, if he is neither 'er 'usband nor 'er brother, 'e'll not mind watching while we mount her one by one—or both of us together!" With his hand he clamped his crotch, grinding his hand against it. "He looks to be a hardy one, eh, Davis? But I'll wager he dinna have a bigger cock than me! But mayhap we'll even give 'im a dunk in her honey-cave, too! And then we'll see, eh?"

Meredith had gone white as a wintry hillside.

The muscles in Cameron's legs tightened. He rolled up on the balls of his feet, preparing to spring. He poised, awaiting the right moment. "I shall warn you only once," he said quietly. "Leave her be."

"And why should we?" the tall one named Davis goaded him. "There be but one of you, and two of us!" He chortled. "Do ye hear that, Monty? He thinks he can best us!"

With that he jerked her against him. Meredith twisted wildly, trying to wrench away. With the back of his hand, Davis dealt her a blow to the head. Then, with a guttural laugh, he dragged wet, open lips down the white arch of her throat.

Fire flared before Cameron's eyes. He waited no longer.

There was a dull crack as an elbow flashed in Monty's face. Without a sound, the man sprawled forward.

Cameron had already reached Meredith. Hands upon her waist, he spun her wide and away. Davis's head came up slowly. His jaw sagged as, with a single slash, Cameron saw to his vow. As his heart pumped its last, Davis's expression was one of bewildered astonishment.

But the other—Monty—had staggered upright. Blood dripped from his mouth, pure malice from his heart. With a venomous snarl on his face, he wrenched his weapon from his boot and hurtled forward.

But Cameron did not see. He had just begun to turn. "Nay!" came a strangled cry.

It all happened in a blur. He caught just a glimpse of slender, outstretched arms flinging high . . . of long silken hair streaming like a glorious copper pennon . . .

There was a vicious, upward arc of the dagger.

A gasp . . . and then nothing.

Meredith had stopped dead in her tracks. Her form wavered, like a frail willow in the wind.

Monty stepped back. His gaze went from his bloodied blade to Cameron's face. But one glimpse of fiercely glowing eyes was enough to start him blubbering.

"Christ, man! I—I did not see her! 'Twas meant for you, not h—"

He never had the chance to finish. Monty died with his eyes wide open, his own dagger buried to the hilt in his throat.

Six

Cameron whirled. Meredith was staring at him, her expression both puzzled and dismayed. Her lips parted, but no sound emerged. A crimson stain bloomed on the front of her gown, a stain that spread sticky and wet.

An awful dread shot through him, like the shaft of an arrow. Sweet Mother of God! Had the swine killed her?

Her knees gave way. She began to crumple. Cameron reached her just before she hit the ground. Catching her beneath the knees, he bore her high in his arms. "*Jesu,*" he breathed.

"Why do you carry me? You—you said that you would not."

Her voice was but a breath.

By the Virgin, what a time for the remembrance! "I said I would not carry you when you faltered or stumbled, and you've done neither."

She turned her face against his throat. "But I did stumble. And you saw—you saw but you said nothing!"

What was this? Was she ashamed? He was awash in amazement, frustration, and desperation—and all at once! Trying to hurry, yet not wishing to jostle her further, he started back toward their camp. Judging from Meredith's limp pliancy, Cameron was certain she'd lost consciousness.

He was wrong. He eased her to the soft, mossy ground beneath the tree. Her eyes snapped open, then sought his. Small fingers wound into the front of his tunic with surprising strength.

"I pray you . . . do not . . . let me die . . ."

His throat tightened oddly. Her eyes fixed him with a desperate entreaty.

"I won't let you die," he said almost fiercely. He swallowed her hand with his own. "Do you hear me, Meredith? I won't let you die."

His heart hammering, he bent over her. A bruise already rose on her temple. The front of her gown was soaked through with blood. Without hesitation, he slid the gaping neckline clear of her shoulders, all the way to her waist.

Her eyes flew wide. "Wh-what are you doing?" she gasped.

His smile was faint. Ah, but she was ever prim, ever righteous! "If I am to save you, lass, I must first see the wound." Grimly he noted that even had she so desired, she didn't have the strength to deny him. One hand fluttered upward, as if to shield herself, only to fall back weakly.

Her lashes swept down. Her gaze veered away and her lashes fell shut. Had she lost consciousness? It would be easier for them both if she had.

He paid no heed to the soft round curves now open to his scrutiny, but concentrated solely on his task. Had the wound been but two fingers' width to her left, her heart would surely have been pierced. The blade had slashed upward toward her shoulder; it penetrated the flesh at the very underside of her breast, there where that tender mound swelled upward. Snatching a linen cloth and his one spare tunic from his pouch, he wiped away the blood. The edges of the wound were clean, not jagged and torn, but he couldn't tell how deep; blood continued to well bright and scarlet. Though Cameron did not consider himself skilled in the arts of healing, he'd helped tend those injured in skirmishes before, and he knew the bleeding must be stopped. Damn. *Damn!* He had no way to close the wound but to bind it tightly.

There was a tearing sound as he plunged his dagger into his tunic. His features taut, he ripped the cloth into strips, wadding one into a thick pad before binding it in place. By the time he'd finished, her face was leeched of all color, the softness of her mouth pinched tight. For now he could do no more. As he covered her naked torso with his plaid, she let out a long, uneven breath.

He knew then that she'd been awake throughout.

In time she dozed. Cameron waited until then to reach beneath his plaid and divest her of the ruined gown; there was little point in her wearing it. The veriest smile touched his lips—she'd have been shocked to the core if she'd known.

Leaning back on his heels, he shook his head. Why the devil had she told that unsavory pair that he was her brother? To protect him? His belly knotted with self-loathing. It was his fault. He'd vowed that the brigand named Davis would die first—and he had. But in his anger, he'd been careless. He should have seen to Monty first, after all.

His sleep that night was fitful. In the morning he woke to ominous gray skies and the rumble of thunder across the hills. Meredith, pale and wan, didn't rouse when he called her name. He stood, his mind turning furiously. He hated to risk moving her, but the damp wet ground was no place for an injured woman—and they were still days away from his keep in the Highlands. He hesitated but an instant, then whistled for Fortune.

He rode the steed hard, back to the place where they had seen the crofter yesterday. Mayhap the crofter would know where they might find shelter.

Instinct served him well. The crofter, a man named Jonas, was only too willing to lend assistance when Cameron relayed how he and Meredith had been attacked by outlaws. Jonas assumed that Meredith was his wife—Cameron saw no need to correct his assumption.

"There is a shepherd's hut not far from where you stay," he told Cameron. "My wife and I would gladly take her in, but the hut is far closer to your camp."

His wife, Johanna, nearly as plump as she was tall, quickly fetched blankets, cloth for bandages, and a healing unguent. Sternly she instructed Cameron that he must keep the wound clean, lest poisons set in. For their generosity, Cameron left them a handful of silver, ample recompense for their services.

It was just as Jonas said—the hut was just atop the rise beyond their camp. It was tiny and crude, with naught but a fireplace and one small window. But at least it offered shelter from the morning mists and cool night air. Hurriedly he gathered fresh straw from outside for a bed, spread it over the dirt in one corner, and draped a blanket over it.

He'd been gone several hours by the time he returned to where Meredith lay. His heart leaped, for it appeared she hadn't moved.

He dropped down beside her. "Meredith," he called. "Meredith."

Her eyes drifted open slowly. He had to bend to hear her.

"You were gone so long. Weren't you afraid I would flee?"

Cameron didn't know whether to laugh or curse. He smiled slightly. "Weren't you afraid that *I* would flee?"

Her gaze skipped away. "I—I thought you did," she confided, a faint catch in her voice.

His smile faded and he scowled blackly. Did she truly think he would abandon her? To do so would have been callous and cruel, and by the saints, he was neither!

"We must go where 'tis safe and dry," he said softly. "We have no shelter here and I fear the rain will soon come."

She nodded, then made as if to rise. "Nay!" he said sharply. "Let me." Tucking his plaid around her, he carefully lifted her in his arms.

Beads of perspiration dotted her forehead by the time he shouldered his way into the hut. Her face was white. He saw the way her teeth caught at her lower lip as he lowered her onto the pallet. He knew the trip must have hurt like the very devil, yet she had made not a sound.

She turned her head ever so slightly. "Thank you," she whispered.

Exhausted, she slept throughout the day. By evening, Cameron had begun to grow alarmed. He'd thought he'd done the right thing by moving her, but where before she'd been a sickly gray, now her cheeks burned ruddy and scarlet. Her breathing was quick and shallow. With a deep furrow etched between the heaviness of his brows, he laid a hand on her forehead.

He swore violently. She was as hot as fire! He stood for a moment, a feeling of helplessness sweeping over him.

Twice now he'd saved her life—and she was a Munro . . . a Munro!

Would Monty have driven home the thrust of his blade had she not stepped between them?

God help him, he didn't know. He knew only that she'd tried to save him . . .

He could do no less for her.

And he'd promised her he wouldn't let her die.

He wasted no more time. Drawing water from the well outside, he stationed himself beside the pallet with a cloth and a basin of water. In one smooth move he swept aside his plaid, baring the whole of her. Wetting the cloth again and again, he drew it slowly over her body from head to toe, cooling the blaze of her skin.

Her head thrashed. Her legs shifted restlessly.

Swearing beneath his breath, he set aside the basin. "Meredith, no! You must lay still, else you will reopen the wound."

She cringed. "My gown . . . Why do you do this? Nay, do not touch me . . . nay, not there! 'Tis wrong!"

Cameron stilled, taken aback. What was this, that she would shrink from him so? This was more than mere modesty—he sensed it with all that he possessed. She had not been so afraid of him this morn! He found the notion immensely disturbing. Indeed, he could have sworn the starkness of terror clung to her voice.

She moaned. "'Tis so dark. I cannot see . . . I cannot see . . . Who are you? *Who are you?*" Her eyes flicked open. She stared at him, wide and unblinking, as if she saw right through him—a look that sent an eerie chill through his bones.

His regard sharpened. It appeared she did not know him—the fever had touched her mind as well.

Putting out a hand, he merely brushed the slope of her shoulder. Giving a half-sob, she scrambled back, curling into herself and huddling into a small ball.

Frustration gnawed at him. Cameron contemplated his dilemma. What the devil was he to do? He had no wish to frighten her out of her wits. But if she wouldn't let him touch her . . .

"Easy, lass. I mean you no harm. You have naught to fear from me."

If she heard, there was no sign of it. Quietly he murmured softly, what nonsense he knew not. Oddly, the mellow depth of his voice seemed to soothe her. Soon her breath was no longer rasping and thin. The unseen tension within her began to loosen, her body to relax.

Holding his breath, he rested his fingertips on her brow, then smoothed damp, stray wisps of hair from her temple. This time she didn't draw away. With his knuckles he skimmed her cheek, a touch that was almost a caress; she turned her cheek in to it. The fever was not gone completely, but she was cooler, and her color was more normal.

Still, she remained slightly restless. Every so often her lips moved. Her fingers plucked at something . . . prayer beads, he realized. With a sigh he suddenly remembered the night he'd stolen her. She'd had them in her hands when his arm stole about her from behind. He shook his head, faintly amused. Saintly little maid! Even in sleep she prayed.

With a faint whimper, she shifted to her back. Cameron froze. The entire sweet length of her now lay bare and open to his gaze. Silken ropes of reddish gold hair were caught beneath her, revealing all that the lass no doubt would wish was *not* revealed, had she been awake. Long dark lashes feathered like dark spikes upon her cheeks. Her lips were slightly parted, lips he suspected would be immensely soft and kissable. Her skin was flawless and unblemished . . .

All of it.

All at once the fever burned in *his* blood. He could not control the rampant course his mind decided to follow—nor the brazen path of his eyes. That she would have taken her vows was almost laughable. He could not imagine such beauty concealed beneath coarse gray wool, forever hidden behind the walls of a nunnery.

Though by doing so he branded himself a rogue, he looked his fill and more. An almost painful erectness stiffened his staff.

There was no help for it. He was but a man who enjoyed the pleasures of the flesh, and one with a hearty appetite, at that—though he was not one to bed any and all, as some men were. He could not deny it . . . she stirred him mightily, stirred all that was male and elemental within him.

He had discovered for himself the fragility of her bones; she'd felt small and slight in his arms, her weight scarcely more than a child's. But there was naught to resemble a child in the woman who lay before him. His bold regard took in the quivering thrust of pink-tipped breasts as her chest rose and fell. Before his very sight, her nipples peaked hard and erect. His gaze dropped to the tender skin below the strip of bandage beneath those tempting mounds.

It struck him that were he to lay his hand between her hips and spread his fingers wide, he could easily span the width of her belly. The sight of that satin-cream hollow drew his gaze endlessly, for there between her thighs nestled a triangular nest of down the same red-gold as her hair.

A dark desire slipped over him. She lay before him, a veritable feast offered to a man who'd not partaken in days, reminding him that it had indeed been weeks since he'd lain with a woman. Her cleft would be tight, he thought suddenly, tight as a glove around the heat of his member . . .

He had touched her dispassionately, with detached indifference as he tended her injury. But now he ached with the need to lave those soft pink peaks with the heat of his tongue. He ached to bury his fingertips through springy red curls and slide a finger deep within her hidden cleft—to discover for himself if her silken channel would cling to his hand as thoroughly as it would cling to his rod.

His blood began to simmer. A ravening heat burned deep in his belly. He had only to reach out . . . The need to touch her was almost ungovernable; the urge that pounded in his veins was unthinkable. Ah, but no doubt the lass would have pronounced it the most grievous of sins . . .

The rational part of him rebelled. His jaw hard, disgustedly he flung the cloth into the basin. Abruptly he drew a thin blanket over her, shielding him from further temptation.

God above, what had come over him to addle his senses so? He was not a man to let lust be his master. She was a Munro. His enemy. Today. Tomorrow. All the days that would follow.

Restlessly he paced the length of the hut and back, then turned and stood in the open doorway. Egan and Finn would soon be home, he thought broodingly. No doubt they would anticipate his arrival within several days of their own. What would happen when he did not appear? He disliked the conclusion which sprang to mind. Would they think this wee lass had slain him? Surely not. Yet Cameron was no fool—his clan would blame the Munros.

The thought of all-out war between the clans made him sick to the depths of his soul. He could not change what he'd done. By God, he would not! Aye, this was the best way, to let the Red Angus believe his daughter was dead. This way he—Cameron— would have his revenge . . . with no more bloodshed.

Thin-lipped and stony, he stared at the sky. Dawn streaked the horizon, a shimmer of pink and gold. He'd been too long without a woman, he decided. Aye, that was it. His body simply commanded that any woman would do—even this one! Scathingly he dismissed his desire. Once they were back on MacKay land, he promised himself, this cursed longing would be extinguished.

He vowed then and there to do all he could to see that she healed quickly.

Seven

Hot. Never had she been so hot. It was as if an inferno raged around her and she was at the very heart of it—even her lungs burned.

Meredith floated in and out of some dark netherworld, drifting between the present and the past. In the murky abyss where she now dwelled, she was hazily aware that she was not in her bed. Her gown had been taken from her and she was naked. Sweet Christ, naked!

She shuddered. There were hands in the dark . . . hands upon her body . . . hands that trespassed where they should not.

She floated back . . . back to that night. Terror iced her veins. She struck out blindly, for shadows surrounded her and she could not see. "Leave me be!" she cried. "I will tell my father!"

Husky laughter rushed past her ear. "Nay, girl, you will not. I know you too well . . ."

That grating whisper . . . it made her cringe. She had the awful feeling she knew it well . . . Her mind screamed, resounding in the hollow of her brain. Who was he? Sweet Christ, who?

"Merry," said the voice. "My sweet Merry."

God . . . oh, God! In some dark corner deep within

her, she knew it was but a dream. For a time at Connyridge, she'd been able to close her eyes and not think of it . . . of him . . . of hands in the dark . . . hands that held her down . . .

Only now there was a face—the cast of his mouth was so very forbidding!—that hovered above her.

"Easy, lass. I mean you no harm. You have naught to fear from me."

Nay, she thought wildly. She had everything to fear from him. In some faraway part of her mind, she knew it was he . . . Cameron MacKay. The man who hated her. The man who used her as a pawn in his game of vengeance.

The arms of oblivion beckoned her anew. She did not fight it, but drifted willingly into the depths of forgetfulness.

Time passed, naught but a blur. She was still so very, very warm, and there was a suffocating heaviness weighting the center of her chest. It hurt to breathe.

It seemed to take a monstrous effort to lift her eyelids. Through a misty haze, Cameron MacKay's handsome features swam before her. "Sweet Lord!" she said faintly. "I am in hell, then, and you are there with me!"

"Nay, lass."

She blinked. "What? And where else would you be? Surely not in heaven."

Something that might have been a smile creased the hardness of his lips. "We are not dead, lass. Of a certainty we are not in hell."

"But . . . we must be. Why else would I burn so?"

"You took a dagger in the breast. You burn with fever from the wound. Do you remember?"

Meredith sought hard to grasp what he said, but it

was so hard to think! Memory emerged in jagged
bursts. There had been two men, Davis and Monty.
Monty had raised his dagger high aloft; Cameron was
unaware of the man's attack . . . There had been a
searing pain . . . but one thought had swirled through
her mind.

Thrice now she'd been thrust upon death's door-
step. Would the next be the last . . . or would this?

Do not let me die.

She was unaware she spoke aloud until she heard
his voice. "Hush, lass."

Lass. Always before the word had carried an acid
rancor. Where was that rancor now? she wondered
vaguely.

"You need your rest to gather strength, Meredith.
Try to sleep."

Sleep, he said. How could she sleep with him so
near? She shivered, and felt something warm placed
over her shoulders.

The burning was gone when next she awoke. Yet
still it hurt to breathe—faith, but she could not imagine why it was so.

*You took a dagger in the breast. You burn with
fever from the wound.*

The wound. With a gasp, she tried to sit up. A
sharp, searing pain shot through her.

There was a vivid curse. "God's teeth! You will
reopen the wound if you persist in moving about so!"

Meredith pressed her lips together. It took a moment before the dizzying pain passed. When it did,
she bestowed him with what she hoped was an ad-
monishing frown.

"You curse too much."

"Indeed. No one but you has ever told me so."

" 'Tis a sin to take the Lord's name in vain."

Somehow the admonishment lacked the necessary heat.

A rakish brow quirked high. "You are convinced I am bound for the fires of hell. Will one less sin make a difference? I think not."

Ah, but it would! The retort sprang to the fore, but for the life of her, she could not summon the reason why it was so. Her mind groped fuzzily for the answer, but she was suddenly too tired to search for it.

Leaden balls seemed to weight her eyes. She could hardly keep them open. There was a sweep of cool fingers on her brow. "The fever has broken," came a low-voiced murmur above her. "You are lucky you yet live."

Lucky. She did not feel lucky. She felt cursed. She should have been back at Connyridge, kneeling in the dirt, tending the crops in the garden. Her mind might have been at rest. Instead she was here with this wretched man who gave her no peace . . .

She must have slept again. When she opened her eyes, he loomed above her, a basin in one hand, a pile of neatly folded linen cloths in the other.

"Good. You're awake. I was just about to change your bandage. That will make it easier." He knelt down near her, turning slightly to set aside the basin and cloths.

His intent registered slowly—and so did the realization that beneath the rough wool of the blanket, she wore not a stitch! Blue eyes flashed with horrified accusation to his face, for this could only be laid at his door.

"What have you done with my gown?"

"I could hardly tend you otherwise. Your gown was filthy and bloodied."

Her lips compressed indignantly. He appeared totally unrepentant, the scoundrel!

"If you think I leered, rest assured I did not, for yours is hardly the first womanly form I've seen and touched."

Nor was he the first man to touch her so . . . She pushed the hated memory aside and concerned herself with the present. With silent indignation, she raised her chin and clutched the blanket to her chest.

"I have already seen all that you would hide. You forget I've changed your bandages these past days. I've touched that which you guard so well—your naked skin. I've touched your naked skin—and aye, even there below your breasts—for who else was there to do it?"

His voice was clipped and impatient—and he was calmly determined. There was no way that she could stop him. Meredith knew instinctively that she was weak as a child, and her body ached all over. Resignation swept over her. She knew it must be done.

Wordlessly she nodded.

The blanket was tugged from her grasp. She had to curl her nails into her palms to keep from snatching it back. Cool air rushed over her flesh. One quick slice from the tip of his dagger and he lifted away soiled strips of linen. With a clean wet cloth, he dabbed at the crusty edges of the gash. Meredith inhaled sharply.

"I'm sorry. I did not mean to hurt you." Their eyes met. Hers quickly skipped away.

It wasn't the pain that made her flinch so—it was his nearness. Unable to stop herself, she glanced down. The sight of her own pink, creamy flesh, tipped by deeper rosebud, seemed to mock her. The stinging heat of embarrassment rose like a flood tide within her. Did he look at her, too? she wondered frantically. Ah, foolish question, that! He could hardly do what he must do and not look upon her flesh. Compelled by a need she couldn't control, she stole a glance at him.

His head was angled away from her, low and bent. Faith, but he was so close! The moist heat of his breath trickled over her skin, the very pinnacle of her breast.

Meredith swallowed. The difference between their skin was readily apparent . . . his so bronzed, hers so fair. Though he was immeasurably gentle, she sensed the latent power there. She couldn't tear her gaze away as he rinsed the cloth, twisting it between his hands. His hands were intensely masculine—big and dark; bristly black hairs scattered across the backs. His fingers were long and lean.

Visions tumbled in her brain, visions to which she dared not give in. She yearned to dive beneath the shelter of the blanket—as if that feeble defense might protect her! If she could have escaped, by the saints, she would have. She felt trapped, as surely as an animal in a snare.

Yet there was naught to threaten her in his manner, nor in his touch—nothing irreverent in either. He tended her wound with the utmost care. His profile bespoke an earnest concentration; it bore no trace of lustful endeavors. Nay, he did not hurt her. Yet it flashed through her mind that it might have been almost easier to bear if he did.

He reached for clean white linen. "Can you arch your back a bit?"

Meredith obliged. From the corner of her eye she saw the bandage dip behind her back. Dismay abounded, for now her breasts jutted forward, as if in offering! She felt naked and exposed, as in truth she was. Mortified beyond measure, she inhaled raggedly as he proceeded to wind the linen around her body.

He stopped almost immediately. A muscle contracted in his jaw. "You must let out your breath, else the bandage will be too tight."

His expression revealed a faint consternation. Slowly Meredith released her breath, unaware she'd been holding it. Only then did he continue, circling her back several more times. A dip of the cloth—the brush of rough, faintly callused fingertips—and it was done. He drew the blanket up to cover her.

Meredith latched on to the edges and turned her head aside. Closing her eyes, she pretended to sleep. It wasn't long before he appeared at her side again, calling her name.

"Meredith."

It crossed her mind to screw her eyes shut, to feign sleep—or unconsciousness. But she strongly suspected he would know the truth.

"I've broth for you. Are you hungry?"

Meredith opened her eyes. He knelt beside her, a rough wooden bowl in his hands. A sumptuous aroma filled the air.

"Aye." She was startled to realize that it was true.

A steely arm slid around her from behind, easing her forward. Tilting the bowl, he held it so that she could drink. To her amazement—and his, she suspected—she drank every last drop, for it was as delicious as it smelled.

Afterward she lay back. She had no energy to spare, yet the thought of sleep held no appeal—she felt all she'd done was sleep of late. She watched as he retreated, crossing to the stone fireplace and setting aside the bowl.

For the first time Meredith became aware of her surroundings. The structure they were in was built of uneven brick; there were gaping holes between many. It was tiny, perhaps only six or seven paces across, with a dirt floor. The only light came from the door, propped open with a stick. Hazy streamers of evening shadows fluttered within. She was lying on a bed of straw covered with a blanket. The obvious surely seemed the implausible. Had he done this for her? Surely not . . .

"Is this your home?" she ventured after a while.

Something flared in his eyes. For an instant she was certain she'd roused his anger. Only then did she realize how foolish was her question. The MacKays were a mighty clan. Of course his abode would not be so humble and small.

"Nay," he said finally. " 'Tis near the place where we were attacked." He relayed how the crofter they'd seen—Jonas—had told him of the hut and lent him assistance.

"How long have we been here?"

"This is the third day."

"The third!" Meredith was stunned.

He laid aside the rusty poker he'd been holding. His gaze now dwelled on a spot just above her left ear. "The bruise there," he said quietly. "Does it cause you pain?"

Her fingers had already slid self-consciously to the spot. "Nay," she said faintly. She felt for herself the swollen, tender lump. "I—I did not even know it was there."

He said nothing, but turned away, no longer inclined to converse. It struck her that he was not a man of many words. But then why should he be? she thought bitterly. He was a MacKay, and she was a Munro.

And it was something neither could forget.

It wasn't long before Meredith began to grow weary. But her eyes flew wide when all at once he drew off his tunic and tossed it aside.

For the space of a heartbeat, he stood poised before the firelight, booted feet braced wide apart. His back was long and sculpted, divided by the valley of his spine. His arms and shoulders were knotted and dense, tapering to hips that seemed incredibly narrow, given the breadth of his shoulders. He bent, stirring the fire with the poker. Meredith stared in both fear and fascination, unable to take her eyes from the rippling undulation of muscle beneath sleek, golden skin. All she could think was that here was a man who embodied both grace and power aplenty . . .

He straightened. Meredith's mouth had gone as dry as bone. Silently—so silently she would never have been aware of it had she not seen him—he came and stretched out beside her on the pallet.

Only the width of a hand separated them, for the pallet was narrow. She squeezed her eyes shut, praying he hadn't seen her watching him. All at once she was reminded anew of her nakedness. How many nights had passed since he'd taken her from the priory? She tried to calculate, then dismissed it. It mattered not. Each one had been spent beside him. This one would be no different, it seemed. He did not ask, nor even demand! He simply acted as if it were his due. And aye, she thought with weary despair, it was.

Not by right . . . but by might.

Was she too tired to protest—or simply too weak? Either way, she decided bitterly, she could not hide from what she was . . .

A spineless coward.

He slept beside her the night through. When the golden haze of morn seeped into the hut, the distance between them had not closed. He had slept deeply, she noted with a sniff, while she had not slept at all! She had wavered between indignation and the fear that he would seize her and have his way with her at any instant. Ah, but she was a fool, for had he not already pronounced his distaste for her?

All too soon the time came to change her bandages. He towered over her, dark and starkly masculine, and all at once the cost to her modesty was too steep.

"I—I can do it."

"How? You cannot see it, nor would you want to." He made the pronouncement flatly.

Meredith flushed and looked away. To her horror she felt her lips quiver. His gaze sharpened; she felt his stare as surely as she felt the prick of a dagger. She couldn't banish the uneasy sensation that he knew precisely what she was thinking—the very feelings that ran through her breast!

Tiny lines had appeared between the slash of his brows, a telltale sign of his displeasure, she'd already learned. "Here are the cloths, then." Abruptly he relented, startling her, for she'd already begun preparing her argument, feeble though it was.

With his help, she was able to sit upright. Her breath caught at the sharp, rending pain the action wrought.

The arm about her shoulder tightened ever so slightly. "Are you all right?" came the voice just above her head.

"Aye," she said weakly, and then again, "aye," this time with more conviction, for indeed, the pain had faded to a dull ache that was not so very unbearable.

Wordlessly he stepped back. Meredith floundered, reluctant to lower the rough wool blanket before his hawklike scrutiny. After a moment, he turned, presenting her with the broad expanse of his back, though he still stood near enough that she might reach out and touch him.

It was difficult, but Meredith managed to unwind the cloths and bathe the wound with the water he'd warmed in a rusty black kettle over the fire. Awkwardly she coiled the linen strip about herself, tucking in the edge as he had done.

" 'Tis done." She pulled the coverlet to her naked breasts, stunned to find she was shaking.

Strong hands caught her beneath the arms, carefully considerate as they lent assistance. Meredith sagged back to the pallet. The effort had cost her strength—but salvaged her pride.

Her head turned slightly. As it did, her lips brushed the chiseled hardness of his jaw. His mouth grew ominously thin. She could clearly make out the tense line of his jaw. He was angry—or displeased, she knew not which. He straightened upright as if he'd been scalded.

Meredith couldn't help it. She felt as if she'd done something terribly wrong. How could he be so gentle one moment, so very cold the next? If he hated her so, why had he bothered to save her? The night he'd taken her, he'd said he must force himself to suffer her presence. Why, then, had he prolonged her life? She didn't understand it, any more than she understood the twinge of hurt that refused to be banished.

When he announced his intent to hunt for food, she gave but a cursory nod. He wasn't gone long. The instant she heard the whinny of his horse outside, she squeezed her eyes shut and feigned sleep.

The door creaked.

It was later that day when he approached. "Do you feel well enough to stand?"

His tone was calmly matter-of-fact. Meredith hesitated. She was about to refuse when she saw he held her tattered gown in one hand.

"Aye," she murmured, then held out her hand.

The gown was dropped into it. He averted his head as she slipped it over her head. She couldn't help but note that he must have washed it. The thought of him doing such an intimate—and womanly—task for her sent confusion running through her. He had fed her, nursed her, seen to her every need—and all with a care that was totally at odds with his grim, stoic visage. Why? her mind screamed. Why should he bother to see to her care and comfort?

Do not let yourself be fooled, warned a voice within. To keep you alive . . . to torment you simply because you are a Munro. He needs no other reason.

She sat up slowly, pushing aside the coverlet. The hands that held such fascination for her closed about her waist. He pulled her upright with effortless ease, and then she was on her feet. She swayed dizzily. She felt suddenly lightheaded and her legs were surely filled with pudding! Dismayed, she clutched at him.

"Wait!" she cried.

Powerful arms drew her close, so close she could feel the corded strength of his thighs against her own. The world tilted, then began to right itself. Dazedly it penetrated that her panic was for naught—he had not released her at all. His hands were snug about her waist. Her own dug into the firm, knotted flesh of his arms.

With a gasp she looked up into his rough, dark face. It gave her a start to see that he was staring straight at her, his eyes almost black.

His gaze lowered slowly to her mouth.

Meredith swallowed. Her heart was drumming so loudly, it sounded like thunder in her ears. A tremor went through her. She did not move, though instinct clamored she do just that—she couldn't even if she'd wanted to! There was something different in the way he held her . . .

For one heart-stopping instant, she had the wildest sensation he would kiss her . . .

But that was absurd.

"Better?" he murmured.

In truth, it was not. For Cameron longed to trap the tempting sweetness of that tremulous pink mouth beneath his. He longed to plunder her lips with his; he wanted it with a need that vibrated in his heart and burned his very soul.

But one thing stopped him.

For he could not forget who she was—who *he* was. He told himself this cursed desire should not be . . . it *could* not be. And so he forced his mind away from this forbidden yearning and steeled himself against her.

She nodded. Her gaze bounced away. Thankfully the dizziness had passed, and her legs were no longer so wobbly.

A turn about the tiny hut and she was exhausted. She would have collapsed were it not for his arm hard about her back.

"I'm sorry. I am weak. Weak in spirit . . . and in body!" She made the outcry before she'd thought better of it. Never had she felt so feeble and impotent. To her horror, she was precariously near tears.

"It will be easier the next time—and the next after that."

His reassurance was unexpected—but most assuredly welcomed. And he was right, thank heaven. The next few days saw a gradual return of her strength. He rarely left her alone, abandoning her only to hunt for food and gather wood for the fire. She sensed the role of caregiver was an unfamiliar one to him. At times he appeared rather restless—he paced outside the hut, for she could hear him. Was it because he was anxious to return to his home?

Meredith, too, chafed. She was used to toil from dawn till sunset, and the hours of inactivity gnawed at her nerves. Yet she dreaded what would come next. When she was well enough, they would leave this place—leave for his home.

And then what would happen?

Her dreams spun adrift one night. She dreamed of Papa's laughing blue eyes, the hearty gusto of Uncle Robert's laughter. Then all at once everything changed. Light became dark, an impenetrable void where the vast depths of gloom lurked all around like the very pits of hell. Warmth became cold. Images swarmed through her mind. She was seized in the dark of night. Hands snatched at her. Fingers plucked at her nipples, pinching them painfully. There was a face above hers, hot breath in her mouth. Greedy hands pried the softness of her thighs apart, spreading them wide . . .

Her eyelids snapped open. She woke with a start, her lungs heaving. Sweat lay like a morning mist heavy upon her brow.

Reality staked its claim. She was with Cameron in the shepherd's hut—she could feel him beside her. Terror still iced her veins, yet she forced herself to

breathe slowly. Never had the night been so dark and
thick, the air so very, very cold! Beneath the wool
blanket, her arms crept around her body. She hugged
herself fiercely.

It was her shivering that woke the man who slumbered so deeply beside her.

An oath rent the air. "God's blood, what ails you?
Are you ill?"

"Nay," she said shakily. She sought desperately to
quell her shivering. Yet her efforts proved futile . . .

For there was nothing so cold as a chill that came
from within.

He raised himself on an elbow to glare at her.
"What, then?"

She felt his gaze like a thistle beneath her skin.
" 'Tis nothing," she denied. "I am merely cold."

Another oath stung the air. She felt him shift, and
then she was caught up against him. Meredith
couldn't withhold a little cry; she wasn't prepared for
his unexpected movement.

"Be still!" he hissed. "I do naught but share my
warmth with you."

Strong arms encircled her, holding her snugly
against the length of his side. Meredith's heart leaped.
Angel of mercy, was he naked? It would seem so, for
her cheek was wedged against the smooth, supple skin
of his shoulder. Somehow her hand had landed
squarely atop the center of his chest—a forest of
dense, wiry hairs tickled her palm.

Yet she couldn't deny the heat emanating from his
body. Time marched by. Neither of them moved. He
was impossibly warm—and she was no longer so
abominably cold. Little by little her anxious dread began to depart.

Her fate could have been far worse, a voice in her

head reminded her. He might have used her for his own pleasure, yet he had not. Nor, it seemed, would he.

Her thoughts grew all amuddle. It made no sense that he should be the one to warm her, for he was the very one who returned her to this path . . . Yet her body yielded of its own accord, seeking and finding the heat offered by his. His body drove away the chill of the night . . .

But not the remembrance buried deep in her soul.

Eight

They left several days later. By this time her wound
had healed sufficiently—the relentless pain had dulled
to an occasional ache. When Cameron had stated his
intention to leave soon, he'd boldly announced that it
would be only after he'd pronounced her well enough
to travel. Though Meredith had no urge to hasten the
journey, neither did she wish to remain in these
cramped quarters with him. Quickly she assured him
the wound had healed nicely. To her shock, he insisted on judging—and seeing!—for himself. Meredith argued; he stood firm. Her ire mounted, but there
was no dissuading him. In the end, her face surely the
color of scarlet, she held a blanket to her chest and
allowed a fleeting glimpse.

It was not the wound that gave her pause—it was
him.

If only she could ignore him. Riding before him as
she did once they resumed their journey, it was impossible. She was awesomely aware of his size and
strength. The corded steel of his thighs supported her
own. His arms were ever present around her, his
hands before her, big and tanned and lean, and far
eclipsing her own . . .

There was no escaping him. Not in the light of day, nor in the dead of night.

Their journey took them ever farther to the north. Deeper into the Highlands they climbed, higher and higher. The landscape grew ever more barren. The forests thinned, but for the places where straggly pines sought a tenuous hold in the rocky soil. The heather, not yet in bloom, looked almost black on the hill-sides—as if it had been poured in shadow.

A meandering brook splashed between two huge boulders. It was there he stopped to water Fortune. He lifted her down, then walked to stand near Fortune, who already guzzled noisily from the brook.

Her gaze trekked over the taut, spare lines of his shoulders. It was she who broke the silence. Fervently she spoke, from the center of her heart. " 'Tis not too late to release me."

Slowly he turned to face her. There lurked on his face the blustery squall she'd prayed would not re-sult—yet had fully expected. He was dangerously si-lent.

She'd promised herself she would not beg or plead, but she was sorely tempted. Hands at her sides, she faced him, ignoring the quiver in her belly.

She moistened her lips. "Let me go," she said again. "You could tell the others—Egan and Finn—that I escaped. That you turned your back and I ran—"

"Nay. It would be a lie. Can you, a woman of God, ask me to lie?"

He mocked her most cruelly. Bitterly she said, "I am not a woman of God, and I *have* lied. I also held a knife to your breast and thought of killing."

He did not like the reminder. She could see it in the sudden tautness of his jaw.

"I can only pray that God will forgive me. That I made up for it in some small way by saving your life. You owe me a debt, Cameron MacKay." Bravely she raised her chin. "You owe me your life."

His gaze pinned her own. "Do I? I could have stopped him. There was no need for you to be so foolish. And do we speak of debts, need I remind you of your own?" His voice was hard. "I saved your life. Twice, to be precise. Or do *you* forget so soon? 'Do not let me die,' " he quoted.

The memory was dim, but it was there nonetheless, and she hated that he reminded her. She had no wish to be beholden to him, yet she was . . .

For her very life.

Doggedly she faced him. "Why?" she said bitterly. "Why did you save me? That day in the river. And with Monty?"

"I could not let you die, nor could I let you suffer. You took the blade meant for me."

"You said you had no wish to hurt me, but it does hurt me, knowing that you hurt my father . . . that even now he believes me dead!" Cameron could not know the pain the knowledge wrought . . . Ah, but she'd forgotten. No doubt that was his purpose, to deal a dual blow to both father and daughter!

At the thought of Papa benumbed by sorrow, her soul began to bleed afresh. She ached, there near the center of her breast, near the gash so recently healed. A pain of the flesh, or a pain of the heart? she wondered starkly. One had mended . . .

But would the other?

His jaw clenched. " 'Tis done, and I cannot change it."

The breath she drew was deep and ragged. "You

are the fool, for I am naught but a reminder of all you should forget—''

He'd been about to turn away. His body turned to stone, his words to ice.

''Forget! Would you have me forget my brothers? My beloved father? They were all that I am and now they are no more! That is something I must live with all the days of my life. And you would have me forget? I think not, for I cannot!''

Too late Meredith recognized the tempest, the seething rage, that brewed within him. Yet when she would have stepped back, he snared her by the waist.

With clenched fists raised high, she sought to push herself away. ''Let me go!''

He caught them in one hand, snatching her close with the other. So close she could see the pale flecks of crystalline gray in his eyes, the bronzed plane of his cheek, the harsh twisting of his lips.

''Nay,'' he said fiercely. ''You will listen, and you will hear what I should have told you earlier. Aye, 'tis time you heard the truth about the Red Angus. You will hear of his butchery . . . of his vile, treacherous nature!

''My father and my brothers and I were on our way back from Inverness. We had just taken our wool to market there. We skirted Munro lands, for we wished no trouble. We were well back into MacKay lands— but two days from home—when we were attacked at the crack of dawn. While my brother Oswald stood guard, his throat was slit—praise God his end was mercifully swift!

''It was the Munro battle cry that woke me, my father, and the rest of my brothers. There was scarce time to rouse from our beds than they were upon us. From a distance I saw the Red Angus—there is no mistaking the flame of his hair. My father leaped to his feet, searching for his sword. It had been stolen from his side in the night, along with the rest of our weapons. Before he could move, he was slain where he stood.''

Meredith could not help it. She shrank back from the brutal anger that blazed across his features.

''I was the next to be struck down—a blow to the head, a sword to the back. Though I tried, I could not move. My youngest brother Thomas was next, but a wee lad of ten! He knew not how to handle a sword, nor did he want to, for he fancied the church! He lay next to me. He stretched out his hand . . . Never will I forget the way he looked—so pleading, so confused! He died reaching out to me! Crying out to me. But I could not save him. *I could not save him!*''

Meredith's stomach lurched sickeningly. She longed to clamp her hands over her ears to shut out the terrible sound of his voice. She'd sworn she would not plead, but God above, she did.

She gave a tiny shake of her head. ''Please! Say no more—''

''But there *is* more, Meredith, much more! I had four brothers left, remember? Though I could not move, I saw all, as if I peered through the sheerness of a veil—my brothers' lives stolen from them. Niall, the eldest. Burke, but a year younger. Kenneth was moaning. Remember I told you of a sword to the belly . . . the most painful of all? I know. I listened to Kenneth scream, a bloodcurdling sound that will haunt me throughout my days. I tried to crawl to him, but I possessed not the strength. Oswald was the only one I did not see die . . .

''Your clansmen thought I was dead. When I woke, I was in the cottage of a crofter who had come upon the massacre. 'Twas he who nursed me and buried my father and brothers—he who told me how in the next village your clansmen boasted how they waited the night through, how well pleased their chieftain was at their triumph—the slaughter of Ronald MacKay and his sons. They sought to render us helpless by stealing our swords—such valiant warriors,'' he sneered. ''They so feared us that they could only face us unarmed! But that was not enough for him, nay, not for the Red Angus. When I made my way home, I discovered what the crofter had spared me.

''The heads of my father, and Niall, his firstborn son, had been delivered to the keep. Niall's wife, Glenda, was the first to see them. She was heavy with child, due at summer's end. The shock of seeing my brother's head sent her into childbed early. Niall's son died, too small to survive—yet another death laid at the feet of the Red Angus! So do not tell me to forget, for I will never forget!''

Meredith felt her belly heave. She was sick, sick to the marrow of her bones. Wrenching away, she fell to her knees and retched.

When her stomach was empty, she leaned back on her haunches. Shaking and weak, she pressed the back of her hand to her mouth. There was scarcely time to recover, even to think, to say a word before he was there, pulling her upright. Her head came up and for one agonizing moment, she met his regard. With the slash of his eyes he scorned her, his gaze fired with a blaze that scorched her very soul. A peremptory hand at her waist, he marched her toward his mount.

Quiet and subdued, she sat before him. She could not deny what he had seen, what he had endured. That her clansmen could be so deliberately cruel . . . For an instant she faltered. Nearly two years had passed since she had seen her father. Could he have changed so very much? He was capable of anger, yes!—for who was not? But atrocities such as Cameron had relayed? She could not fathom her father meting out such brutality, even to a MacKay. She could not doubt his innocence in this. She could not even think of such, for surely he could not have changed so very much!

They traveled throughout the remainder of the day, halting only once. Raising a hand, he pointed toward sprawling fortress that seemed to spring from the mountain behind it.

"There is Dunthorpe," he said.

For a heartbeat, breath was lost to her. An unseen hand seemed to close about her heart. This, then, was to be her prison. He had saved her, only to condemn her.

Stone walls jutted skyward, gaunt and forbidding. A mist curled around the tower. She could almost feel its cold and dampness. Beyond the castle loomed the granite face of the mountain, its sheer walls seemingly untouched by the shadow of time.

Time, she thought with a throb in her breast. Time eternal. How long would she be here? An oppressive burden seemed to settle on her shoulders.

Her future, such as it was, was solely in his hands.

Those hands drew her gaze endlessly. She stared at them, looped on the reins with careless ease. But one thought leaped high aloft: He had no need of a sword to slay her. It could be done with but the power of his hands, lean and dark and strong. A blow to the head. The squeezing grasp of his fingers . . .

"What will you do with me?" She sounded as weary as she suddenly felt.

His gaze resided briefly on her profile. "I've not yet decided."

"What?" She twisted around, that she might see him. All at once she couldn't restrain her bitterness—or the retort that sprang to the fore. "These many days, and you've not yet decided?"

His expression tautened.

Suddenly the rage burned not in him but in her. She resented him as she had never resented another—resented his power over her fate. And she cared not if he punished her, or even how.

Her gaze stabbed into his, afire with indignant outrage. "You took me to assure your revenge," she flung at him. "I am naught but a prize . . . a prize of vengeance!"

"Aye. And I've decided I shall keep my prize. If it will ease your saintly conscience, consider it a pilgrimage."

His arrogant rejoinder only spurred her own. "A pilgrimage to hell, with the devil himself! For you are a bastard," she said feelingly, "a bloody, imperious bastard, and I have naught but contempt for you."

His smile was a travesty. "The saintly maid deigns to curse! Come, now, lass. Does it not feel immensely satisfying to sin?"

Lass. That one word could sound so very different . . . ! Something twisted inside her. The gentleness he had shown her in the hut was gone. His reassurance was no more. The jeer was back.

Meredith choked back the tears that burned her throat, her very soul. She had the awful feeling that whatever the fate he contemplated . . .

It would now begin in earnest.

With every mile that took them closer to his keep, the sky darkened. Black, ominous clouds smothered the sunset. Soon the rain began to fall in leaden sheets from the sky. Her sodden hair streamed down her back. An empty hollow filled her chest. The rain lashed clear to her soul.

A watchman in the drum tower spied the horse that climbed upward from the tiny burn below. A jubilant shout went up as they approached the wooden palisade.

"He's back!" cried the watchman atop the massive south tower. "Cameron returns!"

With every step that took them through the outer ward and toward the gatehouse, Meredith longed to plummet beneath the depths of the earth. A leaden ball of dread lay heavy in her belly.

The iron gate was raised high as they passed into the gloom beneath the towering arch. A guard emerged from the guardroom and stood in the doorway.

He grinned, eyes glinting as they passed by. "We've a place in the pit prison for ye, lady!"

They'd passed into the inner ward. By now a crowd had begun to close around them.

There came a shout nearby. " 'Tis her, daughter of the Red Angus!"

For one never-ending moment, a deathly pall hung in the air. Then it began—the shouts and taunting.

"She be bonnie fair, eh? That is, for a Munro!"

"Bonnie fair!" snorted another. "Nay! She resembles the Red Angus, to the color of her hair!"

Someone spied the broken, puffy skin at her temple. "Ho, but I wish I'd been there when he clubbed her!"

Meredith's face burned painfully. She felt as if an icy wind had blown across her heart. Would Cameron tell them the truth, that not he, but another, had struck her?

It would seem not, the rogue! Behind her, he called out a greeting.

The heckling continued. ''Och, but he'll throw her in the pit prison to be sure!'' One man gleefully rubbed his hands and grinned.

''Aye!'' chimed in a woman with a cackling laugh. ''She won't be so bonnie fair then, now, will she?''

Her heart surely rent in that instant. Darkness stole through her. Her fear and despair and desperation had known no bounds in the days before she'd gone to live at Connyridge. It was there she'd found sanctuary, a haven from the shadows that plagued her. Now she had entered the world anew—only to be thrust into the midst of a clan who hated her and all her kin . . .

And no one more so than Cameron MacKay.

She felt him leap lightly to the ground. Boldly as you please, he set his hands on her waist and swung her down. She'd done no more than raise her head than another figure stepped into her line of vision.

''Out of the way, girl . . . move aside, lad!''

It was Egan. Several paces behind was the other man who had accompanied Cameron to Connyridge— Finn.

''Cameron!'' hailed the scar-faced man. He grabbed his chieftain and gave him a fierce and unabashed hug, then drew back.

''Blood of Christ, man, I feared the worst. I sent men out to search, but they dinna find ye! Finn here was gone nearly a sennight.''

''Aye,'' said Finn. ''We feared the Munros had come after ye and captured ye.''

Cameron raised a brow. ''Why should they come after me? By now the Red Angus has surely received word that his daughter is dead. They have no idea she is even alive.''

''I suppose 'tis true enough,'' Finn admitted gruffly.

Meredith deeply resented all of them for talking about her as if she were not even present.

Egan scowled at Finn. ''I told ye that, man! He's like his da, too smart for the Munros. But I would surely like to know where the devil ye've been!''

Cameron smiled grimly. ''That's a tale for later, my friends. Let it be enough that I'm whole and hearty and safe at home.''

As he spoke, his gaze dwelled briefly on her profile. She maintained what she hoped was a cool aplomb, for she'd not give him the satisfaction of knowing he'd defeated her.

For in truth, that was all that sustained her . . . all that allowed her to hold her head proudly erect.

His smile withered. Tilting his head, he said something in a low voice to Finn. Then he reached out and caught her by the arm. Steely fingers curled into the softness of her flesh. ''Go with Finn,'' he instructed.

And may you go to the devil, she longed to cry. Instead she kept silent, pressing her lips together. Wrenching herself away, she followed Finn, who appeared none too pleased to be her escort.

He led her into the keep, through the great hall and a door on the far right. There they made their way up a steep, twisting stairway to the very top of the tower; Meredith was dizzy and breathless by the time he gestured her through another door.

''You are to wait,'' he growled.

She stepped within. Behind her, the door closed with a resounding thud. To Meredith, it was like the closing of her own tomb. From without, a bolt scraped home.

She stood for a moment, letting her eyes adjust to the gloom. The chamber she was in was small, the furnishings spartan. There was naught but a narrow bed across from the stone fireplace, and a tiny table and chair beneath the window, set high in the wall. Indeed, it was little better than her cell at Connyridge . . . yet far grander than the dank hole in the earth where she would be, had she been relegated to the pit prison.

There was a knock upon the door. Meredith had no chance to respond before the bolt was thrown and it opened. A stout woman stepped within; in her arms was a small round wooden tub.

"His Lordship ordered a bath for ye," was all she said.

Meredith quickly extended a hand to assist with her burden. "Here, let me help—"

"Nay!" The woman jerked away as if she'd been burned.

She refused even to look at Meredith as she marched across the chamber and placed the tub before the fire. Meredith's arms fell to her side. The woman's dislike was like a slap across the face. She stood awkwardly while the woman lit a fire in the hearth. Two young boys followed, toting buckets of hot water. Their manner was as stiff as their mistress's, their faces unsmiling.

Meredith took a deep breath. They might be convinced she was the devil's daughter, but she would not act as such. "Thank you," she said clearly when they'd finished the task.

Not one of the three made any acknowledgment.

Plumes of steam rose from the bath, a temptation

Meredith could not ignore. Putting aside her hurt, she stripped. She was sodden to the skin, and she gasped as she lowered herself into the steaming waters. She soaped her limbs vigorously, then washed her hair. The tub was small, and her knees were jammed against her chest, yet the hot water felt heavenly. She soaked until the water was cold, then dried herself with the length of linen cloth the woman had left, wrapping it around herself as she lingered before the fire.

Distastefully she eyed her tattered gown. A puddle leaked across the stone floor where she'd dropped it. She sighed, resigning herself to the fact that she had no choice but to don it anew—

Another knock. This time it was a woman who was sweet-faced and slender, not so much older than she, Meredith guessed. Chestnut hair waved down her back, swept back from her face with a narrow strip of plaid. Her eyes were wide and thickly lashed, almost the same golden brown as her hair.

"This is for you." Her voice was quiet but cool. With her head bowed low, she slid a tray of food onto the table, then crossed to the bed.

Meredith watched as she deposited several items there. "A clean gown, and a comb—oh, but you cannot know how welcome they are!" The confession emerged unconsciously. The woman was much the same size as she. "Do they belong to you?"

For an instant it appeared she would refuse to answer. "Aye," she said at last.

"Then I must thank you doubly. I promise I shall take good care of them." She hesitated. "Do you . . . have a name?"

The woman's head came up sharply. There was a

flash in those golden brown eyes before she raised her chin. "I am Glenda."

Glenda. Meredith's mind groped fuzzily and then she reeled. Oh, God, it was her. Cameron's brother Niall, the eldest son—this was his widow, the one who'd lost her babe after seeing the heads of her husband and father-in-law!

Meredith could not help it. Her eyes veered to the woman's belly, now flat as her own.

So this was Glenda, no longer heavy with child. Now she understood the silent accusation that glimmered in the depths of the MacKay woman's eyes. Shame such as she had never known rushed through her, shame that singed the very center of her being. Her clansmen—her own clansmen—had robbed this woman of a husband and son.

For the first time the pain of Cameron's loss seemed real, and the knowledge was agonizing.

Glenda had begun to retrace her steps to the door. Meredith realized she was about to leave.

"I pray you, wait!"

Words failed her, for indeed, what could she say that would change Glenda's feelings? Comfort from a Munro? An apology from a Munro? Glenda would neither want it nor accept it.

"I . . . I thank you for your kind generosity," she finished lamely.

"There is no need to offer thanks. I did as I was bidden." Her posture wooden, her manner stiff, Glenda swept from the chamber.

Once again Meredith was alone.

Indeed, she thought bitterly, she might have been a favored guest. A bath, clothing, and food had been provided.

Sighing, she crossed to the bed. Reaching out, she

fingered the soft wool of the gowns—there were three of them, a smock, and even a soft linen bed gown. A wistful smile touched her lips for a fleeting instant. There had been no such luxuries at Connyridge. The habit she wore there had been rough and heavy. Her skin had been red and chafed for many a day until she'd grown used to it.

She slipped the bed gown over her head. The tray of food was left untouched, for she had no appetite. Picking up the comb, she moved to sit before the fire, availing herself of its warmth to dry her hair. It took forever to work out the tangles; her hair had nearly dried by the time she'd finished. Staring into the crackling flames, she wrapped her arms around her knees and hugged them to her chest, dropping her head down.

Oddly, there were no tears. There was no fear. She felt nothing . . . nothing but a vast hollowness inside.

Nine

The great hall was filled with gaiety and song. There were jongleurs and minstrels who sang a rambling song of the lord's belated return. But Cameron had long since vacated his place at the high table. It was too empty. Too lonely. Instead he sat at a trestle table directly below the gallery. Though he was ready with a smile and a greeting for those who passed by or stopped to sit, he felt curiously detached from all the revelry.

" 'Tis good to be home, eh?" With a grin, Egan planted two tankards of ale atop the rough planking and pushed one toward his chieftain.

Cameron glanced up as his friend seated himself on the bench opposite him. He reached for the ale, his expression softening slightly. "Aye," he murmured, for indeed, his heart's realm was the chill and misty Highlands. " 'Tis good to be home." He paused. "And yet, it seems so . . . so different. As if . . ."— though the hall was filled with the sounds of merriment, it was that very thought that echoed in his brain over and over—"as if something is missing."

Egan grew abruptly sober. "Something is," he said quietly.

They both fell silent, lost in the blur of happier

memories, of a time when the brothers MacKay had filled this hall with shouts and laughter—a time when one recounted a tale well told, boasts of manly strength and other attributes, a good-natured challenge quickly taken up by another.

It was Egan who broke the silence. "I noticed you found a way to tame the lass." He tapped his temple meaningfully. "Och, but I canna blame ye. Aye, the wench looks the meek and trembling maid, but the blood of the Munros flows in her veins—"

"I did not strike her," Cameron stated flatly. "There is no honor in striking a woman." He would not keep the truth from Egan—yet neither would he reveal that Meredith had dared to hold a dagger to his breast, for his pride still rankled that he'd been so careless. His thoughts hardened.

"Then who did?"

"We met with foul play." Grimly he told his friend how they'd been surprised by the rogues Monty and Davis. "She took the blade intended for me."

Egan paused, his tankard halfway to his mouth. He stared, dumbfounded. Slowly he lowered the brew to the table. "What, man? Why should she do such a foolish thing as that? Why should a Munro give her life for a MacKay? That cannot be—"

"I was there, Egan. My eyes did not deceive me."

"Mayhap 'twas a death wish! She saw it as a chance to escape. Aye, that must be it."

Cameron was not so convinced. Yet the idea troubled him—troubled him mightily, though it should not have—and that, too, he found rather vexing! Would she have gone to such lengths to be free of him? Nay, he thought. Nay!

It was just as he'd said. She'd taken the blow for him. It still both amazed and confounded him. Egan would have taken the blow for him—but Egan was his greatest friend; indeed, Cameron would have done the same for Egan.

But Meredith had no reason to do so. Especially after what he'd done to her . . .

He was compelled to defend her.

"She would never take her own life. Remember that night at the priory? The note I bade her write to the sisters? She was appalled, for she was convinced that's what I would have her do. ' 'Tis mortal sin,' she said."

"But it would not have been by her own hand," Egan argued. " 'Twould have been by the hand of another."

"Remember she is a woman, and one who was soon to take her vows. The thought is as much a sin as the deed. She took the blade to save my life." Cameron's shrug was deliberately nonchalant. "Though I was never in such danger as she believed." Or so he'd told himself—and her! Ah, but it was masculine vanity that provoked the claim. In truth, he did not know if he would be here now, were it not for her.

He owed her a debt, a debt he must somehow repay. Yet despite the guilt that nagged at him, he could not give up all that he sought . . . he would not!

Thoughtfully Egan fingered his bristly chin. "What will you do with her now?"

Cameron parried the question with one of his own. "You would have killed her, wouldn't you?"

"Aye." Egan's reply was swift and unrepentant. "She is a Munro. These lands would be a better place were there one less. But you chose not to, and so I respect your decision."

Cameron nodded, but his mind had drifted. He recalled his fury this morn. It galled him still that she had dared to suggest he let her escape—that she dared to suggest that he should put aside the death of his father and brothers and forget. Indeed, he could scarcely remember a time when he'd been so furious. A scarlet haze of rage had fired his vision. God's wounds, but the wench bedeviled him as no other—in truth his temper was seldom provoked. A rash anger was rarely wise. His father had taught him that, him and all Cameron's brothers. Nay, 'twas better to contemplate with calm deliberation, to anticipate the actions that might come . . . He should not have lashed out at her as he had. Such gruesome details were not for the tender ears of a woman . . .

Even this one.

His anger had abated. But not the desire. Nay, not the desire . . .

"Will you make a slave of her?" It was Egan again.

Cameron smiled, a smile that was grimly self-derisive. In this, he'd failed his father, for in truth, beyond the driving need for revenge that had consumed his every pore, this was the one thing he'd not considered.

He shook his head. "I've not yet decided," he admitted. His smile withered. "I want her watched at all times, Egan—you and Finn see to it. I'll not take the chance that she'll escape. If she were to run to her father, all would be for naught. The Red Angus is convinced she is dead," he stated flatly. "So I would have him believe, and so it will be."

Despite Egan's animosity toward Meredith, his loyalty was unquestionable. Cameron had no doubt that his command would be obeyed. He trusted Egan implicitly, as surely as he'd trusted his own brothers.

They talked for a while after that, then Egan finally left with several others. Cameron remained where he was.

"I brought ye more ale."

Another full tankard was set before him. Cameron glanced up at the lovely dark-haired woman who had just taken the seat Egan had so recently vacated. It was Moire, the eldest daughter of Moreland, his father's steward . . . nay, *his* steward.

"Moire." He raised the tankard high in silent thanks, then drank deeply.

" 'Tis good that you have returned, Cameron."

" 'Tis glad I am to *be* back," he returned. And all in one piece, he thought, reminded of his dagger-wielding prisoner.

"I trust your journey went well." Large, snapping-brown eyes met his boldly.

"It did indeed." A faint smile of satisfaction curled his lips. Meredith was locked in the tower, right where he wanted her. She wouldn't be leaving anytime soon.

Cherry-red lips curved slyly. "Will you sentence the Munro wench on the morrow, Cameron?"

Meredith, he wanted to snap. *Her name is Meredith.* Instead he said curtly, "I've no intention of sentencing her. She's committed no crime."

Moire's eyes widened. "But surely you mean to hang her!"

"Hang her?" Cameron was astounded. "Is that what everyone believes?"

"Nay," Moire said quickly. "Not everyone. Just . . ."

"Just you?" Heavy brows arose. He didn't bother to hide his admonishment.

Moire had the grace to look sheepish. "What will you do with her, then?"

Cameron was abruptly irritated. First Egan, now Moire. The score was his to settle—no one else's. Why was everyone so damnably concerned about his plans for her?

"I will hold her for however long it pleases me."

Moire paid no heed to the sudden coolness of his manner. " 'Tis said she has the look of her father, the Red Angus."

"Aye." His mouth was no longer smiling.

"I cannot imagine why she sought out a nunnery!" Moire made a face. "Mayhap no one would marry her. Aye, that must be it . . . but such drudgery! Working, praying, working . . . and more praying! 'Tis said they eat but one meal a day there. I can well believe it, for she's a pale, scrawny piece."

Cameron took in Moire's buxom figure. Obviously, he observed dryly, Moire did not subsist on just one meal a day.

Well aware—and aye, well pleased!—Moire reached across the table and plucked an apple from the platter of fruit there. In so doing, her bodice drooped low and Cameron was afforded an uninhibited view of ripe, white-fleshed breasts clear to large, dark brown nipples.

Little wonder that Moreland, her father, was eager to marry off the lass. Indeed, Cameron's own name had been bandied about in tandem with the lady's. But as he'd told his father in private not so very long ago, he would never even consider Moire as his future wife. Though he hadn't confided it to his father, Cameron was well aware that several of his brothers had already plucked from the fruit of the lady's vine. He did not condemn her, for if a man was entitled to lusty endeavors, why should a woman not be as well? Nay, when he married—and he had no doubt that someday he would—it would be to a woman who gave her favors to him alone.

Moire possessed a dark, alluring beauty—that, Cameron did not deny. Though he was not averse to admiring, he experienced a curious distaste for her boldness. Odd, for in truth he was far more tempted by the Munro lass than by this one who so blatantly revealed her bounteous enticements to any and all who cared to look.

Moire studied the apple, then bit into the tender, juicy fruit. With the tip of her tongue she dabbed a trail of juice from the corner of sleek ruby lips. She smiled across at Cameron. "Do ye think ye might take me riding tomorrow?"

The smile he offered was regretful but firm. "I fear I'll be far too busy."

Her smile wavered. Red lips pouted prettily, but it did no good. She departed moments later, the sway in her hips earning more than a few hungry glances. Cameron decided wryly that she would probably not spend the day alone—or this night, either.

He sat there long after the last chord had been played, the last note sung. The hall had grown quiet but for the noisy snores of those merry souls who'd imbibed too much and sought their bed on the nearest bench.

Thoughts of Meredith never strayed far from his mind.

Egan had asked what he would do with her. Moire, too. Ah, he thought with a twist of his lips. What to do with her . . .

A brooding shadow slipped over him. This hall had once brimmed with laughter and life. Indeed, the laughter had been there tonight . . . but the life, the soul of this place he had always called home, was no more.

It was just as he'd told Egan. It had been different. So very, very empty . . .

The bleakness inside him yawned wider.

The way of the clans was the way of the Highlands. Without a chieftain to protect him, a man might lose his lands—his home. There would be no sheep, no crops, no way to feed his family. In times of need, clansmen banded together. To hold one's lands, to ensure the safety of kin, a man might look to his family to help. In this way, the clans were perpetuated. It was, Cameron realized, an awesome duty—one he had never thought to covet, one he'd never dreamed might be his. Though Cameron had never liked to think of his father's death, he'd always assumed that Niall would be the next chieftain. But now that the duty was his, he would not shirk it. He would not fail his father. For many a generation, the Clan MacKay had ruled these hills and glens of the Highlands. So it had been . . .

So it would continue.

Even as the vow hammered through mind and heart, a burning hatred simmered in his breast. He thought of the Munros. His fists clenched hard as he remembered how they had robbed his family of their lives. How *he* had been robbed . . . That was why he had done . . . what he had done. Why he'd stolen Meredith from Connyridge. He had sought to take from the Red Angus what had been stolen from him—and in so doing, impart the hurtful knowledge that the Red Angus was the last of his blood.

His mouth twisted. What to do with her, indeed . . .

Though he had pretended uncertainty with Egan, he knew he would not make a slave of her. Not unless she was his slave alone, he thought blackly, for he was too possessive of her . . .

Something sparked within him.

What was it Egan had demanded? *Why should a Munro give her life for a MacKay?* The words pounded through his brain, over and over.

She was a woman. And she *could* give life.

He, Cameron, was the last of his father's seed . . . as she was the last of hers.

The spark inside him flamed higher.

No, he thought. The idea that burned through his mind and throughout his body . . . it wasn't possible.

It is, insisted a voice deep his soul. And you want her. You know you do. You can have your revenge . . . *and her*.

The idea took root. With every beat of his heart, it grew stronger.

He was on his feet before he knew it, taking the steps to the north tower two at a time.

With one smooth move he threw the bolt and stepped within her chamber.

She was there before the fire, her legs drawn tight against her chest, her head resting upon upraised knees, clad in a thin linen bed gown, her toes peeping out from beneath the hem. It struck him that she looked very young, almost vulnerable.

It took a moment before she discerned his presence. Slowly she raised her head and gazed at him. Her expression was wholly unguarded, her pose oddly defenseless.

For an instant Cameron did not move. For the space of a heartbeat, it was as if he could see clear inside her. His only thought was that she possessed a purity that was disconcerting. She looked so fair. So innocent and humble. Gazing at her thusly, he could almost forget that the blood of the Munros flowed in her veins.

Ruthlessly he pushed the thought aside, scathingly angry with himself. What was this he was about? He could afford no softness. No pity.

He came to stand directly above her. He stared at the vulnerable length of her throat, arched to meet his unremitting regard.

Her beauty struck him like a blow low to the belly. God, that such loveliness belonged to a Munro . . . His mind screamed in outrage. The burning in his veins was no less intense, but now a fire of another kind had kindled in his gut. Her eyes were the color of a sun-washed sky—never had he seen such clarity of color. The curve of her cheek gleamed pale and silken; her lips were slightly parted. He found himself possessed of the sudden urge to press his lips there, against the hollow of her throat, to taste that tempting valley and feel her pulse surge beneath his lips.

Wordlessly he extended a hand.

Her hesitation was marked, but she must have seen the way his jaw thrust out, for she slipped her fingers within his. Cameron pulled her up and onto her feet. As she rose, the light from the fire flared higher—as if solely for his benefit. The lithe, slender shape of her body was clearly revealed beneath the frail cloth. Clearly visible were two round, coral nipples perched atop the mounds of her breasts, a darker, dusky shadow between pale, slender thighs. Cameron could not have called himself a man were his gaze not compelled to linger long and hard.

Desire twisted his gut like a thousand swords. His skin prickled with heat. His rod swelled hard and full. He longed to plant himself heavy and deep within the cavern between her thighs. Bloody hell, he felt like a hound in heat!

Yet there was a part of him that despised himself for wanting her like this. When he'd snatched her from Connyridge, he hadn't been prepared for this—this wretched desire! But Cameron could lie to himself no longer—his attraction to her was something he could not govern at will.

And yet . . . it would serve his purpose well indeed.

She withdrew her hand as soon as she was up and on her feet. He knew from the way she flushed that she was aware of the path his eyes had taken. Was she remembering how he'd seen her naked in the shepherd's hut? God knew *he* was!

He retrieved the straight-backed chair below the window and placed it beside her. "Sit," he told her.

She complied, folding her hands atop her knees. Cameron's gaze sharpened. Did she tremble, or was it his imagination? No, he decided. She was nervous. He wanted her, true, but not all atremble in fear.

A frown pleated his brow as he spied the tray atop the table. Her trencher was untouched. "Why did you not eat?" he growled.

"I have no appetite." She plucked at a fold in the gown; it was there she confined her attention.

"Why not?" A disquieting notion went through him. They'd ridden hard these past days . . . too hard? "Does your wound pain you?"

She shook her head.

"What, then?"

She looked up at him suddenly, her eyes huge and dark and wounded. Cameron glimpsed in those depths something which sent a sliver of remorse through him . . . but no! He refused to give in to it—to her, for mayhap it was naught but a ploy. Ah, he was right, for even now her eyes had lowered, her lashes shielding her every thought.

His mood grew stormy. Mayhap she was convinced if she played the role of meek and humble lady, he would be laden with guilt and allow her to leave . . . why, this very night! She had sought to be a nun, but she employed the wiles of a woman. Ah, but she had much to learn if success would be hers! Guilt was not the way to sway the bend of a man's mind. Oh, aye, he could think of far more pleasurable ways—for both of them!—that a woman might use to entice a man to do her bidding.

"Tell me, Meredith. What were you thinking of when I entered? Nay, let me guess. You were plotting how you might escape, weren't you?"

That brought her head up in a flash. "I was not!" It was an indignant denial.

His hands closed around her shoulders. "What were you thinking of, then?" he demanded.

"If you must know, I—I was thinking about your brothers. Your father—"

"My brothers! My father!" His lips thinned to a stern line. "No doubt you curse them and pray that they burn in eternal flames."

He'd pricked her temper. He saw it in the spark of her eyes. "I pray for them, aye! But I would wish no one to suffer a fate such as that."

His smile was tight. "Not even me?"

Their eyes caught and held endlessly. Hers were the first to slip away. "Nay," she said after a moment. Cameron sensed her anger had died as suddenly as it had erupted. "Not even you."

Her head bowed low. He heard the deep, wavering

breath she drew. Then all at once her gaze lifted to his, dark and pleading.

"I am sorry for your loss," she said, her voice very low. "Truly. I cannot imagine the pain of losing so many you hold dear—and all at once! If . . . if only there was something I could do . . ."

Cameron went very still. "And what would you give to make up for the loss of my brothers and my father?"

She was silent a long moment. He could almost see her mind turning . . . She gave a tiny shake of her head. "Were I a woman of wealth, I would gladly give you all that I have—"

"No. I would not take your coin, even if you had it to give."

"Then I will work for you—"

"I do not want your servitude."

Her shoulders slumped. "Then there is nothing." She swallowed. "You may as well kill me now—"

"What would be gained by one more life gone? I will not kill you, Meredith. Nor will I imprison you."

"What, then?" She cried out her frustration. "There is nothing! I cannot atone—"

"Oh, but you can. *You can*. You can give me a part of all I lost that day."

Their eyes cleaved together. His fervency must have served as a warning, for she moistened her lips with her tongue.

"How?" she whispered.

There was a screaming rush of silence. And it was into that deepening void that his words fell.

"A son. A son . . . and I will free you."

Ten

Meredith's eyes closed. Her strength ebbed. She would have fallen were it not for his hold on her.

Quiet prevailed, a quiet that invaded every corner of the chamber. Jagged bits and pieces of thoughts churned through her mind. What he suggested . . . nay, surely it could not be . . . he could not mean . . .

His features reflected utter calm, a calm she was far from feeling. The slash of those black brows arched expectantly as he awaited her reaction.

Her lips moved, but no sound emerged. It took several tries before she could summon her voice. "You cannot mean that you . . . that I . . . that we . . ."

Her choice of words provoked a faint smile. "That's the way of it, I fear," he said lightly. "I cannot beget a son alone—and you cannot beget my son without me."

"But you could have a son of any woman in this keep. You are chieftain here! You have only to return belowstairs and—and have your pick! Why would you choose me?"

He released her, withdrawing several paces to stand before the fire. Lean hands linked behind his back, strong legs braced slightly apart, he stared into the leaping flames of the fire. The silence thickened—

along with her unease. At last he turned back. His face was in shadow, his expression unreadable.

"Tell me something, lass. Do you wish to remain here?"

Meredith was aghast. "Nay!"

"So you wish your freedom." It was a statement, not a question.

"I do."

"Above all else?"

She eyed him suspiciously. Now what game did he play? "Aye," she said reluctantly.

"You can have your freedom, Meredith, but there is only one way you will attain it." His gaze never left her face. "There is only one way you will ever leave Dunthorpe."

Meredith blanched. Nay, she thought numbly. He could not know what he asked of her. She could never accept him. She could never accept any man!

She pressed her lips together to still their trembling. "Nay," she said, and then again: "Nay! I will be a slave gladly! I will work, work my fingers to the bone! No matter how long—"

His dismissal was curt. "That would give me no satisfaction."

"Then I will find a way to pay you—"

"In your own words, you possess no wealth."

"But my father does! That is why the nunnery took me!"

"Your father believes you dead, Meredith." His eyes grew chill. "I promise you, that will not change."

Ah, but he was cruel to remind her! "Then I will find another way," she cried wildly. "I will pay you any price!"

"If money were my goal, I would have ransomed

you. And you have my price, lass.'' His gaze was
unrelenting. ''Give me a son.''

She felt the stab of his voice as surely as she'd felt
the stab of Monty's dagger.

The breath she drew was deep and ragged. ''Why?
Why?''

''It is true that I could have a son of any woman.
But I do not want a son of any woman. I want a son
of *you,* Meredith Munro. Your family robbed me of
mine. 'Tis only right that a Munro should give it
back.'' Softly he said, ''You are the only one who
can, Meredith. I am the last of my father's seed, as
you are the last of *your* father's—the last of your
father's seed will ensure that my own does not die
off. When you give me a son, you will have returned
a part of all I lost that day. That is why it must be
you. You are the only Munro . . . who can give me a
son.'' His eyes bored into hers like the tip of a lance.
'' 'Tis justice.''

'' 'Tis not justice. 'Tis vengeance!''

''Justice. Vengeance.'' He shrugged. ''Either way,
I will have my son.''

He took a step forward. Meredith took a step back.
A fierce light shone in his eyes, a light that was somehow more frightening than all he had said.

Meredith swallowed. To lie with a man, she
thought sickly . . . and this man, yet! He hated her and
all her clan. Her pain would be his pleasure, his manhood naught but the weapon he wielded against her
. . . inside her!

She couldn't take her eyes from him. He was so
tall, his head nearly brushed the cross-timbers, his
shoulders so broad, it seemed he filled the chamber
to the limit.

Her chest rose and fell. Desperately she sought to

arm herself. "Nay," she said bravely. "I will not do it."

"There will be no negotiating. My decision stands."

Faith, but he was as imperious as ever! He knew no rules but his own! She wanted to grind her teeth in impotent rage; instead she felt her panic spiral. "You cannot want this," she said jerkily. "That night at Connyridge . . . you said that were you in need of a woman, of a certainty 'twould not be me. You said—you said you must force yourself to suffer my presence."

"You are far comelier than I realized." His gaze traversed the length of her, lingering with blatant interest on the arch of her throat, the swell of rounded breasts beneath her gown. "Indeed," he drawled, " 'twill be no hardship to get you with child."

A smile now creased the hardness of his lips. Her nails dug into her palms. Oh, how she wished she possessed the courage to slap his arrogant face! Another time, she promised herself, and she would.

For now, she bolted for the door.

The effort was futile. Ah, but she should have known! He caught her before she could even lay her fingers on the iron handle. She raved in mingled fury and regret. Always he caught her, always he was there, forever barring her way!

A hard arm clamped around her waist, encircling her from behind. The world careened wildly as her feet left the ground. She was borne through the air to the narrow bed against the wall.

A grim-visaged face swam above her. Blindly she struck out, seeking to scratch and kick, anything to disentangle herself from male arms whose reach seemed to span the very seas!

A curse rushed past her ear. "Meredith . . . Meredith, by the Virgin, cease! I have no desire to hurt you, I swear. There are ways to bring you into this gently, and I promise, I will use them!"

That only made her struggle all the more, for she'd heard such promises before and they had been naught but lies!

Cameron was left with no choice. He trapped her wrists above her head with one lean hand, and pinned her to the bed with the weight of his chest against her own. She lay beneath him, gasping and spent.

Slowly he raised his head to look at her. Their eyes locked. She glimpsed in his the unmistakable sheen of triumph.

With the fingers of his free hand he ran the callused tip of his thumb across her lips.

He smiled tightly.

Meredith glared and clamped her lips against him. He persisted, sliding a fingertip along the line of her jaw. Glittering eyes rained down at her. For the space of a heartbeat, she stared helplessly at the hard-featured face of the man above her, a man whose harshly carved lips hovered but a breath above her own.

With thumb and forefinger he caught her chin . . . and then his mouth claimed hers.

Shock rendered her motionless in this, her first taste of his lips. A hundred things went through her mind in that mind-shattering instant. For all the dark intensity of his expression, he did not crush her against him, as she thought he might . . . as she feared he would! Nay, his kiss neither ravaged nor plundered; in short, it was not the brutal assault she expected.

Though she knew his heart lay in his breast cold as a winter morning, his mouth was as warm as a summer breeze. His breath was not hot and fetid. It mingled with her own as she parted her lips in shock or surprise, she knew not which. She trembled, yet not in fear. Not in fear . . .

Yet the terrors of the night which had plagued her for so long returned afresh to haunt her. The dreams which plagued her at the shepherd's hut were too new, too recent. And Meredith was no innocent. She knew where play such as this would lead—indeed, he made no secret of it, for that was his very wish!

Meredith went hot, then icy cold. Her mind flew like a tempest across the seas. She battled a rising hysteria, but it was a battle already forfeit. The past moved in on her. All at once his body was an oppressive weight atop her. She lay beneath him like— like a hare on a spit, and that was how he would use her. Even through their clothing, she could feel him, rigid and thick as a lance of steel. Aye, that is what he would do—thrust his weapon home, deep inside her tender flesh.

An icy dread seeped through her. An enveloping darkness smothered her. It would be just like before, she thought sickly. He would strip her clothes from her. See what only a husband should see. Stroke her body in sinful ways. Suddenly she could not breathe. Very soon he would free his rod into his palm. And then . . .

Already she could feel the change in him. He'd released her wrists, only to slide his arms beneath her back. She was drawn close to him, so close she felt the rampaging throb of his heart as if it were her own.

Her breath grew quick and shallow. A frenzy of fear rushed through her. She shuddered. He said he would not hurt her, but he would. Meredith was as certain of it as she was of her own name. He spoke of gentleness, but she knew it was just a trick—a trick to gain what he sought.

Her fingers came up. She pushed frantically at his shoulders, desperate to dislodge him, but he remained where he was, solid as a boulder, just as immovable.

A low whimper broke from her throat. She tore her mouth away. "Nay . . . *nay!*"

It was a stricken cry, laden thickly with fear. Somehow it penetrated the crimson haze of passion that surrounded him.

Slowly he raised his head. He hovered above her, dark and dangerous. His expression was tight-lipped and stony, his features an iron mask of determination. Powerful arms around her contracted, taut as stone. For one awful moment, she feared he would snap her in two, like a twig between his hands.

Abruptly he released her. Meredith wasted no time scrambling against the wall.

Cameron's jaw clenched hard. What was this? he wondered furiously. He'd felt her tremulous flutter of response—aye, she'd been startled but not repulsed!—her lips had warmed beneath his. He hadn't imagined it! Ego aside, he was far too experienced to have mistaken it. His kiss had not been so abhorrent to her. Why this sudden withdrawal? Did she seek to play some game? If so, he was far from amused!

His face was dark as a thundercloud. "Why do you cower from me so?" he demanded.

She huddled against the wall, her knees clasped against her chest. Pale as the linen she wore, she rocked back and forth, refusing to look at him. "I cannot bear it," was all she would say. "I cannot bear it!" Over and over she said it. Indeed, the wildness he sensed in her reminded him of a trapped, wounded animal.

Scowling, he reached for her anew. She cringed.

Cameron leaped to his feet with a vile, blistering oath. Damn her! he thought viciously. Damn her to hell! How was he to bed her when she quailed like a small child afraid of the dark?

At the bedside he straightened to his full, imposing height. "Look at me, Meredith."

She turned her head aside and squeezed her eyes shut, as if to shut out the sound of his voice.

"Dammit, Meredith, look at me!"

Meredith did, only to regret it instantly. He loomed above her like the fortress in which he dwelled, towering and impenetrable. His gaze scraped over her, cold as the Highland mists.

"You realize, lass, you've already lain with me."

She shuddered anew. "Not like this!"

His eyes narrowed. "If this is a game you play, you gamble greatly, lass, for you might easily have lost all. Indeed, were I not such a considerate, accommodating soul, the heat of my seed would even now flood the gates of your womb! So count yourself blessed this night, lass, count yourself blessed that I've decided to give you time to accept me—to accept the inevitable. You have robbed me of this night, but you'll not rob me of the next. The night will come again . . . and I promise you . . . nay, I *vow*—so will I."

He spun about and was gone—so noiselessly Meredith was left staring slack-jawed at the place where he'd been but a moment earlier.

Softly he had spoken. Quiet as the night. Indeed, it had been little more than a whisper! Yet cloaked within those velvet chords was an iron warning.

He would not let her be.

He would not let her be.

Her breath tumbled out in a rush. She was shaken to the depths of her being by what had happened . . . what had *nearly* happened . . . by what he'd said!

Little by little her trembling ceased. The pounding clamor of her heart eased. She gathered hold of her runaway emotions, pondering her dilemma. Never in all her days had she expected him to demand a child of her—merciful saints, a son! No virgin birth would it be—aye, she thought bitterly, and in a way *he* would never suspect. Nor could she deny that Cameron was a virile, intensely masculine man—no virgin here, either! No doubt he would take immense pleasure in accomplishing the task.

She shivered, slipping beneath the woolen coverings of the bed. He would not be back—instinct told her so. Yet sleep eluded her, for her mind refused to be silent. She had thought to be repulsed by his touch. Yet it was not *him*—indeed, if the truth be told, he was a most handsome man in face and form. Nay, it was what he would do . . . Ah, but this was rich! The one thing he sought . . . was the one thing she'd been so convinced he did not wish of her!

What was it he'd said? *I've decided to give you time to accept me.* Accept him, she thought with a shudder. Nay, she could not! Never in this world.

She'd gained a reprieve. But for how long . . . *how long*?

If she were to heed his warning, but a single night was all she had.

In the tower room directly across from hers, Cameron sought solace in the dregs of a pitcher of wine. His desire was unchecked, his passion unquenched. It was this, the darker side of the soul, that urged him to storm back to her room and take what she refused to give—to teach her that he was master and he would not be ruled by a woman's weakness! Yet Cameron knew that he would not. He'd never taken a woman against her will—indeed, there had never been any need—and he'd not start with this one.

His pride had been stung, he admitted. He stared into his wine, two deep grooves etched between his brows. What the devil had come over her? Naught had gone as planned, as he'd hoped! Aye, he'd expected some resistance, a little maidenly fright, but he'd certainly not considered it an insurmountable obstacle. He was neither selfish nor inattentive when it came to pleasing a woman—her gratification but fueled his own—and so he'd have shown her, had she but given him the chance! He'd thought to kiss her, to seduce her into warm, melting surrender . . . to stroke her lissome young body until she clung to him in fevered ecstasy, panting for his possession.

Meredith had not shivered in ecstasy—she had shuddered in fear. She did not clutch him to her breast, lips moist and upraised and panting for his kiss . . . Instead she had pushed him away!

A fierce inner battle raged within him. He was sorely tempted to do exactly what she suggested— search out another woman. Moire sprang immediately to his mind. Moire, with the dark, gleaming eyes and moist, beckoning lips. Aye, he thought. He needed a woman with full hips and ripe, earthy nature, not a prim, saintly madonna like Meredith!

Yet such an encounter would not serve to banish the burning in his soul, the ache in his loins.

He didn't want to remember, yet he could not forget the feel of her in his arms—so small and delicate, her bones so fragile. Nor could he forget her air of pleading vulnerability . . .

This night had not produced the outcome he'd sought. He'd expected to be sprawled at her side this very moment, her head pillowed on his chest, his body sated and exhausted.

His jaw tensed. In one swallow he drained his wine, grimly resolute as he crawled into his solitary bed. It was just as he'd stated. This night was almost gone, but there would be others. Her resistance but made him burn for her all the more. The time would come. He would have her in his arms again, not quaking in fear, but trembling with need.

For Cameron was determined. He would have his son. No matter what it took . . . no matter how long.

Eleven

Golden sunshine woke Meredith the next morning. Sleep had not come until nearly dawn. She'd spent hours last night listening to the rain beat against the walls, the eerie howling of the wind around the tower, until at last she'd slept in sheer exhaustion. It would have been easy to remain where she was, to turn over and seek refuge in sleep anew, for what had she to look forward to? A day entombed in this tiny chamber?

Perhaps it was the sunshine. After yesterday's storm, it was an unexpected surprise. But she had no desire to laze abed, for she was tired of being afraid. Nay, she decided, she would not waste away in melancholy pity.

Courage, she told herself. Courage and faith. The latter would not fail her, for she could not allow herself to believe that God would desert her. Indeed, Cameron had left her alone last evening. *He* was the one who had retreated. Was that not reason to be encouraged? As for the other . . . well, if she could not *be* courageous, at least she could aspire to it.

She'd just flung back the covers when the door opened. A young girl entered. "Good day, milady. I've food to break your fast."

Meredith thanked her and took the tray from her. There was a generous chunk of bread, a hunk of cheese, and a slice of cold venison. At the sight, hunger gnawed at her belly. Quickly she sat. Her appetite had been nil last evening, but such was not the case now. She ate every morsel, surprised at how hungry she was. She'd just finished dressing and combing her hair when another knock sounded.

"Enter," she called.

The door opened. Egan stepped within.

"Good morning to you, Egan," she greeted him calmly.

Cool blue eyes flickered. He looked a trifle surprised. "Good morning," he said gruffly. "My lord has asked me to show you about."

Fair, slender brows shot high. "So he's decided not to keep me confined in the tower! And you've been given the unlucky task of being my keeper. Tell me, have you displeased him? Fallen into disfavor, that he should give you such an onerous chore?"

Egan drew himself up to his full, lean height. "Nay, lady! I am one of his most trusted men—and also his greatest friend!"

Meredith nodded. "I see. You're being rewarded instead with my company. Well, then, I shall strive to be pleasant. And please do try to keep me out of trouble. I shudder to think what would happen if we both incurred his wrath."

Egan was taken aback by the faint light in her eyes. Did she tease him? Or mock him? Either way, she displayed far more spirit than he'd dreamed she possessed! He would have to be wary of her, he decided—and so would Cameron.

They passed through the great hall on the way to the bailey. As he led her through, a sudden pall fell

over the group that had been talking around the table.
Egan stole a glance at his charge, feeling oddly embarrassed for her. Yet if she took notice, she displayed
no outward sign of it. Her features were unsmiling
but composed, the angle of her chin high.

Outside in the bailey, he cleared his throat. "Perhaps I should show you the outbuildings—"

There was a gentle touch on his sleeve. "I'd be
pleased if you'd show me the chapel first," she said
quietly. "Have I missed morning Mass?"

Egan shook his head. "There is no morning Mass.
There's a priest—Father William—but he only passes
through here every few months or so."

"There's no priest in residence?" Her expression
was one of utter shock.

"Mayhap it is *every* month," he amended quickly,
and then was vastly annoyed at himself. Why the devil was he feeling so guilty? It was hardly his fault
there was no priest in residence; Dunthorpe was deep
in the wild country of the Highlands.

"No matter. Will you please show me the chapel?"

"Aye." He turned and led her past the alehouse
and granary, to the farthest corner of the bailey. It
was quiet and peaceful here. Ivy climbed the rough
face of the stones, clear to the lancet windows set high
above in the north wall. The door was open; she
stepped within. Egan started to follow her.

She turned. "If you don't mind," she said quietly,
"I should like to be alone for my prayers."

Egan hesitated. "I cannot," he said at last.

Something flickered across her features. "Very
well," she murmured.

For some reason he didn't understand, Egan felt
compelled to explain. "I'm sorry," he began, "but—"

"There is no need, Egan"—her smile was fleeting—"I understand that you, too, are only doing as you are bidden."

He watched as she turned and glided down the aisle to the front of the church. Kneeling before the altar, she made the sign of the cross, bowed her head low, and clasped her hands together before her.

Egan felt like a worm. He shouldn't have felt badly, yet he did. Cameron's orders had been strict—he was to watch her at all times. He stood awkwardly in the rear of the nave, branding himself the intruder despite the fact that he was doing his duty. What the devil was wrong, that he should feel remorse? She was a Munro, he told himself. The Clan MacKay's most hated enemy.

Odd, but she looked to be the most pitiful foe he'd ever hoped to defeat.

Not only that, he felt uncomfortably out of place here in the kirk. When was the last time he'd gone to Mass? Faith, but he couldn't even remember! The minutes crept by, and still she did not rise. Egan stared at her small figure. Were her misdeeds truly so many that she must pray so long and so hard for forgiveness? His knees would ache and creak and protest most heartily were he to remain kneeling for so long— he doubted he could have done it, even had he been of a mind to!

He was mightily relieved when at last she rose— and none the worse for it. She glided back to him as effortlessly as she'd left him.

From there he escorted her around the bailey, pointing out the bakehouse and brewhouse, granary, stables, and barracks. Near the stables, she paused, gazing back toward the keep as the wind swirled her skirts and lifted her hair.

She smoothed it from her cheek. A frown had appeared between the smoothness of her brows. "Egan," she murmured, "who is that woman there on the stairs? The young one with the long dark hair?"

The woman had stared at her with open boldness just an instant before. Meredith waited curiously. Egan had turned to follow the direction of her eyes.

"That is Moire. She is the eldest daughter of Moreland, the castle steward."

Even as Egan spoke, Cameron appeared in the wide doorway at the top of the stairs, shielding his eyes against the glare of the sun. The woman Moire had spied him as well. With undisguised eagerness she ran up the stairs, levered herself upward with her hands on his forearms, and pressed a kiss onto his cheek. Even from here, Meredith could see their laughter . . .

There was a strange tightening in her belly. "It would appear she knows Cameron quite well." Not until she heard her voice did she realize she spoke aloud.

"Aye." Egan shrugged. "Indeed, before Ronald died, there were those who said Moire and Cameron would soon marry."

Marry! Meredith was stunned. How, then, had he dared to approach her and demand that she bear his son!

"Egan," she said slowly, "I know of Glenda, Niall's wife . . . his widow." She spoke hurriedly, lest she lose her nerve. "But what of his other brothers? Were any of them wed?"

He shook his head. "Burke and Bryan were to wed Anne and Miriam after harvest. They are there." He pointed to two fair-haired women who strode toward the bakehouse.

Meredith was sick at heart. Was there to be no end to her shame? "So there were no children," she said aloud. "Seven sons . . . and no children."

"None but the babe borne by Glenda." Egan regarded her with a sharp-featured reserve. "The wee laddie died just after he was born."

Meredith's heart ached. Poor Glenda . . . to have lost both husband and son.

And then there was Cameron, who had lost so many more—but nay, she did not want to think of him.

"If you do not mind," she said wearily, "I should like to return to my chamber." The world had gone suddenly dark and dreary. As if to torment her further, their path took them directly before Glenda, who stood wiping her hands with her apron. Meredith's heart leaped. She didn't know what to say or do, but no matter. Though Glenda brushed directly by her, she spared neither glance nor greeting.

Meredith spent the remainder of the day in her chamber. Finn arrived in the afternoon to see if she wished to walk. Meredith declined.

A long time later she stood at the window. Evening sunbeams streaked through a gauzy blanket of clouds to light the mountaintops below with a pale purple haze. She heard the echo of footsteps long before the slip of the bolt from its berth. Thinking it was someone with the evening meal, she remained where she was, her gaze fixed on the distant horizon.

The prickle of tiny hairs on the nape of her neck warned her she was wrong.

She turned to find Cameron a scant sword's length away from her, his hands behind his back as he regarded her. He wore a kilt and a loose white tunic that somehow made him appear broader and taller than ever. The very air seemed to hum and sizzle with the power of his presence—forceful and vital, so very tall and bold as the marauder he was!

Her pulse suddenly beat a rapid tattoo, yet she was determined he would not know the effect he had on her. Raising her chin, she bestowed upon him what she hoped was a gaze of cool and utter disdain.

"Finn tells me you refused to come out this afternoon."

"What do you expect? I am in the midst of the lion's den."

Her tongue was as tart as ever, Cameron noted dryly. In truth, he was secretly relieved that she displayed no outward sign that she'd spent the night weeping or cowering in dread. He'd been half-afraid he might have frightened her forever . . .

"Besides," she went on, "I was out with Egan this morning. Indeed, I wondered what he'd done, that you chose to punish him so."

Cameron frowned, rather puzzled.

"Come, now. We both know Egan would just as soon cut my throat as play the gallant escort. But it appears you command his loyalty."

Cameron raised a brow. It was on the tip of his tongue to admit Egan thought him a fool for allowing her to live, yet such would scarcely reassure her.

"Loyalty is a valuable commodity among one's clansmen. So is trust. I trust Egan implicitly with my life; therefore, I entrust yours to him."

"I may have spent the last few years in a nunnery, shut away from the world, but I am not the fool you think me. Egan is not with me to protect me from harm—he is there as my jailer. And aye, we both know my life holds little value."

"Ah, now, there's where you're wrong, lass. As the

woman who will bear my son, your life is as valuable to me as my own.''

Her eyes flared at this, but Cameron gave her no chance to argue. ''However, I do not wish to bicker with you over Egan's role. Instead I brought you something.'' His hands came out from behind his back; within each one a soft leather slipper was suspended. ''I made a trade for these,'' he said lightly. ''Now you must make a trade.''

He hadn't missed the way her face lit up when first she spied them, but the smile he sought was not to appear. Instead her eyes darkened.

''That is no trade!'' she cried softly. ''I know what you expect of me.''

Cameron scowled. He'd seen her this morn with Egan, barefoot as a child but far more dignified. His conscience had smitten him, for he realized he'd been remiss in not asking Glenda to see to this aspect of her clothing as well. ''It seems to me I've been most generous. Why, the very gown on your back—''

''Belongs to your brother's wife,'' she accused. ''I know you bade her bring it to me, and you did it a-purpose.''

''Aye, I did, for the other was not fit to be worn! And now you would condemn me!''

''Because I know you did not do it out of the goodness of your heart! You went to Glenda to—to shame me, that I would ever be reminded that my clansmen took the life of her husband!''

''I went to Glenda since she is much the same size as you!''

She remained adamant. ''The slippers are naught but a bribe to make me lay with you!'' Despite her bravado, she couldn't quite hide her longing. ''Nay,'' she said stiffly, ''I cannot take them!''

"You," he stated bluntly, "are remarkably stubborn. Tell me, then. What will you do with the gowns? Give them back, too, and run about naked?" His eyes warmed. "I vow such a sight would please many a man here—including me!"

Meredith did not share his sudden good humor. He had her there, and she knew it. Mutely she glared at him.

He sighed. "All right, I admit my deception. A kiss, Meredith. I ask but a kiss, and to demonstrate my good faith, I will wait until later. For now, supper awaits below and you will accompany me." With that announcement he tossed her first one slipper and then the other. Meredith fumed silently, for he left no room for refusal. Bending low, she quickly donned the slippers. Though she would never have admitted it to him, they felt heavenly on her feet.

Yet with every step that took them closer to the great hall, the knot in her belly wound tighter. Surely enough, the great hall was humming with bodies and activity. A long procession of servants carried great platters of food from the kitchen. The scent of roasted meat and yeasty breads filled the air.

Meredith would have much preferred to dine in her chamber alone. The hall was filled with booming voices and boisterous male laughter. The fact that there were so many about—and strangers yet—lent her no ease. Her steps unconsciously slowed, but alas, he did not allow it!

A hand splayed wide at her back, Cameron guided her toward a high-backed chair at the table directly before the massive stone hearth. He took the seat beside her. At the far end were Glenda and several other women; she was spared but a cursory glance. More than anything, Meredith longed to sink through the floor and perish beneath the earth. Finn and Egan were there as well. Finn's shaggy brows shot high in surprise. He glanced quickly at Cameron, who wore an easy smile. Egan's reaction was far less discerning, his expression unreadable.

If anyone was startled by her presence at his side, they did not speak of it aloud. The lull in the conversation when she sat was mercifully brief; it was readily apparent those present would take their cue from their leader. Though no one displayed any outward hostility, neither was there a hint of friendliness. Decidedly ill at ease, Meredith was certainly not wont to draw attention to herself. Cameron kept her cup filled with wine and offered her meat from his trencher. Every so often she sensed his regard on her profile, though he said little, merely inquired about her preferences. Irrational though it was, Meredith welcomed his presence at her side. She gleaned both courage and the strangest sense of protectiveness from it.

That was not the case at the next table. Midway through the meal, a prickle went down her spine. Meredith raised her head, to discover herself the sole object of ill-concealed hatred. Meredith blinked. It was Moire, the woman she'd seen in the bailey earlier with Cameron—was it true they planned to marry? Up close, Meredith was stunned to realize she'd underestimated the woman's beauty. Wavy black hair spilled over white, creamy shoulders. Full lips shone dewy and red, damp with the wine she'd just drunk.

Quickly Meredith recovered. She offered a tentative smile; when it remained unanswered, her own wavered. Moire stared at her coldly. Discomfited, Meredith glanced away. But from the corner of her eye, she saw Moire rise and approach their table. Tall and voluptuous, there was a provocative sway in her hips as she strode straight to Cameron.

A small white hand settled familiarly on one of his shoulders—ah, only now those lips smiled and seduced. Bending low, she whispered into his ear. Meredith reached for her wine, pretending not to notice.

Beside her, there was an unexpected rumble of laughter from his chest. Moire made as if to rise. Cameron caught her elbow and whispered something in return. Tinkling laughter joined his before she moved on.

Just then a little boy raced up, a lad of perhaps seven or eight. He stopped directly before Cameron.

"Ye're Cameron, aren't ye?"

"I am," Cameron said promptly. "You are Marcus, aren't you? And Stephen the wheelwright is your father."

The child beamed at being recognized. His small chest puffed out. "Aye, my da is a wheelwright." He gazed up into Cameron's features. "But you are bigger than my da," he said earnestly.

"I am," Cameron agreed with a nod. "But that does not make your father a lesser man. Indeed, the measure of a man comes from here"—Cameron thumped his chest—"and here"—he tapped his forehead with his fingertips. " 'Tis what my father taught me—what your father will teach you."

The lad frowned. "Why will he teach me that?"

Cameron laid a hand on the back of the boy's head. "Because that is what fathers do," he said softly.

The boy ran off then, but Meredith had gone very still inside. Her heart caught painfully. Cameron's behavior with the boy was wholly unexpected . . . and wholly at odds with his demands of her. She'd been convinced he was the hardest man to ever walk this earth. Now she was not so sure . . .

The thought was abruptly cut short. Beside her, Cameron rose, bidding all good night. "I fear sleep beckons early tonight," he said by way of explanation. There was a deliberate pause. "Meredith?" he inquired coolly.

A glance revealed he'd extended a hand, palm up. Heavy brows raised in expectant silence. She was the sole object of his scrutiny—his and every other's.

His gentleness with the boy was forgotten. All at once fury battled alongside a deep, abiding shame. Meredith's face burned. Why, he might as well have announced that he'd already bedded her, the lout! Ah, no doubt that was his intent! Still, she decided scathingly, she was surprised he hadn't invited the lovely Moire to join them . . . or perhaps he had!

Meredith pushed herself to her feet and turned. Hiking her chin, she brushed by him, ignoring his hand as if she hadn't seen it. Perhaps she was playing with fire, yet it was immensely gratifying when she noticed his features tighten ever so slightly.

On the way to the stair they passed directly by Moire. She inclined her head to Cameron, but her smile turned brittle as her gaze skipped to Meredith.

Meredith didn't know whether to laugh or cry. It seemed she'd made yet another enemy—not by deed or word, but by simple virtue of her existence.

When they left the hall behind, she longed to release a deep-seated sigh of relief. But alas, she was not allowed the luxury. The tall figure beside her was an unwelcome warning that the night was not yet over. His words suddenly played over and over through her head.

You have robbed me of this night, but you'll not

*rob me of the next. The night will come again . . . and
I promise you—nay, I* vow—*so will I.*

Distracted as she was, she scarcely noticed where
they went. It wasn't until they'd passed the narrow
arched doorway which led to the tower stair that she
realized something was wrong.

"Wait," she said. "My chamber is that way." She
nodded back over her shoulder.

"Not anymore," was all he said.

Retreat proved impossible, for now he'd snared her
elbow firmly within his grasp. Her pace was not allowed to falter as he steered her farther down the passageway, beneath a wide stone arch, and into a
narrow, winding stairway. Up they went—and even
farther up—so high that Meredith's legs protested
their burden and her breath grew short. She stumbled
once. Immediately a hard arm caught her and brought
her up against him. For one mind-spinning instant, she
was locked fast against the solid breadth of his chest.
With a gasp she looked up into his face.

The way he arched a single black brow lent him a
decidedly villainous look. "Careful, lass," came his
low murmur. " 'Tis a long way down. A fall might
easily break your frail little neck."

Meredith blanched. A knot of fear coiled deep in
her belly. Saints above, would he murder her yet? The
stairs were indeed steep and treacherous. It would take
but a small push to send her tumbling . . .

He released her. Meredith righted herself, one hand
finding the rough stone as she regained her balance.
Her heart was clamoring so hard she could scarcely
think.

A dozen more steps were all that was left. They
ended before a wide oak door carved with diamond-

shaped panels. Cameron threw it open and gestured her inside.

"Your new quarters, milady."

Her pulse hammering, Meredith stepped into an immense chamber that was easily thrice the size of the one she'd occupied the night before. A fat candle burned near the bed, which dominated the far wall. An assortment of weapons—including a massive claymore—were propped near the fireplace. To her shock, her bed gown had been draped across the bed.

She said the first thing that vaulted into her head. "These are *your* quarters!"

He folded his arms across his broad chest—the bold invader again. "Aye," he said smoothly, "for I missed the night we spent apart. It seems I've grown used to the feel of you beside me."

Her nerves were already screaming. The lazy smile that lurked upon his lips did not bode well for her, she was certain of it. Ah, how she envied him his glib, facile tongue! Her own suddenly seemed all twisted and dry in her mouth. Though she searched frantically for a suitably scathing reply, none came to mind.

His eyes resided on her face. "Ah, you wound me sorely, lass. You look like a lamb about to be slaughtered. I assure you, there is no need—"

Meredith shook her head wildly. "There is every need, for I know why you brought me here. You want me to lay with you!"

"So I do, lass, so I do. But let us speak plainly. Aye, I still want you—and aye, I will have you, just as I will have my son. You are mine, lass, and you will be mine in every way," he promised bluntly, "but I will not take an unwilling maid to my bed— aye, even you!" he said on seeing her eyes widen. "But you *will* lay beside me in this bed, this night and every other after this. Resign yourself to it, for I will not change my mind. Though I dislike it heartily, I will bide my time and wait until you are ready.''

Meredith's mind churned frantically. Give herself willingly to him—to a man? That day would never come. "And who will decide when I am ready? You?" The word was fairly flung at him.

His eyes glinted. "Aye."

Meredith was trapped as surely as an animal in a snare. She decried his arrogance, even as she decried her very helplessness. Wearily she despaired her stormy heart, for she knew not what she should do.

"For now, my heart's only desire is to feel your kiss upon my lips—the kiss we agreed you would give in trade."

Meredith gritted her teeth. How dare he mock her! "I did not agree," she said flatly. "And my heart's desire is to be rid of you!"

"Nor did you disagree," he reminded her. "And so neither of us will sleep this night till I have what I am owed."

Meredith was suddenly too angry to be precisely aware of just what she did. Marching over, she raised herself on tiptoe. Her lips tightly pinched together, she pressed her mouth against his for a fraction of a second. Drawing back, she prepared to savor her triumph, but he was shaking his head.

"That was most unsatisfactory. It will not do, lass, nay, not at all."

His peremptory announcement but kindled the blaze within her. "What! You asked for a kiss and I gave it!"

"That was the kiss of a child. I would have the kiss of a woman." His smile was utterly wicked. "Now, then, put your arms about my neck."

Meredith's lips tightened. Gritting her teeth, she rested the very tips of her fingers upon his shoulders.

He grimaced. "If you lean forward to kiss me, you will surely fall flat on your face," he complained. "Step closer . . . place your feet between mine . . . there, that's it, and for your effort, I shall meet you halfway . . ."

Sweet heaven, he did. His head descended, at the very moment hers lifted.

Their lips met . . . and clung.

A melting curl of heat unfurled in her belly. Her stomach quivered. Her fingers curled into the taut flesh of his shoulders. Confused by the response she couldn't seem to control, she drew back.

He cocked a brow. "That was better. Now. Once more."

A traitorous warmth unfurled within her, like the petals of a rosebud flowering beneath a noonday sun. A strange trembling seized her. It spread throughout her body, clear to her very limbs.

Cameron's eyes opened, dark and heavy-lidded with some strange emotion. A jolt went through her, for only then did she discover a pair of lean male hands had settled around her waist. They were disturbingly warm, those hands. Disturbingly strong . . . and thoroughly unsettling. His nearness wreaked havoc with her senses. Oh, but she should never have complied, for what had she gotten herself into?

"Excellent," he murmured, and then his mouth was on hers anew. His arms tightened, nearly lifting her from her feet. Her heart tumbled to a standstill. The pressure of his mouth deepened. He drew her lower lip into his mouth to suck gently on the tender flesh. Stunned by the force of the strange sensations pouring through her body, Meredith felt the world slip away. She forgot where they were. God above, she forgot *who* they were—that he was Cameron of the Clan MacKay and she was but his prisoner.

She trembled, but not with fear. No, not with fear . . . but with something else. Something she did not recognize—something she was *afraid* to recognize. She could feel the scrape of his beard against her tender skin. Oddly, it was not unpleasant. An endless yearning seemed to well inside her—for what, she knew not. She felt as if she were melting inside, like tallow beneath the flame.

Had she known it was all Cameron could do not to crush her against him, to devour her mouth and let his hands wander where they would, she would surely have leaped from his arms. He felt like shouting his triumph, for whether she knew it or not, she had yielded. He'd been right not to press her, not to force her submission, for he knew full well if he had, she would not be here in his arms, the honeyed softness of her lips clinging sweetly to his.

Through a haze Meredith felt him slowly lift his head, felt the searing weight of his gaze on her face. A finger beneath her chin dictated she meet his eyes.

He gave her a long, slow look. "Now, that," he said quietly, "was a trade worth making."

Meredith flushed, only to realize her arms were still looped around his neck!

Quickly she withdrew them. Had he touted his triumph, her ire and resentment would have known no bounds. As it was, she was shaken and confused by what had happened. Cameron now stood beside the bed.

"This is yours, I believe, mistress." A flutter of white whizzed through the air, straight toward her.

Meredith instinctively raised a hand and caught it—
it was her bed gown.

"Wear it as you please"—a wicked half-smile
curled his lips—"or do not wear it as you please. I
admit, I much prefer the latter." His gaze, thoroughly
assessing, wandered over her. Meredith felt as if she'd
been stripped bare with the mere touch of his eyes.

She glared at him, uncaring that he saw her mutinous indignation. "I concede that I must lay with
you," she snapped, "for as you persist in pointing
out to me, you are stronger and I cannot overpower
you. But by all that is holy, know this, sirrah! Beat
me if you will—throw me in the pit prison!—but I
will not lay naked beside you!"

"Be that as it may." He shrugged. "I, however,
have no such qualms."

His speech thus delivered, he discarded his boots,
then began to unwind his plaid from about his shoulders—and hips. Meredith gaped, for it was soon obvious he meant what he said—he would sleep naked!

She was too shocked to turn away, to squeeze her
eyes shut—as she should have! What protest she
might have made locked tight in her throat. Naked,
he appeared bigger and broader than ever. His chest
was brazenly male, matted with dense, dark fur. His
arms were lean and corded with muscle. Shoulders
that were broad and wide veered to the jutting ridge
of his hips. For one mind-teetering instant, she tested
the courage to venture below . . . and, oh, but surely
she was the most sinful of sinners . . . she could not
suppress the urge to look just once. She caught but a
glimpse of jutting male virility before he started for
the bed. One knee upraised, a pair of hard round buttocks filled her vision before she finally averted her
head. She stood uncertainly, for time unending, it

seemed. Her mind raced. How she could ever look him in the face again and not think of . . .

"I must rise at dawn, Meredith. It would be appreciated were you to come to bed sometime before that."

His voice intruded. The familiar mockery was back—and indeed, she felt much better equipped to deal with it. She regarded him mutely, her lips compressed into a thin line.

"No?" He raised a brow. "You intend to sleep on your feet, then? 'Tis a most uncomfortable way to sleep, I assure you. I know, for I've done it many a time tending sheep when I was young. Indeed, I once tumbled down a hillside." There was a small pause. "I should imagine it will be cold and drafty standing there. The choice is yours, lass. The comfort and warmth of my bed, or the chill of the night."

Meredith hesitated but a fraction of a second. She had no desire to sleep where she stood, or to make her bed on the cold hard floor.

Their eyes met, his inquiring, hers mutely pleading. "Turn around," she said breathlessly.

Cameron very nearly reminded her he'd already seen what she would hide so diligently. But something inside warned him he'd risked as much as he should dare this night. He turned on his side so that he faced the wall.

Meredith shed her gown and tugged the bed gown over her head. She clambered over him, careful not to touch him, just as careful not to lift the sheet too high, lest she see more than she wished to! Hurriedly she slid within.

Cameron faced her, his head propped on an elbow. His smile was gone, his expression unreadable. He

stared at her as if he would pluck her very thoughts
from her mind.

"It occurs to me that you have been sheltered," he
said slowly, "that mayhap you know naught of men
. . . and life." He seemed to hesitate. "What happens
between a man and a woman is not something to be
feared, Meredith. It's where children come from—"

"I know how children are made!" Meredith's face
burned with shame.

"Then why are you so afraid?" he asked quietly.

It was in her mind to pretend she misunderstood—
but it would have been a lie. Clutching the sheet to
her chin, she gave a tiny shake of her head. "Please,"
she said, her voice very low. "I cannot tell you."

Reaching out, he picked up a strand of hair that lay
on her breast. Meredith froze. Her heart surely
stopped in that instant. Now it comes, she thought
despairingly. He claimed he would give her time to
accept him, to accept what would happen, but it was
naught but a lie! Her heart twisted. Ah, but she should
have known!

"Your hair is beautiful—like living flame."

His murmur washed over her, soft as finely
spun silk. She searched his features, stunned when she
detected no hint of either mockery or derision.

She stared at the wispy strands that lay across his
palm, the way he tested the texture between thumb
and forefinger.

"Nay." Her voice emerged unevenly. " 'Tis too
red. Too much like Papa's." Too late she realized
what she had said. She braced herself for the icy mask
of disdain she knew would surely appear.

It did not. Instead he stared at her, solemnly intent.

"They would have cut it, you know," he said suddenly.

Meredith frowned in soft confusion. "What?"

"They would have shorn your hair . . . the nuns. If you had taken your vows, they would have cut your hair." He smiled slightly. "Ah, now, that would have been a sin." As he spoke, he wound the lock of hair around and around his hand.

Meredith froze. But he stopped before the pressure tugged hurtfully on her scalp . . . and trespassed no further. Instead he turned to his back.

His eyes closed.

He and she touched nowhere. Indeed, the width of two hands separated them; those silken strands of her hair were the only link between them. Meredith dared not move. She listened and waited, her heart pounding in her breast . . .

Slumber overtook him. He slept, her lock of hair still clutched tight in his fist.

Only then did she move. Her hand lifted. She touched her lips, there at the very spot he'd possessed so thoroughly. Her pulse quickened as the memory of his kiss flamed all through her. She'd thought it was disdain. Distaste . . .

But she was wrong. In the depths of her being, Meredith was well aware it was something far different.

Her breath came fast, then slow. Something was happening. Something far beyond her experience . . .

Twelve

Egan was worried. He'd watched his chieftain this past sennight . . . watched while Cameron persisted in giving his attention to the Munro wench! He'd known Cameron since they were both young lads—why, they'd tumbled their first wench together! Egan's chest swelled just thinking about it. The woman had later confided that the pair were not her first, and if the truth be told, she'd much preferred Egan over his towering, bony friend . . .

Aye, they'd been through much together. He was the one Cameron had first told of the Red Angus's butchery—how his father and brothers had died. He'd held him close while Cameron's shoulders shook with the force of his grief.

Yet never had he seen Cameron so obsessed with a woman. Always before, the pair had been much the same. Women were a leisurely enjoyment, a pleasure to be pursued but not to distraction. It wasn't that they scoffed at love; it was simply that neither had found the woman whose tender embrace might bind him forever. Of a certainty, while he'd never been one to turn a blind eye to a tasty morsel of feminine flesh, neither had his loins controlled him. It was the same with Cameron, though at times he'd been a bit annoyed that his friend could turn a maid's head without even trying! It was the scar, Egan knew. He'd never be as handsome as Cameron . . .

Yet this was different. *She* was different, the Munro wench—and so was Cameron.

Egan could not say he approved.

He surveyed his friend one night as Cameron kept her leeched to his side—as if he could not bear to be parted! Egan was thoroughly disgusted. It would have been different had it been a matter of control, but Egan was convinced it was she who controlled him— but the wee one did not even know it! Fools they were, both of them! Later he saw the way Cameron bent his mouth to her ear, his words for her alone. Egan's gaze narrowed. He saw the way she immediately shook her head, the way her eyes refused to meet his . . . the way Cameron's mouth turned down. So, he thought. The wench was reluctant . . . or was she? Mayhap it was but a trick. Quietly she withdrew, her head down as she made her way across the hall to the stairway. Even when she was gone from sight, his friend's unblinking regard remained fixed in the place where she had last been.

Egan rolled his eyes. Smitten, he was. Smitten!

Before he knew it, Egan was seated opposite his friend and leader.

"Egan! How goes it this night?" Cameron dragged his eyes from his tender prey.

Egan took a long draught of ale. He'd always spoken plainly with Cameron, and so he would now. He nodded toward the place where Meredith had disappeared and lowered his tankard. "Be wary of her, lad," he warned. "Men, we fight with sword and targe, but women—well, they touch and cajole. They have ways of twisting a man 'round their finger, and not once does he suspect!''

Cameron's jaw thrust out. "What! What have you seen?'' His tone turned sharp. "Is she planning to escape?''

Egan said nothing for the longest time. "Nay,'' he said finally. "She speaks but seldom.''

"To whom does she speak?''

Egan shook his head. "To no one but me. No one speaks to her.'' He paused. "She hides nothing,'' he admitted. "In truth, I've seen no sign that she plans to escape. Nor has Finn.''

"Then why do you alert me?''

"She is a Munro, Egan. I think you forget that.''

Cameron's eyes flashed. "Nay, Egan.'' His lips barely moved as he spoke. "Think what you will, but that is something I *never* forget.''

"You see her as a woman,'' Egan argued, "a desirable woman.''

Cameron smiled tightly. "Perhaps because she is. Be fair, laddie, and acknowledge what your own eyes must surely tell you. She is as fair and comely a maid as any.''

"Aye,'' Egan said gruffly. "She is as fair a maid as any I've seen. But I am not the one who lusts after her, Cameron.'' Baldly he stated his judgment. "You want her, don't you?''

A muscle jumped in Cameron's jaw. He glowered at his friend.

"I've seen the way you look at her, Cameron. Have you taken her to your bed?''

"That, my friend, is not your affair.'' A warning glint appeared in his eyes. "And do not dare to call her a slut.''

Egan returned his glare with equal measure. "I said

no such thing, Cameron, and well you know it!'' He decided to temper his tone. Cameron's temper was not easily riled, yet in a dangerous mood he was a force to be reckoned with. ''Yet you do not have the look of a man well pleasured. And so, as your friend, I must ask again . . . have you taken her to your bed?''

For a moment it appeared Cameron would refuse to answer. ''Nay,'' he said at last. ''She scorns me, as if I am the ugliest of creatures.''

''Well, I won't disagree with that!'' Egan raised his tankard as if in salute, then abruptly lowered it. ''But you must think me addlepated if you expect me to believe you've not yet bedded her. She sleeps in your chamber, in your very bed!''

Cameron tipped his chair back. ''What better way to watch her?'' he countered calmly.

''Post a guard outside her chamber!'' Egan could not help it. He felt betrayed.

''We need the guards elsewhere.'' Cameron's tone was curt. ''She stays where she is.''

Egan was not to be deterred. ''She's no doubt a maiden, man, chaste and untouched!''

Cameron's laugh was tight. ''No one would be more surprised than I were that not the case. She went to the priory straight from Castle Munro. To all accounts she had no suitors. Aye, she's a maid, or I am not Cameron of the Clan MacKay.''

''Do you forget she planned to take her vows?''

''I do not forget.''

''And you would take such a woman to your bed? One who knows naught of the ways of men?''

''She lived among men most of her life, Egan. Indeed, it's only the last few years that she resided in the nunnery.''

''Nonetheless, 'tis not right.'' Egan was adamant.

"Your loins rule you now and not your heart!"

It was Cameron's turn to raise a brow. "What! Do you now defend her? 'Twas you who helped me abduct her. Why, but a few nights past, you vowed you'd have killed her long since."

"That was before I knew what you intended."

Cameron gave a self-derisive half-smile. "Even I did not know what I intended."

Egan stroked the white scar on his cheek. "Moire will not be pleased," he observed suddenly.

Moire be damned! Cameron thought viciously. " 'Twas never my idea to marry her. Nor did I say I would. As for Meredith, you need not worry, Egan. 'Tis a matter of vengeance, that is all. Aye, I want her—and aye, I will have her. But never would I forsake either you or my clan."

His vow seemed to reassure Egan, and the talk turned to other matters. Yet images of Meredith lingered in the back of his mind.

The bruised, wounded look in her eyes the other night filled him with guilt . . . and made him want to shake her senseless! But he was set on his course and naught would sway him. Oh, she spurned him with words, but her mouth had not lied. Her lips had flowered beneath his like a fragrant bloom beneath a noonday sun.

Only this morning she had been plaiting her hair, its fiery length drawn over one shoulder. Her nape lay bare and fragile and vulnerable. His rod swelled thick and rigid as a lance, hidden only by the folds of his kilt. The urge to plant his mouth on her nape, to taste her creamy flesh and drag her into his arms was overwhelming.

He had not.

He had watched her these past days—watched her

and considered, his mind ever churning. She stirred him in ways he'd not thought possible. She stirred him unbearably, as no other woman ever had. Oh, she spurned him with her adder's tongue, but Cameron could not forget her wild panic the night he'd told her she would bear his son . . .

He recalled the way she shrank back whenever he touched her. Still, something in her must have recognized that he would not hurt her, for of late she'd begun to unwittingly ease closer whenever one of his men approached . . .

At last it struck him.

She was uncomfortable in the presence of men.

He'd pondered long and hard. At first he'd thought it was because of the feud between the clans. What woman would not be frightened by her enemies? Then he'd begun to wonder if her sheltered existence was not to blame. Yet it was just as he'd told Egan—it was only the last few years she'd spent at the nunnery. Indeed, she was a woman full grown when she'd departed Castle Munro for Connyridge.

Some little-known sense inside him whispered there was more. Ah, if only he knew! Yet he knew intuitively she would not tell him. She would no more confide in him than she would in any other MacKay.

Yet she sought refuge beside him, pressed herself close though he suspected she knew it not! It pleased him—pleased him mightily. There and then he decided it was but a matter of strategy. It was the way of the Highlanders to strike when the enemy least expected it, where it was least expected. He must breach her defenses. Invade little by little. Aye, he would woo her. School her. Charm and gentle her to his hand.

He was most certainly determined. Now, if only he possessed the patience!

The situation was a trifle different for Meredith. Where Cameron was concerned, she was duly wary. At times he was coolly remote, saying little to her. Yet it was disconcerting beyond measure to turn and discover his gaze full upon her—and not once did he avert his gaze whenever their eyes chanced to meet.

Alas, she was hardly indifferent to him, much as she wished otherwise! He was a man of raw masculinity, and everything within her was aware of it. She experienced a shattering rush of awareness whenever he was near. She was achingly conscious of everything about him—the way he towered above all others, the potent strength of his hands, the heat exuded by his body.

He had kissed her several more times, long, drugging kisses that made her head spin and her heart pound. As if that were not enough, his kiss blazed through to other, forbidden places. The very summit of her breasts, which seemed to swell and grow strangely erect. Last night, when he'd reached across for a hunk of bread, he'd brushed her nipple. A white-hot jolt shot through her. She wondered what it would feel like against her bare skin, with no barrier between . . .

He touched her. Often. Deliberately. She knew what he was doing. He wanted her to grow used to him. Meredith was always careful to preserve her modesty, bathing and dressing once he had gone— thank heaven he had yet to invade her privacy! As for him, it was just as he'd so boldly stated that first night in his chamber—he had no such qualms. He walked about the chamber naked. He slept naked! Meredith always averted her head, though one day he'd caught her staring. Her eyes squeezed shut—yet still she could see the shape of him, tall and sculpted and lean. He'd laughed, the rogue—he'd laughed! And whenever she chanced to meet his gaze, his eyes were ever upon her—within was a simmering heat he made no effort to disguise. For a time she hadn't known what it was . . . but now she did.

It was desire. Stark and blazing and utterly irrefutable.

Indeed, she mused one night as they lay in bed, it was almost worse than before. She could not look at him without remembering what he wanted of her . . . without imagining what he would do . . . what he would have of her! For he was right . . .

It was inevitable. She would be his . . .

The only question was when.

The strain was almost more than she could bear. At times she almost wished he would take her and be done with it—indeed, she wondered wildly why he hadn't.

While her nights were spent with Cameron slumbering by her side, her days were spent in solitude. Self-pity had never been her way, yet never had she been so forlorn, so forsaken. She walked about the bailey as she pleased, but always Egan or Finn lurked somewhere near . . . always. Though she did not hate them, she hated what they did . . . the way it made her feel, as if she'd done something wrong—that she was some abominable outlaw guilty of some horrible misdeed. She bitterly resented Cameron at those times, for she knew it was at his orders that she remained beneath their scrutiny.

There was a small stone bench just outside the chapel where she liked to sit. Here in the far corner of the bailey, she was removed from the bustle all around; here it was quiet and peaceful. Flowers grew in sweet profusion, lending an air of tranquillity where she could forget, at least for a time, that she was a prisoner here.

It was here, one warm summer morning nearly a fortnight after her arrival at Dunthorpe, that she lingered after her prayers; she had been at Dunthorpe nearly a fortnight. With the tip of her finger she traced the mason's mark carved into the stone at the base of the corner, her thoughts on her father.

A trill of feminine laughter floated on the air. Meredith raised her head. Her heart lurched. It was Moire—Moire with Cameron. Small fingers nested cozily in the crook of his arm. Moist, wine-red lips smiled directly up into his face. He said something and laughed down at her.

There was a sharp, knifelike twinge in Meredith's chest—for an instant she thought it was her wound, yet the pain had long since fled.

Why? she screamed inwardly. Why was this happening? Surely she was not jealous. Surely she was not drawn to him . . .

A slight movement from the corner of her eye snared her attention. She glanced over to see a sweet-looking young girl with huge brown eyes staring at her. Meredith judged her to be perhaps four or so.

Her mouth relaxed into a smile. "Hello, there," she said softly.

The child said nothing, merely gazed at her, one finger pressed against her lips.

Meredith tried again. "My name is Meredith." She tipped her head to the side. "What's yours?"

The finger lowered. Rosy lips pursed, as if in deep thought. Then, a whisper: "Aileen."

"Aileen," she repeated, then smiled. " 'Tis a beautiful name." She patted the space beside her. "Would you like to come sit beside me, Aileen?"

The child hesitated, then clambered up beside her. Round eyes peered up at her, intently searching her features. All at once the girl reached out and touched a silken tendril of hair where it trailed across Meredith's wrist. She'd arisen late this morning, and so she'd left it unbound.

"Your hair is bright," said Aileen.

"Aye, lassie, that it is."

"Why is it red?"

There was a painful catch in the region of her heart. "I expect 'tis because my father's hair is red."

Aileen twirled it around her finger. " 'Tis so soft," she said wistfully, "and so long." She emitted a sigh. "I wish mine were as long."

Meredith laid a hand on her mop of dark curls. "It will grow," she predicted softly. "You have only to wait a wee bit longer."

"I dinna think so." Aileen shook her head adamantly. "Mama says I was bald as me da when I was a babe."

Meredith longed to reach out and hug the lass, but she didn't want to frighten her off. She bent her head low. "Let me tell you a secret, Aileen. I, too, was bald when I was first born. My mother often told me so when I was a bairn like you."

"Where is yer mother?"

Meredith smiled faintly. "She died when I was young." She couldn't help but think of Cameron and his brothers. Since coming to Dunthorpe, she'd learned that their mother had died just three winters past. Thomas, she reflected, had been even younger than she—Meredith—had been . . .

"And your da? Is he dead, too?"

Meredith's heart twisted. He might as well be dead
. . . dead as she was to him. "Nay, sweetings. But he
is a long way from here."

Chubby fingers sifted through the trailing ends of
her tresses. Aileen grasped two hunks and crossed one
over the other. Her brow was furrowed in concentration. Her little rosebud mouth pursed. Small brows
drew ferociously over her tiny upturned nose.

Meredith chuckled. "Are you trying to plait my
hair, Aileen?"

"Aye, but I cannot."

She sounded so forlorn that Meredith bit back a
laugh. Gently she eased the strands from the child's
grasp. "Here, lass, let me show you. I know it seems
odd, but you must have three lengths . . ."

It took some time, but at last Aileen managed to
create a loosely woven plait.

Aileen grinned up at her. "I did it!" she crowed.

"Aye, lass, you did—and you did it very well!
Now, if only we had something to hold it." Even as
she spoke, the small plait began to unravel. Aileen
looked ready to cry. Quickly Meredith laid a hand on
her head, seeking to reassure her.

A shadow fell over them. Both woman and child
glanced up at the same time. Meredith's heart seemed
to trip over itself. It was Cameron who towered over
them. Her first instinct was to slide an arm around the
girl. But the child, small though she was, displayed
no fear at this big, brawny man. Before Meredith
could even move, Aileen hopped down, then nearly
threw herself up and into his arms.

"Cameron!"

Before Meredith's stunned regard, he lifted her
high and planted a rather sloppy-sounding kiss on her
cheek. This elicited a high-pitched giggle from

Aileen. Then, bold as you please, he dropped down beside her. Meredith froze. The bench was not particularly wide nor long; with him beside her, they filled it. Indeed, she could not ease over even a hair, else she'd have slipped off! Aileen appeared quite content to sit on his knee.

She peered up at Meredith. "Do you know Leith?"

Meredith licked her lips, conscious of the searing heat of the hard, hairy thigh stretched out beside her own. "Nay, Aileen, I do not."

"Leith is my brother. He was out near the ponds this morn and caught a toad. And do ye know what he did?"

She shook her head.

"He kissed it!"

Meredith blinked. "The toad?"

"Aye, he kissed the toad! Leith kissed the toad!"

A faint smile tugged at Meredith's lips. "Ah," she said gravely. "I, too, have kissed a toad—and found it quite disgusting." Even as she spoke, she cast a meaningful glance at Cameron from the corner of her eye.

Aileen's eyes rounded. "Did he bite?"

Meredith couldn't resist a laugh as she shook her head. She was totally unmindful of the way Cameron's gaze had fallen to her lips.

A slow smile crept across his lips. "The lady says nay. But mayhap," he injected, a sly light dancing in the murky depths of his eyes, "the lady should be more careful, for mayhap the next time the toad *will* bite."

Meredith was not about to be bested. "Then the toad had best beware," she said archly, "lest I decide to bite back!"

To her surprise, he threw back his head and

laughed, a full-blown laugh that caught her wholly off guard. Tiny lines radiated out from his eyes. His teeth were white and strong. For one mind-splitting instant, it was as if the iron-hearted warrior who had captured her did not exist.

He rose, setting Aileen gently on her feet. "Ladies, I bid you good day." With that he strode away.

Aileen turned to her. "Do ye think he likes me?"

Meredith's lips twitched. "I think he likes you very much indeed."

The child beamed and clapped her hands together. "Someday," she announced, "when I am older, I will marry him."

No doubt by then he will be married to Moire. Meredith couldn't withhold the thought that sprang to mind. Her heart squeezed oddly. Yet she said nothing, for she could not bear to squelch the little girl's dreams so cruelly.

After her prayers the next day, Meredith resumed her place upon the bench. It wasn't long before Aileen appeared. With her was her brother, her elder by a scant year or so. The following day, several more came with her. Meredith welcomed their presence, for they did not regard her with frigid condemnation—it seemed the children were the only ones who harbored no animosity toward her. She entertained them with stories from the Scriptures, stories she'd heard when she was but a child at her father's knee. She spoke of Adam and Eve, of Cain and Abel, of the Great Flood and Noah's ark.

It was as the children began to gather around her one day that she noticed several women standing near the corner of the chapel. Among them was Glenda. One of the women planted her fists on ample hips and glared in blatant disapproval. Meredith turned her head and pretended not to notice, yet the woman's voice carried clearly.

"If none of ye will put a stop to this," she declared loudly, "I will! Did ye hear her yesterday? She told of the serpent in the Garden. Aye, and she should know, for she is the serpent here!"

There was a burst of laughter from all but Glenda.

It was she who answered sternly, "Leave her be, Meghan. She but teaches the wee ones of the Lord and His ways. Father William visits but seldom and has little time to spend with them. What, I ask, is the harm in that?"

"Och, and who is she to proclaim the Lord's ways?" Meghan sniffed. "You forget she is daughter to the Red Angus!"

"And you forget," Glenda said sharply, "were she not here, she would already be a nun. Who better to teach them?"

Meredith was stunned. What was this, that Glenda would defend her? She sat at the table with her nearly every night. Though it pained her to acknowledge it, Meredith was well aware her presence was tolerated, certainly not wanted! The knowledge was like a knife in her heart, for she sensed that if she were not a Munro, they might have been friends . . . But Glenda had no eye to spare her, neither a greeting nor even a nod. Always she looked away . . . always.

Meghan protested no more. To Meredith's vast relief, those children who usually gathered around were present the next day. In truth, her existence would have been nigh unbearable were it not for the time spent daily with these bairns.

Somehow she had to find a way to thank Glenda. The opportunity came sooner than she expected.

She rounded the corner of the bakehouse, only to nearly run head-on into another body.

It was Glenda. Her head came up, and she stopped short. They stood face-to-face, eye to eye, one startled, the other distinctly wary. Quickly Meredith spoke before the other woman could flee.

"Glenda, I must thank you for . . . for what you said the other morn to Meghan . . . about my being with the children. I truly mean no distress to anyone, and being with them . . . well, to be frank, it gladdens my heart."

Glenda's brown eyes flickered. "There is no need to thank me," she stated coolly. "I but spoke the truth." Picking up her skirts, she would have stepped around her, but Meredith extended a hand.

"Glenda, wait! I know how you feel about me— who I am—but still I wish to tell you . . . how sorry I am about Niall! Please," she implored, "can we not talk?"

For the longest time Glenda said nothing. Yet when at last she did, her eyes were as tormented as surely Meredith's own must be. "You cannot change who you are," she said, her voice very low. "I cannot change who I am. Neither of us can change what happened. What else is there to say?"

There was much that could be said, Meredith longed to cry. Yet Glenda would not listen. No one would. Perhaps she was right after all, she thought with a pang. Glenda would forever be Niall's widow, and Meredith would forever be the outcast, daughter of the Red Angus. Her heart cried out, for these days had been among the most arduous in her life.

She dreaded the days to come, for she feared they would be no less difficult.

Her step heavy, she started across the bailey. She

hadn't gone far when a little girl appeared before her. She was a wee one, and, from the look of her, one who was just now learning to walk. Even as the thought ran through Meredith's brain, the girl teetered and sprawled upon her hands and knees. Immediately she began to wail. Meredith glanced around, but the child's mother was not there to rescue her.

Two steps took her to the child. She picked her up and hugged her against her breast, savoring the warmth of her small body. She murmured soothingly, she knew not what. The child's sobs ceased. The wee lass drew back and gazed at her with huge blue eyes. Meredith's heart squeezed. For a fleeting heartbeat, she wondered what it would be like to hold her own wee one snug and tight, against her very heart . . .

Something struck the middle of her back. "Leave 'er be!" shouted a young male voice.

Meredith turned, one arm instinctively coming up to shield the little girl. Her stunned gaze beheld two lads of twelve or so a short distance away. The child began to whimper once more.

"Put 'er down, I say!"

This came from the lad who'd just scooped another stone from the ground—it bounced against her shoulder.

Another stone whizzed by, barely missing her temple. A face flashed in her vision—it belonged to a woman, one she recognized as one of the laundress's helpers.

"My bairn," she cried. "Give me my bairn!" Before Meredith could say a word, the woman snatched the whimpering child from her and ducked away. Meredith was stung to the core by the venom in her eyes.

Suddenly Cameron strode into view, his features as grimly forbidding as she had ever seen them. With

both hands, he seized the boys by the collars of their
tunics.

"What the devil goes on here?" he demanded.

"We only meant to teach her a lesson," cried one
of the lads.

"We meant no harm!" whined the other, contrite
now that he'd been caught by his chieftain.

"You meant no harm?" Cameron's expression was
as black as the skies at midnight. "That is not what
I saw! And you could have hit the wee bairn, so do
not tell me you meant no harm!"

"But she is a Munro!" the first piped up anew.

A sudden silence had fallen over the bailey. Nearly
all those present had stopped to watch the scene
played out before them.

The silence had claimed Cameron's notice as well.
The sweep of his hard gray gaze encompassed all. His
voice rang out clear and strong over those gathered.
"I say this not only to you lads, but to all those here.
The Munros are the Clan MacKay's fiercest enemies,
but we will not make war on women and children, on
those who cannot defend themselves! If you cannot
abide by that, then you may leave here and now."

One by one, his people turned back to their work. The
smithy's hammer pounded a dull rhythm on the forge
once more. The squall of a pig filled the air. The chan-
dler wiped his hands on a cloth and resumed his task.
With a scowl, Cameron released the boys. They scrambled away as fast as their legs would carry them.

He turned then, and looked at her. "Come," he
said. It was not a request. It was a demand, pure and
simple, Meredith noted bitterly. It was there in the
thrust of his jaw, in the way he stood before her, legs
braced slightly apart, his features as hard as marble.
Oh, no doubt he would blame her for the fracas!

Suddenly it was all too much: Glenda's rebuff. The woman's glaring distrust. The boys' rancor. Tears struggled to the surface. With a strangled cry she shoved aside the hand that reached for her and ran toward the keep.

Swearing beneath his breath, Cameron swiveled. A hand on his shoulder forestalled him—it was Egan.

"She did nothing. The bairn fell and she picked her up. Then the lads—"

"I know," Cameron broke in tersely. "I saw."

His stride sure and swift, he followed her into the keep. He could hear the echo of her footsteps as she ran up the tower stairs.

The door to his chamber was closed. Cameron shoved it open, only to stop short on the threshold. Meredith was on the floor before the hearth, rocking back and forth.

He stared. Her shoulders were heaving. She was crying, he realized, though she made not a sound.

She'd heard him. She twisted around, one small hand swiping at the wetness on her cheeks. "Can you not leave me be for once? Must you forever plague me?"

The soft curve of her mouth was tremulous. Tears bled through to her voice; they stabbed at him like the point of a knife. He had stolen her, threatened her—through all she'd remained bravely courageous, yet it was this which had finally defeated her. She vexed him as no other woman ever had. He found himself torn as never before. She made him long to protect her from any and everything, even as she tried his patience as no other ever had.

His steps carried him across the floor, until he stood directly above her. "Come," was all he said. "Come," but this time there was gentleness in his tone.

"Nay!" It was a cry torn from deep inside her. She lurched upward, only to find herself caught up against him. She was trapped as ever before, ever and always.

Something broke inside her. She went wild then. With fists raised high aloft, she pounded against his chest. "I hate this place!" she screamed. "I hate being here. Most of all I hate *you*!"

Words. They were just words, uttered in the heat of the moment. Cameron steeled himself against the hurt and wrapped his arms around her, pinning her arms to her sides, quelling her rebellion until she collapsed against him. Without stopping to think, he bent and carried her to the bed, tucking her limp body into his side.

She turned her face into his neck and wept.

"They hate me. They condemn me with their whispers, accuse me with their stares."

The wet heat of her tears dampened his skin. Seeing her like this was like a dagger twisting in his belly. Cameron despised himself as much as she despised him. "Nay—"

"They do. They do! I did nothing to that sweet child, nor to those boys."

His heart knotted. "I know, Meredith. I saw."

Knowing that he had borne witness to her scalding humiliation made it all the worse. A shroud of despair encircled her. She cried even harder.

A strong hand swept the length of her spine. "Hush, Meredith." His voice washed over her, soft as fleece. "*Hush.*"

But it was not so easy. An immense wave of pain crashed over her. She wept for herself, for her father, for a future fraught with uncertainty.

And all the while, he held her. Cameron. He cradled her close against his side, smoothed the errant tendrils of hair from her cheek, and kissed away the tears from her eyes. Ah, but it made no sense that she should find comfort in the arms of the one who caused such stormy torment within her, yet she did. In time her sobs eased. Her shaking ceased, for his embrace was a sheltering cocoon of warmth and strength. He tucked her head into the hollow of his shoulder. With a watery sigh, she closed her eyes, numb and exhausted.

She must have dozed, for when she woke, pale yellow candlelight filled the room. The aroma of roasted meat wafted in the air. Bracing herself on one hand, she sat up.

Cameron stepped forward. He seemed to appear from nowhere. He searched her face intently. Meredith flushed, embarrassingly aware of his scrutiny. No doubt her eyes were swollen and red; she was certain she looked a veritable fright. Yet he must have been satisfied with what he saw, for he said quietly, "There is food. Are you hungry?"

"A little," she admitted. She pushed back the heavy curtain of her hair and arose.

She ate dutifully from the trencher he had prepared for her—haggis, bread, and cheese. She declined the frumenty pudding, but accepted when he refilled her goblet with wine. She drank deeply, then stole a glance at him. He was staring into the leaping flames of the fire. The flickering light cast into prominence the straight blade of his nose, the sensuous curve of his mouth, a mouth that could relax into a boyishly engaging smile or draw into a thin, stern line when he was displeased. An odd little tremor went through her. Lord God above, but he was the most strikingly beautiful man she'd ever laid eyes upon.

"When will you marry her?" The wine was heady and potent—it supplied the courage she so sorely lacked, else she would never have dared to speak so freely.

He appeared startled. ''I beg your pardon?''

Meredith drew a deep breath. ''Moire,'' she clarified. ''When will you marry her?''

He gave her a long, slow look. ''Who told you I would marry her?''

Heat suffused her cheeks. She would not tell tales on Egan. ''I've heard talk . . . that you would marry her . . . and I thought mayhap . . .'twould be when you tired of me.''

A rakish brow rose. Smoothly he said, ''Ah, but how could I tire of you when I've not yet had you?''

Meredith blushed. Too late she realized her mistake—ah, but she'd fallen ripely into his hands with her blunder. Bravely she swallowed. ''I simply thought—''

''I know what you thought, lass. But let me put the matter to rest here and now. I will not marry her. I am not yet ready to marry. Bluntly put, I've no inclination to wed, not to Moire or any other. Now. Does that satisfy your curiosity?''

Her nod was jerky. The sudden glint in his eye warned her not to push the matter any further.

''Good,'' he said pleasantly. ''Now that I've answered your question, you must answer mine. I know you are afraid of me, but I would know . . . is it just me?''

The conversation had taken a direction she hadn't anticipated. Meredith's gaze flew to his, where she read an unfaltering determination. Damnation! she thought. Damnation! Why couldn't he let her be?

''Nay,'' she said jerkily.

''So it's all men?''

"Aye. Any man. Every man." She spoke before she thought better of it.

Little did she know her struggle lay vivid in the depths of her eyes. She lowered her lashes, swiftly veiling her thoughts. But Cameron had already seen. He set aside his wine—and hers.

"No more of that for you, lass." In one fluid move he was on his feet. Two steps brought him before her. Trapping icy cold fingers within his, he tugged her upward . . . up and into his embrace.

Strong fingers caught at her chin and brought her eyes cleaving to his. "Don't you know you've naught to fear from me?" His whisper was low and intense.

Her breath caught. Her lips parted. Whatever she might have said lodged deep in her throat. She had one mind-spinning glimpse of blazing gray eyes before his mouth captured hers. He kissed her then, a kiss of slow, rousing exploration. His lips were like some strange, unknown potion, luring her ever onward into a dark void where naught existed but the pressure of his mouth melting her both inside and out. She moaned—a sound of pleasure, not protest. His arms tightened. For one paralyzing instant she thought she would be crushed. With a groan he lifted her high.

A sense of weightlessness assailed her, and then she felt the hardness of the mattress at her back. He stretched out beside her; the searing fusion of their mouths remained unbroken.

Her hands came up against his shoulders, but she did not stop him. Warm fingers trailed slowly down the column of her throat, then traced the neckline of her gown. Meredith's pulse surely stopped in that instant. For one heart-pounding moment, he hovered there . . . then dipped boldly within the bodice of her gown, pushing aside the cloth and baring her to the waist.

He caught her gasp in the back of his throat. Her hands came up to his shoulders, but he was insistent. Headily persuasive. His tongue touched hers, engaging her in a duel in which both emerged victorious. Those treacherous fingers paused, directly above the pouting tip of her breast. Her nipples tingled and ached, for what she knew not . . .

And then she did. His thumb grazed the very tip, sending myriad sensations radiating outward. It came again . . . and yet again. She nearly cried out. Such sweet, sweet torment. Her body abrim, she arched into that elusive caress. Seeking. Craving, aware somewhere deep within herself that this was what she'd wanted, without realizing it. Him. Desire. Now she knew what it was and she only wanted more. Was she wicked? It felt wicked—his kiss. His hands. Sinfully wicked. But deliciously so. Deliriously so.

All at once she was caught in a maze of conflicting emotions. Since that horrible night so long ago, the thought of lying with a man had brought only fear and disgust. Yet Cameron was different. He made her feel things she'd never thought she could feel with any man. She was reminded of his gentleness with the child Aileen. In truth, he was not so grim as she had once thought. Nor was he unkind.

Yet the thought of being naked . . . of being seen . . . being touched in the way that he would surely touch her . . . She was torn. Torn, and she knew not which way to turn.

"Cameron—" His name was a low, choked cry.

Slowly he raised his head. His eyes were glittering. His hand stilled.

"Cameron, please . . ."

A muscle jumped in his jaw. He gazed at her, at her wide-eyed distress. He felt her trembling against

him. It struck him then . . . she was like a woman who
knew naught of the ways of love . . . or naught but
fear of the ways of love . . .

The thought took root.

Blood pooled thick and heavy there in his loins.
His temples were pounding, his rod pulsing. To touch
at last the hot satin of her skin. To feel the flutter of
moist, soft lips beneath his. To touch and not have
. . . He gritted his teeth and tried to ignore the thick-
ening swell of his rod.

He heard the ragged rush of her breath, saw her
eyes cleave to his.

He wanted her still. He wanted her more than ever,
more than he'd ever wanted anything in his life. Some
strange, twisting emotion unfolded within him. In the
back of his mind, he knew he could not take her, for
she was too disarmingly vulnerable. Yet if he could
not have her, then at least he would have this . . .

A finger on her lips halted the flow of words. "Nay,
Meredith, say nothing. I will not take you," he whispered. "Not now. Not this night. But soon, lass, soon
you will be mine."

Her gown was whisked from her body. Her heart
climbed to her throat as bold glittering eyes roamed
the length of her, dwelling endlessly on the quivering
thrust of firm young breasts, the fiery thatch between
her thighs.

Then his hands were on her anew. He pulled her
close, his mouth claiming hers in a hotly devouring
kiss that left her feeling dizzy and breathless.

The candles were doused. The night closed in. He
lay down, near her but not touching her.

When at last she fell asleep, her lips still burned
with the scorching imprint of his kiss.

Thirteen

She was weakening. Meredith knew it. And so did he. *So did he.*

Cameron was right. It was only a matter of time before she belonged to him completely . . . before her traitorous body betrayed her—indeed it already had! she thought wildly as she lay in bed the next morn. A chilling thought seized her. When that happened, he would discover the truth. Residing in the convent as she had, no doubt he was convinced she was a chaste, innocent maid. Would he be angry? Of a certainty, she decided bitterly. Nay, she could not bear to experience the shame anew. The remembrance made her shudder. She'd felt so dirty. So unclean . . .

She could not stay here. She could not!

Cameron had already risen. Huddling beneath the coverlet, she watched the play of muscle in his bare shoulders as he washed. He half-turned. Immediately she screwed her eyes shut and feigned sleep.

She could hear him drawing on his boots. Footsteps drew near. There followed a ringing silence. Her breath quickened. Her ears strained for some sign of his whereabouts. Where the devil was he?

"Meredith. I know you are awake." The callused tip of a finger traced the line of her jaw.

Her eyes opened. She glared at him. He was now fully dressed and standing beside the bed.

He laughed softly at the defiant flare in those beautiful blue eyes. "Did you sleep well, lass?"

"I slept most soundly."

"Then my snores did not wake you?"

"You do not snore," she said crossly.

"So you've noticed." He sounded pleased. No doubt his good humor would come at her expense, she decided.

The mattress dipped as he sat. Reaching out, he stroked the slope of one bare shoulder. Meredith froze. Saints above, she'd completely forgotten she'd slept naked! She was secretly appalled—never in her life had she done such a thing! Oh, but she had to escape, else she would soon be beyond redemption.

"I've a hard day's ride ahead of me, lass. Finn and I go to pick up some sheep from a farmer to the north."

Meredith's mind began to race. He was heading north. She must go south. Oh, if she could just slip away . . .

His knuckles beneath her chin, he tilted her face up. "Come, now, lass. Will you deliver me into the frosty morn with the warmth of your kiss?"

" 'Tis summer," she told him flatly.

"So it is. You see what effect you have on me?"

"Obviously a chilly one!"

"Hardly." His laughter was low and oddly pleasing to the ear. When he bent and pressed his mouth to hers, she did not fight him. Her body displayed a shocking will of its own. Suddenly all she could think was that this was the last time she would know the fervor of his kiss.

Slender arms crept up and around his neck. Her

mouth clung to his. She felt him start in surprise, and then powerful arms drew her close. The coverlet slipped away, forgotten.

Long moments passed before he raised his head. His gaze rested on her lips, still damp and moist from his kiss. "I will hurry back, lass. On that you may rest assured."

Within seconds he was gone. Excitement gathered within her. She pushed aside the bedclothes and hurriedly washed. A maid brought a tray of food. She did not eat, but tucked away the bread and cheese—she would need it later. All the while her mind buzzed. Of late, Egan had relaxed his guard during her morning prayers—no longer did he remain inside the chapel with her. Indeed, many times he'd been nowhere near when she emerged. And the chapel was far opposite from the drum tower where the watchman was posted.

Her crucifix. She could not leave without her crucifix!

Since the day Cameron had ripped it from her throat, she'd seen no sign of it. Still, she had to try. Hurriedly she searched through his chest, pushing aside his clothing.

A knock sounded on the door. It was Egan, she knew. She bit back a choked cry. Damn—damn! She had no choice but to leave without it, for she might never be granted a chance like this. None of her inner turmoil showed as she opened the door to greet Egan.

By the time she entered the chapel, her heart clamored so that she could scarcely breathe. Egan did not follow her within, but remained outside the doors—Meredith could scarce believe her good fortune. Sinking down on her knees, she prayed it would continue, and finished by asking God's forgiveness for the scarcity of her time with Him this morn. She winced as she thought of Egan—no doubt he would bear the brunt of Cameron's wrath when he discovered she was gone. Though she felt horribly guilty for sacrificing Egan in this way, she could not give in to it.

'Twas a simple matter to exit the chapel through the sacristy doorway. Thankfully, no one lurked near. Hurriedly she placed a gauzy veil over her head to subdue the bright shimmer of her hair as she headed toward the bailey. Bowing her head low, she walked briskly toward the postern gate as if she belonged there. She'd noted several days earlier that often there was no guard present till evening approached—not until this morning had she dreamed she might make use of it.

No one stopped her. No one stepped her way, or even cast a glance at her. Her hands shaking, she let herself out the gate.

Praise the saints, she had made it! The palisade walls were behind her. Now she must keep to the shadows, lest she be discovered . . .

"You mean to tell me she was on foot, your men were on horseback, and still you could not find her?"

"There are several others still searching." Egan's gaze slid away. He could scarcely believe it himself. He'd been stunned when he'd finally entered the kirk this morning, only to find it empty. In truth, he couldn't believe she possessed the daring to actually flee. He felt both humiliated and resentful that she had made such a fool of him.

But the fault was his—no one else's—and so he told Cameron.

"Aye," he said quietly. "I make no excuses. The duty was mine—the fault is mine. I thought she tarried longer than usual at her prayers, yet I waited. After yesterday, I thought mayhap—''

''You need not explain.'' Cameron had gone white about the mouth as he listened. ''You felt sorry for her and she took full advantage of it.'' His thoughts brewed apace with his anger. Had she left because of the incident yesterday? She'd been stung to the core. Or was she ashamed he'd seen her cry? Or because he'd stated anew his desire to make her his? It could have been any of those reasons. All of them. He chafed inwardly. What did it matter why she'd left? She was gone. Relentless purpose filled his heart. But not for long, he decided blackly. No, not for long.

Egan shook his head. ''Coming from the nunnery as she did, I truly did not think her capable of such—''

''I know—such sly deceit!'' His tone was as hard as his expression. He turned and ordered Fortune saddled and brought around again—as well as bread and ale.

Egan stepped forward. ''I will accompany you.''

A hand clapped his shoulder. ''Nay, Egan. I will do this alone.'' His eyes sought Egan's. ''I will be gone for several days. Will you see to things here?''

Egan was puzzled. ''Of course. But Cameron, surely it will not take so long to find her—''

''I know that.'' Cameron's smile was grim. ''But I think it best that . . .''

Egan listened intently. Minutes later, Fortune raced through the gatehouse at his master's command, leaving a cloud of dust in his wake.

Egan watched as Cameron disappeared from sight, his eyes troubled. He'd seen for himself the brittle determination on Cameron's features, and he was certain it did not bode well for Meredith. Oh, but he shouldn't have cared what fate befell the Munro lass! Certainly she deserved whatever punishment Cameron chose to mete out. Yet Egan was almost glad he would not be present when Cameron found her . . .

For Cameron would find her. That was something Egan did not doubt.

Meredith was no fool. She was well aware that Egan would soon discover she was missing. First the keep would be searched. When no sign of her was discovered, he would send out riders. So it was that she did not keep to the rutted roadway, but ducked beneath the shelter of trees. Now and again she peered over her shoulder at the hulking outline of Dunthorpe. A plume of dust spiraled high. She knew then that riders had been dispatched, so she hid among the bushes for what seemed like hours.

Her muscles cramped. Her stomach growled. Her eyes burned from the strain of peering through the brambled foliage. She didn't crawl out from her hiding place until she heard the distant thunder of hoofbeats heading back toward the keep.

She assuaged her hunger with a handful of ripe berries. She felt like crowing her triumph—she'd managed to make good her escape from Cameron! Yet suddenly the weather began to change, as it was wont to do here in the Highlands.

Within minutes the sky was a dark, depthless gray. The wind began to howl, a wind so fierce it whipped the veil from her head and robbed her of breath. Her hair streaming out behind her like a banner of flame, she stumbled back a step. A bush snapped beneath the weight of her foot, upsetting her balance. She went down hard, knocking the back of her head hard against the uneven ground.

The world reeled giddily around her. Meredith staggered upright. Only then did she realize she hadn't been so clever after all. Her spirits plunged. Her heart twisted. Ah, but she should have known she was doomed! If only she could have found her crucifix, perhaps the Lord would have smiled upon her. As it was, her food would not last beyond the morrow. She had no flint and tinder to light a fire. She was a Munro on MacKay lands. What if Cameron's clansmen recognized her as such? She might well be slain on sight. The clouds obliterated the sun. Such weather might well last for days, she realized bleakly. How was she to find her way when she could not tell east from west, north from south?

In desperation she buried her head in her hands. Her throat closed, hot and tight. Her lungs burned as she bit back a sob, cursing her woman's frailty, for what good would it do to weep? Yet she was barely able to keep from breaking down in tears.

That was how he found her—her shoulders slumped as if she carried the burdens of the world, the brightness of her hair caught by the wind and streaming out behind her in wild abandon.

Almost painfully she raised her head, aware that something was different. The hairs on the back of her neck prickled, as they did so often when *he* was near.

Cameron.

From out of the mists they came, man and steed. Cameron and Fortune. The beat of her heart grew still and silent, then all at once pounded so that she feared it would leave the cavern of her breast. She could not move as he reined the great beast to a halt, then dismounted.

For a never-ending moment she felt the brutal

weight of his stare. Wordlessly he raised his hand aloft.

As if he commanded it, the wind ceased to blow— for the space of a heartbeat, it was as if the very world held its breath. Bitterly she despaired her weakness, even as she decried his strength.

Wordlessly she crossed to where he stood. The words he'd used that night at Connyridge returned to haunt her. *Do not try to run, for I will find you. I will hunt you to the ends of this land. Do not try to hide, for I will bind you to my side with a chain that will forever be unbroken.*

Her knees were shaking, yet from somewhere she dredged up the courage to raise her eyes to his. She nearly cried out, for his features were twisted into a dark mask that was terrible to behold.

Her lips parted. ''Cameron—''

''Say nothing!'' he hissed. ''Do you hear? Say nothing!'' His tone cut like a lash. She'd seen him angry before, but not like this—never like this.

She was lifted and set jarringly upon Fortune's back—he followed her up. A rumble of thunder rolled across the land, shaking the very earth. Fortune danced sideways. Cameron laid a hand on his neck and spoke his name. The steed's sleek black flesh quivered, then he quieted.

Meredith stared at his hands, so big and dark. She was like his steed, Meredith thought in half-shame, half-despair. But a touch from those lean-fingered hands and he calmed her, soothed her wild fear with naught but the warmth of his presence.

But not now. She could feel him rigid as a lance behind her; the arms at her sides were taut with restraint.

A heel to Fortune's flank, and they were off.

To Meredith's shock, she hadn't covered nearly the ground she thought she had. Within the hour they were back at the keep. But Cameron didn't ride through the gatehouse as she expected. A curt order to remain where she was rushed by her ear. He dismounted and strode to the guard who had emerged from the gatehouse. Meredith watched nervously as the man handed him a pouch. Finn appeared on horseback and spoke briefly with Cameron.

He returned a moment later. For one shattering instant as he swung up behind her, their eyes collided. His burned like fire, yet never had she seen such coldness. It was little wonder that she dared not ask his intentions. Without a word he wheeled Fortune around and rode away from the keep.

Meredith's mind was muddled. Why had they left? Where were they going? Why did Finn keep pace behind them? To her surprise, they didn't ride far. Before long a familiar scent teased her nostrils—the sharp tang of salt and sea.

She was not given to wonder why for long. Her heart leaped to her throat as Cameron slowed Fortune's gallop to a walk. The steed carefully picked his way down a narrow trail to a small cove edged by a strip of sandy beach.

They halted. Cameron leaped to the sand, then reached for her. His hands displayed no tendency to linger. Meredith glanced toward the waves rolling on the sand. The wind-driven clouds had blown beyond the horizon. Near the headland was a small isle; hills dipped and rolled, carpeted in shimmering green. But this day Meredith had no eye for such beauty, for he had dragged a small raft from between two massive boulders—in the dusky twilight she'd not seen it.

Her gaze trickled from the raft, to the isle, to Cameron's features, now etched in stone. Dread knotted her belly. A helpless despair clamped tight about her breast. He alone knew her fear of water. He alone knew she could not swim. Would he leave her there? Was this his way of seeing that she never escaped? She could scarcely summon her voice.

"Why do we come here?"

His jaw tightened. He made no answer, but deliberately stepped around her.

"Please, tell me! Do you mean to . . ."—her voice quavered—"to leave me there?"

He dragged the pouch from Fortune's back and slung it over his shoulder, then turned back for her. "We've a need to be alone"—his eyes glinted—"you and I."

"Alone," she cried. "There?" She pointed toward the island.

"Aye," he said tautly.

While Meredith digested the full import of that word, Finn gathered Fortune's reins. He tethered the black steed to his own, then galloped off.

The silence of awareness descended, thick and heavy. Meredith knew then what Cameron intended. She had gone too far . . . and the realization came far too late! Sweet Mother Mary! She had incurred his wrath and now it would be her undoing, for she was certain his desire would be appeased once and for all.

One look at his glittering eyes told the tale only too well.

There was no time for further speculation. He caught her hand and pointed to the raft. It was primitively fashioned—rough-hewn logs lashed together with strips of hide.

He spoke but one word. "Sit," he commanded.

Meredith's heart lurched. Would they make the crossing in this feeble craft?

Indeed they did. In Meredith's fear-numbed mind, the journey took forever. Cameron stood near the edge, a long pole in his hands as he guided them ever nearer the island. Raw terror clutched at her insides. Her heart lurched along with the bobbing swell of the raft, for the waters of the cove were choppy and churning. Foam lathered around the rocks that jutted like ragged teeth on the shoreline of the isle. Yet somehow they found their way between, to a tiny strip of beach, where they landed.

Once they were ashore, she caught sight of a small cottage atop the hill that had not been visible from the mainland. Apparently Cameron was well aware of its existence, for he caught hold of her elbow and directed their steps in the direction of the cottage. She nearly retorted that there was no need—there was nowhere she could go that he would not find her.

Aye, she acknowledged bitterly, for was that not what he intended?

The cottage was built of stone, stocky and small. It took a moment before her eyes adjusted to the hazy light. Cameron had no such trouble—he appeared familiar with his surroundings. He strode straight to the table beneath the far window and lit a stubby candle. As the wavering light filled the room, Meredith glanced around. It vaguely registered that the cottage was surprisingly well provisioned, as if in waiting. A pile of logs lay stacked near the massive stone fireplace. On the far wall was a wide bed, the covers neatly tucked and folded. Meredith stood awkwardly in the center of the room while Cameron laid the fire in the grate. Her legs wobbled, for this was surely the longest day of her life.

And it was not yet over.

At last he straightened. Her exhaustion was forgotten. Meredith couldn't help it—her gaze leaped helplessly to his.

His eyes burned like pale torches of silver in the firelight. The very air around him seemed charged and roaring, like the earlier thunder that rolled across the earth.

Slowly he walked around her—a predator circling its prey, she thought hazily. Ah, and now that they were here, it seemed he suffered no shortage of speech.

"Why did you flee, Meredith?"

Beneath his unbending gaze, her own faltered.

"Where the devil did you think you were going?" His features were etched in mocking reproof. "Let me guess. Anywhere, as long as it was away from me."

The very flames of hell seemed alive in his eyes, and all at once she could not bear it. She sought to duck her head, but he would not allow it. His fingers on the point of her chin, he wrenched her regard to his.

"Tell me, Meredith. Where would you have gone? Back to your father—back to the Red Angus?"

Her lips pressed together. She shook her head.

"Where, then?"

"Back to Connyridge," she said, her voice very low.

"To the priory! Why?"

Meredith swallowed. He prodded and probed, like the prick of a knife. Why could he never leave her be?

The tip of a callused finger ran down her throat. "Merry," he said mockingly. "My sweet Merry . . . will you not tell me?"

Merry . . . my sweet Merry. In that instant, her blood surely froze in her veins. For *he* had called her that . . .

She knocked his arm away almost violently. "My name is not Merry! Do not call me that!"

Cameron's eyes narrowed. She had turned utterly white, and her expression was half-wild, half-panicked. He swore to himself. There was something afoot here, and by God, he would know it once and for all.

"Then tell me what I would know," he said smoothly. "I did not misconstrue your concern for your father's safety. Why would you not return to Castle Munro and see for yourself that he is alive and well?"

If anything, her expression grew even wilder. Her lashes fell, swiftly veiling her expression. "No," he said tightly, "do not look away!"

"Then leave me be!" Where before her outburst had been one of anger, now it was a pitiful plea.

He dropped his hands to her shoulders and gave her a little shake.

"Dammit, Meredith, tell me! Why would you not return to Castle Munro?"

She spoke with fervor, straight from the heart. "I will never return there."

"Why not?"

"Because I am afraid . . . I am afraid!"

"Afraid!" Cameron was stunned. He could think of no reason why she should be afraid . . . yet why had she paled when he'd called her Merry? "What, Meredith? What are you afraid of?"

She shuddered. "Of him. I am afraid of him!"

"Who, Meredith? Who?"

He felt the breath she drew—it was deep and ragged. "I do not know . . . don't you see . . . *I do not know*!"

Fourteen

Her eyes clung to his. The fear he glimpsed in their depths sent an eerie prickling down his spine. He grasped her hand—her fingers were icy cold.

He couldn't quell the sensation that this had something—everything!—to do with her fear of men . . . of him!

Drawing her to the bed, he pulled her down beside him. "God in heaven," he said in a strange-sounding voice. "What happened to you, lass? *What happened?*"

Meredith sighed, a sound pulled from deep inside. What did it matter if he knew? she thought dully. He knew almost everything about her—her most innermost thoughts, it often seemed!

Her voice was halting and low. "I was sixteen when it happened. One night, a man crept into my chamber. When I awoke, a hand covered my mouth. He tied my wrists and gagged me." Her voice began to wobble. "Th-there was an empty bedchamber in the tower. It was there that he took me, for there was no one to hear there . . . no one to see."

It did not end there. Indeed, it only began.

"He stripped my clothes from me. I tried to stop him, but he was too strong—too big! He struck me.

He held a knife to my throat and told me he would kill me if I cried out.''

Unbidden, his mind sped back, back to the night she lay ill with fever. What was it she'd said? He pulled the words from deep in his mind.

My gown . . . Why do you do this? Nay, do not touch me . . . nay, not there! 'Tis wrong! Later she had moaned, *'Tis so dark. I cannot see . . . I cannot see . . . Who are you? Who are you?*

Cameron inhaled sharply. He cursed himself roundly. She'd unwittingly revealed it to him that night she'd been sick. Christ, he should have realized! He'd thought it was a dream, that it was him she was fighting, but instead her fevered mind had revived the memory and carried her back to that night.

She began to shiver. He reached for her, but she slipped from his grasp and moved to the center of the room. Her arms came around herself, as if to ward off a chill.

"I was naked . . . *he* was naked. He touched me . . . he touched me everywhere . . . in unspeakable ways. His hands were rough. Hard. They were everywhere, even''—her voice caught—"even inside me. He—he made me touch him! His rod . . .'' Her mouth grew tremulous. "And then he . . .''

An awful tightness crowded Cameron's chest. He knew what she was going to say, even before she said it, and everything inside him raged against it. Her words wrenched at his insides.

Yet by the time she was finished, he was filled with a rage blacker than any he had ever known. This man—this *viper*—had stolen her virtue. Ripped her innocence from her and replaced it with terror. Had the bastard been before him now, he'd have torn him apart limb by limb with the utmost satisfaction.

"Remember you once said I possessed not the courage to take my own life?"

He frowned. "I do not recall—"

"You did. You did!" Her voice went toneless. "A part of me wanted to die. Yet I was afraid of God's wrath—afraid of dying—afraid I would burn in hell for what I had done—"

"Nay! You did nothing, Meredith!" His protest was swift and vehement. "It was not you, it was him!"

"In time, I knew that. In my heart, I knew that God would forgive me. But I could never forgive myself for being so weak. I was so afraid—of him! That it would happen again and again. I felt so dirty—so ashamed!"

"You did not see him? You know not who it was?"

Her gaze lowered. She shook her head. "It was too dark. I saw only shadows . . . I remembered the horrible things he did, the way he whispered 'Merry, my sweet Merry.' "

"That's why you left, isn't it? Why you went to the priory? Because of what he did."

"Aye." She struggled to speak. "I could not stay at Castle Munro. I was afraid to leave my room, afraid of every man I saw. I wondered . . . was he the one? I—I could not stay! I could not!"

Cameron rose. He moved to her, clenching his hands into fists at his sides. He wanted desperately to touch her, to draw her into his arms and offer what comfort he could, yet he sensed she was not yet ready. His soul grew black. Indeed, he thought darkly, would she ever be ready?

"Your father," he said suddenly. "Does he know what happened that night?"

Her eyes avoided his. "Nay. I could not tell him such things—I could not tell anyone!"

And yet she had just told Cameron. Did she even realize what she had shared, what trust she yielded? A faint bitterness seeped inside him. It would seem not.

"My father knew something was wrong. He asked me to tell him, but I never could. I know that you would say differently, but there is no man more kind and tender than my father. I begged him to send me to the priory—I knew he wouldn't refuse. I hated myself, for though he said nary a word, I knew I disappointed him so! I felt that I had failed him as a daughter. I knew he would have me marry in time, and the thought filled me with revulsion. The thought of the marriage bed . . ." Her eyes darkened. "I could not do it! Besides, I knew no man would want me—tainted as I was."

Her gaze slid away. "When we arrived at Connyridge, my heart was in turmoil. 'Twas the hardest thing I had ever done, but I asked that he not visit me, for I knew I might be tempted to leave, yet how could I ever return to Castle Munro?" Her voice plunged to a whisper. "I gazed upon him, and all I could think was that . . . this was the last time I would see him, the last time. I felt . . . as if someone had reached inside my heart and twisted it!" Tears stood high and bright in her eyes. "It was the same for him—I could see it in his eyes! I hurt him—I hurt him terribly! And when I think of him, all I can see is him weeping . . . as he did that day."

By the time she finished, her voice was raw. Cameron had gone very still. Did he love his daughter so very much, then, the Red Angus? For a fleeting instant, Cameron could not reconcile her remembrance

of her father with the butchery he'd witnessed on the
field where his family had been slain. But no . . . *no*.
He steeled himself against it. He bled inside for Meredith, for what she had endured . . . but he could never
bleed for the Red Angus.

A painful silence erupted, for Cameron could not
find the words to console her. Finally, not knowing
what else to do, he raised a hand to her shoulder.

She jerked at his touch.

His hand fell to his side. His mouth twisted. Always
she shunned him. Always. Ah, but he'd forgotten she
wanted naught from him . . . naught but her freedom.

"Go to sleep, Meredith."

Slowly she raised her head. "Cameron—"

"You heard me, lass. Just—go to sleep!"

His voice came out harsher than he had intended.
In the instant before she whirled, she looked utterly
stricken, her eyes huge and glazed over with tears. He
despised himself, but he could not help it, for her
denial had bruised the very center of his being.

With his jaw clenched hard, he strode from the cottage without a word.

Raising his face to the star-flung midnight skies, he
let the moist night air rush over him. It cooled his
skin, but did naught to cool the fever that raged deep
inside.

For days now he'd longed to know what lay behind
Meredith's fear of him . . . Now he did, and Christ!
but he almost wished he did not!

Guilt blotted his soul. She'd been spirited away in
the midst of the night . . . much as he had done the
night he'd taken her from Connyridge. The wounds
her assailant had wielded were on the inside—scars
that had yet to heal. Mayhap they never would. That
was why she had fled to the convent, why she had

remained . . . why she was determined to return.

Yet, knowing this, hearing her recount her ordeal with tremulous voice and floundering courage, he wanted her. Now, as much as ever. *More,* if the truth be told. Yet how could he take her, knowing what he did?

Little did he realize she was in much the same dilemma. Her bed gown had been inside the pouch Cameron had brought—she'd changed into it and slipped into bed. She fervently wished she hadn't told him of that terrible night, yet he'd given her no choice! All the while she spoke, she glimpsed no condemnation, yet why had he dismissed her so curtly? She knew he hadn't left her. Somehow she knew he was near. She cringed inside. What did he think of her? Had he left because he could not stand to look at her? Did he think she was a whore? A pang squeezed her heart. She couldn't bear the thought!

She felt . . . bereft. It was so lonely, here in this bed without him. She missed him—missed him desperately. She missed his warmth, the solid strength of his arms about her back, the steady throb of his heart beneath her cheek. Quickly, before she lost her nerve, she rose and moved to the door. It creaked when she opened it.

For one paralyzing instant she didn't see him. An icy fear ripped through her. Then she saw his form, powerful and tall. He stood not three paces distant, staring out at the moon-drenched darkness. She shifted uncertainly on her bare feet, then spoke his name.

"Cameron."

He remained where he was, his back to her. "Aye?"

She wet her lips. "Will you not come to bed?"

She saw the way his shoulders stiffened. "Nay."

"Cameron, please . . . I cannot sleep . . . without you beside me." The tiny confession was torn from her. Her heart surely dwelled in her throat. Saints above, she couldn't believe what she'd just said.

Slowly he turned. She longed for him to come to her, to kiss her until nothing else mattered. Silence yawned, dark and endless as the seas.

"Cameron, please . . . will you not come inside?"

Two steps brought him directly before her. Still he did not touch her. His features were a mask that shielded his thoughts like a plate of armor. His mouth was ominously thin.

"You must sleep alone this night."

He sounded so hard! His guarded wariness made her long to weep. Her breath caught in her throat. "Why, Cameron? Why?"

Something blazed in his eyes, something that made her pulse pound madly. Then: "You crucify me."

She had to strain to catch the words, yet his tone was taut and utterly fierce.

She gave a tiny shake of her head. "I know not what you mean."

His laugh was mirthless. "Believe me, Meredith, you do not want to know."

"Tell me anyway."

"You would have me lay beside you and not bed you. We share a bed"—his gaze impaled her—"but that is all we share. To lay with you. To kiss you. To taste your mouth, but no more. To touch you, yet *not* touch you . . . You crucify me," he said again.

The words were stark and shattering. The depth of his intensity made her feel all shaky and fluttery inside. Her mouth had gone dry as the deserts of the East.

"I know why you went to Connyridge—I know why you sought to return. You would hide from the world, that no man would see you, that no man will desire you. But you hide from yourself as well. You do not belong in the nunnery. You were meant to have children, a babe at your breast."

Meredith had gone utterly still. In one sweep he laid bare her greatest secret . . . her most fervent yearning.

She ducked her head. Her eyes closed. Her hands upraised, she clenched her fists upon her breasts.

"A babe," she heard herself whisper. "Your son."

"If God so wills it, then it will be."

Her eyes opened, a reflection of her anguish. "That is all you want from me—a son!"

His heart thundered. No man would want her, she had said. But she was wrong.

"It's just as you once said—I could have a son of any woman. But it's you I want, Meredith. *You.*"

That one word sped straight to her heart. Warm, wet tears rose and overflowed, trickling down her cheeks. She made no effort to wipe them away, for heart and mind and body were hopelessly entangled.

"I am . . . impure. Soiled by the hands of another man. I am not a maid! How can you want me? How?"

The broken cry was wrenched from deep inside. Hearing it, Cameron felt his heart squeeze.

Slowly he raised his hands to frame her face. With his thumbs he smoothed the winged grace of her brows. "You are not impure," he chastised roughly. "You are not tainted! Aye, your maidenhead may be no more, but you are a maid as pure and innocent as any I have ever known. How can I want you, you ask?" His head lowered, so that their lips barely

brushed. ''Sweet heaven''—he said against her mouth
. . . into it—''how can I not?''

He kissed her then, kissed her with unbridled longing, with all the pent-up desire buried deep in his
heart, letting her taste the fierceness of his hunger.
With one arm he caught her up against him. In some
far distant corner, he thought she would stop him. She
did not.

For she *could* not.

She was cold—cold to the depth of her bones, and
he alone possessed the power to warm her. Only he
could stoke the fires within her. She had told him of
that long-ago night. She'd entrusted to him that which
she had never told another. And with the feel of his
mouth warm and hard upon hers, the tight knot of
fear inside her melted away. Though she did not understand it, in that moment it seemed only right that
she should yield this, body and soul . . .

They were both trembling when at last he released
her mouth.

Her heart beat high into her throat. Her fingers
curled and uncurled in the front of his tunic. ''Cameron,'' she said faintly. ''You said you would free me,
if—if I gave you a son.'' She couldn't disguise the
ragged edge to her voice.

His gaze sharpened. ''Aye.''

Misty blue eyes lifted to his. The muscles in her
throat worked almost convulsively. ''And will you release me? You will keep your word?''

''I will,'' he said slowly.

There was a heartbeat of silence.

''Then give me your seed. Give me your son.''

Fifteen

Her voice had plunged to a whisper.

Give me your seed.

Cameron stared at her. His eyes darkened. For one mind-teetering second, he was convinced he'd gone mad, that his ears had deceived him. Surely she could not have said . . .

Give me your son.

He was pierced by a bittersweet pang. Even now she wanted nothing from him but her freedom. But his heart had begun to thunder. His blood was burning. He felt purely selfish, purely greedy. Aye, he thought. He would give her what she wanted, for it was just as he'd said.

He wanted her. He ached for her . . . too much to refuse what she offered.

Ah, but would the night's surrender draw the morrow's penance? He had to know—he had to.

"Do you know what you ask?" His gaze probed hers, clear to some unseen place hidden deep within her. "Do you, lass? Say yea or say nay, but say it now!" Even as he spoke, his hands came up to grip her own.

For one perilous moment Meredith's traitorous mind betrayed her and she was reminded of other

211

hands. Hands upon her body. Hands that had forced her down.

Drawn by a force she couldn't command, her gaze trickled down . . . down to where dark fingers caught at her own. They were strong, those hands. Lean and powerful. Tanned and wholly male.

Those hands had grasped her waist, traced the slant of her cheek, skimmed the bareness of her very breast, immeasurably gentle despite their strength. Those hands had made her tremble, but not in fear. Nay, not in fear . . . never in fear.

His hands held no terror for her now.

She trembled anew. Her gaze climbed higher. Her eyes clung to his, trapped by the fiery hold in his. With quavering heart and quaking limbs, she heard her voice, as if from a very great distance. "Aye"— and then again, this time a soft cry—"aye!"

His eyes seemed to blaze. "Then let it be," he whispered. "Dear God, let it be . . ."

His mouth crushed hers, hot and passionate. She felt herself swept high aloft, snug in his embrace. He kicked the door shut with the heel of his boot. Her toes touched the floor. Almost before she could draw breath, her gown was whisked from her shoulders. She could only watch as his clothes met the same end as hers—a forgotten pile on the rough cold floor.

The light from the fire bathed him in pale, firelit glory. Though her cheeks flooded crimson, Meredith could not help herself. Always before, she had hidden her face away, curious but almost desperately afraid to look. Now she could not help herself.

Clad in kilt and plaid, so tall and striking, Cameron was a man whose sheer presence was an over-powering force among those around him.

Naked, he was . . . extraordinary.

He was power and strength. Masculine grace and vitality.

The stark, masculine beauty of his body made her throat constrict. His frame was forged in iron. He was long and lean of limb, the contours of his shoulders were sculpted and round, his arms were sinuously defined with muscle. A dark netting of fur covered his chest and the ridged hardness of his belly. From somewhere she dredged up the courage to gaze the length of him . . . *all* of him.

She dared what she had never dared before. Her regard ventured helplessly lower—what she saw made her eyes widen and her entire body go hot. The bottom dropped out of her stomach. Rigidly unconfined, framed in coarse black curls, his staff stood boldly erect. Meredith let out an uneven breath and transferred her gaze to safer territory, only to discover he'd been watching her all the while!

As if he were precisely aware of where her gaze had resided for long, uninterrupted moments, an odd half-smile curled his lips. He allowed no time for shame. No time for embarrassment. A hand at her hips urged her body against his. His skin was hotter than any fire, the eyes that gazed down at her brighter than any flame—there was nowhere they did not touch.

Did he test her? she wondered frantically. All at once she knew not. She cared not. His fingers twisted in her hair, turning her face up to his. Then his mouth was on hers, a fevered caress that tasted of a tortuous hunger that was strangely thrilling. Warm breath filled her throat . . . *his* breath. Never in her life had she dreamed a kiss could be like this. When his tongue danced against hers, a swirling foray, she felt utterly boneless. She would surely have fallen were it not for the hardness of his arms braced around her back.

She was only dimly aware of being carried to the bed. Firelight flickered over his features as he propped himself on an elbow, his regard utterly intent.

"You know what I will do to you," he said quietly.

She blushed. "Aye."

He ran the pad of his thumb over her lips. "Then listen to me, Meredith, for when I take you . . . it will be nothing like what was done to you before." His tone was low and vibrating. "Nothing at all."

Praise God he was right, for she could not stand to think it might be otherwise.

"You must trust in me, lass. Can you do that?"

Indeed, she thought wildly, she had no choice. Some little-known sense inside warned her they had come too far to turn back now.

"Aye," she whispered. Yet he must have heard the vulnerability in her voice, for his eyes darkened.

"It will not be the same as before," he said again.

With fledgling courage, she laid her fingertips on the bristly plane of his cheek, unable to tear her eyes from his. "Will you swear it, Cameron? Will you?"

His gaze rested on her mouth. "I swear it, lass. *I swear it.*"

This time his kiss was so unbearably sweet, she nearly cried out. He whispered her name, a sound that sent a quiver all through her.

His lips found the corner of her mouth. "Meredith . . . sweet Meredith. You must tell me what pleases you."

With his thumbs he traced slow circles around the boundary of her breasts. "Does this please you, lass?"

She could only nod, for he was drawing perilously close to the delicate roseate peaks. She longed to drag his hands heavy against her swelling fullness, for her nipples thrust turgid and hard, in a way that had only happened with him . . .

"And this?" He grazed the very tips, the merest butterfly caress.

She inhaled sharply. Her breasts seemed to swell still further. That evocative touch came again . . . and yet again. Lightning shot through her, centered there at those dusky crowns. She hadn't realized that he would try to please her. Somehow she'd been convinced he would see to his own pleasure first.

Somehow he seemed to know exactly where she ached, what she wanted. He gave an odd little laugh. "You like that, don't you, lass? Ah, but I knew you would."

His mouth slid down her throat. Heat splintered all through her, even as her mind balked. Nay, she thought hazily. He had touched her there. But surely he would not . . .

She could only watch in mingled shock and fascination as his dark head hovered over her breast. Never had she dreamed he might kiss her there! As if in anticipation, her nipples peaked and hardened. As his mouth touched the quivering tip, she gasped. "Cameron, what—what do you do?"

He raised his head, his smile wicked. "Ah, but there's more, lass. Much, much more . . ."

He began the task anew, but this time . . . this time he trapped the dark rouge center within the hot wet cave of his mouth. His tongue boldly came out to touch the swelling peak, laving and curling, teasing and sucking . . . A sharp stab of pure sensation tore through her. The torment was unceasing. He lashed her nipple with torrid, wanton strokes that made her bite back a cry of sheer bliss.

It was as if a stranger had overtaken her body. She

had convinced herself that she must endure his possession in order to gain her freedom—instead she reveled in his touch, in every kiss, in every mind-stealing caress. She felt her senses widen, expanding like a frail spring blossom beneath the heat of a noonday sun, opening to welcome him . . . but only him. With a helpless little moan she caught his dark head in her hands, as if to keep him there and capture that elusive pleasure forever.

It was no different for Cameron. Had she lain passive beneath him, he knew he would never have forced her. But her mouth clung to his. He felt her shiver with sensation, arching into his hands and mouth as if he were all that she craved. Her blind acceptance of his every caress sent his ardor spiraling. His blood was boiling, his rod near to bursting the bounds of his skin. But he would not hurry his possession of her, for he wanted the memory of this night to remain branded in her heart forever . . .

As he knew it would be in his.

With precise deliberation, the heel of his hand laid claim to the satin hollow of her belly. She inhaled raggedly, but didn't stop him. His mouth gauged the wildly raging pulse at the base of her throat. He buried his fingers in the flaming curls that guarded the center of her womanhood, a plundering quest that did not stop until he touched the very heart of her.

He felt the flutter of her hands upon his shoulders. "Cameron," she said faintly. "Cameron, nay . . ."

His lips swallowed her choked little cry. "It's all right, lass," he murmured into her mouth. "Just let me touch you . . ." He kissed her endlessly, allowing her to adjust to his blatantly possessive touch there between her thighs.

His patience met with reward. His first sweeping

pass grazed soft, dewy folds; the second explored with unerring precision, parting each side of her furrowed cleft to seek the bud hidden deep within. It was there he now worked his magic, circling and skimming that taut kernel of flesh, loving the way her breathing hastened, how her fingers curled and uncurled on his nape—the dew of her passion soon glazed his own. She clutched at him, her breathing as torn and labored as his.

It circled through his mind to sample her sweetest fruit, to taste the spicy tang of her essence full upon his tongue. A fleeting regret seized him, for he knew it was too soon.

With every heartbeat, he wanted her more. He kissed the scar beneath her breast, the hollow of her belly. God, she was sweet. Feeling her tremble with the response she couldn't withhold nearly splintered him apart. The thought of thrusting deep and hard within her velvet heat was almost more than he could stand. He sought to control the rampaging thunder of his heart, the pulsing need soaring ever higher in his rod.

Suddenly it was he who trembled. He was overcome with the need to feel her touch, and his hand entrapped hers, guiding small, dainty fingers down his chest, grazing the plane of his belly, unfaltering in its quest. His fingers caught at hers, searing her palm with the hardness of his shaft, swollen and engorged.

"Feel," he said thickly. "Feel the blaze of my desire for you. No weapon here, lass. Naught but the fierceness of my need for you."

The clasp of her fingers there—*there,* where the pulse of desire throbbed strongest—made both their hearts leap. Pitched into feverish awareness, Meredith couldn't tear her eyes from his face. His words were shattering and raw. Her heart tumbled to a standstill, for she could feel him, hard and rigid in her hand. Above her, his eyes burned like silver torches. The cords of his neck stood out. Only then did she realize the enormity of his restraint.

He was above her now, pressing her back into the bed. Meredith was achingly conscious of the heat and hardness of his body above hers. Her fingers were caught and threaded tight within his, borne to the mattress beside her head. With his knees he splayed her wide, the very tip of his velvet crown snugly embraced by sleek, pink petals of femininity . . . For the span of a heartbeat, she lay before him, naked and vulnerable and helplessly open . . . She could not help it. Dark remembrance scored her mind at the very instant her flesh parted beneath the stunning pressure of his.

She felt her body stretch to accommodate his thrust . . . and then they were no longer two, but one.

Time stood still. Her breath left her in a scalding rush. Meredith was quiveringly aware of the breadth of his shaft buried tight inside her, filling and thick, so deep it seemed he touched her very womb. Yet, impossible as it seemed, her body accepted his as if they'd been made to fit together just so . . .

"Meredith"—her name was a ragged groan—"be not afraid, for I could not bear it if you were."

Be not afraid. His voice echoed through the void of her mind. He'd said that the night he'd taken her, she recalled suddenly. At the time, she'd been terrified . . . But as his mouth now found hers, the tight knot of fear inside her melted away as if it had never been.

His hands released hers. A powerful arm slid down to their hips, binding them together even more tightly.

Traitorous arms locked tight about the binding tightness of his shoulders.

Slowly he withdrew. In the same breath, he moved inside her anew, a blazing shaft of lightning. Again . . . and yet again. Her breath caught. Her body welcomed his of its own volition, clinging to his like a glove.

He was right, she decided vaguely. It was nothing like before. With each carefully gauged plunge of his flesh inside hers, flame licked along her veins. The sensation was indescribably delicious, a veritable feast of the senses. Somewhere in the murky haze of her consciousness, she wondered why she had fought this so hard. Swept into a realm of dark, heady pleasure, her hips taking up the rhythm of his. Arching. Seeking . . .

"Meredith . . . sweet Meredith, give me your lips."

Eyes closed, she raised tremulous lips to his, a willing captive of his passion. Her arms stole about his neck.

For Cameron it was too much. Her sweet surrender was more than he could bear—the feel of his staff clamped tight within the warm, wet prison of her sheath was more than he could stand.

His thrusts quickened. He lunged almost wildly. His climax rushed at him from all sides. The night exploded—and so did he. A jagged groan erupting from deep in his chest, his seed spewing from him almost violently, flooding her with fire.

Sixteen

Sunshine slanted through the shuttered window, gauzy and radiant, proclaiming the arrival of a new day. Meredith awoke slowly, a decided lassitude in her limbs. The fire in the grate had long since grown cold, yet never had she been so snug and warm. The reason for that was clear—she lay within the sheltering protection of strong male arms, her entire length molded against Cameron's side. Her head was pillowed on the sleek skin of his shoulder. Her hand looked small and dainty nestled there amid the bristly curls on his chest; it rested just above his heart, which beat steady and strong beneath her fingertips.

Thrice more he had taken her throughout the long night. The last time . . . ah, the last time. Meredith trembled in remembrance, for the last time had been the best. He was slow and achingly tender and the very thought of it made her tingle all over. It was near dawn before they had finally slept.

She told herself she should rise, yet the thought held little appeal. Indeed, she admitted to herself, never had she felt so safe, so warm and secure—as if nothing or no one could hurt her. Here in his arms, she thought with a pang, was the haven that had always eluded her . . . always until now.

Her gaze wandered up the strong column of his neck, to his profile, relaxed now in slumber. His lashes were long and feathery, shielding the silver of eyes that could snap like a whip—or glow with a bright, sensual haze, as they had last eve. The jutting blade of his nose bespoke an arrogance she knew would ever be present. His mouth . . . ah, his mouth! It was cleanly sculpted, and brought her a rapture she'd never known could exist. A shiver touched her spine, for never had she known a man so ruggedly masculine.

Cameron awoke with the same sense of rightness, of oneness. Though he did not open his eyes, he could feel the silken strands of red streaming across his chest. Her breath misted warmly across his skin. Some powerful emotion surged in his chest. There was something blessedly rich about waking with her in his arms, holding her like this. True, it was not the first time they had lain just so.

But this was different. She belonged to him now— belonged to him as she would never belong to another. Ruthlessly he dismissed the bastard who had stolen her innocence, for he—Cameron—had given it back and she knew it, too. He was the one who had completed her journey to womanhood, who had shown her that lovemaking was something to be shared and neither feared nor dreaded. Aye, he thought with a purely masculine swell of satisfaction, she knew it, too, else she would never have yielded her trust—and aye, her body, too—as she had during the long hours of the night.

She propped herself on her elbow, tugging the sheet so that it covered her breasts. "You are awake, Cameron. I know it."

He sighed and opened his eyes. At the sight of her peering down at him, he smiled.

Her mouth pursed indignantly. "What do you find so amusing?"

"Remember the day you told Aileen you'd kissed a toad—and found it quite disgusting?"

"What of it?"

His eyes gleamed. "It occurs to me you did not seem so disgusted by your toad last eve."

His smile was transformed into a full-blown laugh as she blushed to the roots of her hair.

"What! Am I wrong, then? Ah, clearly you find me lacking! Well, then, 'tis obvious I must endeavor to please you far better. I suppose it is like sword-play—the best way to proceed is through practice . . ."

Meredith found herself seized and hauled atop him. She blinked down at him. "Your swordplay needs no improvement," she gasped.

"Then I must find a place to sheath my sword," he said smoothly. He chuckled heartily as she grasped his meaning, for now his shaft lay sweetly cradled between her thighs. A jolt of longing shot through him. Lord, but she stirred him—stirred him mightily! He knew from the way her eyes widened that she, too, had appraised the proof of his readiness.

Reluctantly he put her from him. His gaze followed her as she slipped from the bed, dwelling long and hard on the dimpled length of her back as she washed. He experienced a twinge of regret, for she did not face him—he knew shyness and modesty precluded it; therefore he contented himself with the glimpse of rounded breast he was given when she tugged her gown over her head. Purposely he waited until she was covered before he arose. He washed and dressed,

while she rummaged through his pouch for the bread
and cheese he'd brought.

When they were done, she brushed the crumbs from
her lap. "Well," she said breathlessly, "what shall
we do today?"

A devilish brow climbed high. Her innocent com-
ment was a tempting inducement. Cameron's blood
fairly sizzled. He craved her with a hunger that startled even himself—never had he experienced a passion so keen as that which he felt for her. Were it up
to him, he would never leave the cottage—indeed,
they would never leave the bed. But above all, he did
not want to frighten her anew.

He rose to his feet and strode to the door, gesturing
her through it. "I've an idea," he said, a secret twin-
kle in his eye. Though she begged to know what they
would do, he would not tell her; rather he teased her
and told her that she must wait.

She glanced at him as they walked along a pathway
that took them inland, farther from the beach. "This
cottage, Cameron. How did you know it was here?"

"My mother was born in this cottage," he told her.
"Her family worked this land for many a year. But
once her parents died, there was no one left. Now no
one lives here."

Meredith glanced around. They had just crested a
small rise. Behind them, the surf rolled upon the
beach. Beyond, the vivid green hills undulated, fold
after fold. "What a pity no one stayed," she murmured. " 'Tis beautiful here."

"Aye," he agreed. "When I was a lad"—there
was the slightest hesitation—"my brothers and I
spent many a happy day on this isle."

His voice had gone low and husky. Meredith's
heart wrenched, for she could hear the loneliness and

longing that dwelled within. Unthinkingly, she slipped her hand in his, a wordless gesture of comfort; it seemed the most natural thing in the world. His grip tightened around hers. Hand in hand, they walked together.

Above them, a hawk turned cartwheels in the deep blue bowl of the sky. Clouds as fleecy white as the belly of a newborn lamb drifted above; their shadows dappled the grassy hills below. Cameron stopped once, putting a finger to his lips, then pointing to where a deer foraged nearby for her dinner.

Soon they came upon a small loch, surrounded by a towering stand of aspen. Sunlight slanted down from above, spilling across the surface of the loch like liquid gold. It was to a small inlet that cut into the shoreline that Cameron strode.

"I thought we might spend the rest of the morning swimming here in the loch."

"I cannot swim, and well you know it!"

"'Tis a matter I intend to rectify. 'Twas here that I learned to swim, and here that you shall as well."

Her gaze swung to the glistening waters of the loch, then back to his face. "Cameron, nay!"

"Come, now, lass. I am a good teacher, am I not?"

Her face turned the color of a glorious sunrise.

She neither agreed nor disagreed. "No doubt those waters are as frigid as—"

"Nay, 'tis warm here in this cove. There is a hot spring that feeds into the loch near that rock." He pointed to a spot near a small pile of boulders.

A slender brow rose. "Should I drown," she informed him loftily, "I will go straight to hell—and I promise I will take you with me."

"And we would not want that, now, would we? Nay, I would much rather be in heaven"—the light in his eyes was irreverent—"as we were last night."

"Cameron! You should not speak of such things!"
His grin made her heart catch. It was difficult to be
as stern as she might have wished.

" 'Tis considered manly to boast of one's prowess
with a woman."

"But should a man boast of his prowess *to* a
woman? I think not!"

"I fail to see the harm in it." As he spoke, he
dragged his tunic over his head. Unabashedly he shed
the rest of his clothing and waded into the water.

The waters of the loch glimmered invitingly, yet
she could not banish a twinge of uneasiness.

"Meredith," he called. "Do you dally a-purpose?"

She glared at him. Perhaps if he had given her fair
warning, she might have been better prepared . . . she
fooled no one, least of all herself! She could make
excuses till the end of her days, and naught would
change. Chiding herself for her cowardice, she decided reluctantly that he was right—she must learn to
swim.

"Mayhap you need assistance."

The wicked gleam in his eyes told the tale only too
well. He would be glad to lend it—and then her les-
sons would never begin! Taking a deep breath, she
discarded her slippers. Her gown followed, but that
was as far as she would go. She would not strip naked
as he did.

Wearing only her smock, she ventured forward tentatively. To her delighted surprise, he was right. The
water was not at all cold. Cautiously, she tiptoed to
where he stood. It was not deep here, but the water
lapped at the jutting ridge of his hips.

The first order of the day was to teach her to hold
her breath. She resisted mightily when he bade her

duck her head beneath the water, but he persisted until at last she complied. Once she was not quite so fearful, he decided it was time she floated on her back. Again she resisted, insisting his hands remain beneath her. When he was comfortably certain she could do it alone, he withdrew his hands.

She never even knew. Her eyes were closed, her hands churning lazily beneath the surface to keep her afloat. Holding his breath, he stepped back. After a full minute—no, two!—softly he called her name.

Her eyes opened. At the sight of him a full arm's length away, she floundered and promptly sank like a stone beneath the surface. She emerged, sputtering and glaring.

His hearty chuckle earned him a stinging spray of water straight in the face. He blinked, his smile wiped clean, and then it was her turn to laugh.

"Rogue!" she threw at him.

"Vixen!" he accused without heat.

By that time the next day, she swam slowly but cautiously across the width of the inlet. Her feet finding purchase in the sandy bottom, she stood upright. Her eyes glowing, she pushed her heavy hair back from her face.

"I did it!" she breathed. "I did it!"

One corner of his mouth tipped upward. Her exuberance made him smile. Flinging her arms around his neck, she pressed a wet, sloppy kiss on his lips.

In that instant, his very heart ceased to beat . . . it resumed with a thick, pounding throb. For she had reached out to him. She had touched him of her own volition. Elation soared within him.

She had realized it, too—her swiftly indrawn breath told him so. She snatched back her hands and would have retreated, had he let her.

He caught her by the hips. "Nay," he said. "*Nay*."

Desire blazed within him, a powerful tide of heat. The cloth of her smock was rendered sheer by the water. Her flesh gleamed white and smooth. The mounds of her breasts rose firm and round, tipped by nipples that stood impudent and erect. 'Twas a sight more brazenly erotic than if she'd stood before him naked, he thought hazily. He wanted to kiss her senseless, until nothing else existed. He wanted to plunge deep within her fiery cave till they were both shaking with need.

Meredith swallowed. The way he looked at her made her mouth go dry . . . as if he would devour her with his eyes.

His gaze dropped to her lips.

Her breath slammed to a halt in her throat. His grip had tightened, burning through the sopping fabric of her smock to sear her very skin. She was suddenly heart-stoppingly aware that her every curve lay revealed to him.

Nearby a procession of ducklings wiggled behind their mother, traipsing across the bank. Insects hummed in the dark netherworld below the trees. A fragrant breeze sighed through the willows. Neither one of them saw, nor heard.

The world veered to a dark void where there was only the two of them.

His voice was low and taut. "You enflame me."

Meredith drew a shaky breath. He touched her with naught but the callused tips of his fingers, yet she felt as if he touched her everywhere—she felt it in every fiber of her being.

"I burn for you. Do you know what that is, lass? To feel a yearning that makes you burn both inside and out?"

The heat of his gaze—and aye, the dark intensity of his words—ripped from her what modesty remained. She stared up at him, caught by the intoxicating web of his gaze, no longer caring that she stood before him almost naked.

"Where?" she asked unsteadily. "Where do you burn?"

"Here." His hand caught hers so that it rested directly above his heart. "And here." His eyes sheared directly into hers as he guided it down . . . ever down . . .

His hand closed around hers—her fingers wound tight around that turgid plane of masculine flesh.

Her pulse leaped wildly. Her gaze dropped helplessly. The water was crystalline clear here. She could see him, all of him, thick and rigid with arousal, surging boldly, for her hand encompassed but half of him.

He saw the way her eyes widened. "Do I frighten you, lass?" No, he thought. Pray God, no . . .

Her gaze shied away, only to return. "Nay," she whispered, and then again: "*Nay.*"

Triumph leaped within him, for her gaze reflected the same intense longing as his. Bending his head, he kissed her with greedy urgency, a deep, ravaging kiss that left both of them gasping.

He dragged his mouth from hers. Shifting his legs wide apart, he filled his hands with her buttocks, then slipped to the backs of her thighs. She caught at the rippling muscle of his arms, her expression dazed.

"Cameron—"

He lifted her astride him. "Wrap your legs around me," he said hoarsely, the sound as raw and molten as his gaze.

She could do nothing but comply, her heels catching together by sheer instinct. She could feel the bulging muscles of his thighs riding beneath her own. For one heart-rending moment, her mind balked at what he would do. Yet even as the thought spun through her, the swollen tip of him breached the velvet petals of her cleft. Then he was driving home, so piercing and deep she burned inside as he had vowed he burned.

A jagged moan caught in his throat. "Sweet heaven," he breathed, the words nearly lost in a rush of air. With his hands he lifted her. For one perilous moment, she was suspended above him, the sleek, ultrasensitive crown of his shaft encased tight within hot clinging flesh.

Smothering a groan, he brought her down upon him, only barely holding his desire in check, for he was determined she find her pleasure first. Again and again he lunged inside her, his hold on her almost frantic as he sought the driving, pumping rhythm that would send them both tumbling over the edge.

Meredith shuddered. His thrusts were torrid and tempestuous. She clutched at the binding of his shoulders. Waves of scorching heat shimmered all through her, scaling ever higher toward something that hovered just beyond reach.

Her hips writhed against his. Straining. Circling. Then she felt it, a starburst of ecstasy cascading all through her.

She cast back her head. He kissed the arch of her throat. Dimly she cried his name, again and again. Stark and shivering, 'twas a sound that drifted aloft to the heavens and above . . .

A sound that sped straight to his heart.

Seventeen

It was several days later when Cameron quietly announced that they would return to Dunthorpe. At the thought, a cold wind seemed to sweep across her heart. By now everyone would know that she had lain with Cameron. She remembered the jeers and leers of his clansmen when she had first arrived. A hard knot gathered in her belly. The thought that she must bear such disdain yet again filled her with dread.

Yet Cameron did not hurry their return. The day was spent lazily, as the others had been, swimming in the cove . . . and wrapped in his arms. The earth lay draped in the midnight haze of nightfall when at last they passed through the gates of Dunthorpe. To Meredith's vast relief, the bailey was nearly deserted, but for a young boy who ran up and took the reins of Cameron's steed.

Cameron pulled her down from Fortune's back. "I must see what has transpired in my absence," he said. His expression was preoccupied, his tone almost curt. "I will be in the hall. Wait for me in the tower."

Meredith nodded. A curious peace—a wondrous closeness—had marked these past days at the isle, an unspoken truce where neither MacKay nor Munro existed. The feud might never have been. For a time, they were but a man and a woman who shared the intimacies of love . . .

Love. The thought brought her up short. She was shocked to her very core, shocked that her mind had dared to conjure up such an absurd notion. Her heart knocked crazily. Surely she did not love him. Surely not!

So absorbed was she that she did not notice the tall figure that had just come around the corner near the tower stairs. She collided full tilt with a hard male form. Her head came up. She stared straight into Egan's unsmiling features.

For an instant it was as if neither knew what to do, what to say. There was a stifling silence.

Something smoldering flared in those icy blue eyes, swiftly masked. "My lady," he greeted coolly. "I take it Cameron has returned."

"Aye." Her nod was jerky. "You'll find him in the hall."

His step wide, he moved around her and would have continued on his way. Meredith turned, watching as his shadow loomed high on the stark stone wall, unable to halt the guilt that flooded her.

She took a deep breath. "Egan, wait!"

He stopped short. His shoulders came up. She read in the rigidness of his posture the desire to ignore her. Yet slowly he turned. The tautness of his jaw was discouraging, but she forced herself to go on.

"I hope that Cameron was not too angry with you, when I . . . when I . . ."

A black brow slashed upward. "When you escaped from the chapel?" he supplied coldly.

Meeting his gaze was difficult. She told herself she had no reason to feel such shame, yet she did. She winced. "Aye," she said miserably.

His eyes seemed to bore into her. "I respected your request, lady. I honored your need to be alone while you prayed."

"I know," she said quickly. She was the prisoner here—why should she apologize? Yet in truth, she could not blame him for his wariness. Still, she felt compelled to explain. "You must understand," she said, her voice low. "I was not brought here of my own free will."

"You have been treated generously, lady. Cameron did not put you under lock and key. Indeed, you have been more guest than prisoner."

Summoning her dignity, Meredith raised her chin. "I betrayed your trust," she stated quietly, "and for that I am sorry. I deceived you, and for that I am sorry as well. Yet I believe I did no more than you or any other would have done in my place. And I regret it sorely if I caused you trouble with Cameron—"

"You did not."

"Good," she said softly. "For that I am glad." The smile she sent him was dazzlingly sweet. "Good day to you, Egan."

He inclined his head stiffly. "Good day to you, lady."

Egan remained standing there long after she had glided up the stairs. Her demeanor had almost made him feel guilty—almost! Did the wench seek to bewitch him as she had bewitched his friend? But he would not be so careless again, he decided. His jaw hardened. He had been fooled once by her guileless shroud of innocence. No, he would not be so easily charmed as his chieftain—or so readily given to forgiveness!

* * *

In his chamber Meredith waited . . . and waited, yet still Cameron did not come. Succumbing to weariness, she finally slipped into bed. Sleep quickly dropped its murky veil around her, and she slept.

It was some time later that the door gave a noisy creak. Meredith came jarringly awake. Her heart bounded, for she was ever reminded of another intrusion in the dead of night.

She peered into the shadows, unable to disguise the tremor in her voice. "Cameron?"

There was a bumping sound, and then a colorfully muttered curse. "Aye," confirmed a disembodied voice.

Relief swept through her. Pushing a wild tangle of hair from her cheek, she turned so that she faced him. There were rustling sounds as he shed his clothes. A moment later the mattress gave beneath his greater weight. Strong arms reached for her, enfolding her snug against his warmth as he pressed a brief kiss upon her lips.

Her fingers tangled in the dark mat on his chest. "You taste of ale," she chided sleepily.

"And you taste of heaven," he whispered as his mouth closed over hers once more. She yielded with a sound that was half-moan, half-sigh, for the instant their lips met, a sizzling heat seared her soul, a heat that met and matched the fire of his passion. Ah, but it made no sense! She had once thought to want no man . . . What madness was this that she should want *this* one? But she could not deny him, any more than she could deny her own traitorous longing.

It was a long time later when desire cooled and their bodies parted. Cameron wound a long silken tress of her hair around his fist, as he so often did, and slept.

Near dawn, he arose. He woke her with a kiss, whispering that he had duties to attend to on his lands and would not be back until the evening meal. Meredith waited until it was almost sinfully late to rise, for with Cameron gone, she had little to occupy her time.

No one was more surprised than she to find that Egan and Finn had gone with him. Still, Meredith did not delude herself. She suspected that if she were to stray anywhere near the outer walls, one of his men would have been there to stop her. Yet her bitterness did not long remain. Late that morn outside in the bailey, she turned to find Aileen and several other children running toward her as fast as their legs would carry them.

"Meredith!" the little girl cried. "We missed ye, Meredith!"

Her brother Leith latched on to Meredith's leg with surprising strength. "Meredith! We thought ye were gone forever. Ye won't leave again, will ye? Please," he begged, "say ye won't!"

Meredith glanced down at their round little faces, their eyes both pleading and elated. Her melancholy melted, along with her heart.

It was nearly noonday when she finally left them. She was nearing the well when a lithe figure planted herself directly before her.

"Well, so you're back, eh?"

It was Moire. The dark-haired beauty proceeded to look her up and down in a way that proclaimed her dissatisfaction more clearly than words.

Meredith took a deep breath and forced a smile to her lips. "Hello, Moire," she said calmly. Despite the other woman's dislike, she did not share her enmity.

Moire ignored her greeting. She planted her fists on

her hips. "Ye should have kept running," she hissed. "Ye should have kept running and never stopped!"

This was not the first time Meredith had glimpsed the other woman's animosity. Yet now she was taken aback by the naked malice that flamed in her eyes. Before she could say a word, Moire's red lips curled into a snarl.

"He took you to his bed, but he will never take you to his heart. Never, for you are the daughter of the Red Angus. I will never forget it. Nor will he! Oh, aye," she went on viciously, "he will tire of you. He will tire of you and then he will turn to me!"

Shaken by the venom in Moire's features, from that day on Meredith did her best to avoid the other woman, for it was almost frightening. She didn't tell Cameron of the incident, for she knew not what he would say. Would he be angry with her? With Moire? Nay, surely not Moire.

He'd told her he would not marry Moire, that he had no desire to wed, not Moire or any other. The very thought of them together squeezed her heart like a clamp. Yet she would not blame him if he were drawn to her. Indeed, she'd seen many a man's eye follow the dark-haired temptress, their lust vivid on their faces. Moire was tall and voluptuous and beautiful, while she was small and plain with gaudy red hair!

Moire predicted he would tire of her—in truth, Meredith was certain that he would! Yet not a day went by that he did not take her. No, he did not put her from his bed or his chamber. Instead their nights were spent in wildly erotic discovery. She wondered what it meant . . . what it would mean, if anything! Or was it simply that he was so eager to get her with child?

In the weeks that followed, boredom vied with loneliness. Cameron brought her several ells of soft wool for some new gowns. Meredith was glad for several reasons. The first was that she intended to return Glenda's clothing as soon as her new ones were ready. The second was that her other gown was so tattered and stained she hated wearing it. She was also glad of the chance to keep her hands busy. Still, she grew tired of the hours spent in his chamber. Few of his people had warmed to her. Though the rancor in their eyes had faded, she wondered if she would ever be welcome—even if she spent a lifetime in this keep! Egan still eyed her with suspicion, as well as Finn. Most of the women remained distantly aloof.

But then something happened that sent her heart tumbling in despair.

Yesterday as she'd walked through the bailey, Thomas from the granary had nudged the man next to him.

"Daniel just returned from the south," he said, "where there was word of the Red Angus."

The other man's lip curled. "What of him?"

Thomas had hitched his chin toward Meredith. "They say that upon hearing of his daughter's supposed death, he shut himself away for more than a fortnight and would speak to no one," he boasted, "and when he finally emerged, he was but a shadow of himself." He smiled broadly. "Mayhap Cameron will send him to his death yet. 'Tis what he deserves, eh?"

The other man's reply was lost on Meredith. Quickly she veered away from the pair, pretending she hadn't heard.

Yet she had worried the night through. Was Papa all right? Was he well? Though she'd been young, she well remembered how stricken he'd been after her mother died. He was no longer a young man. Would grief now send him to his deathbed?

No. *No!* she told herself. She couldn't allow herself to think like this, to believe such a thing might happen. And he was not alone, she reminded herself. There was Uncle Robert to care for him.

Yet her mood remained melancholy. Breaking her father's spirit had been Cameron's intention all along. Now that he had, no doubt, she decided bitterly, he would be ecstatic. Yet he did not speak of his triumph to her; and she would not remind him. Papa was alive, she told herself, and that was the only thing that mattered.

She spent the rest of the morning trying to sew, but her heart was not in it; her seams were crooked and uneven. Finally, she put it aside and wandered down to the hall.

Autumn approached and the day outside was drizzly and wet. Many of the men had already eaten, but a group of women still remained for the noonday meal. She eyed the empty table near the hearth with disfavor; when Cameron was not about, it was where she took her meals. Glancing back at the women, a hint of rebellion squared her shoulders.

She approached the table where the women sat. Among them was Adele—Aileen and Leith's mother—and Glenda as well. Their idle chatter and laughter filled the air. Lifting her chin, she calmly took a seat at the end of the bench.

One by one the voices fell silent. A deadly pall fell over the group. Baleful eyes pricked her with their glare—pricked her very heart.

She was on her feet before she knew it. A hot ache nearly closed her throat, but she paid no heed. Blinking back angry tears, she raised her chin aloft. Her hands balled into fists at her sides.

"What have I done"—she hauled in a deep, unsteady breath—"that you should treat me so? As a child, I lived in fear of the dreaded Clan MacKay. But I have lived among you these many days—lived as one of you—and you are no different than my own people! Your children come to me with arms upraised. I have raised neither voice nor hand to you, nor would I! Yet you shun me as if I carried the taint of leprosy!

"God knows I do not hate you, nary a one of you. Nor do I understand why you should hate me so, for never have I harmed you!" She set free the storm in her soul, her voice shaking with the depth of her emotion. "Aye, I am a Munro, but I am not your enemy and I do not regard you as mine! 'Tis men who continue to fight," she declared fervidly, "men who prolong this bloody feud. The little ones I held in my arms only yesterday—Aileen and Leith and all the others—there are children just as young and innocent at Castle Munro. It makes me bleed inside to know that very soon hatred will darken their hearts—and why, I ask? Because our fathers and husbands and brothers say it is so, that it has always been so! Yet we all pay the price for their stubbornness, every one of us, and for the life of me, I know not why this feud began! I know only that I fear it will never end!" With that she spun and fled toward the stairs.

In the hall there was a stunned silence. A dozen pair of rounded eyes glanced at each other.

It was Judith, sister to Meghan, who said slowly, "Why *do* we feud with the Munros?"

One woman nodded sagely. " 'Tis because they refused to let us cross their lands."

"That is not what I was told," protested her neighbor. " 'Twas because they stole our sheep!"

"Nay, 'twas not sheep that was stolen! 'Twas the chieftain's favorite gyrfalcon."

"Which chieftain was that?"

" 'Twas Alexander, grandfather to Ronald."

"Alexander! That is not right!" This came from Meghan. "The trouble began when Edgar was chieftain!"

"Nay, 'twas Edgar's bride who was stolen away!"

"I shall ask my husband," Meghan said stoutly.

"Yer husband!" another scoffed. "Do ye think he will know any more than we do? The girl is right. This feud has gone on for a hundred years or more and we know not why!"

Meredith did not know that Cameron had seen her jump up from the table. On his way to the gatehouse, her outburst stopped him cold. He paused just inside the doorway listening, for her voice carried clearly. He caught just a glimpse of her as she charged toward the tower stairs.

Tears shone bright and glistening in her beautiful eyes.

A pang shot through him. He had deliberately blinded himself to how lonely she must be, ever the outcast, to all but him. Guilt rode heavy on his soul at the helplessness, the sadness he sensed in her. It was his fault, he realized, his alone.

The thought was not particularly palatable.

In truth, he had not wanted to examine too closely his reasons for keeping her with him. He'd brought her here in order to take his revenge upon the Red Angus . . .

He'd kept her solely for himself.

Almost from the beginning, he'd wanted her.

Wanted her with a raging fever he'd never felt for another. He'd given little thought to her feelings. And only now did he admit the truth . . .

Her beauty was not just in face and form, breath-takingly lovely though she was. No, he thought slowly, hers was a beauty that resided in the heart as well. Many a time he'd seen her with the children—she was caring and kind and loving to all.

It was later that day when he entered his chamber. Meredith sat on the side of the bed, pale but dry-eyed. He would take his cue from her, he decided in that instant. If she mentioned the incident in the hall with the women of the keep, he would not keep from her the knowledge that he'd witnessed her outburst; but if she chose to ignore it, then so would he.

Peeling off his tunic, he dropped it on the floor. He was wet to the skin, having just crossed from the stable in a downpour. "Meredith," he called, "would you fetch a dry tunic from my chest?"

Wordlessly she arose. Opening his chest, she pulled the soft woolen garment from atop the neatly folded pile of his clothing. She was just about to close it when the glint of metal in the corner caught her eye. Bending low, she peered closer, then caught her breath.

It was her crucifix, the one he'd snatched from about her neck the day he'd stolen her away from Connyridge. But it was no longer intact; one of the shining silver links was detached from the other so that it could no longer be worn.

Raw pain sliced through her. She felt as if a piece of her heart had been chipped away.

As Cameron stepped near to retrieve the tunic which hung over her arm, he saw the chain dangling from her fingers.

At his approach, she looked up at him, her expression stricken. " 'Tis broken," she said faintly. "My crucifix is broken."

Cameron had dropped the necklace in his chest upon his return from Connyridge. In all honesty, he'd forgotten it was there.

Disappointment was plainly written on her features. " 'Tis but a cross," he said quickly. "Another can easily be gained."

" 'Tis not the same." She shook her head. " 'Tis not the same!"

He frowned. "Do you value it so highly, then?"

"I valued it above all else," she said, her voice very low.

"How came you by it? Did the sisters—"

"Nay." Her voice cut across his. She hesitated. " 'Twas a gift from my father," she confided. "He gave it to me the day I entered Connyridge. He reminded me that God would always be with me—as would he."

At the mention of her father, the muscles of his face seemed to freeze. His expression grew painfully aloof. She could almost see him curling inside himself. Before she could say anything more, he plucked the necklace from her palm. She watched as he crossed to his chest and dropped it within. Her heart twisted.

It seemed his hatred was fired as keenly as ever. Without a word, he left the chamber. Indeed, she wondered that he did not destroy it then and there.

He didn't return until late in the evening. The cast of his profile was not so grim as before, yet Meredith was not given to leniency just then. She ignored him as he strode to stand before the fire. With her lips compressed, she confined her attention to combing her hair, aware of his scrutiny. The lengthy strands crackled and flowed out about her shoulders and down her back, a mantle of living flame. But to Meredith it was wild and untamed. She pulled the comb through the strands once more, then dropped it in frustration. Pulling it into a long rope over one shoulder, she separated it into three lengths with her fingers.

"Nay," came his voice. "Do not plait it."

Her chin firmed. "I want it plaited. It gets too tangled if it is not."

"You've not slept with it plaited since you came to me," he pointed out.

Meredith's eyes flashed. "I did not come to you!" she flared. "You stole me away! And I did sleep with it plaited. Always until then!"

All at once he was there before her. Strong hands curled about her own. He tugged her to her feet.

"What is amiss, Meredith?"

She gazed up at him, the soft line of her lips faintly defiant. Yet deep within her, she knew it was but a token gesture. There was a frown etched between his brows. His expression was fraught with concern.

Meredith trembled inside. Ah, but she wished he would rage and storm. Then she could have hated him, defied him . . . or at least tried to!

"Can you not tell me?"

A maelstrom of confusion warred in her breast. He was so gentle. So sweetly tender. Once she had been afraid of his strength . . . but now she feared his tenderness far more. She should have hated him for all he had done to her, yet she could not. Indeed, when his mouth brushed hers, it was all she could do not to twine her arms about his neck and cling to him.

She could lie to herself no more. The very sight of him made her knees weak and turned her blood afire. Oh, she'd told herself she yielded to him because it was the only way she could gain her freedom. But once she'd lain with him, her passion rose up to meet his own. Aye, she thought bleakly, she had been tempted by the pleasures of the flesh—she had bowed to their lure with pitiful resistance.

And now . . . now she was ashamed of her weakness, that she had allowed him to make his will her own.

Fiercely she berated herself. Always she was afraid. Of water, though she had at last learned to swim. Of men. Of the uncertainty of the future . . .

A finger beneath her chin, he brought her face to his. "Meredith," he said again, "can you not tell me?"

The breath she drew was deep and ragged—it felt like fire in her lungs. "You leech my will from me," she said, her voice very low. "You render it your own and I—I hate myself, for I am ever meek and fearful!"

Cameron was sorely tempted to laugh. Meek? he wondered in amazement. Fearful?

"Surely you jest!"

"I do not. Women are weak"—bitterness edged her tone—"and I am weaker than most!"

Cameron could not help but be reminded of all she'd said at the noon meal.

"Is there no strength in softness?" he noted quietly. "A man tests his might with his sword arm. He fights with dagger and dirk. But women possess a strength that cannot be seen. They wait while the men ride off to war, tending to children, even defending their home if need be. They share the burden when their men falter." Lean hands closed over her shoulders. His gaze delved directly into hers. "As for you, you were incredibly brave the night I took you from

Connyridge, braver than many a man.'' She had taunted him as many a man would never dare to do, and so he told her. "Never," he finished intently, "have I met a woman with more courage and strength than you."

Her eyes grew stormy. "You say that only because you wish to bed me!"

"Oh, aye, that I do"—a gleam in his eyes, he swept her high in his arms—"but I say it because it is true." Laying her on the bed, he kissed the mutinous swell from her lips—kissed her until the faint accusation in her eyes glimmered no more and they were both left breathless and gasping.

As always when he touched her, his body clamored for release. But Cameron did not take her, for she seemed disarmingly defenseless just now, her emotions laid naked and bare before him. He sensed her admission cost her pride greatly, and everything within him compelled him to offer what comfort he could. Instead he wrapped her in his embrace, nestled her tight against his side. Urging her head into the hollow of his shoulder, he brushed his mouth across the softness of her temple and buried his lips in the flaming cloud of her hair. He was feeling protective of her just now, though he dared not ask himself why.

It was a long time later that he broke the silence that had enveloped them.

"Meredith," he said quietly.

"Aye?" She stirred. He knew by the blurriness of her voice that she'd been on the verge of sleep.

"The man who took you from your bedchamber at Castle Munro. He spoke to you. Called you by name. He was not a stranger, then, was he? It must have been someone who knew you—who dwelled within the castle walls."

She hid her face against his shoulder. "I don't want to think about it," she said, her voice muffled. "Please, I cannot!"

He felt the shudder that went through her—the memory haunted her still! His arms tightened. "I'm sorry, sweet. I'm sorry. I should never have spoken." Brushing his lips against her temple, he cursed himself for distressing her so.

In time she fell asleep. Yet her sleep was restless. In the night, she wept, tears that blotted his soul like blackened stains. She was miserable, and the blame rested solely on his shoulders. So what the devil was he to do? Send her back to the Red Angus? Or back to Connyridge?

His jaw clenched hard. Nay, he thought blackly. *Nay!* The thought of either was untenable. In that moment, he sealed a bargain within his own heart. He would never let her go. Never.

She was his . . . and so she would remain.

Eighteen

When Meredith awoke the next morning, Cameron was gone. With a sigh, she shifted to her side. Unbidden, her hand crept out to touch the place where he'd lain—the sheets were still warm from his body.

Her eyes grew cloudy. She didn't understand him. Indeed, she feared she never would. When he'd learned her crucifix had been a gift from her father, she'd felt his coldness like a vast sea of ice. The certainty was like a thorn in her heart. He hated her father so . . . did he hate her, too?

Silly fool! scoffed a voice in her head. Does he treat you as if he hates you?

Little by little, the tension seeped from her limbs. He did not. He'd been achingly tender last night, his arms a haven that shielded her from all harm. But in all the weeks since they'd returned from the isle, this was the first night he'd not bedded her.

Her mind raced and there was no help for it. Had his desire waned already? Had he abandoned his quest for a son of her?

A niggling voice within whispered she should have been relieved, for mayhap he would release her. Ah, but would he turn to Moire, then? At the thought of Cameron with the dark, voluptuous beauty, there was

246

a betraying little catch in her breast. Why? her heart cried. Why was it so? She shouldn't have cared who he bedded, as long as it was not her! God knew she could never hate him, but she should have been glad of the chance to gain her freedom.

Long minutes passed before she told herself to rise. A frown pleated her brow, for of late it had been a supreme effort to drag herself from bed in the morn. At the priory she had always risen promptly at dawn, coming instantly awake, yet now the thought of rising so early wrought a groan. Chiding herself for her laziness, she swung her feet to the floor and rose.

For an instant her head spun dizzily. Her belly heaved, like giant waves sloshing in her middle. Saints beware, was she sickening? This had happened nearly every day for the past fortnight. Several times she'd even lost her morning meal. Too, her breasts seemed swollen and sometimes hurt to touch. Was it the same sickness? Yet by the time she'd washed and dressed, the dizziness and queasiness had passed.

Downstairs in the great hall, she winced, unable to smother her dismay. The women of the keep were gathered at a table. In order to exit the hall for the chapel, her path would take her directly past them. For a moment, she thought to flee before she was seen.

But that was the coward's way, she told herself. She would not quail in her room, feeling sorry for herself. Dredging up the strength from somewhere deep inside, she angled her chin high and moved forward, determined not to let their coolness wound her anymore. She glanced neither to the right nor the left.

"My lady, will you break your fast with us?"

Her ears had surely deceived her. Surely one of them had not said . . .

"Meredith! Meredith, please stop!"

There was no mistaking the sound of her name. Meredith's pace slowed to a halt. Ah, but she was sorely tempted to ignore the call. Yet something inside would not let her. Squaring her shoulders, she summoned both pride and dignity and turned to face the table.

From the corner of her eye, she saw Glenda. Like yesterday, Moire was not present. But it was Adele—Aileen and Leith's mother—who rose to her feet, glancing at the others as she did. Odd, Meredith noted dimly, but Adele looked as frightened as she felt. Yet Meredith was determined not to show her fear.

"Aye?" she said quietly.

Two bright spots of color had appeared on Adele's plump cheeks. "Lady," she said quickly, "we have thought much on all you said yesterday. We have talked . . . all of us here . . . and—and 'twould seem we have misjudged you. You are right. As women, we share a bond that . . . that men canna understand. And 'tis our hope that—that mayhap we can learn from each other."

"Aye," someone called from the far end of the table, "she speaks for all of us, she does."

"Aye, we are heartily ashamed of our pettiness, and ask your forgiveness."

This last came from Meghan, who had once denounced her so cruelly. Meredith was stunned, scarcely able to believe her ears. She searched the faces of those present, yet neither mockery nor disdain dwelled within their faces. All appeared contritely earnest—all but Glenda, who sat at the far end with her hands folded before her, her lashes lowered.

Meredith's throat constricted. This was one morning her prayers could wait, she decided suddenly, for the impossible had happened; these women had extended a hand of friendship, and she would not thrust it aside.

Somehow she managed a watery smile. She saw them all through a misty blur. "Ladies"—she couldn't control the slight quaver in her voice—"I would be glad to break bread with you."

Hands tugged her down on the bench. "Och, now, lassie, dinna cry!" An arm slid around her shoulders and gave her a quick hug.

Across the table there was a toothy grin. "Ye've a heart of puddin', 'tis plain to see!"

The morning passed far more quickly than she could have imagined. For the first time a tiny kernel of hope took root in her heart; for the first time she felt she might not forever be the outcast. Yet when next she glanced at the end of the table, she discovered that Glenda had slipped away.

It was several days later as the women left the table that a tremendous wave of giddiness caught her in its sway.

"Meredith," said a voice. "Meredith!"

It seemed to come from an immense distance. Spots of black and gray swam before her. A roaring sound buzzed in her ears. She stretched out a hand, for the floor beneath her feet tilted alarmingly.

The next thing she knew, she was lying prone on the rushes. A dozen faces peered down at her.

"Give 'er some air," someone said, "and fetch Cameron."

"Meredith. Meredith, can ye speak?"

"Aye," she said unsteadily. She stretched out a hand to push herself to a sitting position.

A hand slipped into her elbow. "Careful, now, lest ye fall and give us a fright again!"

It was Adele. Meredith took a deep breath while the world righted itself. "I didn't mean to frighten anyone." She gave a slight shake of her head. "It isn't like me to be so sickly, but I fear I've had such spells often of late."

Several of the woman exchanged glances. "Have ye been feeling poorly in the morn?"

Meredith tipped her head to the side and regarded Meghan. "Aye. I have. But how did you know?"

No one answered. Instead someone said, "Have ye lost yer meals?"

"Indeed I have. Several times, in fact."

Still no answer. "Yer courses, milady. When did ye last have yer courses?"

Meredith flushed, then pondered a moment. "Just before I came here." Again that strange look passed among the women. Meredith frowned. "What is it? Do you know what ails me?"

"Dinna worry"—someone flashed a grin—"it will not last much longer."

"Hah!" came a vehement protest. "I retched nearly every day!"

"No doubt 'twill not be verra long before yer belly begins to swell."

Her bewilderment had turned to outright fright. "What!" she cried anxiously. "What is wrong with me?"

"Ye were too long in the convent," Miriam said cheerfully. "Yer breeding."

"Breeding," Meredith repeated, then blanched. "Do you mean to say I'm . . ." Faith, but she could scarcely bring herself to say it.

Meghan had no such trouble. "There can be no doubt, lassie," she said with a lusty chuckle, "yer with child."

The announcement could not have come at a worse time. With a gasp Meredith looked up to see that Cameron had stepped up. He towered over all of them. Another time, and the expression of astonishment that washed over his features would have struck her as humorous.

But not just now. Sweet heaven, not now . . .

For he laughed, the wretch—he threw back his head and laughed!

There could be no doubt he was pleased. The women parted in unison as he made his way forward. His eyes alight, a smile upon his lips the likes of which they'd not seen for many a month, he stooped and gathered her against his chest. In one swift move he was on his feet. The women whispered among themselves as he bore her toward the stairs.

"Do ye think the babe is his?"

"Of course it's his! He took her to his bed all but that verra first night!"

"Did ye see the look on his face? Oh, I vow he'll be a proud papa indeed."

" 'Tis exactly what he needs. With a child he'll not grieve so over the loss of his father and brothers."

"Do ye think he'll marry her?"

"Marry a Munro? Once I would have said never in this world! But he is fond of her, so who can say?"

Someone sighed. "Ah, but I wish my 'usband would look at me the way he looks at her."

Meredith did not hear their whispers. As Cameron whirled and turned toward the tower stairs, she caught a glimpse of Moire over one broad shoulder. What she saw nearly made her cry out. Moire's eyes glittered with ill-concealed malice.

In his chamber, her heart thumped wildly as he eased her onto the bed.

"How are you now, lass?"

Meredith was still reeling. She was with child—with child! Saints, but it all seemed like a dream!

She took a deep, fortifying breath. "Better," she murmured.

He laid his palm against her cheek. His gaze captured hers.

"You did not know, did you?"

Though she longed to look away, she couldn't. "Nay," she said faintly. "In truth, I had no idea what to expect . . . what to look for."

His lips twitched as he fought against a smile. "Miriam was right. You were too long in the convent—though I can see why they did not speak of such things." He paused. "I'm surprised your mother did not tell you."

"She died when I was but eight. When I started my monthly flux"—she felt her cheeks heat, but she plunged ahead anyway—"one of the elderly women told me it was the curse of Eve. She said that it was her penance for sinning in the Garden, a penance that must be paid by all women. She said that the pain of childbirth was the most terrible pain a woman could bear." She shivered, for she'd forgotten those words until this very moment.

Cameron cursed the woman vilely, for he could hear the sudden fright in her voice. Weaving his fingers through hers, he brought her hands to his lips. "Don't be afraid, lass." His eyes held hers. "I will be at your side, I promise." A faint smile formed on his lips. "Besides," he added, "where else would I be when my son is born?"

Her eyes flared. "Your son?" she snapped. "What makes you so certain this babe is yours?"

"A silly question, lass, and well you know it. But

I see, you seek to wound me. Yet today . . .'tis impossible!''

Her attempt at a glare failed miserably. His eyes were dancing, as clear as a rushing stream. Something caught at her heart, something she could not deny. Never had she seen him so happy, so clearly elated. And when he stretched out beside her and brought her mouth to his, she parted her lips with a tremulous little sigh. Her arms crept tight about his neck.

As always, her nearness made him throb. But when he felt those slender arms steal around his neck, the way her lips parted beneath his with a breathy sound of pleasure, his chest filled with a wild elation. His hands moved restlessly over her back. Filling his palms with the roundness of her buttocks, he rolled suddenly.

Now she was the one who lay atop him. With a soft cry, her mouth broke free of his. She half-rose above him. He smiled at her bewildered confusion.

''Cameron—''

''Hush, lass.'' Burning inside, he tugged her gown down over her shoulders, baring her to the waist.

His eyes darkened. His smile faded.

Even as she watched, he splayed his fingers wide over both breasts. The contrast between his tanned fingers and her pale white flesh was riveting. His fingers shifted so that her flesh jutted high and full. In some faraway corner of her mind, she noted that her breasts were fuller, her nipples tinged a darker hue of rose. His thumbs raked across the turgid peaks. Gentle though he was, she winced.

Gray eyes flashed to her face. ''Are you tender there, sweet?''

''A little,'' she admitted.

She felt herself drawn down against him. Husky

laughter drifted across her cheek. "Then I'll have to find some other way to please you, won't I?"

In seconds they were both naked. He fed on her mouth endlessly.

He raised his head, his eyes glittering. One lean hand rested possessively on the silken hollow of her belly, for she was still as slender as ever. "Aye, this child is mine, and I'll kill any man who dares touch you."

His whisper was heated and intense; it sent a thrill all through her. With a moan Meredith caught his head in her hands and guided it to hers.

But he was not content with only her lips. A brazen finger slid through the soft down at the joinder of her thighs, then dipped boldly within. Heat unfurled within her, for now he traced a shattering path along her furrowed channel. Another finger joined the first, their wicked rhythm a tempting inducement of what was to come.

His mouth followed suit, trailing a forbidden pathway down the ladder of her ribs, across the satin plane of her belly. Down, ever down . . . until his lips grazed the thatch of curls that guarded her innermost sanctum.

Her breath caught in her throat. Her head rose off the pillow. "Cameron!" she said faintly. "Cameron, nay!"

He did not stop.

"Aye, lass. *Aye!*"

His tone was starkly compelling. Dazedly she felt the powerful sweep of arms around her hips. Her heart lurched. Instinctively she tried to clench her legs together, but he would have none of it.

He gave an odd little laugh. "Nay, sweet, do not deny me." Even as he spoke, with the breadth of his shoulders he spread her quaking limbs, leaving her open and vulnerable to his hands, his eyes . . .

And his mouth.

Her cheeks flooded crimson. Her pulse thundered in her ears. To her utter shock, warm breath swirled against her, stirring damp red curls. He kissed the tender inside of each thigh. With his thumbs he parted her.

She gasped at that first wanton stroke of his tongue, for never in her life had she imagined such an intimate caress. His mouth was tormentingly elusive, coming close to yet never quite touching the center of sensation hidden within sleek pink folds. A thousand shivers raced along her spine. She thrust her cleft against him, a wordless plea for him to end this torture.

God above, he did.

At last he breached her, the lash of his tongue blatantly erotic against her swollen core, tasting the dew of a passion that spun wild and out of control. Dimly she heard herself cry out as pleasure reached its zenith, carrying her to the stars and beyond.

She was still moaning when he braced himself above her, his eyes blazing, his arms bulging. He filled his hands with the smoothness of her buttocks. She couldn't look away as he came inside her, tight and thick, embedded so deep that coarse dark hairs mingled with the flame of hers.

"Meredith," he said tautly. "*Meredith!*"

There was no holding back for either of them. The kiss they shared was fiercely ravenous, his thrusts torrid and hot. Feeling the hunger in him, the silver glitter of his gaze, knowing he wanted her so made her all giddy and hot inside. Her hips began to circle and writhe, churning with the tempo of his. She felt her passage tighten and contract around his rigid thickness, again and again. Then everything exploded inside and she was flung high aloft yet again.

Her convulsive shudder but spurred his own. His breath ragged, Cameron kissed the arch of her neck, the place where her pulse thrummed wildly at the base of her throat. He plunged wildly. Once. Twice. Thrice. With a jagged groan, his scalding seed erupted deep within her.

In the aftermath his fingers twined with hers. Easing to his side, he carried their joined hands to the center of his chest; his hand engulfed the small one curled trustingly within his own.

A son, he thought in amazement. I will have a son! A laugh of sheer pleasure rumbled from his chest.

But Cameron was not laughing several days later. In three days Meredith had eaten nothing and drank little, for when she tried, her stomach rebelled. Desperate, he sought out Glenda, for he was well aware she knew of the travails of pregnancy. Hurriedly he told her of Meredith's plight.

"She is so weak she can scarcely lift her head from the pillow," he finished grimly. "Can you help her?"

Glenda's hesitation was almost nonexistent. Her heart went out to him, for Cameron's expression was harried—he was clearly distraught. Concern for his child? she wondered. Or both . . . ?

She strongly suspected it was both. Laying her hand on his forearm, she gave it a reassuring squeeze. "I will go to her," she promised softly.

Abovestairs, Meredith's head still whirled. She'd just stumbled back to the bed from the chamber pot, which now held the contents of her stomach. The door creaked. Footsteps approached.

The thick, dull pounding of her heart seemed to echo through her entire body. "I will be fine," she muttered, thinking it was Cameron, too exhausted to open her eyes. "Just give me a moment."

She heard the splash of water in the basin. The mattress dipped. Vaguely it registered in her mind that the weight there was not enough to be Cameron. At the same instant, a cool wet cloth swept down her cheek. She turned into it gratefully, for she felt both clammy and hot. Beads of perspiration dotted her upper lip.

The cool wetness settled on her forehead. Her eyelids fluttered open. Glenda's sweet features swam before her. Meredith would surely have gaped in startled surprise, had she possessed the energy.

Instead she heard herself mutter, "You should not be here." Her lids drifted closed. She welcomed the darkness that swirled around her and let exhaustion lead her to sleep. She dozed lightly, and when she opened her eyes, the room was much brighter.

Glenda was still there.

Seeing that she was awake, the other woman moved to the bedside. Gentle hands eased her back to the bed. "Do not rise yet"—the command came in firm but dulcet tones—"for I would have you eat something first."

Meredith paled. "I cannot eat."

"You must," Glenda encouraged, "for the sake of the babe. Please, 'tis but dry bread. Will you at least try?"

Doe-soft eyes met those of fairest blue, one pleading, the other guardedly wary.

Finally Meredith nodded. One morsel at a time, Glenda handed her the dry, crusty bread, instructing her to stay as still as possible while she ate. A full quarter hour later, Meredith was shocked that she'd not had to bolt from the bed and rush for the chamber pot.

Glenda came near. "How do you feel?"

"Better," Meredith admitted.

"You look better," Glenda observed. "There is more color in your cheeks."

Meredith turned her head so that she did not have to strain so to see the other woman. "How is it you knew 'twould help?" she asked after a moment.

Glenda smiled slightly. "My mother was a midwife in the Border lands, before her hands became so gnarled with age that she could no longer use them. She knew much about the birthing of babes, and I listened well." She paused. "It may help to keep dry crusts of bread at your bedside, to eat when you first awaken, but before you rise. 'Tis a remedy passed on from my mother, from her mother before her, and hers before that."

Meredith nodded. An awkward silence cropped up. She sensed that neither she nor Glenda knew what to say.

"Glenda, there is no need for you to remain. I know you are here because Cameron bade you come." It slipped out before she could stop it, and then she could have kicked herself. She hadn't meant to sound petty and mean, yet one glimpse of the distress on Glenda's face and she feared she had. Yet before she could say a word, Glenda raised her head. Tears stood high and bright in the golden brown of her eyes

"That is why I came," Glenda said slowly, "but that is not why I stayed." She paused. "I must be honest," she said in a low, choked voice. "I hate what your clansmen did to Niall, to his family . . . but I can-

not hate *you*. Oh, I wanted to''—suddenly it was all
tumbling out in a rush, and she could not stop it—
''aye, I tried so very hard! Yet the more I saw of you,
the more I *see* you, the more I come to know you . . .''
Her tears spilled over into her voice. She began to
sob. ''Oh, Meredith, I cannot do it. What you said a
few days ago—you are right. We are no different than
you! As women, we share a bond that mayhap no man
can ever understand. Oh, don't you see . . . I—I cannot hate you!''

Meredith was struck dumb. Then, as she realized
what Glenda was saying, a wellspring of emotion
poured through her. She pushed herself from the bed.

Her arm slipped around the MacKay woman's
shoulder. ''Glenda. Glenda, please, do not cry—else
you will make me weep as well! For nothing would
please me more than to call you my friend!''

''Truly?'' Glenda's gaze sought hers.

''Oh, aye, Glenda. Aye!''

Suddenly they were hugging each other, both weeping and laughing at one and the same time.

A short while later Meredith tipped her head to the
side. ''You said your mother was from the Border
lands. How did she come to live in the Highlands?''

''She didn't,'' Glenda said quickly. ''Both of my
parents were Lowlanders. I did not come to live in
the Highlands—here at Dunthorpe—until after my
marriage to Niall.''

Meredith was stunned to learn that when Glenda
had first arrived, she, too, had felt like an outsider.
Highlanders were a breed unto their own, and often
looked askance at Lowlanders. Nor, Glenda confided,
had it been easy to come and live among strangers.

Nor was her marriage to Niall a love match, at least
not at first. Indeed, Glenda did not lay eyes on him

until the day they were wed! Their fathers had fostered together and grown to be great friends, so much so that they pledged their firstborn son and daughter would marry, did God allow it.

The hours sped by; Glenda stayed well into the afternoon. It was odd, yet Meredith felt she'd known Glenda all of her life! Somehow she'd known it would be so. By then Meredith was feeling much more like herself. She was painfully ignorant of such matters as carrying a babe, but Glenda was patient and she felt no embarrassment. By Glenda's calculations, Meredith was stunned to learn, she was nearly three months gone.

It was much later that Meredith walked her to the arched doorway.

Glenda reached out and gave her a quick hug. "I'll check on you in the morn," she promised. "If you're feeling up to it, will you share the morning meal with the rest of us?"

Meredith swallowed. "Everyone knows, don't they?"

Glenda's heart went out to her. "Aye," she said softly.

Meredith's heart plummeted. Hot shame washed through her. "How can I?" she said miserably. "How can I ever hold my head up again? Everyone is surely convinced that I am a harlot—and I am!"

Glenda spoke firmly. "Nay, you are not! No one will condemn you for what he did. He took you to his bed and you had no choice in the matter! There are times a man will have his way, and there is little a woman can do."

Meredith's eyes avoided hers. "You do not understand. I am. I am a harlot, a Jezebel!"

Glenda was puzzled. "Meredith, it was bound to

happen, so do not judge yourself so harshly! Oh, I know not why, but this babe will be a kind of healing not only for Cameron, but for everyone! And I am not the only one to think thusly!''

"That is not why he wanted this child . . . why he wants a son! 'Tis to make me pay, a way to give back a part of what my clansmen took from him. He said that if I gave him a son he would release me!'' Self-loathing poured through her, like boiling oil. "And I agreed—I agreed!''

Glenda was stunned. "What! He said he would free you, if you gave him a son?''

"Aye.''

"But Meredith . . . how can you bear this babe, and then leave?''

Meredith went utterly cold inside. "I do not know,'' she whispered. "God help me, I do not know!''

She was suddenly shaking from head to toe. What had she done? she thought helplessly. Sweet Jesus, what had she done?

Nineteen

In the weeks that followed, it was a question that plagued her no end. Meredith was more confused than ever. In those wondrous days that followed their time together on the isle, she had put the possibility from her mind—the chance that his seed would find fertile ground within her—foolishly. Oh, so foolishly! Though she longed to feel frozen inside, she could not.

Yet now the moment of truth was upon her. Until now, she'd dared not think of it. But now she had no choice. A child grew inside her, a child of her own blood. Long before the day she felt that first faint flutter of movement in her womb, she knew . . .

She could never give this child up. She could never abandon her bairn.

Yet how could she forsake her very heart?

She thought of her father. How did he fare now that he thought his only child dead and gone? If Cameron had his way, it would always be so, for she was certain he would never discharge the vengeance in his heart. Aye, if Cameron had his way, Papa would never know of his grandchild, the grandchild that would have brought sunshine into his life and tears of joy to his eyes.

Bleak acceptance was not so easy.

So what was she to do?

She might well have been cleaved in two, caught between the man who had sired her . . . and the man who had seized her very heart for his own as surely as he'd seized her from the priory.

For when night cast its murky veil upon the earth, she could not deny her own treacherous longing. In the dark of night—and aye, even sometimes in the day!—he whispered tenderly of the delight he found in her embrace.

Cameron was clearly elated at her pregnancy. At times, Meredith couldn't help but resent him for it. Deep in her heart, she knew that Glenda was right— he would have had what he wanted whether she wished it or no. He had imposed his will upon her, and her swelling belly was but the proof. He would have what he wanted, and no doubt a son!

Yet he was caring and tender—he treated her as if she were precious! She had only to rise and he was there, lending his arm. Glenda was convinced it was her he wanted, but Meredith was not deceived. She was but the receptacle that housed his child.

It was Glenda who helped her through the early bouts of sickness. In the short time that they had grown to know each other, Meredith came to love her as surely as she would have loved her own sister. She knew it was difficult for Glenda, having endured the loss of her own bairn—a bairn she'd waited nearly five years to have. Indeed, Glenda had thought she was barren. Somehow that only made her loss all the more heart-rending. She ached inside for Glenda, and could only hope that Glenda might someday find a man to love and cherish her as Niall had done.

She voiced the concern one day. "Glenda, what of

you?'' she asked. ''You have remained here these many months. Do you ever long to return to your home in the Borders?''

For an instant, a faraway wistfulness dwelled in Glenda's golden eyes. ''Sometimes,'' she said after a moment. ''But my parents are gone, taken three winters past. My uncle still lives in the keep. During my time here, I came to know and love Niall's brothers as my own. Dunthorpe is my home now and 'tis hard to think of leaving.''

Meredith reached out and touched her hand. '' 'Tis my hope that you will someday find someone to love as you loved Niall. You are so young to be widowed and—and it pains me greatly to think that you might be alone for the rest of your life. I will pray that—''

''Nay, Meredith, do not, for such a thing can never come to pass!'' Glenda's tone was low and fervent. ''I have resigned myself to widowhood. Never will I marry again—never. Oh, I know you do not understand! But I could not bear to lose a husband and child ever again. 'Tis far better that I am alone.''

Her words were scored with bitterness. Though Meredith did not entirely agree, clearly it was a subject best left alone for now.

It was some weeks later that she found herself confiding she was hardly averse to Cameron's touch.

A faint blush stole into Glenda's cheeks as she remembered how she'd gone eagerly into Niall's arms, almost from the very first . . . to the very last. '' 'Tis no sin to enjoy fleshly pursuits with a man,'' Glenda said softly.

''It is when the man is not your husband.'' It was a painful truth that Meredith admitted. No matter that he'd taken her to his bed, no matter that he was solicitous and sweet, he did not love her. Of a certainty

he would never marry her. How could he? she reflected bitterly. He would never forget that she was a
Munro. No doubt he still regarded her as his fiercest
adversary.

It was a burden that dragged at her spirit. To be
unwed, yet bear a babe . . . she felt dirty. Shamed. Yet
again she despised her weakness, weakness of both
body and will. She could only pray—and she did!—
that God would forgive her transgressions . . . that he
would forgive her many failings.

For Meredith could not forget what Moire had said.
*He took you to his bed, but he will never take you to
his heart. Never, for you are the daughter of the Red
Angus.*

Of late it took but a single thought and her throat
grew tight with unshed tears. Though Glenda had assured her that women in her condition were inclined
to weepiness, it seemed her emotions ran riot. To
Meredith it was but one more sign of her weakness.

She caught sight of Moire and Cameron one drizzly
morn from the tower window. The day was dark and
dreary, an ominous reflection of her mood. The rain
began to fall in drenching sheets from a leaden sky.
Cameron raised his plaid high above her head to
shield her. Together they ran across the bailey, dodg-
ing puddles. Near the doorway of the stable, Moire
lost her footing. A sinewy arm reached out and caught
her up against him. For one timeless moment, Moire
braced her hands against Cameron's chest. She gazed
up at him, a smile full upon glistening red lips, a smile
he returned in equal measure and more.

An oppressive weight settled on Meredith's breast,
until she felt she was being crushed. With a cry she
wrenched away from the window. She could stand no
more. She could *watch* no more, but she could not

stop her mind from meandering down a path that led
to the future. She was suddenly terrified. What would
happen when this bairn was born? Would he cast her
out? What if their child was a daughter? Would he
cast them both out? And if their child was indeed a
son, would he rip the babe from her arms once he had
what he wanted and she was no longer needed?
Would Moire stand as mother to her child? She could
not bear the thought.

You are a fool, a niggling voice jabbed in her head.
He can do whatever he wishes, for this is his keep
and he is chieftain here. As he once took great pains
to remind you, he is the stronger . . .

The depths of despair encircled her breast. She sat
in the chair, staring into the dancing flames of the fire,
seeing naught but a future barren of happiness. Never
in all her days had she felt so empty inside!

When Cameron strode into his chamber, he was
whistling a merry little tune. "Meredith? Meredith,
where are you?" He peered into the evening's gloom,
then frowned. Why hadn't she lit the candles? He finally made out her form, huddled in the chair before
the fire.

"Ah, there you are, sweet."

He strode to her, pulling her up from the chair. But
when he tried to take her in his arms, she was limp
and unresponsive. He gazed down at her, puzzled and
just a trifle hurt.

"Meredith?" He queried her uncertainly. Suddenly
fear leaped high within him. "Are you ill, sweet?"

Sweet. Meredith's heart squeezed. Was that what
he called the lovely Moire?

"I am fine," she said curtly. There was a pause.
"Cameron"—she spoke his name quietly—"what
will happen if this child is a lass and not a lad?"

"A lass," he repeated. He blinked, as if the possibility had never occurred to him, never until now.

"Aye. What if I do not bear a son?"

"Meredith, do you forget I had six brothers? My father sired seven sons—seven!" A laugh erupted, deep and resonant. "Can you doubt I would have a son?"

His arms were still looped around her. Her fists came up to lodge on his chest, not resisting, yet not yielding, either.

"You cannot be certain of that. I may very well carry a daughter and not a son. What will happen then?" She was insistent.

He was determined. "Well, then, we shall just have to make certain the next is a son."

"The next." Meredith blanched. "Do you mean to say you would—"

"I would." His smile was boastful, his eyes agleam as he stepped back. His gaze swept the length of her. "As with the first, it would be no hardship. And I did say I would have a son."

Meredith stiffened. "You would force another babe upon me?"

His smile was wiped clean. His features hardened, brittle as a thin layer of ice. His lips barely moved as he spoke. "I did not force you, Meredith, and well you know it."

Meredith pressed her lips together.

He gritted his teeth at her withering expression. "Do not look at me like that. What have I done that is so terrible?"

"You got me with child!"

"You wanted this child. Need I remind you of what you said at the isle? 'Give me your seed. Give me your son.' " Anger forced the remark from him.

"You would have had what you wanted anyway," she flung at him. "When the choice is but one, there is no choice at all!"

In some far distant corner within him, Cameron knew she was right. Had she not surrendered, he would have had his way, even if it were under the guise of seduction. Ruthlessly he pushed aside his guilt. But he would not admit it to her, not now!

"You will not find me so obliging a second time." With an effort she held his stormy gaze. "You leave me no choice, Cameron. Release me." She would not allow him to know she could scarcely bear the thought of leaving him.

"Release you!" He glowered at her. "So we are back to that, are we?"

Her spine went rigid. Lord, but he infuriated her as no other! Reckless anger lent her courage. "Release me," she said again. "Now. This very night."

He scoffed. "To go where? To Castle Munro? From your own lips, you said you would never return there. The man who abused you, who took you from your chamber . . . no doubt he is still there, Meredith."

Meredith's breath caught. Ah, but he was cruel to remind her of that which tormented her so . . . that which was best forgotten.

"Even if I did return you to your clan, what would you say? When it came out that I took you from Connyridge—that you carry a child of MacKay blood—your clansmen would retaliate. The feud would begin anew. Nor will I allow you to wander at will carrying my child. As for the nunnery"—his lip curled—"it was never meant to be. Admit it, Meredith. Indeed, I doubt you would ever have taken your vows."

She trembled. It was as if he saw inside her, clear

to her very heart, and she hated him for it. For seeing what she would rather keep hidden. She gave a cry of impotent rage.

"God, but you are a vile bastard!"

His teeth shone white against his bronzed face. He cast his gaze briefly heavenward. "Lord, will you listen to this? I vow you had best close your ears, for sweet, saintly Meredith has deigned to curse. I must admit, sweet, it springs to your lips quite readily."

His mockery cut deep. "This child is mine," she flared. "Need I remind you who carries it?"

"And need I remind you who gave it to you? This child is just as much mine as yours."

Her breast rose and fell. Blessed be, but there was no arguing with him there. She spoke the first thing that vaulted into her mind.

"If you will not release me, then I will escape. You will not know when or how, but somehow I will find a way!"

A tempest flared in eyes that impaled her with their fierceness. He snatched her up against him. His tone was blistering, his features taut with anger.

"Hear me and hear me well, Meredith. I will not release you, nor will you escape me. Never will I let you go, even if I must chain you in this chamber!"

Her last vestige of control slipped away. A crippling wave of pain slammed through her. He was right. She could not leave here, for where would she go? Back to Connyridge? No, she could not endure the pity of the sisters. Nor could she return to her father—or anywhere on Munro lands. If anyone, especially Papa, should discover that she had been at Dunthorpe these many months, the feud would ignite once more. The thought pierced her to the quick. Dear

God, what if Cameron should die? Killed by one of her own?

Nor was there any need for him to chain her, she realized achingly. For she was already enchained. Chained not by fetters of iron, but enchained by the heart. The soul.

She loved him. She loved him madly, but she would never dare admit it to him. Nay, not when he harbored no such affection for her!

Cameron's mood was black as a moonless night. Conflicting urges tore at his breast. He was torn between the need to storm back to his chamber and shake her senseless . . . and to make love to her until nothing else mattered, until all the angry words between them turned to gasping sounds of passionate rapture.

Did she truly think he would release her? He was both amazed and furious. Nay, he would send her nowhere—not to Connyridge or Castle Munro. For he knew her, his pious little maiden. She would be broken and defeated, her pride in shreds, ashamed and degraded. His clansmen might have called it the sweetest revenge of all . . .

But Cameron could not do it. He could never hurt her like that.

It was Glenda who noted the discord between the two. Cameron spent three straight nights on a bench in the hall, while Meredith spent hers alone. In the morn—indeed, throughout the day!—Cameron snapped at any and all who were unwise enough to cross his path. Meredith's eyes were red-rimmed and swollen. The mere mention of his name caused her lips to tremble. Tears flowed she could not control.

Glenda felt like throwing her hands high in mingled disgust and frustration. She had bided her time these

many weeks, for she'd been convinced the pair would
see what *she* could see. But it appeared they were too
blind. Or too stubborn. Perhaps both.

She waylaid Cameron one afternoon when the hall
was deserted. "You are a lout," she told him.

A black brow slashed upward. "Indeed," he
drawled. "What have I done to warrant my sister-in-
law's displeasure?"

"You know far better than I what you have done,"
Glenda retorted, "but 'tis Meredith who pays the
price."

His eyes narrowed dangerously. "Glenda," he said
coolly, "you have never been one to meddle in another's affairs. I pray you, do not meddle in mine."

"You are right. 'Tis not my way."

He inclined his head. "Excellent," he murmured.
"I shall be on my way, then—"

Deliberately she placed herself in his path. "Yet I
fear I must make an exception. Have you noticed how
melancholy Meredith is of late?"

His heart leaped. Was that a good sign? Perhaps
she had reconsidered her stance, he reflected in satisfaction. Yet in the very next instant, he was abruptly
anxious. Or was it because of the bairn? Christ, was
she ill? What if all was not well?

He was sorely inclined to reply that he could hardly
know she was melancholy when she refused to speak
to him, to even look at him! Mayhap 'twould be best
to listen to what Glenda had to say. Thus armed, he
disguised his alarm.

"Melancholy? I cannot imagine why."

Glenda glared at him. "Nay, I suppose you cannot.
Shall I tell you why?"

"I suspect you will anyway." His smile was grim.

"Meredith has said nothing to me of late," she informed him curtly. "But I know she is saddened because she will soon bear a bairn, and she is unwed." Glenda spared him nothing. "I know of no one more deeply devout than Meredith, lest it be Father William. Aye, she will soon bear a bairn, and this goes against all she has ever believed in, her very faith. I cannot imagine the shame she feels, especially since she once planned to take the veil."

A pang shot through him. Somehow Cameron had never thought of it quite like that. "What, then? Would you have me marry her? Glenda, she is a Munro, daughter of the Red Angus!"

"That did not stop you from taking her to your bed!"

A sliver of guilt nagged at his gut. He had no answer for that.

"Tell me, Cameron. Will you deny the bairn is yours?"

"Nay!" His protest was vehement. "The child is mine, and I claim it as mine!"

Glenda spoke with quiet intensity. "Then I would have you think on this. Unless you marry her, this child will not be born to the Clan MacKay." She paused. "Unless you marry her, this child will be a Munro."

She left him alone to ponder.

And ponder he did. He rode hard, to the very top of the mountain pass high above Dunthorpe. There he paused, gazing at the vast panorama spread out before him in noble majesty. All around, peaks jutted high in stark grandeur, cloaked in swirling mist. Far below, the valley bowed low. The hills undulated gently as far as he could see. All was still and silent. 'Twas as if the very world held its breath.

Immense pride swelled his chest. These were

MacKay lands. *His* lands. Lands that would someday be his son's lands, for somehow Cameron knew, with all that he possessed, that his child would be a son.

Yet all at once he was caught in the rampage of a wind that blew fierce and cold. His mind was caught in the same tumult.

To marry a Munro, daughter of his father's murderer . . . sweet Jesus, would his father ever forgive him? Yet if he did not . . .

Would his son?

His plaid twisting madly behind his shoulders, he closed his eyes. All he could see was her . . . *Meredith*. Meredith, with the red-gold hair and eyes as blue as the skies of heaven. Meredith, small and delicate, gently rounding now with the weight of his son.

The merest smile tugged at his lips. Meek she thought she was, but in truth Cameron had never known a woman of such valor. He thought of how she slept nestled tight against his side, one small hand curled trustingly in the middle of his chest. In truth, he was amazed she had ever yielded! Nay, he thought, she had not surrendered—she had battled him every step of the way. It had been no easy task to bring her into his arms—and his bed. Indeed, his craving for her had only sharpened. No matter how many times he took her, it was never enough.

It would never be enough, he realized, for she brought to him a fulfillment greater than any he had ever known. Oh, he'd told himself what he felt was lust. But it had never been lust. What he felt was far deeper even than desire. Somehow she had seeped into his very bones . . . Aye, he'd stolen her away from Connyridge . . . and lost his very heart and soul in the bargain!

Yet he could not deny he'd brought Meredith to

Dunthorpe against her will. He'd snatched her fate from her. A voice in his head reminded him that he'd not known of her vulnerability, of the terror that had driven her to Connyridge. Still another taunted that even when he'd known, his course had not been swayed. He'd planted his child in her, and aye, she was right—she was given no say in the matter. He thought of how she must feel, all hope extinguished . . .

He rode back to Dunthorpe at a breakneck pace, as if he were beset by demons—as indeed, he was—the demons of his conscience! It was late by the time he arrived. The great hall was deserted but for a few of his men who lingered at their ale.

Grabbing a candle from a spike upon the wall, Cameron strode with unwavering intent toward the north tower stairs.

The door creaked as he pushed it open and stepped within the chamber. It was dark, he noted. Meredith was already in bed. The light from the candle caught her in its wavering glow as she sat up.

"Cameron?" She pushed thick, wavy tresses from her face to peer at him sleepily.

He set the candle aside. Three steps brought him to the bedside. A deep breath, and the burden that seared his being the entire journey home was no more.

"Marry me," he said baldly. "Marry me."

Twenty

Meredith's heart stood still.

She stared at him, convinced she must have conjured him up from the depths of her dreams. The world seemed to teeter and dip, then abruptly righted itself.

This was real. *He* was real, standing before her in the flesh. Anguish wrenched at her insides, for this should have been everything she wanted . . . it should have been *all* she wanted.

She clutched the covers to her breast and gave a tiny shake of her head. "Why?" she said, her voice very low. "Why would you do this?"

His gaze bored into hers. "I am this bairn's father. We must," was all he said.

The bairn. Ah, but she should have known! Anguish rent her soul, yet she was suddenly so angry she was shaking with it.

She straightened her shoulders, her demeanor regal despite the fact that she was clad only in her bed gown. "The night you took me from the priory, you said that were you in need of a woman, 'twould not be me. Well, I tell you this, Cameron of the Clan MacKay. Were I in need of a husband 'twould not be you!"

His jaw locked hard. "Lady," he growled, "you *are* in need of a husband. And here is the proof!" Deliberately he pushed aside the covers and laid his hands on the curve of her belly, splaying his fingers wide.

Meredith pushed them away and sprang from the bed. "I will not marry you, for I am but the instrument of your revenge! 'Tis just as I once said—I am your prize of vengeance!"

"That is not true—"

"If it is not, then let my father know that I yet live!"

Cameron's eyes flickered. He said not a word, yet there was no need—his stony expression said it all.

Meredith gave a jagged cry. "You see, you cannot. You *will* not! And I will not marry you!"

There would be no reasoning with her. He could see it in the wildness of her eyes. He swore vilely. By God, he would not beg!

"Say what you will," he told her tightly, "but this does not end here."

"And I say it does! You made me come here. You made me your prisoner. You shamed me. Humiliated me. You put your bairn in my belly, but you cannot make me do this! I would not marry you if you had a priest before me in this very chamber!"

The words dropped into the air with the weight of a boulder. For never-ending seconds he stared at her. Another time and she might have retreated from the surge of anger that rushed into the frigid gray depths of his eyes. The sizzle of his gaze nearly scorched her.

Somehow she possessed the courage to stand her ground. Just when she could stand the taut silence no longer, he spun around. For the second time that day he departed without a word, his spine as rigid as his shoulders.

The world seemed to blacken all around her. Meredith sank to a heap on the floor. Her legs would no longer hold her. "Cameron!" she choked out. "*Cameron!*"

Cameron did not hear. Indeed, Cameron did not return that night. Or even on the next . . .

Desolation such as she had never known rent her apart. In her heart Meredith could not believe what she had done. Marriage to Cameron . . . was she mad? Dispossessed of her wits? She had refused the very thing that should have been the answer to her prayers.

She spent the next sennight in a daze. She could not speak of what had transpired between them, not even to Glenda. Nor did Glenda know where he had gone. It occurred to Meredith that perhaps Egan did. But she was afraid to query the hard-faced warrior, for he gazed at her with as much dark suspicion as ever.

She knew Cameron would be back. But when . . . *when*? And saints beware, what would happen when he did? She told herself over and over that she didn't care when he returned—or even if he did . . .

But her heart knew. Her heart gave the lie to the torment in her soul. As the days stretched one into another, she fretted and stewed. Was he safe? Had he come to some grievous harm? Had her clansmen seized him? Did he even now lie cold in the ground, his heart as still and lifeless as his father's and brothers'?

He was in her every prayer, her every thought.

A full fortnight later, there were shouts in the bailey early one afternoon. Tired, for she'd not been sleeping well of late, Meredith had just lain down for a brief nap. With a sigh, she finally arose and peered outside. Figures scurried to and fro across the bailey, but she saw nothing unusual. Her head had just lowered to the pillow once more when Glenda burst inside. Excitement glowed in her wide golden eyes.

"He is back!" Glenda announced.

Meredith propped herself on an elbow. One slender brow rose aslant. She feigned a calm she was far from feeling. "Who is back?"

"Och, you know very well who! 'Tis Cameron!" Glenda had already snatched the cover from Meredith's shoulders. "Quickly now, Meredith, you must rise, for he wishes to see you. He awaits you in the hall!"

Meredith was sorely of a mind to retort that if he wished to see her, he should come to her. But there was something about Glenda's manner that stopped her. The other woman's expression was both harried and excited. When she asked her sharply what was amiss, Glenda shook her head adamantly.

"Naught is amiss," was all she would say. Glenda seized her hands and pulled her up. "Here, I will help you."

Meredith was puzzled, for though Glenda commanded she hurry, she insisted Meredith change her wrinkled gown into one of forest green lamb's wool. The gown was finely woven and soft, and as Glenda noted, complemented the rich fire of her hair.

"I fail to see why it matters what I wear. There is none that hides the shape of me." Grumbling as Glenda twitched the skirt into place, Meredith bemoaned her ripening shape. "I fear I am growing plump as a ripe pear."

"You are expecting a child," Glenda said briskly. "No one expects that you remain slender as a reed. Now come, let me brush your hair."

Glenda brushed her hair to a glossy satin. When Meredith would have wound it into a fat plait over one shoulder, Glenda stopped her.

"Nay, do not bind it! It looks lovely as it is, flowing down your back."

There was a pinch in her heart. Meredith couldn't help but recall that Cameron preferred it just so, loose and tumbling free.

At last Glenda pronounced her ready. Though her heart had bounded high with the news of Cameron's return, Meredith couldn't help but recall their last bitter exchange. All at once she was scarcely eager for this meeting—especially when the two of them would not be alone.

She descended the stairs with Glenda, filled with trepidation. To her consternation, the hall was packed with his people. Yet she had no trouble singling out Cameron. His profile strikingly rugged, he stood near the high table, clad in plaid and kilt, towering over all others.

She was suddenly quivering inside. Were it not for Glenda tugging at her sleeve, she would never have found the strength to cross to him.

Just then he spied her. He inclined his head slightly. "Meredith," he greeted coolly. "At last."

Ah, but she both envied and resented him, for he was clearly at his ease. Before she could say a word, he turned and beckoned to someone near the hearth.

The man stepped to Cameron's side. Small and frail-looking, his eyes were gentle as he gave her a smile. He was completely bald, his head round and shiny. He was garbed in dark vestments. Meredith stared numbly. Merciful angels, this could only be . . .

"This is Father William," Cameron stated smoothly. "I brought him here to marry us."

Meredith's heart knocked wildly in her chest. Ah, but he was as imperious as ever! He did not ask or plead or sweetly cajole, but did the deed as it pleased him!

He gripped icy cold hands in his. "Well, lass? 'Tis my son that rounds your belly. I've a priest here before you in this very chamber. So what do you say? Will this day see us wed?"

It was a challenge—a challenge akin to the one she'd thrown at him before they last parted. What was it she'd said? *I would not marry you if you had a priest before me in this very chamber.* His expression was solemn, his mouth unsmiling. Yet mingled within those silvery depths was a wholly unexpected tenderness.

She felt like weeping. He was neither humble nor ashamed, but as audacious as ever. Yet it made him the man he was.

The man she loved.

She could not speak for the lump lodged high in her throat. She knew not what to say. She knew not what to do, for it was just like him to bring her before his people—before the priest!—for no doubt he was convinced she would not refuse him again!

She could not . . . yet neither could she say yea.

She faltered, blinking back tears. Through a watery haze, her gaze slid beyond the broadness of his shoulders to Glenda, whose eyes were as moist as her own. Glenda gave a slight nod.

Her lips parted. Her eyes lifted to Cameron's. "I must confess," was all she could say. "I must confess!"

For one mind-bending instant, a dark cloud seemed to flit across his features. Then he gave a slight nod and stepped back.

It was Father William who led her from the hall and into the chapel. There in the cramped closeness of the confessional, it all poured out. Her days at Connyridge, how she'd agonized over taking the veil. How Cameron had stolen her from the priory. Her eventual capitulation to his ardent embrace.

Hidden behind the screen, Father William nodded. Shaggy brows shot high as he listened to her tale. He was surprised at Cameron's actions toward the lass, though he reminded himself of all Cameron had lost. In truth, though he was a priest, he could see why Cameron had been tempted. He was not blind to her beauty— and he sensed her inherent grace and goodness.

"None of us on this earth is free of sin," he said slowly when at last she finished.

Closing her eyes, Meredith dipped her head low while he pronounced her penance. The burden carried on her shoulders was far lighter than when they entered the chapel. And yet . . .

"Father, please!" she said, her voice very low. "You must help me. I said I would not marry him, yet now that he is here with you"—she floundered— "I want to, and yet I am so afraid!"

Father William's voice was very gentle. "You love him, don't you, lass?"

Meredith swallowed. "Aye," she said painfully.

"I fear the choice is yours, lass, for I will not—I cannot—marry you if you are unwilling, regardless of what Cameron may demand of either of us. I must have your mutual consent. I will say only this. I do not condone what Cameron has done, for 'tis my belief this feud has gone on far too long." He paused. "You must look within yourself, lass. 'Tis a choice only you can make. Or perhaps you should look for guidance from a heavenly power far greater than my own."

Her heart said marry him. Her heart said someday he might grow to love her. Despair wrenched at her. Why couldn't it be today? a voice screamed from within. Why not now?

She clasped her hands together and squeezed her eyes shut. She prayed as never before.

She and Father William left the chapel for the hall but moments later.

With every second she was gone from sight, Cameron chafed. What the devil kept her? His scowl was as black as his thoughts. Reluctantly he reminded himself that while he had always considered the confessional an unpleasant duty that must be attended as little as possible, a woman of Meredith's faith would hardly view it the same. Her sins could hardly be so many as to keep her so long! He thought of what Glenda had told him. *She will soon bear a bairn, and this goes against all she has ever believed in, her very faith*. But that was not her fault, for it was he who had led her down this very path!

As the minutes crept by, it whirred through his mind that perhaps she'd enlisted Father William's aid in helping her escape! How he stopped himself from charging into the chapel after the pair and invading the sanctity of the confessional, he would never know.

Indeed, just as he was about to, she and Father William reappeared. His heart leaped, for he had gambled greatly by bringing Father William here. Yet he knew it was the right thing to do, the *only* thing to do, and Meredith would see it, too, once they were wed . . . wouldn't she? He cursed long and hard, then damned himself as he remembered Father William's presence. He could read nothing in Meredith's expression, neither anger nor a taunting refusal. Instead she kept her eyes downcast as she made her way toward him.

Her footsteps carried her directly before him. He held his breath as she slowly raised her head. Cameron beheld her, her eyes as breathtakingly blue as the skies on a warm sunny day—for once it was he who envied her composure, for uncertainty marched like a marauding army inside his breast. Displaying a presumption he truly did not experience, he extended his hand, palm up. For one awful moment she did not move . . . His heart lurched.

Their fingertips barely brushed. With a faint blush, she laid her fingers within his.

Some nameless, powerful emotion flooded his entire being. His hand curled around hers; tucking it into his elbow, he turned to Father William.

To Meredith it was all a daze. Her head swam dizzily, until she heard Father William proclaim them man and wife.

Only then did reality surface. The ceremony was over. She was Cameron's wife—his wife! Their child would not be born a bastard. Even as the thought raced through her mind, hard arms snared her close. Meredith drew a startled breath and then his mouth captured hers. He kissed her for all to see, a surprisingly intimate kiss given their audience.

When it was over Meredith sought to glare in mild reproof, but she could not, for she was too elated. She could not withhold the smile that crept to her lips, nor did she want to. Holding their hands high, Cameron turned toward the crowd gathered around and said simply, "My lady."

For an instant, all was hushed and quiet. Then someone behind them began to clap. A cheer went up, and then there were shouts and laughter all around.

But there were two who did not join in the roar of approval. Meredith saw Moire stalk from the hall, red lips curled in disgust. And Egan stood near the far wall, his visage grim, his mouth a taut, straight line. But even that was not enough to dim her joy.

Afterward a steady procession of servants streamed from the kitchens bearing food and wine and ale. The minstrel played a host of lively, merry tunes. Boisterous laughter bounced from every corner of the hall. The atmosphere was gay and festive. Meredith chuckled as one reveler went to reclaim his seat on the bench. He tucked his bottom beneath him and ducked low, only to completely miss the bench. Clearly he'd imbibed a little too freely from his cup.

It was then Meredith spied Aileen, peering at her from alongside Adele, her mother. Her eyes were dark and baleful, her lips pursed in a frown. Meredith crooked her finger to beckon her, but Aileen promptly shook her head. All at once she had a very good idea what was amiss with the little girl . . .

Cameron had already noticed where her gaze rested. He tipped his head to hers. "What is wrong with Aileen?" he murmured.

Meredith sighed. "I fear I've forever lost favor with her, for it seems I've claimed her prince."

"Her prince?" Cameron was puzzled.

Meredith's brows shot high. "Do you mean to say you've never noticed? Aileen is quite taken with you, sir—and meant to someday claim you as her husband."

"Indeed." Cameron rubbed his chin and pretended a thoughtful concentration. "Why, who knows? By the time she is old enough, mayhap I'll have a yearning for a much younger bride."

Meredith gave a mock indignant gasp. "What! Do you commit me to the ranks of the aged already?"

"Nay, wife." His eyes were dancing. "And I fear

I must reconsider. I'm quite content with the bride I have and do not wish for that to change.''

Wife. It gave her an odd thrill for him to address her so.

''But I cannot have the child angry with my lady,'' he went on. To her surprise, he rose and strode toward Aileen. Meredith watched curiously as he sat on his haunches before the little girl. She couldn't hear their conversation, but he returned a few minutes later.

''All is well,'' he told her mildly. ''You are no longer in disfavor.''

''Never tell me. You told her you would marry her when she is older.''

He shook his head. A smile lurked about his lips. ''I assured her we would name our firstborn daughter after her.''

''You what!'' Meredith was aghast.

''Aye,'' he said with a wink. ''But before we have a daughter, we will have a son.'' He swung her high into his arms.

''Cameron! Put me down!''

''I think not, lass. I will have but one wedding night—and I do believe it should begin this very moment!''

Amidst bawdy shouts and laughter and cheers, he strode across the hall and toward the stairs. And suddenly she was laughing, giddy with relief and delight and happier than she had ever known she could be.

In his chamber he lowered her to the floor. Gently he touched her cheek. '' 'Tis good to hear you laugh with me,'' he said quietly.

She cupped her hand to his cheek. ''Aye,'' she agreed, a small catch in her voice, for his eyes were achingly tender. '' 'Tis good.''

He brought her hand to his lips and kissed her

knuckles. "Wait," he said suddenly. "I have something for you." He touched the tip of her nose with a fingertip. "Close your eyes."

Her eyes flashed to his. Her laugh was breathless. "Cameron, what—"

"Shhh! You must close your eyes or you may not have it."

Drawing a deep breath, Meredith did as he bade. Heavy footfalls crossed the room. There was a creak, and she guessed he was rummaging in his chest. A moment later she felt him something slip over her head.

Her breath caught—and so did her heart. Surely it was not . . .

Her hand came up. Saints be praised, it was. She touched the finely etched surface of her crucifix. "Cameron . . . how? 'Twas broken—"

"I had it repaired."

Meredith's mouth had gone dry as dust. "Cameron," she said tentatively, "does this mean that you've forgiven my fa—"

He didn't give her the chance to finish. " 'Tis for you, Meredith. I returned it, for I know you treasure it." His response was carefully guarded. "As for all else, may we please not speak of it? This night is for us, Meredith. Only for us."

She swallowed a pang. She knew then that his feelings had not changed—yet it did not change her own. Mayhap he was right, that the feud had no place in this moment, for this was their wedding night. Thoughts of no other should intrude. God willing, there might come another time . . .

For in truth, Meredith was touched beyond measure. All at once, 'twas not the gift, but the giving of it that was beyond price.

"Thank you," she murmured. Her eyes shining,

she slipped her arms around his neck. Tangling her fingers in the dark hair that grew low on his nape, she drew his head down to hers.

The moment their lips touched, a heady possessiveness swept over him. The contact sent a jolt all through him. He felt the way her lips trembled beneath his, the way she arched against him, and joy shot through him. She was here in his arms, agonizingly sweet and tempting, and she was his wife. His heart thundered. Dear God, he thought in amazement, my wife. His arms stole about her. With a groan he almost crushed her against him. What might have been meant as a gentle offering dissolved into a blistering passion. His tongue delved into the honeyed warmth of her mouth, again and again.

It was a moment no less intense for Meredith. She was trembling as he divested her of her gown and his own clothing. The need to feel his hard length, to feel the pulse of his desire throb against the very gates of her womb was almost more than she could bear. But when he would have scooped her up and borne her to the bed, she stopped him with a fist centered squarely on his chest.

"Wait," she pleaded. "Wait."

Meredith drew a slow, uneven breath. Many a time he had kissed every silken hollow of her body, even there at the cleft below her spine, rendering her a boneless heap by the time he turned her over and plunged deep within her. Suddenly all she wanted was to please him the same way he pleased her. She kissed the squareness of his jaw, the corded length of his throat, the discs of his nipples hidden beneath crisp, curling hair. All the while she ran her hands over the gleaming satin of his shoulders, the plane of his back, the flexing steel of his buttocks. She even dared to taste the hollow of his navel, the bulging swell of his thighs. She thrilled to the feel of rock-hard muscle sheathed in bronzed, gleaming skin. A reckless abandon washed over her then, as she dared still more . . .

Slowly she knelt between his thighs.

She brushed her lips across the grid of his belly, then drew back to see his response.

He swelled before her very eyes.

''Oh, my,'' she whispered. Her eyes widened as she beheld his rigid length.

Her shocked whisper was almost his undoing. He made a sound that was half-laugh, half-groan. Through some miracle, he'd kept his hands at his sides. Now he reached for her.

She shook her head. ''Nay, Cameron, not yet.'' She was determined to give him the same exquisite pleasure he gave her. Always he was unselfish in his loving. Always. And now, so would she be just as unselfish. For one never-ending moment, she paused, poised between his thighs.

With her tongue she touched him.

His heart leaped. Nay, he thought. Nay . . .

And then there was no further thought of stopping her, for he could no longer think. He could only feel . . .

His blood was scalding. Every sensation was centered there, at the overwhelmingly sensitive part of him that betrayed his need of her. Mesmerized and unable to move, he couldn't tear his eyes from the sight. It spun through his mind that this was the most gloriously erotic moment of his life. To think that she would do such a thing—and to the part of him she had once so feared . . . The flaming curtain of her hair skimmed over his thighs. Her tongue was a divine torment. Swirling daintily.

Darting boldly. Tasting every inch of him, even the pearl of desire that glazed the arching tip.

A shudder wracked him. His hands plunged into the streaming skeins of her hair. His fingers skimmed her nape, the bareness of her shoulders. His breath grew harsh and rasping.

"Sweet Jesus," he said hoarsely. "I can stand no more!" With a cry, he caught her and dragged her upward.

Two steps and they were at the bedside. He pulled her astride him.

His eyes sheared directly into hers. "Remember the day you told me you would ride neither before me nor behind me?"

"Aye." Steadying herself against his chest, she gazed down at him.

"Now you will ride upon me." His smile was wicked and wanton.

She needed no further guidance. A twist of the hips and his thickened spear was deep within her. His hands found her breasts. He stroked her nipples until they stood hard and taut against his palms. When he kissed her she tasted his essence on her tongue.

They were both roused to a fever pitch, their hips churning in a wild frenzy as they scaled the heights toward completion. Gritting his teeth against the eruption he felt building inside him, he plunged his thumb within her nest of curls and stroked her pleasure button. She cast back her head, her eyes smoky and dazed. The walls of her channel contracted around him, again and again. With her release came his own. Their mingled cries reached beyond the stars and shattered the very heavens.

Twenty-one

Winter descended brutal and hard upon the land. Many a day was long and dark, scoured by the relentless blast of winds that whipped down the passes. High above Dunthorpe, the mountains stretched across the sky, beautiful but daunting, the rugged crags of granite garbed in their wintry armor, locked in snow and ice.

Many within the keep commented that never had there been such a frigid winter. Yet they bore the rigors of nature well, venturing without into the snow and cold as needed and tending their duties with cheerful vigor.

There were several instances, however, that marred the peaceful days. One was when a flock of sheep disappeared—stolen, it was claimed, by the Munros. The other was when two young men—both belonging to the Clan MacKay—wandered onto Munro lands. The men were held for several days before being released by the crofter who had captured them. Meredith was saddened greatly by the continuing hostility between the clans; yet there was no bloodshed in either case, and for that she was eternally glad. Oddly, even during those days of heightened tension when word came of the strife, there were few hate-filled, suspicious glances directed her way. Since she had married Cameron, much had changed. As his wife, she was accepted as she might never have been otherwise. For that, too, Meredith was grateful.

And so, although her days were not spent in glowing happiness, there was at least a measure of contentment. She treasured the long nights huddled cozily beneath the blankets, anchored against her husband, his powerful arms snug and warm about her body. Every morning when he left, he pressed a lingering kiss upon her lips—and the swell of her belly.

As the days slipped into weeks, her body grew heavy with the weight of the child within her. Yet Cameron took an avid interest in her pregnancy. He inquired daily about her health. Though Meredith occasionally bemoaned the babe's animated activity in her womb, Cameron was raptly absorbed. He would lay for hours beside her, his hand cupped possessively on the mound of her belly, feeling the babe's undulating movements beneath his palm.

"A lively wee lad, is he not?" he boasted one evening as a tiny elbow or foot jabbed his hand.

"Aye, a lively wee *lassie*," Meredith emphasized with a toss of her head. "And determined to keep her mother awake in the hours of the night when she should be sleeping!"

"Then you have only to wake the lad's father"— a teasing, unholy glint appeared in Cameron's eyes— "for you need not lie awake alone, sweet. I am only too happy to provide another diversion, one I think both of us would find extremely pleasurable."

His crooked, irreverent grin made her heart turn over. He was achingly tender, ardently sweet. His touch spoke not only of comfort and concern, but of stirring passion. Though Meredith felt ungainly and clumsy, Cameron declared she was more beauteous than ever. His husky assertion made her melt inside.

A wellspring of hope had begun to gather within her. They talked for hours on end, about little things, silly, mundane matters. His gaze made her shiver with awareness, for it was ever upon her . . . as he was ever in her heart.

The one thing they did not speak of was the feud between their clans. Meredith was reluctant to break their fragile truce. She could only pray that when their child was born, Cameron's hatred of her father would blunt and soften.

And she dared to pray for more . . . that he might someday love her in return. Love her as wholly and completely as she loved him.

One evening in the last month of her confinement she wanted to surprise him, so she arranged for them to dine alone in their chamber. Though she did not care for hot mulled wine, Cameron was fond of it, so she asked that it be brought, along with several other of his favorites—fresh-baked bread wrapped in a clean linen cloth, fat sausages steeped in meaty juices, a tray of honeyed cakes and pastries to indulge his sweet tooth. All in all, it was an evening filled with quiet serenity.

After they had eaten, Cameron drew her down upon his lap. His nearness made her quiver inside. He was so handsome, so splendidly lean and strong. Unable to help herself, Meredith wrapped her arms about his neck and laid her head on his shoulder.

He laid his hand upon her belly. "It will not be long now," he murmured.

Her lips brushed the bristly hardness of his cheek as she shook her head. "Nay," she agreed. "Glenda feels it will be soon. Indeed, it could be but a matter of days.''

His knuckles grazed the softness of her cheek. Fingers beneath her chin, he brought her gaze to his. ''Are you afraid?''

Meredith could not control the bend of her mind. She recalled how Glenda's babe had been born dead. What if that should happen to her own? She couldn't withhold the quiver of fear that shot through her. Yet again she despised her weakness.

She lowered her eyes. ''Aye,'' she admitted, her voice very low.

Cameron made a sound deep in his throat. ''Meredith! Be not afraid, sweet. Be not afraid, for I swear I will let nothing harm you.''

''You said you would be with me,'' she reminded him.

Cameron's heart contracted. Both her voice and her mouth were tremulous. ''I will,'' he promised anew. When she lifted her face, he spied the tears that threatened to overflow. His embrace tightened. ''Meredith! Do not weep. I will protect you, sweet. I will protect you always.''

His caring speared her heart, his words a healing balm to her wounded soul. She clung to him as he kissed away the tear that slipped from the corner of her eye.

It was later, as he prepared for bed that night, that he brought a hand to his abdomen. A grimace of pain sped across his features.

Meredith raised up on an elbow. ''Cameron, what is it? Are you ill?''

A sheen of perspiration dotted his upper lip. '' 'Tis nothing,'' he insisted.

''Cameron, are you sure? You look unwell—''

Before she finished, he crashed to the floor.

Meredith slipped from the bed as quickly as her condition would allow. "Cameron!" she cried. "Cameron!"

His skin was ashen gray and clammy to the touch. Even as she dropped to her knees beside him, he writhed in pain and clamped a hand to his belly. Meredith pushed it aside. The whole of his abdomen was a tight hard knot; she felt it cramping beneath her fingertips.

His lips were bloodless. "Daggers . . . turning inside," he groaned. He managed to push himself to his knees, only to drop his head and retch violently.

Meredith raced to the door and opened it. "Egan!" she screamed. "*Egan!*"

It seemed to take forever before Egan rushed in. At a glance he took in Cameron's distress. It was he who lifted Cameron to the bed.

By morning the bed was drenched in sweat. There was no ease from the violent spasms that now shook his entire body. Meredith sat beside him, bathing his brow and face. Never had she felt so helpless!

She shook her head and glanced at Egan, who stood at the end of the bed. "He needs more help than we can give."

Their eyes met; his were as frightened as her own. His glance sought Glenda's, for she hovered behind Meredith. Glenda gave a nod.

Egan strode to the door and threw open the oak portal. His bellow surely shook every timber of the keep.

"Send Finn for the physician!" he shouted.

Once again, it seemed to take forever before the physician finally appeared. He was a small man with hands as slight as a woman's, and there was an air of capability about him that could not be denied. He listened while Meredith and Egan described Cameron's malady, then quietly asked to be alone to examine Cameron.

Egan reluctantly withdrew, but doggedly remained outside the door.

Meredith hesitated. Glenda placed a hand on her arm. "Come," she murmured softly. "We must do as he asks."

Meredith nodded. But unlike Egan, she did not remain, for there was a place where she might do far more good . . .

In the chapel she sank to her knees before the altar. Trembling, she clasped her hands to her breast. Her eyes squeezed shut. Her lips parted. "Heavenly Father . . ." she began.

How long she remained there on her knees, she knew not. A long time later, the door behind her creaked on cumbersome hinges. Emptying her lungs with a long sigh, she started to rise. She was not given the chance. Fingers of steel snared her elbow, jerking her upright.

With a gasp, she looked up into Egan's scarred face. "Egan!" she cried softly. "You're hurting me—"

"Be silent!" he hissed. His grip on her arm tightened until she nearly cried out. He dragged her from the chapel and toward the south tower. Meredith could do naught but stumble after him. He did not stop until they reached the chamber at the top. He thrust her inside and stepped in after her.

Meredith noted dimly that this was the chamber where she'd spent the very first night. Her eyes locked on Egan's face. He looked for all the world as if the demons of hell resided within him.

Her heart was pounding. "Egan! Egan, why are you acting like this? Sweet Lord, is it Cameron? Tell me. Tell me, please! What is wrong with him?"

"As if you do not know!" he sneered.

"I do not!" Only one man had frightened her more than he did now—that was Cameron, the night he'd stolen her from Connyridge. "Please, Egan, tell me what is wrong!" An awful thought crowded her heart. "Never say he is dead!"

"He is not, despite your most diligent effort." Harsh lips twisted. "Tell me, Meredith. Just now in the chapel—did you pray that he would die?"

"Nay! I prayed that he will soon be well again!"

"And you had best hope that he is. For if he dies, lady, so do you!"

Meredith's heart was beating so hard she could scarcely draw breath. She stretched out her hands. "Egan, why do you do this? Tell me what is wrong with my husband!"

"Ah, lady, you feign ignorance so well! But you do not fool me. I know very well what you did. He may well die because of you!"

"What I did . . ." Meredith felt the blood drain from her face. "Egan, I tried to help him! I summoned you for help."

"A ploy, that you might later proclaim your innocence."

"Nay!" she breathed. "Nay!"

"Who else, then, I would ask? You supped with him. You ordered mulled wine—and but one cup. The servants tell me that you do not drink it." Those cold blue eyes fairly simmered with accusation.

"Only because I do not care for it!" Meredith's mind was all awhirl. Was this really happening? Merciful saints, it was a nightmare! "Egan, please," she implored. "Is Cameron all right?"

"He lives. That is all I will say." He strode toward the door, then turned. "By God, lady, you may count yourself blessed. For did you not carry Cameron's child, you would even now dwell in the cold and damp of the pit prison! Were it not for that, I would kill you myself! So use your time well. Pray that your husband lives, else your time on this earth is measured."

Meredith shrank back. His voice was like a whip, each word a lash tearing into her flesh. The depth of his rage vibrated like blackened thunder in the air.

When he was gone, she trembled in fear—yet not because of Egan's warning. Tears rained freely from her eyes. Her only thought was of her husband. Cameron, she thought achingly. *Cameron!* Was his condition so very dire, then? The thought that he hovered at death's door was like a knife in her heart.

When Cameron awoke, he felt battered and bruised, as if he'd been trod upon by a thousand horses. Summoning both breath and strength, he called his wife's name.

It was not Meredith who loomed at his bedside, but Egan.

The grim-faced warrior cocked a heavy brow, noting with approval the tinge of color in his chieftain's skin. " 'Tis good that you are finally awake," he said softly. "How do you fare?"

"As if I've been turned inside out." Cameron could not help his grumbling.

Egan smiled slightly. " 'Tis little wonder. The physician gave you a purgative."

"A purgative! Why?"

Egan's smile withered. "For the poison."

"Poison . . ."

"Aye." Egan spoke the word as if it were a condemnation. "You were poisoned."

Cameron's gaze sharpened. "Where is my wife? Where is Meredith?"

"Do not concern yourself with her." Egan's reply was terse.

"And why the devil not? She should be here, not you! 'Tis a wife's duty to attend her husband."

And the last time she tended him nearly killed him! Egan fought to hold his tongue. Instead he said tersely, "She is in the south tower."

"What is she doing there?"

"It was either there or the pit prison."

"The pit prison!" Cameron swore. He pushed aside the covers and swung his legs to the floor. For an instant his head swam dizzily. "What the blazes has come over you?" he demanded. "I know you have never liked her, but God's blood, she is my wife. And if you have harmed her—" Cameron stopped.

"If I have harmed her! You fool, the witch poisoned you. Remember the meal brought to you here in your chamber?"

"Aye, we shared it! There was no poison!" Cameron protested as vehemently as he was able.

"Aye," Egan said. "All but the wine, I dare say! She knew full well that you would not suspect should she not partake of it!"

Cameron shook his head. The notion that Meredith would try to poison him was too much to comprehend. Too much to bear. "Nay. Nay, I say."

"And I say aye! She sought to protect herself by calling for me! I've talked with the servants, Cameron. All are loyal to you, as loyal as I! Who else could it be but her?''

He may well be right, Cameron thought. Indeed, 'twould not be the first time she sought to see you dead. Remember she held your dagger to your breast?

But could not do the deed!

And now she had!

It was as much exhaustion as shock that made him fall back weakly. Egan grabbed his legs and hiked them to the bed.

Cameron's features were drawn and white. ''Have you accused her? Before all here?''

Egan hesitated. ''Nay. I've not accused her openly, though I did confront her.'' His lips compressed. ''She denied it.''

His gaze sought his friend's. ''Tell me it is not true. Tell me she did not betray me!''

Egan's harsh features softened, for he well knew his chieftain's dilemma. He shook his head. ''Were it within my power I would, Cameron. But all points to her, and however painful it may be, the truth does not lie.''

His body would heal. This Cameron did not doubt. Ah, but what of the rending in his soul? Never had he been so torn! Yes, he thought with blistering irony, he'd taken Meredith's body. Given her his seed that even now flourished in her womb. Everything within him cried out in stark bitterness. But would he ever have her trust? Her heart?

Yet Egan was his greatest friend. He would not hesitate to put his life in Egan's hands. No, he could not put aside his friend's judgment so easily. Egan believed that Meredith had sought to see him dead . . . And she had sought to escape him. So many times she had pleaded for her freedom.

His death was one way to assure it.

"Say nothing of this to anyone," he ordered. "I will find out the truth for myself."

"But Cameron—"

Cameron turned his head aside. "Leave me," he said dully. "Leave me."

It was through Glenda that Meredith learned of Cameron's condition. He had survived, but it would be several days before he regained his strength. And it was Glenda who reluctantly disclosed that Cameron had been poisoned.

A splinter of shock resounded all through her. "What! But who would do such a thing?"

There was an uncomfortable silence. Glenda would not meet her eyes. And in that instant, Meredith knew . . .

"He believes I am guilty?"

"He is a fool," Glenda said quickly. "His illness has addled his reasoning."

A crippling anguish went through her. Meredith swallowed it and raised tear-glazed eyes to her friend. "What of you, Glenda? Do you believe I poisoned him?"

"Once I might have. But not now. Take heart, Meredith." She reached out and hugged Meredith's shaking shoulders. "Take heart and believe that all will be well, as Cameron must surely come to believe in your innocence."

They wept in each other's arms.

By morning Meredith was dry of eye . . . and full of outrage.

The bolt scraped noisily. The door swung open.

She did not turn from her place near the window. Thinking it was the servant with her morning meal, she called, "Please take it away. I am not hungry."

There was the sound of the tray slipping onto the table. "You must eat, lass, for I would see my son alive and healthy and well."

Meredith froze. Oh, but her thoughts were suddenly not nearly as composed as she wished them! The sight of him nearly brought her to her knees. For the space of a heartbeat anger flagged. His nearness called to her. She longed to launch herself against him, to comfort him, for his features reflected his ordeal. He was paler than he should have been, his lean frame thinner. The smudges beneath his eyes made them darker than usual.

But then she remembered. He had no need of her. How could he, when after all this time he could believe she had sought to murder him?

Determinedly she straightened her spine. Deliberately she looked beyond his shoulder. "What? Do you come alone? Why, I wonder that you dare! Do you not fear for your life now that you are alone with me?"

His smile was tight. "Malice does not become you, Meredith."

"And what does? The murder of my husband?"

He widened his stance ever so slightly. Powerful arms crossed against his chest. There was an arrogant lift of one dark brow. "I do not know, wife. Suppose you tell me. Was it the wine, I wonder? Or the honeyed cakes? You partook of neither."

Meredith compressed her lips. "I have naught to tell you," she stated haughtily.

"You have naught to tell me—and everything to deny?"

"That is true," she said, her eyes flashing. "Who laid the blame on me? Egan?"

His eyes rested long and hard upon her. He said nothing.

Meredith made a sound of mingled anger and frustration. "He hates me. He has always hated me and you know it. Mayhap he is the one who did it—and sought to blame me!"

All at once there was a dangerous glint in his eye. "There is no one who would wish me dead here," he stated flatly. "This is Dunthorpe—my home. So watch what you say, lass, for I trust Egan with my life. I always have and always will."

"And you trust me with nothing!"

"That is not true, sweet. I trusted you with my heart!"

His heart? She could no more banish the relentless hurt that ripped at her insides than she could the love that surged unbidden in her heart. A part of her longed to clutch at him, to beg him to believe in her, to confess that she loved him too much ever to harm him. But pride kept the words locked fast within her.

No, she could never confide her love, not to this cold-eyed stranger before her. In all the months she had been here, naught had changed.

The breath she drew was sharp and painful. "You trust me with nothing!" she charged bitterly. "You swore you would protect me. Yet you defend Egan and condemn me. You forever hold me guilty because of who I am—the daughter of the Red Angus. After all this time, you cannot see beyond that, nor do you wish to! You wrong me in this, Cameron, for by all that is holy, I did nothing to harm you!"

Something flickered across his features, something she couldn't decipher. He stretched out a hand. "Meredith—"

She slapped it away. "Do not touch me, Cameron.

Just leave me be. Leave me be!'' She would have said more, but all at once there was a tight drawing across her lower back. There had been a nagging ache in her back when she'd risen this morning; but this was different. Vaguely she wondered if it was the bairn.

Her hand went to the small of her back. Nay, it was but a cramp, she decided, her fingers seeking the knot. Yet her slight grimace must have given her away.

He swore. "Jesus, Mary, and Joseph! Is it your time?"

Her lips compressed. "Nay," she said shortly, for she was still bitingly angry with him. "It cannot be. 'Tis my back, not my belly."

Cameron was not so certain. Her expression had been most odd, and he would take no chances. He bolted through the door and into the hall in search of Glenda.

By the time the pair returned, a second and yet a third twinge had occurred.

Glenda's cheeks were flushed crimson with exertion. "Meredith! Cameron says the bairn comes."

"The bairn . . ." Her lips turned down as she grumbled. "How the devil would he know? How many children has he given birth to, I ask?"

"Quickly, Cameron. Take her to the bed!"

She might as well have been a buzzing fly in the midst of an uproar, for all they listened to her. She drew herself upright.

"Now see here, the both of you! Even if it were my time, which it is not, I am fully capable of walking that meager distance on my own—"

Her protest went unheeded. Her feet were swept out from beneath her and she felt herself borne high in the air. He whirled. His head swiveled in the direction of the narrow bed in the corner. Though she did not know it, in but a heartbeat his decision was made.

He strode from the chamber and down the stairs. Glenda snatched up her skirts and hurried behind them.

Meredith clutched at him. "Cameron! Where the blazes do you think you're going? Take your hands off me!"

His gait was as unwavering as his tone. "I think not, sweet. This bairn will be born in my bed—the bed where my father and I and my brothers were born."

Meredith's jaw clamped shut. She glared at his profile, the arrogant tilt of his jaw. She was sorely tempted to argue, yet what was the use? Before his will, her own was forfeit. Ah, but if she could have delivered this child on the stairs he now descended, she would have, if only to spite him! Indeed, she was not yet convinced the babe was about to make his appearance—or rather, *her* appearance, she decided defiantly.

In his chamber he lowered her carefully in the center of the bed. A maid had scurried in, and Glenda was already briskly issuing out orders.

"We will need a fresh gown for Meredith, and clean linen for the bed. And swaddling for the bairn . . ."

Meredith was about to snap that there was no hurry, when suddenly a cramping band of iron stole around to the front of her belly, so intense she gasped.

She was no longer tempted to argue that this babe would not be born today. When the pain eased, she saw that Cameron had drawn up a chair near the side of the bed.

"You cannot mean to stay!"

"Your memory fails you, lass. Do you not remember I promised I would remain here with you?''

"I do not hold you to it. You may leave," she informed him imperiously, for she was still inclined to be less than lenient toward him.

He laid his hand on her belly. "I cannot," he said simply. "I will be here when my son is born."

Meredith pushed at his hand, longing to screech at the top of her lungs. Faith, but he was infuriating! She gritted her teeth. "You will *not* be here when my daughter is born!"

"If you wish me to leave, then you will have to remove me yourself."

Meredith's eyes darkened. "I do not want you here," she said with a low, choked sound, "not when you think me so vile that I would poison you. Look to your own that might betray you, but do not look to me, for I did not do it!"

Cameron cursed beneath his breath. "Speak of it no more!" he commanded. "Save your strength, for you may need it later."

Little did he know . . .

She was stripped to her underdress. Though Glenda assured them both a first birth could take many hours, it was not long before the pains grew sharper. Meredith caught her breath, releasing a long sigh of relief when they eased. Just when she thought that it was not so bad—that the pains were not so unbearable, that childbirth could be endured and was not the ordeal she feared—her womb was gripped by a ferocious cramp that seized the whole of her belly. She bit back a cry, for above all, she was determined to be strong. And so she held back, clenching her muscles, holding her breath until the spasms ebbed.

But they came so close now. Harder and stronger than ever.

Glenda clucked with exasperation. "Meredith, do not hold back so! It only makes it harder. Why, I screamed so loudly I was surely heard in the next valley."

Meredith sank back against the pillow. "I will not," she gasped. "I . . . am weak in all else. I will not . . . be weak in this."

"The devil, I say! Meredith, cease such prattle! You are strong and full of pride and courageous as— as any Highland warrior!"

Cameron's voice reached her. Her eyelids drifted open. Through a haze of torment she saw him. For all the fierceness of his gaze, his fingers were incredibly tender as he pushed aside the damp strands curling across her forehead.

"Why are you still here?" Dimly she heard herself.

His lips curved in a faint smile. "Ah, lass, but you've not yet given me my son."

Her eyes flashed. "My daughter!" she flared.

He bent and kissed the mutinous pout of her lips. "That's the spirit, sweet."

She gritted her teeth. " 'Tis just like you! Were you in my place, you would not be so amused."

"Were I in your place, I would not be so brave as you!"

She glared at him, or tried to. Yet curiously, she was heartened by his words—and aye, though she would never admit it, by his steadfast presence. He bathed the sweat from her brow and clasped her hands within his. Through a haze she heard his low masculine murmurs of encouragement.

The darkness of night crept within the chamber. Fat candles cast flickering shadows on the walls. Glenda, bless her sweet, gentle soul, sought to assure her, telling her that it would not be long now . . . yet still the pains came unendingly. Frightfully strong, and now along with the pain came an immense pressure from within. As the contraction ebbed, she sank back, shaking and wet.

At the foot of the bed Glenda had raised her smock above her knees. "Oh, Meredith! The bairn is almost here. When next you feel the pain, love, you must push."

The world was dull and hazy, her mind filled with fog. She longed to cry out her despair, but she didn't have the strength. She was so immeasurably weary, and she could stand no more.

"Meredith!" a sharp male voice rapped out sharply. "Do you hear, lass? You must take my hands and push."

She blinked, bringing into focus dark, forbidding features that hovered above her.

She gave a tiny, stricken cry. "Why are you angry? You are always angry with me. Ah, how foolish of me. 'Tis because I am a Munro."

Her eyes were glazed, her lips swollen and bloodied from biting back her cries. Her hair streamed across the pillow, the fiery skeins a wild, matted tangle. Seeing her thus, so limp and exhausted, Cameron's insides knotted.

He bent and framed her face with his hands. "You are my wife, Meredith, my wife, and I hold you dear above all else." The breath he drew was deep and ragged. "And as God is my witness, I love you."

A tearing pain clawed through her. Her nails dug into Cameron's palms. Certain she was being torn apart, she cast back her head and cried out her anguish.

The babe slid from her into Glenda's waiting hands.

"A wee laddie!" Glenda gave a joyous half-sob.

"Meredith, you have a fine, healthy son!"

Meredith turned her head. Swaddling trailed from Glenda's hands. She caught a glimpse of a tiny red body, a dark, slick head. She heard a thin, mewling cry and it spun through her mind that she should have known—that Cameron would ever have his way. A tremulous smile graced her lips, for it was the greatest joy she had ever known, for she had a son . . . *a son*.

Blackness engulfed her.

Cameron was only half-aware as he got to his feet, not entirely steady. Numbly he realized it was over. Yet it didn't seem real until a beaming maid pressed a tiny bundle into his arms. He stood awkwardly, afraid to move, to breathe, for this bairn was the tiniest creature he'd ever seen in his life.

A solemn little face regarded him in turn. He beheld pink, rosy cheeks. Dark brows arched over blue, opaque eyes. A cap of hair he guessed was as black as his own . . . The babe screwed up his eyes and mouth and let out a wail.

Cameron started. His laugh was rusty. A son, he thought in amazement. This is my son. Pride swelled his chest till he thought he would burst.

"Meredith," he said aloud, "we have a son!"

But Meredith did not answer. Footsteps echoed on the floor. Figures rushed by him.

"Please God, not now. We cannot lose her now!"

He looked up and saw Glenda on the bed, kneading Meredith's belly. A frantic looking maid was shoving a wad of cloth between her thighs. Almost before that was done, the edges were stained crimson . . .

Glenda chose that moment to glance up. He caught her eyes and held them. Hers were dark and shimmered with tears. He glimpsed her frantic fear.

"There's too much blood," Glenda cried. "There's too much blood and I cannot stop it!"

He passed the babe into someone's arms. Meredith's pallor struck him like a blow to the middle; her face was an ashen gray. A chill ran down his spine.

Fear clamped down upon him. He reached for her hand. Her fingers dangled limply. "Meredith," he breathed, and then it was a ragged cry. "*Meredith!*"

Glenda dashed a tear from her cheek. "Cameron, please leave us! You can do no good here."

There was a hand at his elbow, tugging and pulling. "Aye, 'tis for your wife's good, my lord. 'Tis women's work we do here, and we do it best alone."

The door was slammed as he left. How long he stood there, he knew not.

He couldn't erase the choking fear inside. Guilt seared his soul. Christ, he'd done precisely what Egan had predicted. His loins had ruled and not his heart. He had demanded a son of her. He'd wanted her— and he'd taken her. He'd seen her delivered into his greedy arms . . . into her worst nightmare, for she had not wanted him. She'd wanted no man! Yet he would ever have his way . . . And now he had his son.

And it might well cost him his wife . . . it might cost Meredith her life!

His mind blurred. He moved without conscious thought, guided by instinct alone. He found himself in the chapel, alone within its lofty walls.

He swallowed. Something had drawn him here, something beyond his power to control. This was the one place he had not come when his father and brothers had been murdered. He'd screamed and cursed the very heavens, for he'd felt so abandoned and forsaken. So very, very angry that so much had been taken from him. Yet now . . .

He sank to his knees and prayed.

Not for his own forgiveness, but for Meredith. His life. His love. For without her, his own meant nothing.

Some far distant corner of his being was still amazed . . . Whoever would have thought it could be? A MacKay and a Munro . . .

It was in the early hours, as dawn's first light cleansed the night's gloom, when he retraced his steps to his chamber. Vaguely he noticed Glenda in the corner, rocking the babe, yet his eyes were only for his wife.

She lay so still that for an instant his heart leaped. She was so very pale, pale as the sheet drawn over her breast. Her eyes were closed, the sweep of her lashes thick and dark against the whiteness of her cheeks.

Raw emotion scored his very heart. His lungs burned so that he could not breathe. Christ's mercy, surely she was not *dead*.

In a heartbeat he was kneeling beside her. A hoarse sound escaped—the sound of her name.

At first he thought he was dreaming. Her eyelids fluttered open. Cool fingertips came to rest upon his unshaven cheek.

"We have a son, Cameron." Her voice was so faint he had to strain to hear. But she was smiling, the merest wisp of a smile that pierced his heart. "We have a son."

With a jagged cry, he wrapped his arms around her, bowed his head to her breast, and wept.

Twenty-two

She had a son.

Depleted of strength as she was, joy lit Meredith's heart. It was sometime later that she woke to the low murmur of voices in the room.

"... I'm sure we can find a wet nurse."

Somehow the words penetrated the haze surrounding her. She gasped as she realized what they were about. Tears sprang to Meredith's eyes as she tried to sit up and failed. Yet her protest was surprisingly strong and decisive.

"Nay," she cried. "Nay!"

Two stunned pairs of eyes turned her way.

It was Cameron who spoke. "Meredith, there is no need to burden yourself—"

"Burden myself! I am his mother!"

Cameron and Glenda exchanged glances. "She can easily lay on her side and nurse him."

That was precisely what she did, for she was too depleted of strength to sit up. The next few days passed in a haze. She woke only to nourish her child and eat.

A week passed before she was allowed—or able— to leave her bed. Her limbs felt like porridge and she swayed dizzily once she was on her feet, but her first insistence was on a bath. With Glenda's and Miriam's assistance, she eased into the round wooden tub that sat before the fire. Miriam changed the bed linens, while Glenda helped her wash her hair. Though the effort taxed her sorely, it felt good to be up and about.

She was no sooner tucked back into bed than a mournful wail rose from the cradle in the corner. Eagerly she held out her arms. With pillows propped behind Meredith's back so she could sit, Glenda laid her son in the crook of her arm. Rather awkwardly, she slipped her bed gown from her shoulder and bared her breast. The babe rooted frantically, then latched on almost ferociously to her nipple. His greediness made both her and Glenda laugh.

A flood tide of love rushed through her. He was perfect, she thought, tracing the arch of one dark brow. A fine dark fuzz covered his scalp—his coloring was undoubtedly Cameron's. He was a handsome little lad, as handsome as his father, she decided proudly.

Her heart abrim, she cradled his head in her palm. "Angel," she crooned adoringly, "my sweetest little angel."

"Ah, but I fear we cannot call him 'angel,' else he will be the laughingstock of the Highlands." A thread of laughter laced that deep male voice.

Meredith glanced up to find Cameron in the doorway. Her heart lurched. Tall and bronzed and commanding, he strode within the chamber, so strikingly masculine a tremor resounded all through her.

By the time he sat upon the bed, Glenda had slipped from the chamber. The door eased shut with a quiet creak; they were alone.

All at once Meredith was quiveringly aware of his nearness; he sat so close, an iron-hard thigh rode gently against her own. His gaze roved searchingly over her features.

"You look much improved," he said softly.

Meredith blushed, feeling rather naked and exposed, with her gown fallen completely down her shoulder. Yet she was suddenly very glad that she had bathed and combed her hair, which now lay in a fiery curtain about her shoulders, the ends faintly damp and curling.

"I am," she murmured, wanting to lower her gaze but unable to tear it from his.

His regard seemed to deepen. Many times throughout this past week she had sensed his presence, heard the deeply resonant chords of his voice. Many a time she'd felt the brush of faintly callused fingertips upon her brow, for she would have known his touch anywhere. And she could have sworn warm lips dwelled fleetingly upon her own. Or did she but dream it?

Still another vague, elusive remembrance snatched at the fringes of her mind. *You are my wife, Meredith, my wife, and I hold you dear above all else. And as God is my witness, I love you.*

Something painful squeezed inside her chest. Had he really said that? Or was it but the foolish, fanciful meanderings of a memory hazed in pain?

If only she knew. If only she dared ask. If only she dared *hope* . . .

His gaze fell to their son, still suckling avidly. He laid his hand on the soft down of the babe's head. For a heart-stopping instant his fingers lay perilously near the naked flesh of her breast. The heartfelt simplicity of that gesture made her heart bleed afresh, yet Meredith was determined not to cry.

He ran a finger down the bairn's cheek. The babe's mouth stopped working. Tiny, fuzzy brows drew together over his wee nose, as if in puzzlement. They both laughed, though hers was rather shaky, as the child resumed his meal.

"It's time this lad had a name, don't you think?"

"Aye," she agreed, hoping he wouldn't hear the slight catch in the word.

"It should be something on which we both agree."

"Aye," she said again.

He appeared as hesitant as she. "I was thinking . . . mayhap Brodie Alexander. I've always had a fondness for the name 'Brodie.' And Alexander was one of my forebears."

"Brodie Alexander," she repeated, testing the name on her tongue. "Do you know, I—I like it very much. And he looks like he should be named Brodie Alexander, don't you think?"

"I do indeed." His gaze resided briefly on her lips, smiling now in pleasure. Cameron nearly groaned. God, she was sweet! Her cheeks were flushed the becoming pink of a newly bloomed rose, her eyes a pure, serene blue. His gaze moved hungrily down the slender column of her throat. The naked slope of her shoulder tempted him mightily. He yearned to run his fingers over her skin, knowing he would find it smooth and warm and as soft as fleece. Her breast was creamy and full, and her nipple was damp and glistening as she moved the babe to the other breast. Though he sensed her shyness about nursing before him, she made no effort to withdraw from either his nearness or his scrutiny.

And Meredith was indeed nervous beneath his unwavering regard. "If you mean to send me away, Cameron, I warn you I will not allow you to take my babe from me." Her arm tightened around the child. Where the announcement came from, she knew not.

But now that she had made it, she would not back down.

A brow shot high. A smile tugged at his lips. Ah, but she was a far cry from the wide-eyed, trembling maid he'd kidnapped those many months ago, he decided with amusement. Yet even then she'd defied him, frightened as she was . . . She was so brave, so full of courage, yet he suspected she knew it not.

In the next instant, his smile was gone. "I have no intention of sending you anywhere. You are his mother and he needs you. But I will not give him up, either." He paused. "Therefore, we must make this marriage work."

"How? There is much between us. My clan and your distrust."

An odd expression flitted across his features. He said nothing.

The breath she drew was deep and ragged. She was certain the tightness in her throat would surely strangle her. With trembling fingers she lifted the gleaming silver crucifix from where it hung about her neck and held it toward him. Tears glistened along her lashes, tears that darkened her eyes to sapphire. "I swear, upon this cross, that I did not poison you. I did not—I *do* not—seek to see you dead. I cannot prove my innocence. I can only claim it—and hope that you believe me."

Their eyes collided, hers pleading, his wholly unreadable. The tension was drawn out endlessly. Just when she thought her heart would surely break, his hand came up. Holding her gaze, with his thumb he blotted the single tear that slid down her cheek.

"And if I say that I believe you, will you cease these tears?"

Her heart caught. She was almost afraid to believe

what he was saying, just as afraid not to . . . "I will."
Her vow came out a low, broken whisper.

Something flashed in the bright silver of his eyes,
something she could have sworn was tenderness. He
leaned close, so close the heat of his breath mingled
with her own.

"Then dry your eyes, lass, for this should be a time
of joy, not tears."

The low vibrancy of his tone made her ache inside.
Did he but seek to appease her? She longed to throw
her arms around him and press herself tight against
his heart, but encumbered as she was with Brodie, she
could not.

His gaze dropped to her lips. For one heart-rending
moment, she thought he would kiss her, and oh! how
she wanted him to. She yearned for it with every fiber
of her being. But, alas, he did not. And then the moment was gone, for somehow Brodie's mouth had
slipped from her nipple. He howled fiercely at this
loss, and his clamor made them both laugh shakily.

It was several days later, when Meredith was finally
able to rise from her bed, that Cameron introduced
their son to his clansmen. The residents of Dunthorpe
gathered in the great hall, filling it to overflowing;
they spilled through the wide oaken doors and onto
the stairs that led down into the bailey. Men lifted
their bairns to their shoulders as all strained to catch
a glimpse of their chieftain and his newborn son.

Cameron stood upon the dais with Brodie in his
arms. An expectant silence rippled across the crowd.
He stepped forward.

He lifted the babe high in both arms. "My son,"
he called, "Brodie Alexander of the Clan MacKay."

At precisely that instant, Brodie wiggled. He let out

a demanding cry, surprisingly strong for so wee a form.

A roar started to go up, but Cameron was not yet finished. He beckoned for quiet, then turned ever so slightly to where Meredith sat, observing all with a slight smile.

He extended a hand to her.

Meredith caught her breath. Numbly she rose to her feet.

His fingers closed around her own, warm and strong. For a fleeting instant, their eyes met and held. "And my wife"—he raised their joined hands high— "the woman who gave him to me."

The cheers that filled the hall were deafening. Unexpected tears rose in Meredith's eyes. She couldn't help but recall the day she had ridden through the gates of Dunthorpe, a prisoner of the man who was now her husband. Never in all her days had she thought she would hear his people cheering her.

But they were no longer just his people. They were hers as well . . .

Touched though she was, she couldn't help but think of her father. There had been no news of the Red Angus for a long time now. Had his heartache eased? For his sake, she prayed it was so. Though she longed to send word that she was well—that he had a grandson—she knew Cameron would never allow it.

And yet in that moment, with their joined hands linked before his people, she felt very close to him.

Ah, if only such closeness could have continued . . .

Yes, both Meredith and Cameron took immense pride in their son. The arrival of the chieftain's son brought cheer and gladness within the lofty walls of

Dunthorpe. Gifts and fond wishes abounded for their newly born son.

Yet in the weeks that followed, husband and wife were alone but seldom. During those rare times when they were, an air of uncertain restraint marked their encounters.

Meredith worried anew. Was Cameron still convinced she had poisoned him? Perhaps he'd eaten something that had been tainted. A part of her scoffed that someone here at Dunthorpe would deliberately seek to poison him. Still, he was the only one who had sickened. It was odd, most odd. Too, it chilled her to know that Egan was convinced she was to blame. For a time the stoic Highlander's manner had softened. But once more his gaze and manner were chill, his eyes as cold as the mists that hovered on the mountaintops. She longed to cry out her innocence to him, yet she did not, for he was so very fierce! It occurred to her yet again that perhaps Egan was the one who sought to blame her, for she well knew his hatred for the Munros equaled that of his chieftain's. Could *he* have poisoned Cameron? Yet that made no sense, either . . .

She and Cameron had not slept together in the same chamber—in the same bed—since the night before he had sickened. Instead, he had moved his belongings to the chamber directly below hers. A month passed, then another and another. It frustrated her no end, for their relationship might have as well been that of brother and sister. Since Brodie was born, he had yet to kiss her, to hold her tight within his binding embrace. They did not touch, not even the merest brush of his fingers upon hers! She chanced to catch the weight of his eyes upon her one day after supper— for an instant her pulse quickened. A tempest of longing swirled inside her. But it was for naught, for alas, he did not return her smile, not even in part. Indeed, his features were shuttered. She could read nothing of his thoughts, for it was as if there were a shield of iron between them. He appeared stark and remote and more distant than ever! Abruptly he turned away. Her heart twisted in mute despair, for the hurt was almost more than she could bear. She fled to the sanctuary of her chamber, her lungs burning as she fought back a sob.

He'd said they must make their marriage work, but had he changed his mind? Could it be that the moment she had feared would come had indeed arrived? Had motherhood doused his desire for her? She took pains with her appearance, wearing her hair loose and tumbling over her shoulders the way he had always liked. Glenda had remarked on how quickly she had regained her figure after the birth. Though her breasts were fuller from nursing Brodie, her hips and waist were as slim as ever. Yet the love she craved was nowhere to be found.

A bittersweet pang rent her breast. Aye, she'd quickly regained her figure, the bloom of health in her cheeks. But inside she wilted with every day that passed and Cameron gave no sign that he would return to their bed . . . to *his* bed. Her body had mended . . . but would her heart? He loved their son, and for that she was heartily glad. Ah, but if only he loved his son's mother!

She did not know that Cameron's guilt was like a blight upon his soul. In those awful hours when Meredith's life had rested in God's hands, he had come to realize he loved her above all else. That he had ever accused her of trying to kill him was a remembrance that filled him with deep, scalding shame. For months his hatred of her clan had blinded him. She could never be so devious. His foolish stubbornness had stopped him from seeing her as she really was—the most caring, giving woman he had ever known. There was a calm strength about her now, a mature serenity that made him love her all the more.

Yet he was tormented as never before. He hated having her so near at hand, yet being unable to touch her. It was Glenda who had hinted he might reclaim his husbandly rights—ah, if only he could, he thought blackly. The very sight of his lovely wife made his head swim. She aroused him beyond reason. Motherhood had made her shine like the brightest of jewels; she was more breathtaking than ever. Her hair was unbound, a fiery cloud about her shoulders. He longed to twist his fingers in the silken mass and bring her mouth to his. Her skin shimmered like the finest of pearls. He'd seen this only yesterday, as he'd gone to retrieve the keys to the storeroom. Meredith was sitting in the chair before the fire, holding Brodie. She had looked up quickly, as startled as he.

He'd stopped in his tracks. Her gown was open to the waist. The babe was asleep. His mouth was half-open; it had fallen away from her nipple. Her breast was temptingly full, round and tipped with rose. His breath dammed in his throat; for an instant he could not breathe. A hungry desire quested within him, knotting his gut. His fingers fairly itched with the need to push aside the rest of her gown and bare her completely, to share that succulent fruit with his son. Without a word he'd turned and retraced his steps. It was the only way he could stop himself from lifting his son into his cradle, dragging her into his arms, carrying her to the bed, and making love to her until they were both exhausted. But he knew if he did, he would not end there.

Only one thing made him hesitate.

He had once taken all from her and demanded everything of her . . . and in so doing, she'd nearly lost her life. He paled whenever he thought of it. He could not forget how frail and weak she'd been, how he'd watched her strength seep away, breath by breath. Praise God she'd regained her health quickly! She now appeared vibrantly healthy. Yet he shuddered to think what bearing another child might cost her. The easiest way to rein in his desire was simply to refrain from being alone with her.

Nor was that the only burden he carried. Cameron had his pride, too. He would not return to his bedchamber—to *their* bedchamber—unless she asked. And since she did not ask, he had grimly decided that he had forced his will upon her for the last time. No, he would snatch her will from her no more.

If she wanted him, then she must be the one to let him know it.

Summer came to the Highlands, warm and sweetly scented. The mists lifted, and sunlight sparkled on verdant green hillsides. Radiant flowers bloomed across the meadows. Like the crops that filled the fields, their child thrived. His cheeks grew round and plump. Chubby legs pumped and kicked. He gazed avidly at all around him. The deep murkiness of his eyes had lightened to the brilliant color of a sunwarmed sky . . . his mother's eyes.

Passing through the great hall one day, Meredith heard a tiny, cooing laugh that sounded amazingly like Brodie's as she passed a small adjacent chamber. Curious, she pushed open the door.

Cameron sat in a high-backed chair. Brodie lay on

his thighs, his swaddling pushed aside. A dark finger swirled an idle pattern on the roundness of his tummy; Brodie chuckled delightedly. The sight of this lean brawny man, so big yet so gentle with this tiny infant, was a sight that never failed to move her to the core.

He glanced up then; a slight sheepishness crossed his features. She sensed he was embarrassed, and it made her smile.

She watched as he replaced Brodie's swaddling and lifted him to his shoulder. In the instant before he rose to his feet, she caught a faint wistfulness in his expression.

"Cameron?" She frowned, tilting her head to the side. "What is it? What are you thinking?"

He looked away—deliberately, she knew. Before she thought better of it, she laid a finger on his sleeve.

"Cameron, please tell me!"

Slowly his gaze returned. It traveled from her face to his son's. Dark fingers stroked the babe's cheek. His voice, when at last it came, was very low. "I was just thinking . . . that I wish my father could have seen him."

Her breath caught.

Her heart went out to him, for she heard the raw pain in his tone. Her throat tightened oddly. "So do I, Cameron. Oh, so do I, more than anything! And . . . oh, I do not mean to be cruel, but . . . but your father is gone—Brodie's grandfather is gone. But Brodie has another—a grandfather who yet lives . . ."

His features seemed to freeze. "What do you mean? The Red Angus?"

"Aye," she said, and then it was a broken cry: "Aye!" Suddenly it was all spilling out. Everything she had not dared to think of, for the pain it wrought. "I have carried this in my heart these many months.

You believe that my clansmen killed your brothers and your father. You saw their plaid, and you heard their battle cry. I—I believe you, Cameron, but no matter what you say, I cannot believe my father was there! He is a man of honor, a just, fair man. He would not murder for murder's sake alone. He would not surprise those who slept and steal their weapons, even his enemies! Say what you will, but I know he would not!'' She drew a deep breath, her eyes mutely pleading. ''You led him to believe that I was dead—but what of Brodie? How long will this go on? Cameron, 'tis not right! My father has a grandson, and 'tis only right that he should know!''

His jaw jutted out. Damn her, he thought. Damn her! The one thing she would ask of him was the one thing he would not give . . . could not give!

Curtly he spoke. ''Brodie is my son, Meredith. He was born a MacKay—''

''A MacKay with Munro blood! No matter how you may hate it, you cannot deny it. Aye, this is your son, but he is mine, too! So tell me, Cameron. Will you teach our son to hate the Munros—to hate the Red Angus? To hate his own grandfather?''

His tone was sharp. ''You could just as easily teach him to hate the MacKays!''

''When he lives here among the MacKays?'' Her chest was heaving. ''That will not happen, Cameron, and you know it as well as I!''

''What, then? Do you wish to go to Castle Munro? Need I remind you that 'twas you who said you would never return there?''

A tremor went through her. Now it was she who hesitated. ''I do not know,'' she cried brokenly. ''I do not know!''

For an eternity his gaze rested on her, cool and

chill. "So what would you have me do? Ask him to come here? He would not, Meredith." Flatly Cameron made the pronouncement. "He would think it was a ruse—a trap."

It came to her then, as suddenly as a storm in the mountains. She drew a ragged breath. "Nay," she said quietly. "He would not." Her hand crept to the silver chain about her throat. "Not if you sent him this."

Twenty-three

A brooding darkness slipped over Cameron throughout the night, for this was a decision he did not want to make. A part of him was furious with Meredith for even suggesting it . . . To think of the Red Angus here at Dunthorpe!

Still another part of him whispered that this was inevitable. When Brodie had been born, Cameron had deliberately put the feud—and the Red Angus—out of his mind. At the time he'd thought it best that the Red Angus never know his daughter was alive, that he had a grandson.

He could not ignore the truth. Meredith was right. Their child was a MacKay . . . a MacKay with Munro blood. And raised here at Dunthorpe, influenced by his clansmen, Brodie might easily grow to despise the Clan Munro.

The very notion was disturbing—nay, unpalatable! No matter his own feelings, it wouldn't be right if Brodie were to decry his own kin.

And he could never hurt Meredith like that—never in this world. She had forgiven him much, he admitted. Could she ever forgive him if he refused her in this?

It was a chance he would not take.

Yet ultimately, the choice was taken from him, in a most unexpected way.

It was Moire who announced casually at the table one morning, "They say the Red Angus is dying."

A dozen pair of shocked eyes fastened upon her. "What!" someone said. "Where did you hear that?"

"From the peddler at the gates last eve." Moire defended herself staunchly. "He passed through Munro lands on his way here."

Within the hour it was the talk of the keep. It was Glenda who sought out Cameron and told him. Cameron wasted no time climbing the tower stairs. His step was heavy, for this was a task he did not relish.

As the door opened, Meredith straightened from the cradle where she'd just placed Brodie. "Good morning." If she was a trifle cool as she greeted her husband, she could not help it. He had yet to speak further of allowing her father to see Brodie.

He stepped before her. One look at his face and she knew instantly that something was amiss. Beneath his tan, he was distinctly pale.

"What is it?" she said quickly. "What is wrong? Is it Glenda?"

He shook his head. "Glenda is fine. Meredith . . . it seems your father is dying."

Meredith put a hand to her throat. "That cannot be," she said in a half-strangled voice. "You say this only to hurt me!"

"Believe me, this brings me no pleasure, Meredith. But I thought it best if the news came from me."

She swayed. Blackness stole all through her. For one perilous moment she thought she might faint.

His hands came out to catch at her shoulders. "Meredith!"

She pushed him away. "I am fine!" Suddenly she

was babbling. "I must go to him. I must!" She turned toward the cradle. "Brodie. I must gather his things. And he should be fed . . ." She stretched out a hand. "And Glenda. I must tell Glenda—"

"Meredith—"

"No, Cameron, you cannot stop me!" she cried wildly. "He is my father! If he is dying, then I must go to him. I must be with him. If you will not take me, then I will find my own way."

"Meredith. Meredith, *hush*!" Strong arms closed around her. "I will not stop you! But you must calm yourself—"

"I cannot! There is much to be done. Brodie's things must be packed. We must have food for the journey—"

"And we will. I will send Glenda to you. Feed Brodie, and then rest while you can, for the journey is a long one." He gave her shoulder a reassuring squeeze, then departed swiftly.

Meredith had just finished feeding Brodie and laying him in his cradle when Glenda burst into the chamber.

"Meredith, Cameron told me you must make ready to journey to Castle Munro."

Meredith nodded. "Aye. My father . . ."—she couldn't help the betraying catch in her voice—"he is dying."

Glenda laid a hand on her shoulder. "I heard, Meredith. I heard. And . . . oh, I know there has been much distrust between the Clan MacKay and the Clan Munro, but I am truly sorry."

Meredith's throat clogged tight. Papa . . . dying. She could scarcely stand to think of it. It was still so hard to believe . . .

She couldn't withold the tears that sprang to her

eyes. Seeing them, Glenda's arms came around her. Meredith drew both comfort and strength from Glenda's embrace.

After a moment she drew back. "I am fine. Really. Now . . . do you mind helping me gather our clothing?"

"Of course not—that is why I came. Oh, and I stopped by the kitchen and ordered bread and cheese packed."

Between the two of them, it did not take long to collect the necessary belongings. Picking up the pouches, Glenda put them near the door.

Meredith had started toward Brodie's cradle just as Glenda turned. It seemed the tears were now in Glenda's eyes—a sight that made Meredith stop short. "Glenda," she cried. "What is amiss?"

" 'Tis nothing." Glenda dashed at the dampness in her eyes and sought to smile.

Meredith shook her head. "Nonsense," she admonished. "If 'twere nothing, then you would not weep."

"You are right," Glenda admitted. " 'Tis just that . . . I will miss you dreadfully, Meredith. You will return, will you not?"

The odd note in her voice made Meredith's gaze sharpen. She looked at Glenda oddly. "Why would you think I would not return—" All at once she understood. "Ah," she said softly. " 'Tis because we go to Castle Munro, is it not?"

Glenda nodded, her golden brown eyes wide and distressed. "You are my greatest friend in all the world, Meredith. If this is the last time I shall see you—"

"It is not." The lump was back in Meredith's throat as well. "Glenda, it is not! This is my home now. This is where I belong.'' She reached out and grasped Glenda's hands in her own. "And I will miss you, too," she said simply, "for you are like a sister to me."

"Meredith. Oh, Meredith, I feel the same!" The pair hugged each other once again, their smiles shaky as they drew back.

Suddenly Glenda's faded. "Meredith," she said quietly, "mayhap I meddle where I should not, but . . . oh, I know you have said nothing to me—indeed, I do not blame you—but I know that matters between you and Cameron are not what you wish. Yet I know in my heart that he loves you. I *feel* it. And so I would ask you to have faith. Have faith and believe that all will be well, for I truly believe it will."

A pang rent Meredith's heart. If only it was so . . . for she could not bear to think she might spend her life loving a man who might never love her in return.

Outside in the bailey, Cameron had ordered that the horses be readied and supplies gathered. It was there he saw Egan and told his friend of his plans.

"You go to Castle Munro!" Egan's regard was tight-lipped and disapproving. "By the shroud of Christ, that woman will be the death of you yet!"

Cameron's eyes glinted. "Be careful where you tread, my friend," he warned softly. "She is my wife, and I will tolerate no disrespect for her, even from you."

Egan sighed, the sound heavy. "I know that, Cameron. But I dislike the idea of you traveling alone on Munro lands." He made a sudden decision. "Let me gather some men—"

"No. A large party will garner too much attention.

I think it best if we travel discreetly.'' Cameron was adamant.

But so was Egan. ''Aye, you are right, of course. But I will not let you go alone, Cameron. 'Tis too risky.''

In the end, Cameron decided Egan's suggestion was sound. If something should happen to him, he could trust Egan to get Meredith and Brodie to safety. In truth, it was one less worry. By noonday, they were well on their way.

Though Meredith made no protest, Cameron was anxiously aware that she was exhausted by the end of each day of travel when he lifted her from her mount. She was unused to riding, as he was. Brodie, lamb that he was, obliged both mother and father greatly by proving to be an excellent traveler. Cameron fashioned a sling to carry the lad on his back, and Brodie seemed to delight in it. He gazed brightly around at the vivid green landscape. He did not fuss or cry, except when he was hungry and sought his mother's breast. If they but had more time, Cameron would have insisted on a cart and pony where Meredith and the babe could sit or ride at their leisure. Yet he knew Meredith would have chafed at the delay.

The next day, they crested a small rise. They followed the road, which skirted the edge of a dense forest. All at once an odd feeling slithered down his spine. He glanced over at Egan. But a glimpse of Egan's frosty blue eyes yielded what he already suspected—they were being watched, and Egan knew it, too.

Something unspoken passed between them; Egan gave a slight nod. Raising a hand, Cameron called a halt. Meredith, who was holding Brodie, flashed a grateful smile. Brodie had begun to squirm, rooting against her, for he was hungry. Strong hands on her waist, Cameron swung his wife and child to the ground. He bent low so that he spoke directly in her ears.

"Say nothing, lass, but go behind that boulder and do not move until I come for you."

Meredith's gaze flashed to his. His stern warning came as a surprise, but she was too alarmed by his fierceness to do anything but obey. Hurriedly she did as he bade her, shushing Brodie. She had just ducked behind the boulder when footsteps pounded behind her. Hoarse shouts erupted.

Cameron and Egan were already turning as three great brutes dressed in blackened leather rushed at them. One carried a battle-ax, while the other two were armed with dirks. Sunlight caught the glint of steel as they ripped their swords from their scabbards.

The trio was no match for the two men of the Clan MacKay. The battle was over almost before it began. Shaken and dazed, Meredith was ushered back to her mount by her husband. She gasped as she spied the three broken bodies.

"Cameron!" she gasped. "Who are they? Why did they attack us?"

"Thieves," he said smoothly, "from the look of them. They care not who they prey on."

A shiver went through her. Back at Dunthorpe, she had not been pleased when she saw that Egan meant to accompany them. Yet now she was heartily glad of his presence.

It was much later that she slept in utter weariness. But there was no sleep for Cameron. He paced restlessly beside the fire.

From where he sat before the flames, Egan looked

up at him. "Those men today," he said suddenly. "They wore no plaid."

"I know." Cameron continued his pacing.

"It was just as I thought—a trap," he spat. "They knew we were coming. They were lying in wait."

Cameron made no answer, but continued his pacing.

"Why"—Egan voiced aloud the thought that had been in Cameron's mind since the attack—"do I have the feeling that we were not meant to reach Castle Munro?"

Only then did Cameron come to a halt. "Because we were not," he said grimly. "Which means we shall have to be very, very cautious from here on out."

It was the following afternoon when Castle Munro came into view. Perched on a bluff overlooking fields of grasses that undulated in the breeze, its tall stone walls glittered in the sunlight. Overhead the sky arched brilliant and sunny. Though it was not so massive as Dunthorpe, it was still a castle of considerable size.

With every step that took them closer, a feeling of dread coiled in Cameron's belly. For the first time, he understood what Meredith must have felt as she'd passed through the gates of Dunthorpe. Yet his lovely wife had borne it bravely, her head held high . . .

And so would he.

In case something should go wrong, Cameron insisted that Egan remain behind and stand watch. Egan liked it not a whit, but he did as Cameron asked. Later, when he was assured of all of their safety, he would send word to his friend. If all was well, he would see that Egan was admitted.

As they approached the outer walls, a sentinel appeared at the gatehouse. Before Cameron could announce them, Meredith pushed back the drape of her hood and revealed her face.

Another time, and Cameron might have chuckled at the amazement that washed over the sentinel's features. He dropped to his knees and made the sign of the cross.

"Dear Lord, am I seein' a ghost, then? Surely I've gone mad, for this cannot be! 'Tis dead ye be!"

Meredith's lips quirked. "I assure you, Ranald, you've not gone mad. 'Tis I, Meredith, and I am as alive as you. But please, tell me"—she couldn't hide her worry—"how is Papa? He yet lives, does he not?"

Ranald's eyes drew together, as if in puzzlement. "Aye," he said slowly, "he does."

Meredith sent a fervent prayer heavenward. "Thank you, Ranald, thank you."

They ventured farther within. Once they reached the inner bailey, Cameron leaped lightly to the ground, then helped Meredith to her feet. Brodie was sleeping soundly, cradled in the crook of her elbow.

By then, they'd begun to attract notice. There were shocked whispers from several people nearby.

" 'Tis her! 'Tis Angus's daughter!"

But Cameron had been recognized as well. "Do ye not know who he is?" someone shouted. "Look at his plaid!"

"He is a MacKay!" someone thundered.

A mighty blow from behind knocked him to his knees. Meredith gasped and whirled on the giant who had struck him. "Leave him be!" she cried indignantly. "He is with me!" She extended her free hand to Cameron, who accepted it and rose to his feet. He said nothing, but his lips were a taut, straight line. His expression was nearly as hostile as those who had gathered around them.

"What goes on here?" demanded yet another gruff male voice. "Step aside, and let me have a look!"

Meredith turned . . . and came face-to-face with her father.

Every drop of color drained from Angus's face. He staggered, as if he would fall. Anguish crept into his eyes, a world of it.

"Papa!" Meredith cried. "Papa, do not look at me so!"

He shook his head. "I see what I do . . . yet I cannot see what I am seeing!"

Meredith smiled mistily. "I am here, Papa. Your eyes do not deceive you."

"God in heaven," he breathed. "My jewel is alive. My jewel is alive and whole and well!" Tears filled his eyes, tears that made Cameron both wince and smile.

Unable to speak for the joy that surged within him, Angus held out his arms. Meredith laid her head on his chest and closed her eyes.

At length he drew back, clearly in a daze. "I still do not understand. The sisters at Connyridge told me you were dead—that you had taken your own life! Meredith, it has been nearly a year! Where have you been all this time? Why did you not send word?"

"I would not let her." Cameron stepped forward. "I was the one who led you to believe she was dead. My men and I found a woman dead on the road near the priory—a woman who bore a faint resemblance to Meredith. After I stole her away from Connyridge, my men dressed the woman in Meredith's robes and threw her over the cliff."

"But the note she left—"

"Was written at my instruction." Cameron paused. "Since the night I stole her away from Connyridge those many months ago, your daughter has been with me . . . at Dunthorpe."

"Dunthorpe," Angus echoed. Shaggy brows drew together over his nose. "But that is the MacKay stronghold!"

Cameron raised his chin. "Aye," was all he said.

For the first time Angus seemed to notice the man at his daughter's side. "Who the devil are you?" he demanded.

Cameron raised his chin. "I am Cameron, of the Clan MacKay."

Angus looked as if he might explode. "MacKay," he repeated through his teeth. "By God, that you should dare to set foot in my home, and with my daughter, yet . . . Seize this man!" he shouted. "Seize this man and take him—"

"Papa, no, for I tell you now, where he goes, I go as well!" Her eyes ablaze, Meredith stepped close to Cameron's side.

Angus's face was like a thundercloud. "Meredith, are you daft? Why do you defend this man . . . a MacKay, yet?"

"Because he is my husband, Papa. He is my husband and I love him"—her voice rang out clearly—"and we have a son." Her hand went to the blanket that covered her slumbering child. She pushed it aside to reveal his form. "This is Brodie, Papa. Our son." The merest smile played over her lips as she added softly, "Your grandson."

As if he knew he was the subject of discussion, Brodie stirred. The babe yawned, and waved a sleepy fist high in the air. His eyelashes fluttered just as Angus stepped close.

He beheld eyes as blue as the skies above . . . as blue as his own.

For the second time in a few short minutes, Angus wept.

Cameron had never been as proud of his wife as he was in that moment when she stood before her father, defiant and determined as she claimed him as her husband before all . . .

She was so brave, so courageous. She risked her father's wrath, for him. *For him.*

And she loved him. Sweet Jesus, she loved him!

He was still reeling when they adjourned to the great hall. It was here that Angus first held his grandson. An odd sensation closed Cameron's throat as he watched the Red Angus with his son—he held Brodie as if he were the greatest of treasures. After Angus gave the order that food was to be prepared, Cameron decided it was safe for Egan as well. It was Angus who rode out with him to find Egan. By the time the three returned, a meal had been laid out. Someone had fetched a cradle, and Brodie now slept there, his mouth open, his little rump curled high in the air.

It was then that Robert, Angus's brother, strode into the hall. Taller and less stout than Angus, his hair was a shade darker than Meredith's and her father's, and not quite so bright. His eyes were different, too, a deep, dark brown.

He strode straight to her chair. Meredith stood while he embraced her. "Meredith! My God, lass, I could scarce believe it when I heard the news. Why, you've risen from the dead!"

Meredith gave a shaky laugh. "Not quite, Uncle."

His sharp gaze took in Cameron, who had also risen. "Ah, and who have we here? Your husband, I take it?"

Cameron inclined his head. "Aye, sir. I am Cameron."

"Well, well, it appears I am just in time for supper." He glanced between Cameron and Angus. "A MacKay and a Munro sitting together at table. Why, 'tis surely an occasion not to be missed."

His lightness was forced, his manner a bit stiff. Meredith decided it best to ignore his discomfort. Her gaze moved to her father. Nearly three years had passed since she'd seen him, she realized. More gray threaded the strands of his fiery red hair and brows, and he was not so heavy as she remembered, yet she had expected him to be in his sickbed, not up and about, and so she commented.

"What! Why would you think such a thing?" Angus was puzzled at her admission.

"We received word that you were dying, Papa. Have you not been ill?"

"Nay! Oh, I admit, when word of your death came to me, I did not leave the grounds for many a day, but I was hardly on my deathbed. And that was months ago."

Meredith did not miss the way Egan's eyes met Cameron's—nor did Angus.

"Do you think you were lured from your home, lad?"

Cameron's reply was cool. "I do not know, but aye, now that I see you are well, it does make one wonder."

"That it does, lad, that it does. But come, let us eat. The three of you are no doubt ready for a good meal after so many days in the saddle. How long a journey is it from Dunthorpe?''

''Nearly five days, sir.'' Cameron could not help but be suspicious. Angus had been so angry in the bailey, yet now there was no sign of it. Yet, the old man's manner toward him was not particularly amiable; rather, it was as if he weighed and measured his new son-in-law.

Indeed, Cameron realized, the Red Angus's manner was much the same as his own. *My father is not a murderer.* Meredith's plea tolled through his mind. Well, he would see. Aye, he would see what the Red Angus had to say about the butchery of his father and brothers.

The time came soon enough, once the last dish was served and the platters and trenchers were cleared from the table. Angus raised a grizzled brow. ''Now, then. I should like to hear precisely what precipitated your abduction of my daughter from Connyridge.''

Cameron met his challenge with one of his own. ''Murder most treacherous, sir,'' he said softly. ''The murder of my father and my brothers.''

Angus was astounded. ''What! And you blame me? Because of the feud between our clans?''

Cameron's voice was tight. ''Nay. Not because of the feud.''

''What, then? I cannot deny, I'd heard the MacKay chieftain and his sons were murdered by brigands and thieves—''

''Nay. Not brigands and thieves, but men who wore the Munro plaid. Men who gave the Munro battle cry . . . and were commanded by a man with red hair.'' Grimly he relayed the details of the attack.

Angus was on his feet in a heartbeat. ''Do you accuse me?''

Cameron countered with a question of his own. "Did you order the murder of my family?"

Angus's denial was a roar. "Nay, I did not! Deceit is not my way. Ask any who knows me!"

"And what if I say I saw you?"

Gray eyes locked with blue in a sizzling battle of wills. All at once the tension in the room reached a fever pitch. Even Brodie began to cry. As she reached for the babe and settled him on her lap, Meredith's heart froze in her chest. She did not know what terrified her more—her father's unfamiliar, forbidding countenance or the icy cold mask of her husband's.

It was Angus who let out his breath slowly. "I do not know who you saw, lad, but it was not me. It may well be that this foul deed was done by my clansmen—but I swear I had no knowledge of it—not until this night."

"So you deny all knowledge of the murder of my father? Of my brothers?"

"Dear God, aye! This feud has simmered between our clans for many a year—yet not since I was a child have I heard of such bloodshed as you have described. I pray that never again will I hear of it! But first I must know . . ." His gaze turned to Meredith. "He sought vengeance through you, lass. Did he harm you? Did he hurt you in any way . . . ever?"

Meredith heard the slight break in her father's voice. She felt his anxious fear with all that she possessed, just as she felt the way Cameron had gone rigid and stiff beside her.

Her hand came out to cover Cameron's where it lay on the sturdiness of his thigh. "Nay, Papa. Never has he hurt me. Not ever. For you see"—she smiled, not caring that her love was undisguised—"my husband is a man such as you."

Angus nodded, his relief audible. "Then know this, lad. I will do all within my power to see that those who murdered your family are found and sentenced."

Cameron went utterly still. For the very first time, doubt crowded his every pore. Could it be that he had been wrong all this time? Could it be that he had wrongly accused the Red Angus? He did not want to believe it, and yet . . .

His heart told him otherwise. Meredith had told him the Red Angus was a man of honor . . . and somehow he was beginning to believe it.

"Wait," he said suddenly. "We have yet to speak of the feud."

"What of it, lad?"

Cameron's heart squeezed. *Lad*. Angus did not seek to needle him. He spoke the word with a natural ease, as casually as his own father once had.

Meredith's fingers slipped between his own. At the contact, Cameron swallowed. Her hand looked pitifully small there against his palm. The contrast between their skin was riveting. Soft against hard, he noted dimly. Dark against fair.

His gaze was drawn helplessly to her face. She was smiling ever so slightly, her head tipped to the side as she gazed at him, her eyes full of some emotion he dared not name.

He looked into her eyes . . . Angus's eyes, he realized. His son's eyes . . .

There was a terrible tightness in his chest—it hurt to breathe. Sheer pain ripped through him, for an instant rendering him wholly immobile. For there was an agonizing struggle being waged in the center of his breast . . . The past against the present, the future. MacKay against Munro . . .

He moved without conscious volition. He stood,

pulling her up beside him. For all at once he knew what he must do . . . and why.

It was not easy—indeed it was the hardest thing he'd ever done! Yet he heard himself speak the words he'd never thought to say . . .

"It must end. Dear God, this feud must end."

Twenty-four

It was over. The feud was over.

Meredith stepped inside her bedchamber a short time later. Her head was still swimming as she laid Brodie in the cradle that stood before the fire. It was still so hard to believe the feud was over . . .

At Cameron's insistence.

Her father—bless his soul!—had agreed it was long past time the antagonism ended.

It would not be easy. Both men were aware that their clans would not dismiss their hatred so readily, for their hatred stretched back a very long time—the possibility had kept them at the table for a long time afterward. Yet both Cameron and Angus were in accord on one very important point . . .

No matter what the provocation, the hostilities must not be renewed.

It was much later when the discussion was at last concluded. They all arose—Meredith, Cameron, Angus, and Robert. Angus cleared his throat.

"I would like a word alone with my daughter."

Meredith's gaze swung immediately to Cameron—an uncharacteristic uncertainty flickered across his features. Offering what she hoped was a reassuring smile, she passed Brodie into his father's arms.

"I won't be long," she murmured for his ears alone. Raising her head, she glanced at her Uncle Robert. "Uncle, would you please show my husband and our son to my chamber?"

Robert stepped forward. "Of course," he said smoothly.

Cameron said nothing, but moved to follow Robert toward the stairs.

Meredith and her father were left alone.

Without a word Angus opened his arms.

Meredith wasted no time, but stepped within his hearty embrace.

Angus rubbed his cheek against her hair. "Meredith," he said, and then again: "*Meredith*! My child, you cannot know how I've felt these many months without you! 'Twas just like when your mother was taken from me—it was as if a part of my soul had been lost and would never be found. Yet here you are before me . . ." He broke off, his every emotion reflected in the unsteadiness of his voice.

Tears misted Meredith's vision. She made a small choked sound and raised her head. "I know, Papa, I know, and I am so sorry! I tried to escape, but Cameron found me, and then . . . then somehow I was falling in love with him . . . Papa, I was so torn, between him and you!"

Angus's body had turned to stone. "I know what you said in his presence, Meredith. But I must hear it again. Did he harm you? Hurt you in any way?"

Meredith shook her head. "Nay, Papa. *Nay!* Why, he defended me before his own clan. Oh, at first I was so very frightened, for he was so fiercely determined! But then I began to see the man beneath the vengeance. Indeed, 'twas the loss of his brothers and father that provoked his vengeance. Papa, in so many way he reminds me of you. He is unquestionably loyal to his clan, so protective of those he holds dear . . . and I love him. Papa, I do!''

"Aye," he said slowly, "I can see that you do." His expression softened. "You trust in your heart, and I must trust in you."

Not long thereafter, she kissed him good night and climbed the stairs to her old chamber.

A glowing fire now burned in the hearth; she spied Cameron stretched out in the chair before it. Brodie slumbered in the cradle which had been brought up and placed near his feet.

He glanced up when the door opened. By the time she crossed to him, he was on his feet. He gazed searchingly into her face. "All is well?"

"Aye."

Shyly she raised her eyes to his. "Cameron, I want to thank you for what you did in the hall—ending the feud. I know what it cost you."

He shook his head. "There is no need to thank me, Meredith. I did what was right. I could not live with myself were my son—*our* son—to grow up despising his grandfather and all his clan." His features turned pensive. " 'Tis odd, really," he said slowly, "but I feel as if an oppressive weight has been lifted from me."

And so do I, Meredith echoed silently. Before she could say a word, Brodie began to squirm and fuss. Meredith's breasts began to sting as they filled with milk. She'd been able to soothe him in the hall, but it had been some hours since he'd eaten and she knew he was impatient. It was Cameron who fetched him, his big hands immeasurably tender as he lifted Brodie from the cradle. He brought the babe to her, laying him in the crook of her arm.

"He needs you," he said simply.

Meredith settled herself in the chair before the fire. The evening had turned chill, and she watched as Cameron threw a chunk of wood onto the flames. In a few minutes she switched Brodie to the other breast. Thus far he'd given no indication that he intended to leave—that he wished to sleep elsewhere, as he had for so long now. He stood near the hearth, his hands linked behind him. Staring at the taut, spare lines of his shoulders, her yearning for him ripened.

All she wanted was to feel his arms snug and warm about her back, the drumbeat of his heart strong and steady beneath her ear. She craved his nearness with a force that made her tremble inside. Yet she was afraid to hope he might stay—just as afraid not to.

She'd managed to hold the thought in abeyance until now—now she could no longer avoid it. As overjoyed as she'd been to see her father, the thought of spending the night alone here—here in the chamber where she'd once been snatched from the bed—made her stomach cramp with fear. A trickle of apprehension snaked down her spine. It was all she could do to stop her gaze from skipping to the door again and again.

Soon Brodie slept. Meredith laid him in the cradle, then drew a deep, uneven breath.

Somehow she managed to disguise her true feelings. "Would you like me to see if another chamber can be found?"

"There is no need. I will sleep here this night." Looking deeply into her eyes, he raised a brow questioningly. "Remember what you told your father? That where I go, you go?"

She locked her hands together to stop them from trembling. "Aye."

"So you said—and so say I." He was utterly grave. "I would not sleep elsewhere, even if I wanted to."

"If you wanted to!" A faint bitterness bled through to her voice. "Why should you want to, when you have slept elsewhere these many weeks?"

There was a small silence. His gaze seemed to delve deep into hers. " 'Tis not what you think," he said finally.

All at once she was perilously near tears. If he remained, she told herself, it was solely for her father's benefit—so Angus would not know that anything was amiss with their marriage.

She turned away, for she could no longer endure his piercing scrutiny. An elusive hurt stabbed at her, but she was determined not to let him see it.

"Must you make this more difficult? There is no need for you to remain with me. I—I know you find me distasteful."

Cameron stared. "Distasteful! Meredith, nay. Nay, I say!"

"You do! Since Brodie was born, you avoid me. When we are alone, you—you quickly find some excuse to leave. You do not share my bed. Well, I am not a fool, Cameron. I know when I am not wanted!"

He was quiet for a moment. "It is true," he said at last, his tone very low. "I have made excuses so that I am not alone with you." He gestured vaguely. "Meredith, I know not how to explain, but . . . it hurts to be with you. It hurts to—to want you."

Everything was coming apart inside her. "And is that so terrible? To want your wife? Ah, but I forget that *you* cannot forget. I am the daughter of the Red Angus. Ah, and to think I was foolish enough to believe that you truly wished to end this feud."

"I do want it ended! And I am the fool, not you."

She said nothing. Her shoulders had begun to heave.

"Meredith. Meredith, come here!" Lean hands caught at hers. She resisted when he tried to tug her close, but he wouldn't allow it. Finally, with an impatient sound, he snared her around the waist and caught her up against him.

"I am the fool, not you," he said again. His knuckles beneath her chin dictated she look at him. His eyes captured hers.

"Listen to me, sweet. When Brodie was born, I knew a fear such as I had never known! The memory haunts me still, for it was my fault that you nearly died."

Meredith caught her breath. "You? You were afraid?" It seemed strange, that this strong, powerful man might be afraid . . .

"Aye." With the pad of his thumb, he caressed the pouting fullness of her lower lip. "All I could think was . . . what if I lost you? You are more precious to me than anything in this world. I cannot be near you without craving you, without wanting to hold you tight against my heart, to claim you for my own . . . 'Tis you and you alone who fill my every moment, you who light the fire in my heart, the questing in my soul . . . you alone who can satisfy me. And yet I dare not touch you for fear that my seed will lodge in your womb, that you might suffer yet again the agony you suffered when Brodie came into this world. For if I lost you, I would lose my very heart."

His fervent admission made her quiver inside. Never had it occurred to her this might be the reason he held himself so distant. Indeed, it sounded almost as if he loved her . . .

" 'Twas not your fault," she said with a tiny shake

of her head. "I scarcely remember the pain, and I did not die. I am well and healthy and . . . and I cannot bear to go on like this! I need you, Cameron. I need for you to hold me!" The confession broke from her with a ragged sob, before she could stop it. "I love you, Cameron! I love you!"

A powerful tide of emotion rose inside him, taking from him the ability to speak, even to move. Then, with a groan, he engulfed her in his arms, for Cameron could no more deny her offering than he could the depth of his longing. He trapped tremulous lips beneath his own.

As Cameron carried her to the bed, Meredith buried her face against the hardness of his shoulder, savoring the warm haven of his embrace. His lips grazed her temple. Yet all at once a shiver coursed the length of her.

"Cameron, though I am heartily glad, 'twas most odd, finding Papa well. Do you truly think we were lured from Dunthorpe? That those men who attacked us were lying in wait?"

His arms tightened. "I was mistaken, sweet." He would not nourish her fears further, though in truth he still questioned the coincidence. He masked his unease with a faint smile. "Go to sleep, love, for I know you are weary."

He was satisfied just to hold her, not with passion's urge but with a basking contentment that came only when she was in his arms. Before long, her limbs grew limp. Her lungs rose and fell deeply. Soon she slept.

For Cameron, sleep was impossible, for he was still reeling at her declaration. Mother of Christ, to think that she loved him, after all he had done! He had wrested her away from the priory, commanded that she bear his son and then wed him! He should have told her, he realized with a twinge of regret, told her that he loved her. In light of all he felt, the sentiment seemed so frail and hardly enough to express the boundless surge in his heart.

It was later that his mind eventually turned back to the feud. Aye, he thought with the greatest relief, he was glad it was over. It would take some time for his people—and the Red Angus's—to accept, but in time they would understand and be grateful that the hostilities had ended.

Angus had sworn he would find those responsible for the murder of his brothers and father. Damn, but he'd been so certain he'd caught a glimpse of the Red Angus! Could it be that his hatred had somehow conjured up the vision in his mind? Nay, he thought. There had been someone . . .

He was right. And that someone had watched the evening's events unfold with venomous disgust. For in this man's view, if the world existed with one less MacKay, it was a far better place.

Such was the churning of this man's mind as he crept up the stairs toward the chamber where Cameron and his wife lay in sleepy repose. He vowed that before the hour was through, Cameron MacKay would blacken this earth no longer.

A thin sliver of yellow appeared as the door gave way beneath his hand, lit from the rushlight that burned in the hall outside. It was that which roused the two inhabitants of the bed.

Still caught in the heavy drape of sleep, Meredith raised a hand to protest the light. Full wakefulness struck as air rushed by her and Cameron's figure charged from the bed.

In the still of the distant night beyond, the risen moon emerged from behind a froth of clouds and spilled through the open shutters. Against that yellow haze, two figures grappled with each other. Meredith bolted upright the second she saw a hand shift high aloft. Moonglow glinted off the gleaming blade of a dagger. Even as a cry spilled from her throat, the dagger carved an arcing path downward. The man on the right flung up an arm, but it was too late.

He crumpled to the floor.

A hand like a claw dragged her from the bed. Meredith let loose a piercing scream. There was a vile curse. A hand clamped over her mouth, drowning the sound. She was spun around and brought up against a hard male form. "Merry," grated a raspy voice in her ear. "My sweet Merry."

Meredith's blood turned to ice. She knew that voice. Knew it well indeed . . .

"Uncle Robert," she whispered. "Oh, sweet heaven, it was you who stole me from this very chamber. You who took me away and—" She could not go on.

His eyes gleamed. "Ah, Merry, but I have such fond memories of that night! I could never look at you again without remembering how you felt naked against me!"

Meredith was sick to the core of her being, for it was he who had abused her. He who had hurt her that long-ago night, who had so terrorized her and driven her from her home.

"But you didn't know until now, did you, lass?" he taunted. "I always wondered if you knew, or if you were too much the coward to say so. But I am not a coward. It was I who killed Ronald MacKay and his sons," he boasted, "and now I've killed your husband."

No. *No!* Cameron lay on his side, still and motionless. One lean hand lay palm upward. A horrible dread ripped at her insides, for she could not bear to think he was dead!

"The man Cameron saw that day. It was not Papa, but you!"

"A pity he did not die that day. I thought he had. Indeed, 'twas some while before I learned that he had survived. I sent a spy to Dunthorpe, one who found work with the smithy—oh, aye, a big, handsome lad . . . and he found a pretty, dark-haired beauty so angry that the new chieftain had married another."

"Moire," she breathed.

"Aye." Robert's smile was gloating. "She was only too willing to slip poison into his wine. Ah, but she was furious that he did not die! I do believe, lass, that in time you would have been next. But then we came upon the idea of bringing you both here to me! She proved most resourceful, I must say!"

So it was Moire who had also begun the talk that her father was dying. Meredith was suddenly filled with a rage such as she had never known.

"So it was you who arranged to have us attacked when we drew near." Her stare was infinitely cold.

"Oh, aye, sweet Merry. But alas, your devoted husband will not escape this time. I have already seen to it, have I not?" His gaze rested briefly on Cameron's prone figure, then returned to her face.

His eyes filled with lust. "Merry, ah, my sweet Merry, I could not resist you once you were grown! You remind me so of your mother. You won't tell, will you, sweet Merry? You wouldn't then and you won't now." His grin was leering. "Ah, but you disappointed me when you ran off to Connyridge, Merry. I intended far more than just that one sweet taste of you, you know. And now I shall have it.''

His head descended. Meredith did not think, but reacted with all the anger in her heart. Doubling her fist, she swung at his face with all her might.

There was a satisfying thud. Robert's head snapped back. Blood poured from his nose.

His eyes glittered. ''By God,'' he snarled, ''you'll pay for that!''

He got no further, for suddenly an arm shot out and swiped at his knees. Flung off balance, Robert went down hard upon the floor.

Robert's blade had bit deep into Cameron's shoulder, leaving him stunned for a moment. When the mist of pain had cleared, he'd heard Robert's confession—heard it and been filled with a vile rage more potent than any he'd ever known. He'd awaited the right moment, feigning a mortal wound until at last the moment came. He leaped to his feet, but damn! his sword was across the room, propped near the bed.

In the corner, Robert now sprang upright as well, his features contorted in a feral snarl. He gripped his dagger in his hand.

But in his haste to creep into the chamber, he had left the door ajar. Meredith's screams had awakened others in the household. And now Robert noticed Angus in the doorway. A glimpse of the blazing fury alight on his brother's features told him that Angus had heard all.

His breath hissed inward. By God, it mattered not. He was set on his course and he would not allow his weakling brother to stop him.

His lips curled back over his teeth. With a bellow

of rage, he hurtled toward Cameron, his dagger poised high.

The blade never fell, for another sliced up and outward, stopping him cold. An instant later, Robert slumped to the floor. The dagger slipped from his lifeless fingers.

Angus stood over his brother's form, his sword still in hand. He had always believed in loyalty to clan and family above all else. But in that moment when he lunged toward Robert, he did not see his brother. He saw only the man who had betrayed his trust, the man who had misused his beloved Meredith, the man who had turned her laughter into quaking fear.

Thankfully, Cameron's injury was not as serious as Meredith had feared. He assured her he'd suffered far worse, yet Meredith fretted anxiously until the bleeding stopped and the wound was bound with clean white strips of linen. Egan had charged into the chamber just as Angus attacked Robert, for he, too, had heard Meredith's screams.

Robert's body was removed from the chamber. After Meredith finished tending her husband, she walked with Angus to the door. There she paused, gazing upward into his face.

"Thank you, Papa, for saving my husband's life."

"I could not stand by and watch Robert slay him as well." Angus's blue eyes darkened. He laid a hand on his daughter's shining head for a fleeting moment. The tide of emotions inside him was all at once too great to contain. "Lord, Meredith"—his voice was half-choked—"when I think of what he did. That it was he who drove my poor child away—"

Meredith stopped him with a shake of her head. "Please, Papa. Let us not speak of it. Let us put it behind us and look to the future instead."

Angus gazed deep into her face and saw no remnants of shadows there. Some of the anguished bleakness lifted from his breast. "I love you, Meredith. 'Tis good to have you here." The words were simple but heartfelt. "Now that you are here, will you stay?"

A strong hand descended on Meredith's shoulder. It was Cameron who answered firmly, "Aye, we will stay awhile, but only if you promise to visit us at Dunthorpe."

" 'Tis a journey I may be making far sooner than you think." Angus's gaze slid toward the cradle. "I should like to see my grandson grow." He chuckled. "Though I cannot believe the boy slept through all this clamor!"

He kissed Meredith gently on the cheek and departed, thinking that if the warmly possessive light that shone in his son-in-law's eyes was anything to go by, his grandson would not long be the only child.

Once Angus was gone, Egan stepped forward as well. His actions were the last thing in the world Meredith expected.

He drew his sword and laid it at her feet, then dropped down on one knee. He bowed his head before her.

"Lady," he said haltingly, "my sword belongs to you, as surely as it belongs to your husband. I have wronged you—wronged you grievously, for in my heart I thought you guilty of seeking your husband's death. I can only pray that you will be generous. That you will forgive me, for I am not certain I can ever forgive myself."

His voice was gratingly low. The depth of emotion she heard there made her heart turn over.

The sight of this fierce Highland warrior stunned

her so that she could scarcely speak. "Egan," she said shakily. "Egan, of course I forgive you! Now rise, for there is no need to humble yourself so."

He seized her hand, brought it to his lips, and kissed it. Slowly he raised his head. "Mistress"—he was solemnly intent—"you are the greatest lady I have ever known." With that he rose to his feet.

His declaration brought an aching lump to her throat. Meredith reacted without thinking. With a misty smile, she raised herself on tiptoe and kissed the hardness of his cheek. She sensed that she had startled him, yet the merest smile grazed his lips— she realized it was the first time she had ever seen him smile.

When the door closed behind him, a wispy sigh emerged from her lips. The impossible had happened this day; Egan no longer regarded her as his enemy, and the blood feud between the Munros and the MacKays was no more.

Beside her, Cameron arched a brow. "Careful, wife," he teased, "else I will think your affections given elsewhere and another feud will begin."

The light in his eyes was purely tender as he drew her into his arms. Meredith felt her heart soar clear to the heavens.

She placed her fingertips lightly upon his chest. "My heart belongs to you, Cameron. To you and no other."

"And mine to you, wife." He was silent for a moment. "You need not worry ever again about Moire, lass. When I first brought you to Dunthorpe, she was anxious to see you thrown in the pit prison. But methinks she and your uncle's spy may both find themselves the next occupants."

"I see," she said gravely, but her eyes were shining. "So you are no longer entranced by the lovely Moire?"

"Ah, but I never was entranced." He touched his forehead to hers. " 'Tis you I love, sweet, beyond all measure."

Gladness spilled all through her. "And I love you, Cameron of the Clan MacKay," she breathed, raising her lips to his.

The kiss they shared was long and unbroken. When at last they parted, Meredith twined her fingers in the dark hair on his nape and glanced at Brodie's cradle.

"Papa was right," she murmured. " 'Tis hard to believe Brodie slept through all."

"Aye. How will he make it through a night of tending sheep?" Cameron mused aloud. "He will surely tumble down a hillside, as I did!"

Meredith's laugh was breathless. However, in the next instant, she marched a provocative fingertip up to his mouth. "However," she went on, "he will soon be awake to break his fast. And I do believe, husband, 'tis time we broke ours."

Cameron's lips quirked. "A wise woman, you are. And brave, too, to have married a rogue such as I."

"Aye, that you are!" she agreed without heat. "Remember the night we first arrived at Dunthorpe? You commanded that I give you a son. 'Give me a son and I will free you,' " she quoted. It was her turn to raise a slender brow. "But now the tables have turned, and I have a command for you."

He was already backing her slowly toward the bed. "And what is that?"

Slender arms twined about his neck. "Give me a daughter," she invited huskily, "and I will ensnare you forever."

He smiled against her lips. "Sweet love, you already have."

Have you ever wondered why opposites attract?

Why is it so easy to fall in love when your friends, your family . . . even your own good sense tells you to run the other way? Perhaps it's because a long, slow kiss from a sensuous rake is much more irresistible than a chaste embrace from a gentleman with a steady income. After all, falling in love means taking a risk . . . and isn't it oh, so much more enjoyable to take a risk on someone just a little dangerous?

Christina Dodd, Cathy Maxwell, Samantha James, Christina Skye, Constance O'Day-Flannery and Judith Ivory . . . these are the authors of the Avon Romance Superleaders, and each has created a man and a woman who seemed completely unsuitable in all ways but one . . . the love they discover in the other.

Christina Dodd certainly knows how to cause a scandal—in her books, that is! Her dashing heroes, like the one in her latest Superleader, SOMEDAY MY PRINCE, simply can't resist putting her heroines in compromising positions of all sorts . . .

Beautiful Princess Laurentia has promised to fulfill her royal duty and marry, but as she looks over her stuttering, swaggering, timid sea of potential suitors she thinks to herself that she's never seen such an unsuitable group in her life. Then she's swept off her feet by a handsome prince of dubious reputation. Laurentia had always dreamed her prince would come, but never one quite like this . . .

SOMEDAY MY PRINCE
by Christina Dodd

Astonished, indignant and in pain, the princess stammered, "Who . . . what . . . how dare you?"

"Was he a suitor scorned?"

"I never saw him before!"

"Then next time a stranger grabs you and slams you over his shoulder, you squeal like a stuck pig."

Clutching her elbow, she staggered to her feet. "I yelled!"

"I barely heard you." He stood directly in front of her, taller than he had at first appeared, beetle-browed, his eyes dark hollows, his face marked with a deep-shadowed scar that ran from chin to temple. Yet despite all that, he was handsome. Stunningly so. "And I was just behind those pots."

Tall and luxuriant, the potted plants clustered against the wall, and she looked at them, then looked back at him. He spoke with an accent. He walked with a limp. He was a stranger. Suspicion stirred in her. "What were you doing there?"

"Smoking."

She smelled it on him, that faint scent of tobacco so like that which clung to her father. Although she knew it foolish, the odor lessened her misgivings. "I'll call the guard and send them after that scoundrel."

"Scoundrel." The stranger laughed softly. "You *are* a lady. But don't bother sending anyone after him. He's long gone."

She knew it was true. The scoundrel—and what was wrong with that word, anyway?—had leaped into the wildest part of the garden, just where the cultured plants gave way to natural scrub. The guard would do her no good.

So rather than doing what she knew very well she should, she let the stranger place his hand on the small of her back and turn her toward the light.

He clasped her wrist and slowly stretched out her injured arm. "It's not broken."

"I don't suppose so."

He grinned, a slash of white teeth against a half-glimpsed face. "You'd recognize if it was. A broken elbow lets you know it's there." Efficiently, he unfastened the buttons on her elbow-length glove and stripped it away, then ran his bare fingers firmly over the bones in her lower arm, then lightly over the pit of her elbow.

Goosebumps rose on her skin at the touch. He didn't wear gloves, she noted absently. His naked skin touched hers. "What kind of injury are you looking for?"

"Not an injury. I just thought I would enjoy caressing that silk-soft skin."

She jerked her wrist away.

What could be more exciting than making your debut . . . wearing a gorgeous gown, sparkling jewels, and enticing all the ton's most eligible bachelors?

In Cathy Maxwell's MARRIED IN HASTE, Tess Hamlin is used to having the handsomest of London's eligible men vie for her attention. But Tess is in no hurry to make her choice—until she meets the virile war hero Brenn Owen, the new Earl of Merton. But Tess must marry a man of wealth, and although the earl has a title and land, he's in need of funds. But she can't resist this compelling nobleman . . .

MARRIED IN HASTE
by Cathy Maxwell

"I envy you. I will never be free. Someday I will have a husband and my freedom will be curtailed even more," Tess said.

"I had the impression that you set the rules."

Tess shot him a sharp glance. "No, I play the game well, but—" She broke off.

"But it's not really me."

"What is you?"

A wary look came into her eyes. "You don't really want to know."

"Yes, I do." Brenn leaned forward. "After all, moments ago you were begging me to make a declaration."

"I never beg!" she declared with mock seriousness

and they both laughed. Then she said, "Sometimes I wonder if there isn't something more to life. Or why am I here."

The statement caught his attention. There wasn't one man who had ever faced battle without asking that question.

"I want to feel a sense of purpose," she continued, "of being, here deep inside. Instead I feel . . . " She shrugged, her voice trailing off.

"As if you are only going through the motions?" he suggested quietly.

The light came on in her vivid eyes. "Yes! That's it." She dropped her arms to her side. "Do you feel that way too?"

"At one time I have. Especially after a battle when men were dying all around me and yet I had escaped harm. I wanted to have a reason. To know why."

She came closer to him until they stood practically toe to toe. "And have you found out?"

"I think so," he replied honestly. "It has to do with having a sense of purpose, of peace. I believe I have found that purpose at Erwynn Keep. It's the first place I've been where I feel I really belong."

"Yes," she agreed in understanding. "Feeling like you belong. That's what I sense is missing even when I'm surrounded by people who do nothing more than toady up to me and hang on my every word." She smiled. "But you haven't done that. You wouldn't, would you? Even if I asked you to."

"Toadying has never been my strong suit . . . although I would do many things for a beautiful woman." He touched her then, drawing a line down the velvet curve of her cheek.

Miss Hamlin caught his hand before it could stray further, her gaze holding his. "Most men don't go beyond the shell of the woman . . . or look past the fortune. Are you a fortune hunter, Lord Merton?"

Her direct question almost bowled him off over the stone rail. He recovered quickly. "If I was, would I admit it?"

"No."

"Then you shall have to form your own opinion."

Her lips curved into a smile. She did not move away.

"I think I'm going to kiss you."

She blushed, the sudden high color charming.

"Don't tell me," he said. "Gentlemen rarely ask before they kiss."

"Oh, they always ask, but I've never let them."

"Then I won't ask." He lowered his lips to hers. Her eyelashes swept down as she closed her eyes. She was so beautiful in the moonlight. So innocently beautiful.

Across the Scottish Highlands strides Cameron MacKay. Cameron is a man of honor, a man who would do anything to protect his clan . . . and he wouldn't hesitate to seek revenge against those who have wronged him.

Meredith is one of the clan Monroe, sworn enemies of Cameron and his men. So Cameron takes this woman as his wife, never dreaming that what began as an act of vengeance becomes instead a quest for love in Samantha James's HIS WICKED WAYS.

HIS WICKED WAYS
by Samantha James

Cameron faced her, his head propped on an elbow. His smile was gone, his expression unreadable. He stared at her as if he would pluck her very thoughts from her mind.

"It occurs to me that you have been sheltered," he said slowly, "that mayhap you know naught of men . . . and life." He seemed to hesitate. "What happens between a man and a woman is not something to be feared, Meredith. It's where children come from—"

"I know how children are made!" Meredith's face burned with shame.

"Then why are you so afraid?" he asked quietly.

It was in her mind to pretend she misunderstood—but it would have been a lie. Clutching the sheet to her chin, she gave a tiny shake of her head. "Please," she said, her voice very low. "I cannot tell you."

Reaching out, he picked up a strand of hair that lay on her breast. Meredith froze. Her heart surely stopped in that instant. Now it comes, she thought despairingly. He claimed he would give her time to accept him, to accept what would happen, but it was naught but a lie! Her heart twisted. Ah, but she should have known!

"Your hair is beautiful—like living flame."

His murmur washed over her, soft as finely spun silk. She searched his features, stunned when she detected no hint of either mockery or derision.

She stared at the wispy strands that lay across his palm, the way he tested the texture between thumb and forefinger, the way he wound the lock of hair around and around his hand.

Meredith froze. But he stopped before the pressure tugged hurtfully on her scalp . . . and trespassed no further. Instead he turned his back.

His eyes closed.

They touched nowhere. Indeed, the width of two hands separated them; those silken red strands were the only link between them. Meredith dared not move. She listened and waited, her heart pounding in her breast . . .

. . . Slumber overtook him. He slept, her lock of hair still clutched tight in his fist.

Only then did she move. Her hand lifted. She touched her lips, there at the very spot he'd possessed so thoroughly. Her pulse quickened as the memory of his kiss flamed all through her . . . She'd thought it was disdain. Distaste.

But she was wrong. In the depths of her being,

Meredith was well aware it was something far different.

Her breath came fast, then slow. Something was happening. Something far beyond her experience . . .

What could be more beautiful than a holiday trip to the English countryside? Snow falling on the gentle hills and thatched roofs . . . villagers singing carols, then dropping by the pub for hot cider with rum.

In Christina Skye's THE PERFECT GIFT, Maggie Kincaid earns a chance to exhibit her beautiful jewelry designs at sumptuous Draycott Abbey, where she dreams of peacefully spending Christmas. But when she arrives, she learns she is in danger and discovers that her every step will be followed by disturbingly sensuous Jared MacInness. He will protect her from those who would harm her, but who'll protect Maggie from Jared?

THE PERFECT GIFT
by Christina Skye

Jared had worked his way over the ridge and down through the trees when he found Maggie Kincaid sitting on the edge of the stone bridge.

Just sitting, her legs dangling as she traced invisible patterns over the old stone.

Jared stared in amazement. She looked for all the world like a child waiting for a long lost friend to appear.

Jared shook off his sense of strangeness and plunged down the hillside, cursing her for the ache in his ribs and the exhaustion eating at his muscles.

He scowled as he drew close enough to see her face.

Young. Excited. Not beautiful in the classic sense. Her mouth was too wide and her nose too thin. But the eyes lit up her whole face and made a man want to know all her secrets.

Her mouth swept into a quick smile as he approached. Her head tilted as laughter rippled like morning sunlight.

The sound chilled him. It was too quick, too innocent. She ought to be frightened. Defensive. Running.

He stared, feeling the ground turn to foam beneath him.

Moonlight touched the long sleeves of her simple white dress with silver as she rose to her feet.

He spoke first, compelled to break the spell of her presence, furious that she should touch him so. "You know I could have you arrested for this." His jaw clenched.

Her head cocked. Poised at the top of the bridge, she was a study in innocent concentration.

"Don't even bother to think about running. I want to know who you are and why in hell you're here."

A frown marred the pale beauty of her face. She might have been a child—except that the full curves of her body spoke a richly developed maturity at complete odds with her voice and manner.

"Answer me. You're on private property and in ten seconds I'm going to call the police." Exhaustion made his voice harsh. "Don't try it," Jared hissed, realizing she meant to fall and let him catch her. But it was too late. She stepped off the stone bridge, her body angling down toward him.

He caught her with an oath and a jolt of pain, and then they toppled as one onto the damp earth beyond the moat. Cursing, Jared rolled sideways and pinned her beneath him.

It was no child's face that stared up at him and no child's body that cushioned him. She was strong for a woman, her muscles trim but defined. The softness at hip and breast tightened his throat and left his body all too aware of their intimate contact. He did not move, fighting an urge to open his hands and measure her softness.

What was wrong with him?

Imagine for a moment that you're a modern woman; one minute, you're living a fast-paced, hectic lifestyle . . . the next minute, you've somehow been transported to another time and you're living a life of a very different sort.

No one does time-travel like Constance O'Day-Flannery. In ONCE AND FOREVER Maggie enters a maze while at an Elizabethan fair, and when she comes out she magically finds she's truly in Elizabethan times! And to make matters more confusing, the sweep-her-off-her-feet hero she's been searching for all her life turns out to be the handsomest man in 1600's England!

ONCE AND FOREVER
by Constance O'Day-Flannery

Maggie looked up to the sky and wished a breeze would find its way into the thick hedges; she couldn't believe she was in this maze, sweating her life away in a gorgeous costume and starving. Thinking of all the calories she was burning she wondered, who needs a gym workout? Maggie stopped to listen for anyone, but only an eerie silence hovered.

Suddenly, she felt terribly alone.

Spinning around, she vainly searched for anyone, but saw and heard nothing. "Hello? Hello?" Her calls went unanswered. She stopped abruptly in the path. She felt weak. Her heart was pounding and her head felt light. Grabbing at the starched collar, she released the top few buttons and gasped in confusion. Okay, maybe she could use that shining knight right about now. She didn't care how or where he appeared, as long as he led her out, for the air was heavy and still, and Maggie found it hard to breathe.

"Help me . . . please."

Silence.

Her heart pounded harder, her stomach clenched in fear, her breath shortened, her limbs trembled and the weight of the costume felt like it was pulling her down to the ground.

Spinning around and around, Maggie experienced a sudden lightness, as if she no longer had to struggle against gravity and push herself away from the earth. Whatever was happening was controlling her, and she was so weary of struggling . . . flashes of her ex-husband and the alimony, her failed job interviews, the bills, the aloneness swirled together. It was bigger, more powerful than she, and she felt herself weakening, surrendering to it. The hedges appeared to fade away and Maggie instinctively knew she had to get out. Gathering her last essence of strength, she started running.

Miraculously, she was out. She was gasping for breath, inhaling the dust and dirt from under her mouth when she heard the angry yell that reverberated through the ground and rattled her already scrambled brain.

She dare not move, not even breathe. If this were a nightmare, and surely it couldn't be anything else, she wasn't about to add to the terror. She would wake up any moment, her mind screamed. She *had to!*

Drawing upon more courage than she thought she had left, Maggie slowly lifted her head. She was staring into the big brown eyes of a horse.

A horse!

She heard moans and looked beyond the animal to see a body. A man, rolled on the side of a dirt path, was clutching his knee as colorful curses flowed back to her.

"Spleeny, lousey-cockered jolt head! Aww . . . heavens above deliver me from this vile, impertinent, ill-natured lout!"

Pushing herself to her feet, Maggie brushed dirt, twigs and leaves from her hands and backside, then made her way to the man. "How badly are you hurt?" she called out over her shoulder.

The man didn't answer and she glanced in his direction. He was still staring at her, as though he'd lost his senses.

Shoulder-length streaked blond hair framed a finely chiseled face. Eyes, large and of the lightest blue Maggie had ever seen stared back at her, as though the man had seen a ghost. He was definitely an attractive, more than average, handsome man . . . okay, he was downright gorgeous and she'd have to be dead not to acknowledge it.

Wow . . . that was her first thought.

Everyone knows that ladies of quality can only marry gentlemen, and that suitable gentlemen are born—not made. Because being a gentleman has nothing to do with money, and everything to do with upbringing.

But in Judith Ivory's THE PROPOSITION Edwina vows that she can turn anyone into a gentleman . . . even the infuriating Mr. Mick Tremore. Not only that, she'd be able to pass him off as the heir to a dukedom, and no one in society would be any wiser. And since Edwina is every inch a lady, there isn't a chance that she'd find the exasperating Mick Tremore irresistible. Is there?

THE PROPOSITION
by Judith Ivory

"Speak for yourself," she said. "I couldn't do anything"—she paused, then used his word for it—"unpredictable."

"Yes, you could."

"Well, I could, but I won't."

He laughed. "Well, you might surprise yourself one day."

His sureness of himself irked her. Like the mustache that he twitched slightly. He knew she didn't like it; he used it to tease her.

Fine. What a pointless conversation. She picked up her pen, going back to the task of writing out his progress for the morning. Out of the corner of her eye, though, she could see him.

He'd leaned back on the rear legs of his chair, lifting the front ones off the floor. He rocked there beside her as he bent his head sideways, tilting it, looking under the table. He'd been doing this all week, making her nervous with it. As if there were a mouse—or worse— something under there that she should be aware of.

"What *are* you doing?"

Illogically, he came back with, "I bet you have the longest, prettiest legs."

"*Limbs*," she corrected. "A gentleman refers to that part of a lady as her limbs, her lower limbs, though it is rather poor form to speak of them at all. You shouldn't."

He laughed. "Limbs? Like a bloody tree?" His pencil continued to tap lightly, an annoying tattoo of ticks. "No, you got legs under there. Long ones. And I'd give just about anything to see 'em."

Goodness. He knew that was impertinent. He was tormenting her. He liked to torture her for amusement.

Then she caught the word: *anything?*

To see her legs? Her legs were nothing. Two sticks that bent so she could walk on them. He wanted to see these?

For anything?

She wouldn't let him see them, of course. But she wasn't past provoking him in return. "Well, there is a solution here then, Mr. Tremore. You can see my legs, when you shave your mustache."

She meant it as a kind of joke. A taunt to get back at him.

Joke or not, though, his pencil not only stopped, it dropped. There was a tiny clatter on the floor, a faint sound of rolling, then silence—as, along with the pencil, Mr. Tremore's entire body came to a motionless standstill.

"Pardon?" he said finally. He spoke it perfectly, exactly as she'd asked him to. Only now it unsettled her.

"You heard me," she said. A little thrill shot through her as she pushed her way into the dare that—fascinatingly, genuinely—rattled him.

She spoke now in earnest what seemed suddenly a wonderful exchange: "If you shave off your mustache, I'll hike my skirt and you can watch—how far? To my knees?" The hair on the back of her neck stood up.

"Above your knees," he said immediately. His amazed face scowled in a way that said they weren't even talking unless they got well past her knees in the debate.

"How far?"

"All the way up."